cont

How to Master Your Marquis

Juliana Gray

BERKLEY SENSATION, NEW YORK

THE BERKLEY PUBLISHING GROUP
Published by the Penguin Group
Penguin Group (USA) LLC
375 Hudson Street, New York, New York 10014

USA • Canada • UK • Ireland • Australia • New Zealand • India • South Africa • China

penguin.com

A Penguin Random House Company

HOW TO MASTER YOUR MARQUIS

A Berkley Sensation Book / published by arrangement with the author

Berkley Sensation Books are published by The Berkley Publishing Group.
BERKLEY SENSATION® is a registered trademark of Penguin Group (USA) LLC.
The "B" design is a trademark of Penguin Group (USA) LLC.

For information, address: The Berkley Publishing Group,
a division of Penguin Group (USA) LLC,
375 Hudson Street, New York, New York 10014.

ISBN: 978-0-425-26567-3

PUBLISHING HISTORY
Berkley Sensation mass-market edition / January 2014

PRINTED IN THE UNITED STATES OF AMERICA

10 9 8 7 6 5 4 3 2 1

Cover art by Alan Ayers.
Cover design by George Long
Interior text design by Kristin del Rosario.

To Mr. Gray,
who also rows.

ACKNOWLEDGMENTS

Thanks are due, as always, to my agent, Alexandra Machinist, at Janklow & Nesbit, who keeps finding new ways to amaze me, and to the marvelous team at Berkley who transforms the words on the screen into books in bookstores: my editor, Kate Seaver; her assistant, Katherine Pelz; the heroic art, marketing, publicity, and sales departments; and a copyeditor who sees all, knows all, and tactfully conveys all.

PROLOGUE

Old Bailey, London
July 1890

The courtroom was packed and smelled of sweat.

James Lambert, the Marquess of Hatherfield—heir to that colossal monument of British prestige, the Duke of Southam—was accustomed to the stench of jammed-in human perspiration and did not mind in the slightest. He feared, however, for the young woman who sat before him.

Hatherfield couldn't watch her face directly, of course, but he could sense the tension humming away in her body, like the telephone wire his stepmother had had installed into her private study last year, in order to better command her army of Belgravian sycophants. He knew that her back was as straight as a razor's edge; he knew that her eyes would appear more green than blue in the sulfurous light waxing from the gas sconces of the courtroom, and that those same eyes were undoubtedly trained upon the presiding judge with a fierceness that might have done her conquering Germanic ancestors proud.

He knew his Stefanie as he knew his own hands, and he knew she would rather be boiled in oil than sniff a human armpit. His darling Stefanie, who thought herself so adventurous, who had proved herself equal to any number of challenges, had nonetheless been raised a princess, with a princess's delicate nose.

The judge was droning on, *precedents* this and *brutal nature of the crime* that, and Latin tags strewn about with reckless enthusiasm. He was a man of narrow forehead and prodigious jowl; the rolls about his neck wobbled visibly as he spoke. A large black fly had discovered the interesting composition of the curling white wig atop his pear-shaped head and was presently buzzing about the apex in lazily ecstatic loops. Hatherfield watched its progress in fascination. It landed atop the fourth roll of wiry white hair with a contented *bzzz-bzzz*, just as Her Majesty's judicial representative informed the mass of perspiring humanity assembled before him that they were required to maintain an open mind as to the prisoner's guilt *ad captandum et ad timorem sine qua non sic transit gloria mundi et cetera et cetera et cetera.*

Or perhaps he was now addressing the jury. Hatherfield couldn't be certain; the man's face was cast downward, into his notes; or rather into the jowls overhanging his notes. Like that chap at Oxford, that history don, the one who would insist on taking tea at his desk and dropping bits of crumpet unavoidably into the jowly folds, to be excavated later as he stroked his whiskers during lectures. On a good day, the dais might be strewn with the crumbly little buggers, and a positive trail left behind him on the way back to his chambers. What had they nicknamed him? Hatherfield screwed up his forehead and stared at the magnificent soot-smeared ceiling above.

Hansel, that was it.

A flash of movement caught his eye. Something was going on with Stefanie's fingers: She was scribbling furiously on the paper before her, biting her tender lower lip as she went. She looked up, locked eyes with him, and flashed the paper up and down again, the work of an instant. He saw the words, nonetheless. They were written in large capital letters, underlined twice for emphasis:

PAY ATTENTION!!

Ah, Stefanie. He tapped his fingers against the rail before him and composed his reply in Morse code:

I AM PAYING ATTENTION. TO YOU. YOU LOOK EXCEPTIONALLY HANDSOME IN THAT WAISTCOAT. I SHOULD VERY MUCH LIKE TO KISS YOU.

He watched as her eyes dropped down to his fingers. He tapped the message again.

She changed color. Well, he couldn't see her well enough to verify, but he knew anyway. The flush would be mounting up above her stiff white collar, spreading along the curving wedge of her regal cheekbones and beneath her mustache. The tip of her nose would be turning quite pink right about . . . now. Yes, there it was: a little red glow. Just like when he . . .

With her elegant and agile fingers, Stefanie tore the paper in half, and in half again; she assembled the quarters together and tore them rather impressively once more. She hid the pieces under a leather portfolio and locked her hands together. Her knuckles were bone white; Hatherfield could see that from here.

Familiar words struck his ear, jolting him out of his pleasant interlude: his stepmother's name. ". . . the Duchess of Southam, who was found murdered in her bed in the most gruesome manner, the details of which will become clear . . ."

The Duchess of Southam. Trust her to toss her bucket of icy water over his every moment of happiness, even from the grave, merely by the sound of her name in a room full of witnesses. He had tried by every means to deny her that power over him, and still she laid her cold hands on his body.

Hatherfield found he couldn't quite bear to look at Stefanie now. He trained his gaze instead on the judge. The fly had disappeared, frightened away perhaps by the thunderous vibration of those tempting white curls, as the speaker worked himself up to an indignant climax—a theatrical chap, this judge, for all his comical jowls—and asked the prisoner how he pleaded.

Hatherfield's hands gripped the rail before him. He straightened his long back, looked the judge squarely in the eye, and replied in a loud, clear voice.

"Not guilty, my lord."

Devon, England
Eight months earlier

Princess Stefanie Victoria Augusta, a young woman not ordinarily subject to attacks of nerves, found to her horror that her fingers were twitching so violently she could scarcely fold her necktie.

True, it was a drab necktie. She had longed for one in spangled purple silk, or that delicious tangerine she had spotted through a carriage window on a dapper young chap in London, before she and her sisters had been hustled away by their uncle to this ramshackle Jacobin pile perched on a sea cliff in remotest Devon. (For the record, she adored the place.) But the array of neckties laid out before her on the first morning of her training had offered three choices: black, black, and black.

"Haven't you any *interesting* neckties?" she had asked, letting one dangle from the extreme tips of her fingers, as if it were an infant's soiled napkin.

"My dear niece," said the Duke of Olympia, as he might say *my dear incontinent puppy*, "you are not supposed to be interesting. You are supposed to be the dullest, most commonplace, most unremarkable law clerk in London. You are *hiding*, if you'll recall."

"Yes, but must one hide oneself in such unspeakable drab neckties? Can't they at least be made of silk damask?" Stefanie let the necktie wither from her fingers to the tray below.

"Law clerks do not wear silk damask neckties," said her sister Emilie. She was standing before the mirror with great concentration, attempting a knot under the anxious supervision of His Grace's valet.

"How do you *know* they don't?" asked Stefanie, but Olympia laid a hand on her arm.

"Stefanie, my dear," he said affectionately, for she was his favorite niece, though it was a close secret between them, "perhaps you don't recall what's at stake here. You are not playing parlor games with your courtiers in charming Hogwash-whateveritis . . ."

"Holstein-Schweinwald-Huhnhof," said Stefanie, straightening proudly. "The most charming principality in Germany, over which your own sister once reigned, if you'll recall."

Olympia waved his hand. "Yes, yes. Charming, to say nothing of fragrant. But as I said, this is not a friendly game of hide-and-seek. The three of you are being hunted by a team of damned anarchist assassins, the same ones who killed your own father and kidnapped your sister . . ."

"*Attempted* to kidnap," said Princess Luisa, smoothing her skirts, except that her hands found a pair of wool checked trousers instead and stopped in mid-stroke.

"Regardless. No one is to suspect that you're being scattered about England, dressed as young men, employed in the most invisible capacities . . ."

"While you and Miss Dingleby have all the fun of tracking down our father's murderers and slicing their tender white throats from end to end." Stefanie heaved a deep and bloodthirsty sigh.

Miss Dingleby had appeared at her other elbow. "My dear," she'd said quietly, "your sentiments do you credit. But speaking as your governess, and therefore obliged to focus you on the task at hand, I urge you to consider your own throat instead, and the necktie that must, I'm afraid, go around it."

Four weeks later, the neckties had not improved, though Stefanie had become a dab hand at a stylish knot. (*Too stylish*, Miss Dingleby would sigh, and make her tie it again along more conservative lines.)

If only she could make her silly fingers work.

The door opened with an impatient creak, allowing through Miss Dingleby, who was crackling with impatience. "Stefanie, what on earth is keeping you? Olympia has been downstairs with Sir John this past half hour, and we're running out of sherry."

"Nonsense. There are dozens of bottles in the dungeon."

"It is not a dungeon. It's merely a cellar." Miss Dingleby paused and narrowed her eyes at Stefanie's reflection in the mirror. "You're not nervous, are you, my dear? I might expect it of Emilie and Luisa, straightforward as they are and unaccustomed to subterfuge, but *you*?"

"Of course I'm not nervous." Stefanie stared sternly at her

hands and ordered them to their duty. "Only reluctant. I don't see why *I* should be the law clerk. I'm by far the shadiest character among the three of us. You should have made me the tutor instead. Emilie will bore her pupil to tears, I'm sure, whereas *I* would . . ."

Miss Dingleby made an exasperated noise and moved behind her. "Take your hands away," she said, and tied Stefanie's black neckcloth with blinding jerks of her own competent hands, to a constriction so exquisitely snug that Stefanie gasped for breath. "The decision was Olympia's, and I'm quite sure he knew what he was doing. Your Latin is excellent, your mind quick and retentive when you allow it to concentrate . . ."

"Yes, but the law is so very *dull*, Miss Dingleby . . ."

". . . and what's more," Miss Dingleby said, standing back to admire her handiwork, "we shall all be a *great deal* reassured by the knowledge that you're lodged with the most reputable, learned, formidable, and upstanding member of the entire English bar."

Stefanie allowed herself to be taken by the hand and led out the door to the great and rather architecturally suspect staircase that swept its crumbling way to the hall below. "That," she said mournfully, "is exactly what I'm afraid of."

Olympia and his guest were waiting in the formal drawing room, which had once been the scene of a dramatic capture and beheading of a Royalist younger son during the Civil War (Stefanie had verified this legend herself with a midnight peek under the threadbare rugs, and though the light was dim, she was quite sure she could make out an admirably large stain on the floorboards, not five feet away from the fireplace), but which now contained only the pedestrian English ritual of a duke taking an indulgent late-morning glass of sherry with a knight.

Or so Stefanie had supposed, but when she marched past the footman (a princess always greeted potential adversaries with aplomb, after all) and into the ancient room, she found herself gazing instead at the most beautiful man in the world.

Stefanie staggered to a halt.

He stood with his sherry glass in one hand, and the other perched atop the giant lion-footed armchair that had been

specially made a century ago for the sixth duke, who had
grown corpulent with age. Without being extraordinarily tall,
nor extraordinarily broad framed, the man seemed to dwarf
this substantial piece of historic furniture, to cast it in his
shadow. His *radiant* shadow, for he had the face of Gabriel:
divinely formed, cheekbones presiding over a neat square jaw,
blue eyes crinkled in friendly welcome beneath a high and
guiltless forehead. He was wearing a dark suit of some kind,
plain and unadorned, and the single narrow shaft of November
sunshine from her uncle's windows had naturally found him,
as light clings to day, bathing his bare golden curls like a
nimbus.

Stefanie squeaked, "Sir John?"

The room exploded with laughter.

"Ha-ha, my lad. How you joke." The Duke of Olympia
stepped forward from the roaring fire, wiping his eyes. "In
fact, your new employer has the good fortune of traveling with
company today. Allow me to present to you the real and genuine Sir John Worthington, Q.C., who has so kindly offered to
take you into his chambers."

A white-haired figure emerged dimly from the sofa next to
the fire and spoke with the booming authority of a Roman
senator. "Not nearly so handsome a figure as my friend, of
course, but it saves trouble with the ladies."

With supreme effort, Stefanie detached her attention from
the golden apparition before her and fixed it upon the source
of that senatorial voice.

Her heart, which had been soaring dizzily about the thick
oaken beams holding up the ducal ceiling, sank slowly back to
her chest, fluttered, and expired.

If Stefanie had been a painter of renown, and commis-
sioned to construct an allegorical mural of British law, with a
judge occupying the ultimate position in a decorous white wig
and black silk robes, bearing the scales of justice in one hand and
a carved wooden gavel in the other, she would have chosen
exactly this man to model for her and instructed him to wear
exactly that expression that greeted her now.

His eyes were small and dark and permanently narrowed,
like a pair of suspicious currants. His forehead was broad and
steep above a hedgerow brow. His pitted skin spoke of the

slings and arrows of a life spent braced between the dregs of humanity and the righteous British public, and his mouth, even when proffering an introductory smile, turned downward at the ends toward some magnetic core of dole within him. Atop his wiry frame was arranged a stiff gray tweed jacket and matching plus fours, with each leg pressed to a crease so acute that Stefanie might have sliced an apple with it.

If Sir John Worthington *had* ever encountered trouble with the ladies, Stefanie judged, it was not without a significant intake of champagne beforehand. On both his part and hers.

Still, Stefanie was a princess of Holstein-Schweinwald-Huhnhof, and what was more, she had never yet met a living being she had not been able to charm.

"Good morning, Sir John," she began cheerfully, and tripped over the edge of the rug.

Time was supposed to slow down during accidents of this sort, or so Stefanie had heard, but all she knew was a flying blur and a full-body jolt and a sense of horrified bemusement at the sensation of threadbare carpet beneath her chin. A feminine gasp reached her ears, and she was nearly certain it wasn't her own.

A pair of large and unadorned hands appeared before her, suspended between her face and the forest of chair and sofa legs. "I say. Are you quite all right?" asked a sonorous voice, which in its velvet baritone perfection could only belong to the Archangel.

Was it manly to accept his hand in rising? It was a marvelous hand, less refined than she might have expected, square and strong boned, with a row of uniform calluses along the palm. The fingers flexed gently in welcome, an image of controlled power.

Stefanie swallowed heavily.

"Quite all right," she said, rather more breathily than she had planned. She gathered herself and jumped to her feet, ignoring the Archangel's splendid hands. "New shoes, you know."

A little giggle floated from the sofa.

Among the sounds that Stefanie could not abide, the female giggle ranked high: well above the drone of a persistent black fly, for example, and only just beneath the musical efforts of a debutante on a badly tuned piano.

She shot the sofa an accusing glance.

A young lady sat there, utterly dainty, perfectly composed, with a smug little smile turning up one corner of her mouth. She was beautiful in exactly the way that Stefanie was not: delicate features, soft dark eyes, curling black hair, rose-petal skin without the hint of a freckle. Though she reclined with languorous grace upon the sofa, one tiny pink silk slipper peeking from beneath her pink silk dress, she was clearly of petite proportions, designed to make the long-shanked Stefanies of the world appear as racetrack colts.

Except that Stefanie herself was no longer a young lady, was she?

"Charlotte, my dear," said Sir John, "it is hardly a matter for amusement."

"Nothing is a matter of amusement for *you*, Uncle John," said his dear Charlotte, with a sharp laugh.

Stefanie expected Sir John's face to empurple at this saucy (if accurate) assessment, but instead he heaved a sigh. "Mr. Thomas, I have the honor to introduce to you my ward, Lady Charlotte Harlowe, who lives with me in Cadogan Square, and who will, I'm sure, have as much advice for you as she does for me."

Lady Charlotte held out her spotless little hand. "Mr. Thomas. How charming."

Stefanie strode forward and touched the ceremonial tips of her fingers. "Enchanted, Lady Charlotte."

"Indeed," said Sir John. "And I believe you've already made acquaintance with the Marquess of Hatherfield."

"Your friend is a marquess?"

"Yes. Hatherfield practically lives in our drawing room, don't you, my boy?" Sir John looked grimly over her shoulder.

Stefanie turned. "Lord Hatherfield?"

She spoke with solemn composure, but her head was spinning. The Archangel was a *marquis*? Good God! What other gifts could possibly have been lavished on his head by an adoring Creator? Did he spin gold from his fingertips?

A marquis. Practically living in his drawing room, the old fellow had said.

God help her.

The Archangel Hatherfield grinned widely and shook her hand. The calluses tickled pleasantly against her palm. "It's a great pleasure to meet you, Mr. Thomas. I admire your pluck enormously, entering into Sir John's chambers like this. I daresay you charm snakes in your spare time?"

"Oh, I gave that up long ago," said Stefanie. "I kept tripping over the basket and losing the snake."

Hatherfield blinked at her once, twice. Then he threw back his head and howled with laughter. "Oh, Thomas," he said, wiping his eyes, "you're a dashed good sport. I like you already. You've got to take good care of this one, Sir John. Don't let him near the cyanide tablets like the last poor clerk."

"Really, Hatherfield," said Sir John, in a grumbly voice.

"Well, well. This is charming," said Lady Charlotte, looking anything but charmed. "I look forward to hearing Mr. Thomas's witticisms all the way back to London. How lucky we are."

The Duke of Olympia, who had been standing silently at the mantel throughout the exchange, spoke up at last. "Indeed, Lady Charlotte. I do believe that you will profit enormously from Mr. Thomas's company, both on the journey to London and, indeed"—he examined the remains of his sherry, polished it off, set the empty glass on the mantel, and smiled his beneficent ducal smile—"in your own home."

Lady Charlotte's already pale skin lost another layer of transparent rose. "In our home?" she asked, incredulous, turning to Sir John. "Our *home?*" she repeated, as she might say *in my morning bath?*

Sir John, impervious Sir John, iron instrument of British justice, passed a nervous hand over the bristling gray thicket of his brow. "Did I not mention it before, my dear?"

"You did not." She pronounced each word discretely: You. Did. Not.

"Well, well," said Hatherfield. "Jolly splendid news. I shall look very much forward to seeing you, Mr. Thomas, when Sir John can spare you. You *will* spare him from time to time, won't you, Sir John?"

"I will try," said Sir John, rather more faintly than Stefanie might have expected.

She was not, however, paying all that much attention to Sir John and his ward. Hatherfield had fixed her with his glorious blue-eyed gaze in that last sentence, and she was swimming somewhere in the middle of him, stroking with abandon, sending up a joyful spray of . . .

"Nonsense," said Lady Charlotte. "Clerks are meant to work, aren't they, Sir John? It costs a great deal to educate a young man in the practice of the law, and it must be paid *somehow*."

"Why, dear Lady Charlotte," said Hatherfield, without so much as a flicker of a glance in her direction, still gazing smilingly into Stefanie's transfixed face, "you speak as if you've ever done a moment's useful work in your life."

A strangled noise came from the throat of the Duke of Olympia. He covered it quickly, with a brusque, "In any case, my friends, I see by the clock that you will miss your train if you delay another moment. I believe young Mr. Thomas's trunk has already been loaded on the chaise. I suggest we bid one another the customary tearful farewell and part our affectionate ways."

Hustle and bustle ensued, as it always did when Olympia issued a ducal decree. Stefanie's hand was shaken, her overcoat found, her steps urged out the front hall and into the chill November noontide, where the Duke of Olympia's elegant country chaise sat waiting with pawing steeds. To the left, the landscape dropped away into jagged slate cliffs, awash with foam, roaring with the distant crash of the angry sea.

"Cheerful prospect, what?" said Hatherfield.

"Barbaric," said Lady Charlotte. She reached the open door of the chaise and stood expectantly.

Stefanie, feeling lighthearted and therefore (as her sisters well knew) rather mischievous, grasped Lady Charlotte's fingers to assist her into the chaise.

A little gasp escaped her ladyship, an entirely different sort of gasp from the one that had greeted Stefanie's arrival on the threadbare rug of Olympia's Devon drawing room. She jerked her hand away as if stung.

"Is something the matter, Lady Charlotte?" asked Lord Hatherfield solemnly.

She raised one delicately etched eyebrow in his direction. "Only that I require your assistance into the vehicle, Hatherfield."

Hatherfield handed her in with a smile, but what Stefanie noticed most was not that golden smile, nor the unexpectedly gut-churning sight of his strong fingers locked with those of Lady Charlotte, but the expression on her ladyship's face. It had changed instantly at the point of contact, from sharp hauteur into something softer, something dulcet and melting and almost longing, something rather akin to . . .

Adoration.

The Marquess of Hatherfield swung himself into the carriage and tapped the roof with his cane. In deference to both Lady Charlotte and her august guardian, he took the backward-facing seat, next to young Mr. Thomas.

Mr. Thomas. Mr. Stephen Thomas. He glanced down at the plain wool legs next to his. Rather skinny legs, at that; particularly in comparison to his own, which were thick and hard, the quadriceps hewed into massive curves by nearly a decade spent powering racing shells through the rivers and lakes of England in an attempt to outpace the skulking shadows in his memory.

Yes, Mr. Thomas's legs had a curiously slender cast, beside his.

Which was only to be expected, of course, and not curious at all. For Hatherfield had gathered at a glance what the supposedly keen-eyed Sir John and the reputedly sharp-witted Lady Charlotte had, by all appearances, not begun to suspect.

It was quite obvious, really.

Mr. Thomas's legs were slender because *he* was a *she*.

A brash, clever, amusing, lovely, and elegant *she*. How she'd sprung right back up to her feet after her humiliating fall, how she'd joked about it afterward. A *she* for the ages.

The Marquess of Hatherfield straightened his gloves, settled back into his cushioned seat, and smiled out the window.

ONE

Old Bailey
July 1890

The prosecution called Sir John Worthington to the witness box at the end of a brutally hot afternoon, just before adjournment.

Stefanie looked up at the face of her former employer. Though she'd seen him just this morning over breakfast, he seemed to have aged a decade. His skin had grown pallid, and shone with perspiration in the heavy atmosphere of the courtroom. Even his magnificent whiskers drooped in exhaustion. She lifted her pen over the paper before her, as if that little act might somehow have a similar effect on Sir John's defeated spine.

"Sir John," said the counsel for the prosecution, brusque and rather offensively energetic in the face of the withering heat, "how would you characterize your relationship to the accused?"

Sir John cleared his throat, and his spine straightened a miraculous inch or two. He said, in a voice accustomed to ringing through courtrooms, "I would characterize him as a friend of the family, a close friend."

"As a second son, perhaps?"

"I have no first son."

The prosecutor smiled. "As a kind of protégé, then. A young man who spent a great deal of time in your home."

"Yes."

Stefanie's clenched organs relaxed a fraction. Of course Sir John knew how to answer these questions. Simple, without elaboration. Give the prosecutor nothing to pounce on.

After all, hadn't she herself learned all this in Sir John's own chambers?

"Would you say you had a fatherly affection for him, then?"

"Certainly I had an affection for him."

The prosecutor turned to where the Duke of Southam sat, white-haired and unsmiling, his cane propped beside him, in the second row of benches. He stretched out his arm, palm upward, and stretched his face into an expression of confusion. "But the accused already had a father, did he not?"

"Yes, he did."

"And yet Lord Hatherfield breakfasted at your house every morning, did he not, instead of that of his father and stepmother."

"He often breakfasted at my house."

"So you must have been familiar with the state of Lord Hatherfield's mind. With the nature of his relationship with his parents." The prosecutor inserted an emphasis on the word *parents*.

"We did not discuss Lord Hatherfield's family."

"Did you have the impression, then, that relations between Lord Hatherfield and his parents were not warm?"

"I had the impression that Lord Hatherfield was a dutiful son."

"But not an affectionate one."

"I can have no opinion on that matter."

The prosecutor's eyes narrowed slightly with frustration. He turned around and, in a sweeping gesture, brought his hand to rest on a stack of papers at his table. "But can we not conclude that since Lord Hatherfield lived entirely on his own, took his breakfast each morning in the home of Sir John Worthington, and by all accounts saw almost nothing of his parents, that relations between them were not only not warm, but in fact quite cold? That Lord Hatherfield was not—as you say—a dutiful son, but rather a hard-hearted and even unfilial son, who paid his parents little attention and rendered them even less service?"

Mr. Fairchurch shot to his feet at Stefanie's side. "My lord! This is pure speculation on the part of my learned colleague."

"Proceed with your questioning, Mr. Duckworth," said the judge, "and stick to the facts, if you please."

"I beg your pardon." Mr. Duckworth patted his brow. "As a father myself, I find the subject close to my heart. Sir John, I will rephrase the question, in deference to my learned colleague's delicate sensibilities. Where would you judge that the Marquess of Hatherfield spent the chiefest part of his time: at your house, or at the home of the Duke and Duchess of Southam, God rest her soul?"

Sir John looked neither at the duke nor at Hatherfield. He fixed his eyes on Mr. Duckworth, and his expression no longer sagged under the oppressive weight of the late July heat, but had hardened into a mask. "At my house."

Stefanie's fingers grew damp around her pen. She glanced at Hatherfield in his box. He stood with his usual expression of mild interest, hands resting lightly on the rail, a small smile curling the corner of his beautiful mouth. As if they were not discussing his father and stepmother at all, but rather two strangers whose names escaped him at the moment.

Mr. Duckworth smiled and turned to the jury. "Thank you, Sir John. I believe that settles the question of Lord Hatherfield's filial affection to the court's confident satisfaction."

TWO

❧

Among the many virtues owned by Her Royal Highness Stefanie, youngest Princess of Holstein-Schweinwald-Huhnhof, the earliness of her hours was not conspicuous.

"One final admonition," Miss Dingleby had said, sharp of eye and sharp of voice, that last morning in Devon. "You are now a member of the professional classes. Early to bed, early to rise."

"Of course!" Stefanie had replied cheerfully, lifting her teacup in salute. "The easiest thing in the world. Healthy, wealthy, and wise!"

That was yesterday morning, however, with a civilized breakfast spread out before her and a decent cup of tea spread out inside her. This morning, the picture was altogether different. Stefanie opened her eyes in a bare little bed to a bare little room, no breakfast within sight, no tea within scent, while a cold rain rattled against her gloomy window glass. She did the sensible thing. She rolled onto her empty stomach and went back to sleep.

An instant later—it seemed like an instant, anyway—a furious knocking started up in Stefanie's brain. She cracked open one eye.

To her mild confusion, the knocking seemed to be coming from the door instead of her head. Well. How terribly rude.

She said so.

"How terribly rude!" she called out. "There's no need for that sort of thing!"

A slight pause in the racket. "Sir?"

Oh. Her voice. Of course. Stefanie cleared her throat and added a little heft. "There's no need for all that knocking. I shall be up in due course."

"Sir!" *Knockknockknock.* "Sir John, he says you're to come downstairs directly this moment, he's to leave for chambers in ten minutes!" *Knockknockknock.* "Come on, now, sir! He'll have me head if you're not dressed and ready!"

Stefanie heaved herself up and shook her head. She glanced at the plain white clock on her plain white nightstand—seven forty-six, how ghastly—and then at the plain white nightshirt covering her torso. Her wits began to gather themselves.

Slowly.

Slowly.

Oh, Lord. Now she remembered.

The long, wet day of travel yesterday, crushed up against the massive thighs of the Marquess of Hatherfield. The steely glare from that steely china doll, Lady Charlotte. Sir John, buried in papers. The train, the carriage to Cadogan Square. The austere supper of bread, cheese, and Madeira with a silent Sir John in the Gothic dining room (Lady Charlotte had flounced upstairs to take supper on a tray). The rain, the rain. The itch of her glued-on mustache. The dull black necktie, sinking her further into gloom.

The rain.

The weight of all these recollections sank into her dismal mind. Really, it was a wonder she could stir herself at all this morning.

"Coming," she called, sotto verve.

Knockknockknock. "Now, sir! They'll have me head, they will!"

Stefanie swung her legs to the floor and summoned herself. "You may tell Sir John," she said, quite deeply and quite clearly, "I shall be downstairs, dressed and shaved and ready, in exactly three minutes."

Another slight pause. "Very well, sir." Footsteps, in blissful retreat.

So much for the knocking, then. Now for the toilette.

The shaving part was easy, as she had no actual whiskers to whisk off, only a bristling dark mustache to glue on. (She had thought it rather dashing, yesterday. Now she cordially hated the itchy thing.) Instead, Stefanie found her black trousers and thrust her legs into them; she found a shirt and buttoned herself in. She applied jacket and necktie in swift strokes; she splashed her face with icy water and slicked back her auburn hair with oil. Toothbrush, tooth powder. Dabs of glue, then the mustache. Shoes. Damned buckles.

She clattered downstairs at double time and came to a perplexed halt at the bottom of the steps. "Sir?" inquired a passing footman, bearing a tray.

"The breakfast room?" she gasped.

"If you'll follow me, sir." The footman moved off at a stately pace. Stefanie jogged behind him. The scents trailing through the hall made her want to swoon: rich and meaty, toasty-browny, spice and milky. Tea and all good things. Stefanie adored breakfast. On Sunday mornings, when Miss Dingleby allowed the lesson schedule to relax a trifle, Stefanie might linger over the table for an hour, stuffing herself silly, a dollop of this and a fat sausage of that. Tea and more tea. That dreadful section of grapefruit, upon which the governess insisted.

Stefanie's belly made a prolonged and undignified sound, to make its intentions clear.

The footman swerved to the left, and Stefanie followed him into an elegant breakfast room, plated at one end by a set of French doors that allowed in as much light as the weather and the surrounding houses would permit. But Stefanie's eyes didn't linger curiously at the gray view of Sir John's courtyard garden, not when a sideboard full of breakfast stood promisingly to her right. She veered foodward and snatched a plate.

Sir John's voice ground into the air behind her. "Why, good morning, Mr. Thomas. At last." The last two words bit deep.

"Good morning, Sir John. A trifle gloomy, wouldn't you say?"

"My dear young man," said Sir John, in a way that suggested she was anything but. "Whatever are you doing?"

"Gathering breakfast, of course." Stefanie placed an egg in

her cup and hovered between the sausage and the kidneys. "The most important meal of the day, according to that American fellow, whose name escapes me. The chap with the electricity."

"Indeed." Dryly. "Which is why I so deeply regret that you will miss it."

"Miss it? Whatever for?"

"Because we depart this house for my chambers in four minutes, Mr. Thomas."

A faint titter.

Stefanie turned from the sideboard, plate in hand, mouth open to object, and only then did she realize that the room contained three occupants. Sir John at the head, gray of hair and flushed of face. Lady Charlotte, exquisite at his right, like a pastel drawing of a medieval shepherdess.

And the Marquess of Hatherfield.

He sat to the left of Sir John, with his back to the sideboard, wearing a pale gray suit of fine wool that stretched and stretched across the width of his shoulders. But he had turned his head in her direction, and Stefanie's gaze drifted to a halt somewhere in the middle of his amused blue eyes, the fresh-scrubbed skin of his cheeks and neck. He looked delicious and dewy and edible, every muscular, lovingly crafted inch of him, and he seemed to be suppressing something in his throat.

Something rather like a prodigious bout of laughter.

"I beg your pardon, your lordship," Stefanie said. "Were you going to say something?"

He dabbed at his lips. "Benjamin Franklin."

"Benjamin Franklin?"

"The American chap. With the electricity. Though he was not, in fact, a notable proponent of breakfast, merely early hours in general."

"Oh, right. Of course. Thank you." Stefanie eased herself into a chair and signaled for the footman to address her with the teapot. "In any case, I shan't be above ten minutes, Sir John, I promise. Thank you, my good man." This to the footman, who set down the teapot with grave ceremony. She poured herself a cheerful cup and bent close to inhale the scent. "Have you any fresh toast? This seems to have cooled."

Another titter.

Stefanie eyed Lady Charlotte from the rim of her teacup. She had spent all day yesterday enduring her ladyship's telling titters, her superior giggles, and really. Enough was enough.

"Something amuses you, Lady Charlotte? Or does the old lace itch something dreadful this morning?"

A slight movement of his lordship's shoulders at her side.

"Not at all," said Lady Charlotte. "I was only observing the expression on Sir John's face."

Stefanie turned in surprise to Sir John. The chandelier overhead, wired for electricity and blazing with unseemly enthusiasm, illuminated his face in lurid detail: the purpling skin, the wide-open eyes, the outraged brows, the staggered chin.

A gulp of hot tea, which had been on the point of swishing itself comfortably down Stefanie's esophagus, spilled over into her windpipe.

"I say," said the marquess, pounding her back. "Nasty thing, tea."

Sir John rose from his chair and tossed his napkin atop his empty plate. He pulled a gold watch from his pocket—quite needlessly, for a clock ticked away on the nearby mantel—and consulted the dial. "My chaise departs this door every morning for Temple Bar at eight o'clock precisely. *Precisely*, Mr. Thomas. In consequence, if you yourself are not present on the front doorstep at precisely eight o'clock, you shall be obliged to make your own way to my chambers. We begin work at eight thirty, Mr. Thomas."

Stefanie nodded helplessly to the rhythm of Hatherfield's open palm on the back of her drab black coat. Through her watering eyes, she saw Sir John stride out the door in a flash of electric light against his gray head.

"I suppose we ought to have warned you about my uncle's punctual habits." Lady Charlotte smiled benevolently.

The tea had finally found its way out of Stefanie's lungs. "Really. A matter of a few minutes. Is he ordinarily so inflexible?"

"How unfortunate it's raining. You won't find a cab, poor fellow." Lady Charlotte spread another slice of toast with the thinnest possible layer of butter. "But no doubt the walk will lift your spirits."

"Your concern touches me deeply."

"Lady Charlotte is renowned for her generous spirit," said Hatherfield. He folded his napkin neatly and laid it next to his plate.

Lady Charlotte turned to him. "Are you leaving, James?"

For some reason, the intimacy of Hatherfield's given name on those flawless rosebud lips made Stefanie's innards revolt. She set down her fork.

"I'm afraid I must," Hatherfield was saying, "loath as I am to leave poor, young, unsuspecting Thomas trapped between your playful claws, my dear."

There was an odd silence. Stefanie glanced up from her tea.

Lady Charlotte's gaze rested to Stefanie's left, on Hatherfield's rising body. Her lips had parted slightly, her eyes had grown wide and uncertain.

But the expression lasted only an instant. In the next, Lady Charlotte turned to Stefanie herself, all softness and solicitation. "Yes. Poor Mr. Thomas. You must have an umbrella. I shall see to it myself. Must you leave your breakfast behind, however? A horrid shame. Tyrannical Sir John. He really is impossible."

The Marquess of Hatherfield was on his feet. "Indeed. On second thought, I perceive a splendid solution to this unfortunate dilemma."

"You do?" said Lady Charlotte.

"You do?" said Stefanie, setting down her empty teacup.

"I do. Mr. Thomas, you may finish your breakfast at your leisure, and ride in perfect dryness and comfort to Sir John's chambers."

"Really, James? Are you going to head out into the rain and fetch him a hansom yourself?" asked Lady Charlotte dryly.

"Not at all. I shall simply take him there in my own hansom, which awaits us in the street outside this very moment. Mr. Thomas? Does this suit you?" Hatherfield turned to Stefanie and made a little bow.

Stefanie returned Lady Charlotte's astonished gaze with a wink. She finished her toast, dabbed her mouth, and rose from her chair, all the way up to the tip of Lord Hatherfield's straight golden nose.

"How very kind, your lordship. I should like that very much."

The rain crackled earnestly against the window of Hatherfield's hansom, filling in the silence. He settled into the corner and crossed his arms. Young Thomas had his—*her*—hands twisted together on his—*her*—lap. She stared at the window as if counting the raindrops on the glass.

"Nervous?" he asked.

"Me?" She turned to him. "No, not at all. I'm not the nervous sort. I was only reflecting."

"Of course you were." He paused. "May I be so unpardonably rude as to ask the subject?"

The subdued light in the vehicle softened her face, making her sex so obvious it took him by the chest. In the breakfast room, she had looked so sturdy and young-laddish, with her brave cheekbones and bristling mustache and short, sleek hair. He'd had to concentrate to shift the image in his mind, to see her properly, as she really was.

Here, now, it was much easier. Hatherfield wanted to reach across the few feet of damp space and take her hand.

Take more than that.

She was still looking at him, not replying. Good Lord. Could she read his thoughts?

"I was thinking about my family," she said. "My sisters."

"Left behind?"

"Yes."

"Ah. You must miss them a great deal."

She opened her lips eagerly as if to say *Oh, very much!* But at the last instant she checked herself. "Oh, a little, I suppose." She shrugged and looked back out the window. "They're only girls, after all. Not much company for a young fellow like me."

"Ah, no. Of course not. I quite understand. Have a few sisters myself. All that nonsense about dresses and ribbons and lapdogs. Appalling rot."

"Yes, quite." She sounded as if she might choke.

"We men, on the other hand, have much weightier things to discuss. Politics, for example. Tell me, what's your opinion of this Corrupt Practices Act? I don't think there's enough bite to it, myself."

"No, not at all. Much more bite is required. Corrupt practices are . . . simply . . . dreadful things."

"I quite agree. Any sort of subterfuge undermines the trust."

"The trust?"

"Yes. The public's trust in its political institutions and services. Disguise, underhanded dealings, it's all most distressing. Most un-British, wouldn't you say?"

"I . . . yes. Most un-British."

Hatherfield uncrossed his arms and stretched one hand along the back of the seat. "The worst sort of punishment should be reserved for such devious malefactors. Nothing's too severe for them, really. It makes my fingers tingle with eagerness to deliver the proper justice." He wiggled the fingers in question to emphasize his point.

At which time Thomas's spine went stiff as a pole. She turned back to him and shot him a look of such haughty severity from those green blue eyes, it nearly pinned him to the seat. "You're up early today, your lordship," she said crisply.

"I beg your pardon?"

"The hour. I thought idle young aristocrats such as yourself were only just retiring as dawn breaks over London."

"Ah, well." He spread out his hand. "I'm sorry to disappoint you, then. But habits are habits."

"You make a habit of rising at seven o'clock in the morning, in order to secure a breakfast at Sir John's table? Are Lady Charlotte's charms so terribly irresistible?" Her eyebrow rose, as if she'd just delivered a blow of mortal proportions.

He laughed. "No, no. Charming as the lady is, the habit is of much longer standing than my acquaintance with her. No, the thing is, I row."

"Row?"

"A boat." He motioned with his arms. "In the river, each morning."

"In the *river*?" Aghast. "Each *morning*?"

"Yes, indeed. Bright and cheery. Up around Putney Bridge. A number of boathouses there. I belong to one."

"But . . . why on earth?"

The expression on poor Thomas's face was priceless. Such a mixture of horror and bemusement, eyebrows perched high on her forehead, jaw dipping low. How plump, those parted lips. Hatherfield could almost see the tip of her tongue, beckoning within.

She'd just asked a question. What was it? Oh, right.

"Exercise, Mr. Thomas." He plucked at a piece of invisible lint on his trouser knee. "I find I'm rather addicted to it. And the early hour, if you care to gaze upon it, is really quite good for the soul."

"The soul." As she might say *the tooth fairy*.

"Yes, the soul. Even in London, even in the incessant drizzle." He nodded to the window. "Just you, in a light little well-behaved racing scull, and the water, and your own muscles working in rhythm. Not another care in the universe."

Her eyes were on his face, now. He rather liked them there, earnest and curious.

"Aren't you cold, out there?"

He shrugged. "A little. But the exercise warms one up wonderfully. And then breakfast, of course. You have me there. Sir John lays a much earlier table than my own family. I take shameless advantage."

"They don't seem to mind."

The hansom lurched around a corner. Hatherfield glanced outside. They were turning into the muddy Strand now; almost there. Somerset House slid past in a monumental charcoal blur. "No, they don't," he said. "He does have a kind heart, Sir John, under all that bluster. You might wish to consider cooperating with those early hours of his. It's not that hard, really. A little discipline goes a long way."

She made a little noise of laughter, a delightful bell-like sound. "Oh, that's easy for you to say, you paragon. You're accustomed to rising at dawn."

"So I am," he said, "but that doesn't make it any easier."

"Then why torture yourself?"

Why, indeed? Why torture himself? Why rise at dawn every morning and push his body through a wall of pain, beyond the limit of human endurance, beyond memory and conscious thought, out there in the fog-shrouded Thames with no one to see or hear him?

Because it was better than lying sleepless in his bed, staring at the ceiling.

Hatherfield felt Thomas's gaze on his face, this stranger with her elegant bones and white unmarked skin, all buttoned up in her sober man's suit, on her way to begin a day's work in the chambers of Sir John Worthington, Q.C., in Temple Bar. The two of them in his own carriage, masks in place, outer shells fully hardened to protect the secret centers within.

What was she doing there? Why? A hot little flame burned inside Hatherfield's chest, a most uncharacteristic desire to know her, to look inside her secret center.

Dangerous business, secret centers. Who knew what he might find?

"It's not torture," he said. "You only have to retire at a decent hour, set your alarm clock—you do have an alarm clock at your bedside, don't you, Mr. Thomas, working man that you are?—for half four in the morning . . ."

"Half *four*!"

The hansom made another sharp turn, jolting them both. Hatherfield put out an instinctive hand to steady her. The clattering rhythm slowed.

"Here we are," he said. "You have your umbrella?"

"Right here." She held it up, just as the carriage came to a stop. Her lips parted uncertainly. "Thank you, Lord Hatherfield. It's very kind of you. I confess, I've never ridden in a private hansom before."

"Not at all. An eccentricity of mine, I suppose, but a hansom is a great deal nimbler than a proper four-wheeler, to say nothing of economical. I drive it myself from time to time. Anyway, it was no trouble at all. I couldn't have lived with the picture of you arriving here late, all wet and wilted, to face Sir John's secretary for the very first time."

"His secretary?"

Hatherfield opened up the door and gave her a nudge. "Give him my warmest regards!" he said cheerfully, and that was the last he saw of poor young Thomas, her face registering stricken trepidation, her luscious round, young bottom outlined against her drab black trousers as she pitched herself out the hansom door.

Hatherfield fell back against the cushion and stared at the ceiling of his carriage.

The little front window opened. "Back to the Mansions, sir?" inquired the coachman.

"Back to the Mansions."

Back to his own rooms in Albert Hall Mansions, where he would take out a sheet of paper and compose a friendly man-to-man telegram to the Duke of Olympia: Warmest regards, faithful servant, et cetera, and what the devil sort of mischief was he plotting with this Mr. Stephen Thomas, whose luscious bottom was quite demonstrably *not* that of a mister?

THREE

Sir John's secretary.

Nobody had warned Stefanie about a secretary. But here he stood before her, black of eyes, thin of hair, gimlet of face, his bony shoulders squared for battle. He said, in a voice both high-pitched and menacing, "You're wet, Mr. Thomas. Wet and late." The word *late* was uttered with particular distasteful emphasis, as he might say *infected with clap*.

But Stefanie was not the sort of princess to allow a mere underling to get the moral advantage of her. She placed her hat on the hat stand, removed her damp coat, and straightened her lapels before answering.

"It's raining," she said, "and half eight is a most uncivilized hour."

The outrage on the secretary's face turned so livid, Stefanie could almost smell it. Or perhaps that was the chap's own scent, redolent of mothballs and hair oil.

He thrust his finger at the clock on the shelf. "Do you see what the time is, Mr. Thomas?"

"I do, Mr. . . . er . . . I beg your pardon. Have you a name?"

A faint titter sounded from some distant corner. The secretary whirled about, and for the first time Stefanie noticed the room in which they were standing, a large and stately chamber

lined with shelves and shelves of legal texts in handsome gold-
stamped bindings. Down the exact center of the room marched
two rows of elderly wooden desks, containing four young men
in threadbare black suits identical to her own, with identical
brown whiskers bristling about their jowls in an extremely
businesslike fashion. Four identical pens scratched in unison
across the four identical desktops. Stefanie gazed in horror.

The tittering quelled instantly.

The secretary turned his gimlet face back to her.

"My name is Mr. Turner, and you would do well . . ."

"Turner. Charmed." Stefanie cast a disdainful glance at the
plain black-and-white clock ticking dolefully on the shelf and
pulled her own watch from her pocket, a handsome gold piece
given to her by a particularly generous stepmother for her
eighteenth birthday, and which she had been sternly instructed
to leave behind in Devon. "It is eight thirty-six in the a.m.,
Turner, and . . ."

"*Mister* Turner."

Stefanie favored him with an indulgent smile. "*Mister*
Turner. It is eight thirty-six in the a.m., and if those six minutes are of such critical importance to you and Sir John, I shall
be happy to make them up at the end of the day. Now. Where
is my office, Mr. Turner?"

"Your office!" Mr. Turner's face, alas, had already gone as
scarlet a shade as his circulatory system could support; the
valiant old capillaries could apparently do no more. "You have
a desk, Thomas. A . . ."

"*Mister* Thomas."

Another titter interrupted the even scratching of the identical pens.

Mr. Turner's black eyes narrowed even farther. More, and
they would squint shut entirely.

"*Mister* Thomas. You have a desk. Right there." Mr. Turner
pointed a long and bony finger toward a battered wooden con-
traption in the back corner of the room, the last in the right-
hand row.

Stefanie turned and gazed at the desk in question for a
weighty moment. She swiveled back to Mr. Turner. "This is
entirely inadequate, to say nothing of the lack of privacy. I
shall require my own office."

"Your . . . own . . . *office*?"

"Yes." Stefanie removed her gloves in a few brisk tugs. "Nothing large or elaborate, of course. A nice little box will suffice, so long as there are sufficient shelves and a sturdy desk." She cast a disapproving eye at the dull piece of furniture in the corner, which seemed, if she wasn't mistaken, to tilt at least half an inch to the left-hand side. "And a fireplace, of course. I do dislike working in the cold."

"Oh, I see. A fireplace, naturally."

Stefanie began to tick off the items on her fingers. "A window for natural light, such as it is in this godforsaken fogbank of a city. Oh. And a rug. So much easier on the feet."

"A rug!" Mr. Turner smacked his forehead. "Of course! How could I neglect such an important furnishing for Your Royal Highness! Shall I arrange for a personal servant to toast your crumpets and polish your crown?"

A squeak, as of hilarity barely contained.

Stefanie opened her lips to tell Mr. Turner that sounded very agreeable indeed, the sooner the better, though naturally one should really employ a professional jeweler for the second task, ordinary servants being so unfamiliar with the delicate and specialized treatment of precious minerals.

Then she remembered herself.

"A servant is quite unnecessary, Mr. Turner," she said. "I am shocked you would consider such an extravagance. I will not report what I've heard to Sir John—I should never stoop to telling tales—but I shall bear it in mind." She tapped her forehead.

"The cheek!" Mr. Turner said.

"Yes. Isn't it, rather. But don't worry, my good man. I'm sure we shall grow used to each other in no time, learn to appreciate in full the other's sterling qualities. Fast friends and all that. Do you think . . ."

A loud bang rattled the books in their bindings. The pens stopped scratching. Stefanie spun about.

Sir John Worthington stood in the doorway, hands on hips, judicial robes dangling from his shoulders, white wig just a trifle askew. Stefanie's hand itched to set it right.

"What the devil is going on here? Turner? What's this racket?"

"Sir, I . . ."

"Dash it all! I'm off to court in"—a glance at the clock—"seven minutes precisely, and you look quite distinctly as if you're about to have an apoplexy on the floor of my chambers. Bad form, Turner. Very bad form."

At these damning words from his employer, Mr. Turner's scarecrow throat seemed to clog with fear, or rage, or nervous anxiety, or some other emotion beyond the power of Stefanie's comprehension. "Oh, but sir . . . Mr. Thomas, sir . . ."

Thunderous. "What about Thomas? Spit it out, man!"

"He . . . he . . ." An asthmatic wheeze.

All at once, Stefanie understood. She was a princess, after all; she had witnessed more than one underling turned into primordial jelly in the face of Royal Disapproval. Perfectly natural, if not particularly brave. Her heart softened. In such cases, the strong must naturally protect the weak.

"The thing is, Sir John," said Stefanie, casting her eyes down contritely, "I was being cheeky."

"Cheeky!"

"Yes, sir. Very, very abominably cheeky. A bad habit of mine, I'm afraid."

"I say. Is this true, Mr. Turner?"

Mr. Turner's mouth worked. He cast a desperate glance at Stefanie. He straightened his bony shoulders, clutched his hands to the small of his back, and tilted his chin. "Cheeky, sir? *Cheeky* does not begin to describe the scope of Mr. Thomas's insolent lack of respect for his superiors. This . . . this *young fellow*"—as he might say *young fornicator*—"this young fellow had the temerity to ask for an office, sir. An office! With . . . with a window!"

"And a rug," Stefanie said modestly. "So much easier on the feet."

A swift twitch disturbed the stern line of Sir John's judicial mouth. "Shocking. Shocking, Mr. Thomas. You should be aware that in these chambers, only I and my fellow counsel Mr. Norham are privileged to inhabit private offices. The clerks and secretaries perform their duties in a shared space, in order to promote that atmosphere of open-minded collegiality without which learning and innovation cannot take place." He waved a withered hand to indicate the open-minded collegiality, the learning and innovation with which the atmosphere apparently vibrated.

"I see. Of course," said Stefanie. "Quite laudable, sir. I shall keep that in mind henceforth."

"You will allow me to observe, Mr. Thomas, that you have not made a particularly auspicious beginning to your law career. It is not yet nine o'clock on your first morning, and you have already demonstrated a propensity to both tardiness and"—another twitch—"cheekiness. This must be nipped in the bud, Mr. Thomas. In the bud."

Someone coughed at the back of the room. The sound echoed delicately from the ceiling plasterwork.

"Yes, sir."

"You must endeavor to keep your cheeky remarks to yourself in these chambers. You will also keep strictly to the stated hours of business."

"Strictly!" piped up Mr. Turner, with raised finger.

"To that end, Mr. Thomas, I shall assign you to prepare a summary of the relevant case law for a matter just brought to my chambers on Friday. A most extraordinary case. Mr. Turner will give you the necessary details and direct you to the necessary resources. I expect to find this summary on my desk when I arrive in these chambers tomorrow morning. Is that understood?"

"Tomorrow morning at half past eight!" shrieked Mr. Turner. "Not a minute later!"

"Yes, sir," said Stefanie.

"Mr. Turner, my briefcase," said Sir John.

Mr. Turner scuttled into the office like a bony black beetle, leaving Stefanie and Sir John in the vast book-lined hall with the battered desks and the identical clerks and the monochrome clock ticking steadily away. Sir John's eyes were grave and slightly pink at the corners. "Mr. Thomas," he said, not unkindly, "I perceive you are not a young man accustomed to discipline. But the law is exact and demanding, and you must learn to adjust your own habits, for I assure you the legal system of Great Britain will not adjust itself to yours."

"Yes, sir."

"I admire your pluck, however." He turned in a swish of black robes, just as Mr. Turner emerged through the office door, bearing a large leather suitcase in his hands as if it were a holy chalice. "Thank you, Mr. Turner," he said, and strode to the door.

"Wait, Sir John!"

The man turned in an astonished jerk, eyebrows high.

Stefanie walked up to him and reached for his head. "Your wig. It's gone lopsided, I'm afraid."

A gasp rent the air behind her.

Stefanie tugged the wig into place and stood back critically. "Much better."

Sir John's lips trembled. A flush pinked the tip of his nose. "I will have that summary on my desk on the dot of half eight, Mr. Thomas, or this day in my chambers will be your last. And Olympia can bloody well hang himself."

And he stalked out the door with a crash of his briefcase against the wood.

B y eight o'clock in the evening, Stefanie's back felt as if it had turned into metal wire and been left out in the rain to rust.

A summary. It had sounded so simple. A summary: How difficult could that be?

Very difficult indeed, as it turned out. Thirty or forty pages' worth of difficult, of deciphering the dry legal language in the books stacked at her desk and on the floor next to her feet. Of organizing and describing each precedent, its similarities and points of departure to the case in question. All this, when she had no earthly idea of British law, or any law at all, for that matter. Thank goodness she retained her Latin, or rather thank the diligent and determined Miss Dingleby, because goodness had had nothing at all to do with it.

Stefanie glanced at the clock, that dashed tyrannical clock on the shelf, and allowed herself to link her fingers together above her head and stretch. Oh, heaven. Long and high, that was it. Her startled vertebrae rattled together like dominoes. The swathes of linen binding her chest strained and strained. She'd imagined that dressing as a man would free her body— all those skirts and petticoats and corsets, how she'd hated them—but this was just as bad, in its way. Just as constricting.

God, what she wouldn't give to loosen them, to let her poor crushed bosom breathe for a moment. An instant or two of physical freedom, just a taste of her old feminine self.

Stefanie cast a speculative look at the window. The glass had gone black long ago, the other clerks had left for their comfortable dinners and comfortable beds. She was quite alone.

Why not?

Stefanie twiddled her fountain pen between her thumb and forefinger, and then she set it down and shrugged off her jacket. She unbuttoned her drab waistcoat and pulled her shirt from her beastly black trousers, and then she slid her hands upward along her soft female skin to the edge of the linen band and . . .

The door flew open.

"Hullo there, Thomas!" called out the cheerful voice of the Marquess of Hatherfield. "I've brought you a spot of supper, what?"

Stefanie whipped to face the bookshelf, stuffing her long white shirt in fistfuls back down her trousers. "Supper!"

"Yes, supper! Sir John informed me of your little, er, predicament, and I said to myself, dash it all, that's no way to . . . I say, I haven't caught you out, have I?"

Stefanie's fingers flew at her waistcoat buttons. "Not at all. Only . . . just . . ."

"Making yourself a bit more comfortable, eh? Nothing to be ashamed of, old boy. We're all guilty of it, from time to time." A plonk, as of something soft and heavy on a wooden surface.

Stefanie tugged her buttoned waistcoat in place, along with her dignity. She turned. The Marquess of Hatherfield it was, right enough, standing before her like a Thoroughbred in the sales ring, hair glossy, eyes bright, clothes molded lovingly around his triangular torso. She aimed her gaze between his arrow-straight eyebrows, the better to avoid the mesmeric power of those dancing blue eyes. "I haven't the faintest idea what you mean. Is that Bordeaux?"

"Rather. A sixty-two Mouton Rothschild, if you like that kind of thing."

"Egad."

"I thought a celebration of some sort was in order. Your first day of gainful employment." Hatherfield set down the bottle and swung his jacket from his shoulders, arranging it about a nearby chair with a bullfighter's flourish. He plucked a corkscrew from the hamper and applied himself to the matter at hand. "Ghastly place, these chambers of Sir John's. The flesh positively shuddered at the thought of you slaving away all night, not a soul for company."

Stefanie was trying to keep her eyes fixed on the bottle, instead of the play of muscle beneath his white shirt as he twisted the corkscrew. Her brain was still reeling in shock. Hatherfield. Here. Amid the books, the battered desks. A few feet away, gathering up all the meager light and energy in the room and radiating it back outward like a beacon of divine hope. Apollo come to life. "I can manage well enough."

"Ah. You were planning to work all night with no sustenance at all?" The cork slid free with a faint relieved pop.

"I . . . well, I hadn't thought of that." Which was quite true. Stefanie hadn't given supper the slightest consideration. After all, food simply arrived at the appointed hours, didn't it? Borne by servants, prepared to varying degrees of excellence, piping hot and accompanied by the appropriate garnish.

Except when one was a lowly law clerk slaving away unnoticed and unaccompanied in Temple Bar.

"You see?" Hatherfield tapped his temple and poured out two glasses. The liquid slid downward in a silky curl. Stefanie's mouth tingled.

"It was very kind of you to think of me. To come all this way."

"I hadn't anything better to do." He handed her a glass. "To your health, my good fellow."

"To your health." She clinked and drank. Oh, heaven. A masterful vintage, a masterful wine, thick and plummy and perfect, all the more so for arriving so suddenly and unexpectedly in the middle of her loneliest hour. She opened her eyes, which had closed briefly in ecstasy, and found the gaze of the marquis fixed intently upon her face. "Sir?" she said, and her voice, good Lord, it *squeaked!* Stefanie had never squeaked in her life, not even when confronted in the middle of the night by the mayor of Huhnhof Baden while exchanging his prize bull for a rather bad-tempered white goat.

But that *gaze* of his, all blue and alive. God in heaven. You could almost touch it. You could die from it, if you weren't careful.

The obvious question began to form in Stefanie's discombobulated brain: Why, exactly, had the eminent and Apollonian Marquess of Hatherfield troubled himself to bring the unremarkable Mr. Stephen Thomas a picnic supper in Temple Bar this evening?

"Ah. You're probably wondering why I've troubled myself to come so far this evening," said Hatherfield. "Cheese?"

"Yes, please."

Hatherfield brandished an ivory-handled knife, sliced a wedge, and placed it on a soft white roll. "To be perfectly honest, Mr. Thomas, I'm curious about you."

"Curious. About me?" Stefanie accepted the bread and cheese with her best innocent air. She was rather good at innocent airs, or so she flattered herself. God knew she'd had ages of practice. When the Archduke of Schleissen-Pleissen stormed downstairs to breakfast complaining publicly of a bed short-sheeted the night before, an innocent air might prove the only thing standing between a certain mischievous young princess and a week spent with the solid weight of a Gutenberg Bible balanced atop her head.

"Yes, Mr. Thomas. About you. You don't seem the ordinary sort of law clerk at all." Hatherfield served himself and slumped with massive masculine grace into the chair behind him, dangling his wine from one hand and his bread and cheese from the other, glossy blond hair flopping in an irresistible wave onto his forehead. Apollo transformed to Dionysus.

Hmm. Stefanie rather liked Dionysus.

She slumped into her own chair, not to be outdone, and propped her foot upon the desk for good measure. "For that matter, your lordship, you don't seem the ordinary sort of marquis, if you don't mind my observing. All this rowing business. Fetching supper for lowly clerks, unannounced. Haven't you a club in which to drink yourself silly and gamble away your fortune? A mistress on whom to get a bastard or two?" A luxurious sip of wine. "Explain yourself."

Hatherfield coughed. "You first."

Stefanie gestured outward with her wine hand. "Nothing to tell. I am as you see me. Humble fellow seeking to make his fortune in the law."

"Really."

"Really."

Hatherfield bit into his bread and cheese and ate without hurry. His gaze settled at the top of her head and traveled warmly downward, bite by bite, lingering on the buttons of her waistcoat, the seam of her trousers, until he reached the tip of her shoe where it rested atop the desk. He swallowed his last. "How fortunate, then, that you can count on the patronage of the Duke of Olympia in your quest for professional glory."

Stefanie's skin tingled, her clothes itched. Could he see the lurch of her heart beneath her waistcoat? She kept her limbs still under his lazy stare, her face mild, but the effort required all her concentration. He'd asked a question. What was it? "Olympia?" she said feebly.

"Yes. A lucky coincidence, having such a powerful chap so thoroughly in your corner."

"We are related. On my mother's side."

"I see. Eat your supper, Thomas. You need your strength."

Stefanie, not ordinarily an obedient sort of girl, found herself biting into her bread with vigor. "And you, sir?" she asked, through her full mouth, as slovenly and unfeminine as she could manage. "Isn't your mistress expecting you this evening?"

"I don't have a mistress, Mr. Thomas."

Was that a trace of emphasis on the *Mister*? Was that a smile lurking at the corner of his mouth? Stefanie lifted her other leg to the desk and crossed it over the first.

"Come now, your lordship," she said. "We are both men of the world, aren't we? A gorgeous young fellow like you, a fine, healthy animal. A chap has his needs, hasn't he? Nothing to be ashamed of."

"I'm flattered by your assessment of my charms, Mr. Thomas, but I'm afraid I must disappoint you there." He spread his hands. "No mistress."

"Ah. You're between lovers, then?"

"In fact, I've never kept a mistress." Hatherfield shrugged and drank the rest of his wine, without moving his eyes so much as a millimeter away from the center of Stefanie's gaze. He leaned forward and refilled his glass.

"Oh. I see." Stefanie had just opened her mouth to ask why, when an Awful Possibility occurred to her.

No mistress. Warm gaze traveling down the length of

Stefanie's trousers. Masculine beauty beyond the range of ordinary human imagination. That absent mustache, those shaved cheeks, as sleek as a boy's.

Stefanie's mouth went dry with disappointment. Well, not disappointment, surely. It wasn't as if she'd ever contemplated . . . After all, she had her disguise to maintain . . . Well, really, she was a princess, and once she regained her title, there could be no . . .

Oh, but still. He was so . . . so . . . delicious. Sprawled there in his chair, simmering with gorgeousness and strength and a sort of intent inventiveness, his red wine balanced in his palm. Like a golden leopard, ready to pounce. Her insides grew warm, just looking at him. Thinking about those large and calloused hands on her skin, that broad chest against hers . . .

What a shame. Not to be, apparently. Not that it ever *had* been to be, so to speak.

"I see," she said again, and hid her face in her wine. "I expect the women of London are prostrate with disappointment."

"I don't know about that," said Hatherfield, "but the fact is I'm a dull fellow, really. Up at dawn, in bed by ten. A few solitary habits. An investment or two to inspect, now and again. Not much to interest a lady."

"Obviously, I wouldn't know about that."

"No, of course not." Hatherfield set his wineglass on the edge of the desk and leaned forward. He steepled his fingers and contemplated her, smiling. "You, on the other hand. I have the distinct feeling there's all sort of interesting things going on in that head of yours."

"No, no. Not at all." Stefanie swung her legs to the floor and shuffled a paper or two. "Nothing, you know, but my passion for the law and all that."

"Tell me about this case you're working on."

"*This* case? Oh. No." Stefanie's face, already a trifle flushed, grew distinctly warm. "No, no. Very, very, extremely, just really quite a dull affair. Of no interest whatever."

"Surely not that bad." Hatherfield whisked a sheet of paper from the desk.

"Look here, that's . . . a client . . . quite confidential, I'm sure . . ." She held out her hand. "Give that back."

"Tell me what it's about."

"Give it back!"

Stefanie lunged forward. Hatherfield pulled back. She crashed into his chest.

"Careful," he said, holding the paper just out of reach. His damned eyes danced a wicked blue dance.

Stefanie pushed against his chest (oh, marble-hard pectorals beneath a silky wool waistcoat, God save her!) and climbed to her feet. With great dignity she snatched the paper from his hand.

"If you must know," she said, "it is a criminal case."

"So I supposed. Who's the criminal?"

"A . . . um . . . a dustman."

"A dustman! What the devil has the dustman done to warrant the attention of the great Sir John Worthington?"

"He's . . . well, he engaged in . . . with a woman . . . not his wife."

"I say! Is that all? Not terribly cricket of him, but hardly a crime."

Stefanie heaved a sigh, straightened her waistcoat, and sat back down in her chair. "If you must know. A very commonplace affair, really. The usual sort of thing. Husband works at night, his old childhood friend the dustman comes in at dawn pretending to be husband, engages in relations with wife . . ."

"What the devil?"

"I told you it was nothing of any real interest."

"On the contrary. I'm immensely interested. Do you mean to say that the dustman just decided to creep in one morning and . . . and . . ."

Stefanie coughed. "The, er, the matter in question took place over the course of some months. Apparently."

Hatherfield sat back in his chair. "Well, I'm dashed. Horrified, but dashed. Didn't she realize something was off, in all that time?"

"She says she was half asleep and couldn't tell the difference."

"I say. And the dustman? What's his defense?"

"Well, that's the thing. He says she knew it was him, that

they were simply having an affair, as it were. And when the husband came home early one day and surprised them, the wife turned on him."

"Has he any proof of this? Love notes, that sort of thing?"

"Not that he's presented so far."

"Extraordinary. Still, either way, the dustman's a black-guard." Hatherfield rose from the chair and snatched his wine-glass. "Creeping into her room like that, night after night."

"But if she invited him in . . ."

He spoke to the wall of books. "What if she thought she couldn't refuse him? If he threatened to tell the husband? To hurt her?"

"She has no proof. It's his word against hers."

"Yes, that's the trouble. The law's no help at all, is it?"

"The law is prosecuting him for rape. That's something."

"Yes, but what does the wife get, either way? Nothing. If her husband believes her, she might have a marriage left if she's lucky, but it will never be the same, will it? Everybody knows what happened in that room. Everybody knows her shame. Her husband, her friends, her family. She'll be shunned."

"But if she was a willing participant . . ."

Hatherfield's fist slammed against the shelf, rattling the books, spilling his wine on the rug. "But if she *wasn't*, Thomas! What then?"

Stefanie watched him in amazement. His body, having released its thunderbolt of energy, now stood absolutely still against the bookshelf, his white shirtsleeves stark against the dark leather bindings, his head bowed to the floor. Only the slight movement of his breathing disturbed the granite smooth-ness of his back.

"Then you're right," she said. "Then there's no real justice. Except in the hereafter, I suppose."

"The hereafter is a very great distance away, Thomas."

What could she say to that? Stefanie was no theologian. She went to church, she took the sacrament, she believed—more or less—during that hour or so each week. She humbled herself, she promised reform, and then she went out into the broad daylight and lived her life with very little thought for either eternal reward or eternal punishment. Simply doing her best to be a decent sort of person. She drummed her fingers on the papers before her and said, "I suppose life isn't fair for anyone. High or low."

"No, I suppose not."

"Still, your concern for the wife's plight is laudable. Not many men would spare much pity for an adulterous woman, willing or not."

Hatherfield's head lifted. He turned slowly to face her, and by the time his eyes met hers again, his expression was perfectly composed. Smiling, even. He tipped the wineglass to his lips and drank deep. Stefanie watched the muscles of his throat work up and down.

"Well, there you are, Thomas. Perhaps I'm a bit unusual after all."

Stefanie swallowed. "I had better get back to work. I'll be up another few hours at least, finishing this summary."

"What a nuisance. Making his point, isn't he, that Sir John." Hatherfield began packing the food back into the hamper.

"I suppose I asked for it."

"Did you, now?"

"I was cheeky."

Hatherfield tilted back his head and laughed. "Yes, I expect you were. Well. Enjoy your just deserts, Mr. Thomas. Let me know when you're finished with the work and ready to head home."

"What's that?"

"Why, you don't think I'd let you travel all the way back to Cadogan Square in the middle of the night, do you? By yourself?" Hatherfield shook his handsome head and tsked. "I'll be in Sir John's office, soaking up the comfort of his sofa. Wake me when you're ready to leave."

"But you . . . but . . . I can't possibly ask you to . . ."

"No, of course not." Hatherfield closed the lid of the hamper, latched it, and set it on the floor. "Which is why I'm not giving you a choice in the matter."

He picked up his jacket and slung it over his shoulder with a broad wink, and then he strode off confidently for the darkened door of Sir John's private office.

FOUR

The heat, if possible, was even worse this morning. The night had hardly cooled the courtroom air at all, and Stefanie's shirt was already stuck most uncomfortably to her back. Her necktie she longed to wring about the throat of the smug Mr. Duckworth.

She looked up anxiously at Hatherfield, who had just been brought in. As calm and unaffected as ever, of course, as if the heat couldn't reach him, as if he hadn't been up for hours already. He'd requested his own custom-built rowing machine to be brought into his cell each morning, and being Hatherfield had somehow convinced the prison staff to allow it, and he stroked for at least an hour before dawn broke, in that meditative trance she knew so well.

The way he used to do, on the river.

The crowd lining the courtroom was even thicker today, for the Duke of Southam himself had just been called to the stand. If Sir John had looked pallid and exhausted, the duke looked like a cadaver. His skin hung slack from the gaunt bones of his face, and he had neglected to pomade his hair, which frizzed thinly about his skull. The prosecutor gave him a sympathetic smile.

"I ask your pardon, Your Grace, for forcing you to this

ordeal. No doubt the past several months have proved very hard on you."

The duke stared at him and did not answer.

"You must miss the duchess a great deal, Your Grace. Don't you?"

The duke's lips moved. "Yes, I do."

"And your own son stands accused of her murder. It must be very hard."

Silence, and a cold ducal stare.

Mr. Duckworth dropped his eyes, cleared his throat, and took a long breath. Despite herself, Stefanie was impressed. Even beaten down as he was, the duke could still fell an eager prosecuting attorney with one look from those pale blue eyes.

"Naturally a man does not want to think his own son capable of murder. But we are gathered here in this courtroom to discover the facts and administer justice, are we not, Your Grace?"

"Of course."

"I'm sure you wish to see justice administered for your wife, the duchess, who has been murdered in such an unfathomable and—you will pardon me—brutal manner."

"Of course."

"To that end, I must ask you a few questions about the Marquess of Hatherfield, your son. Would you say that the two of you harbored a close affection for each other?"

The duke glanced at Hatherfield's face, with its gentle smile, and turned back to Mr. Duckworth. "I am sorry to say I would not."

"I understand—again, you will forgive me, Your Grace— that the estate to which Lord Hatherfield was entitled, on the unhoped-for event of your death, had encountered some financial difficulty. Is this correct?"

The duke straightened in his chair. "An estate so extensive as mine is costly to maintain, Mr. Duckworth."

"I must beg you to answer the question directly, Your Grace."

A long, slow breath. "Yes. I had recently encountered some reverses."

"Did you confide these facts to your son?"

"I did."

"Did he appear sympathetic to your troubles?"

Another quick glance in Hatherfield's direction. Stefanie pressed her lips together, hard, and counted the beats of her heart.

"Your Grace? If you would kindly answer the question. Did the Marquess of Hatherfield appear sympathetic to your troubles? Did he offer you any assistance, either moral or physical, in your distress?"

The duke blinked, as if holding back tears. His knuckles grew white where they gripped the wooden rail before him.

He closed his eyes.

"No. No, Mr. Duckworth, he did not."

FIVE

November 1889

The Thames lay gray and greasy around him, encased by fog. Hatherfield concentrated on the solid feel of the blades in his hands, the slick slide of his seat on the rails, the rhythm of his legs as he pushed *off* . . . and *off* . . . and *off* . . . and *off* . . .

A steady rhythm, a hard and powerful rhythm. Rhythm was the key. Let the rhythm do the work. You could go on forever if you had the right beat in your legs and arms.

Sometimes, he thought he might just do that. Go on forever. Down the Thames, out the estuary, and into the North Sea.

Hatherfield had acquired an instinctive feel for the traffic of the Thames by now, such as it was at this dark and early hour. A lantern shone at the bow of his boat; he knew by the movement of the water when another boat was approaching. A glance over his shoulder, a minute adjustment of the oars, a pair of shouted *halloos* exchanged as his wooden shell slid by.

In truth, he preferred rowing farther upstream, at Windsor or Henley; on the Cherwell at Oxford, where he had learned the sport. But December was drawing closer, and the chance of ice was too great outside the busy metropolis, and besides, he would have to pay for lodgings. London it was, with its searing yellow fog and multitude of barges and boats. At least the chaps at the boathouse were a pleasant sort, a few friends from school days, all understanding one another in this love for the water, for the exhilaration of a boat gliding like a rocket up the river, for that moment when the pain in your lungs and chest and muscles disappeared and you were simply part of the boat, a flawless machine, not even human, invincible. Emptied of thought, emptied of sin and stain. Washed clean by the wind of your own draft.

Yes. That.

The shadow of Hammersmith Bridge passed overhead, black against the charcoal sky. Hatherfield gathered himself for the final stretch, the last long yards. His limbs sang. He felt the thud of his heart in his chest, the pull of his breath in his lungs, the stretch and flex of his mighty tendons. The happy symphony of his body, every instrument in tune, despite the late and broken rest of the night before, looking after young Thomas. He had expected to wake up this morning tired and reluctant, regretting those lost hours of sleep, but instead he'd felt . . . well, good. A bit of Christmas morning, the way Christmas morning had felt when he was very young. A pair of mischievous eyes seemed to be smiling upon him as he rose from his bed, as he changed into the exercise clothes his valet had laid out for him, as he drank his glass of water.

Her voice, deep and mock-contrite, making him smile into the black early morning: *I was cheeky.*

The dark banks of the river blurred past, the trees of Barnes, and then he was home, Boathouse Row, a few miserable lanterns shining out from the odd window. Rowers were early risers, but he was the earliest. The docks were still quiet. In an hour, the sun would be up, the boats would be out. He would be eating breakfast in Cadogan Square. Thomas would be there, sitting next to him at the table, brimming with fresh air and exuberance.

Thomas.

He aimed for shore, relaxing his pace, allowing the boat to glide smoothly to the side. The moon had gone, the sun was not yet risen. He could hardly make out the shape of the boathouses to his left, the lights of Putney Bridge to his back. The boat bumped gently at the landing. He steadied the oars and unlaced his feet from the stirrups. From his exhausted body

came a sated hum, that familiar fleeting sense of self-satisfaction.
How long would it last today? As long as breakfast, surely.
Breakfast with sharp young Thomas. He smiled and stepped
into the cold water.

"Hatherfield!"

His fingers froze around the side of the boat.

"Hatherfield, I say! Hurry up with that nonsense."

The voice was hard and short with impatience, a voice
accustomed to giving orders and having them obeyed.

Hatherfield squared his shoulders.

"One moment, Father."

"I must speak with you immediately, Hatherfield."

"I've got to take the boat in first, Father."

A muttered curse, and the bang of a carriage window
shoved back into place.

Hatherfield unshipped the blades and laid them on the
dock, and then he grasped the edges of the shell and lifted it
over his head in a single smooth heave.

"Hurry it up, then!"

Hatherfield carried the boat into the dank cavern of the
boathouse and laid it carefully on its horse. He went back to
the dock and brought the oars in, and then he found a wool
jumper from his cubbyhole and pulled it over his head. His
cotton-clad body, wringing with sweat, was already beginning
to feel the cold in the air.

"For God's sake," said the Duke of Southam, "I don't
understand why you persist in this hobby of yours."

Hatherfield placed his hands on the edge of the carriage
door. "Was there something you wished to tell me, Father?"

"Come inside the carriage."

"I'm not dressed."

"You can dress at home."

"My home is the Albert Hall Mansions now, Father. My
own rooms, you know. The old bachelor establishment."

The duke's fist crashed against the doorframe. "Climb in, for
God's sake. I shall catch a chill in a moment."

Two men walked past, heading into the boathouse. Chittering
and Monmouth-Farraday, going out in their usual pair, casting
him a look of friendly and barely disguised curiosity. As if to say,
Trouble, old chap?

Hatherfield shrugged. "I've got to send my own driver off."

He went behind the boathouse and informed his driver that he would be making his own way home, and then he returned to his father's carriage and climbed inside. It lurched forward instantly, clattering over the cobbles and up the approach to Putney Bridge.

"By damn, you smell like a stable," said Southam, holding a handkerchief to his nose.

"I meant to bathe and change first." Hatherfield kept his voice civil. He folded his arms across his chest.

Southam let out a put-upon sigh and cracked open the carriage window. "I suppose I can bear it until we reach home."

Hatherfield looked out the opposite window, where the feeble London dawn spread promisingly beyond the rooftops. They had just crested the middle of the bridge span, and the Thames glittered and shifted in the growing light, already filling with boats. Inside the carriage, the air was cold and humid, filled with the smell of Southam's peppermint hair oil and Hatherfield's own hard-earned sweat.

He plucked at a stray thread of wool on his sleeve. "I gather you had something important to tell me?"

"Yes." The duke hesitated, and all at once Hatherfield was conscious of an uneasiness lying beneath his father's stern voice, his air of arrogant command. "It has to do with your duty, Hatherfield. Your duty as the heir to this storied title, this dukedom that has passed down through eight generations without interruption . . ."

"Ah. The duchess has been gambling again, has she?"

"You will not speak of your mother with disrespect."

"She's not my mother, sir." The word *mother* tasted like poison in his mouth.

"She has cared for you since you were ten years old, Hatherfield. She's the only mother you have."

Hatherfield said nothing.

"In any case, and as you know, the income from our various estates has been falling every year, as rents decline . . ."

"And your expenses continue to climb, and you refuse to do anything to modernize the estates, or to invest in anything that gives off the slightest whiff of a profitable enterprise . . ."

"That will be enough. You will have ample opportunity to

ruin the dukedom when your mother and I are dead. For the present, you have a duty to preserve the honor of your name, the privileges you have the immense good fortune to inherit, by whatever means in your power."

"Father," said Hatherfield wearily, "for the last time. You know I've invested every penny of the trust in the Hammersmith project. I'm living on nearly nothing as it is."

"You have fifty thousand pounds, Hatherfield! The entirety of your mother's dowry, compounding interest for nearly twenty years."

"I invested it all, the instant I came into the money, as you know. The project's only half finished. I can't sell at this point, and I can't pull any money out." He had made bloody well certain of that, in fact, knowing his father's skill at extortion. Such as the one he was attempting right now.

The duke harrumphed. "There is another option, of course. Eminently easy. Efficient. Gentlemanly, not like this damned row of houses you're building in Hammersmith."

Oh, for God's sake.

"Father, I am not going to marry Charlotte Harlowe."

"Two hundred thousand pounds, Hatherfield!" The duke's voice burst within the interior of the carriage.

"It might as well be two hundred million. I won't marry her."

"For God's sake! She's beautiful, she's clever, she's charming. She quite plainly adores you, God knows why. Your damned looks, I suppose. Who the devil *will* you marry, if not her?"

"Whom I please, Father. But not her."

"Why the devil not?"

"Because I don't love her. Because I have the settled conviction that we should make each other miserable."

"Because you wish to disgrace your family," said Southam, in a bitter voice. "You wish to have your revenge on us, for all our imagined crimes, by watching the title fall into ruin, the houses sold, the estates broken up . . ."

"Nonsense. No doubt I shall find an agreeable heiress to marry at some point. Or perhaps I'll amaze you with the success of my houses in Hammersmith, and I shall have the blunt to bail you out myself, from time to time. You have only to wait. Perhaps retrench an inch or two, in the meantime. Perhaps even do the unthinkable, sir, and focus your capable mind on marshaling the immense resources of the dukedom to more profitable use. Instead of the simple and rather base expedient of putting your only son out to stud."

The duke picked up his cane and jammed it into the floor of the carriage. His voice shook with passion. "That is the point, damn it all! We have no resources! You have no inheritance, Hatherfield. An empty title, mortgaged to the limit. There is nothing, nothing!"

"Oh, come, sir. Nothing? You are the Duke of Southam."

The carriage staggered to a stop. A delivery wagon, probably. Hatherfield looked out the window, where the shops of the King's Road sat quiet and shuttered, waiting for the midmorning tide of commerce to rise.

The duke spoke quietly. "Our mortgage obligations currently exceed our rent-roll by approximately eleven thousand pounds per annum. When the next payment comes due, we have not enough cash on hand to meet it."

"Are there no more banks willing to take on your overdraft?"

"I will not suffer the indignity of being refused credit."

"Father, you've got to face facts. Agricultural incomes have been plummeting for years. Decades. If the dukedom is to survive, you've got to sell up and invest the proceeds elsewhere. Do as I've done with Mother's money."

A dry laugh. "Invest what proceeds? If I sold every acre, it wouldn't cover the mortgages upon the property."

"The duchess's dowry?"

"Spent. The rest went to the girls' marriage settlements."

Hatherfield swore.

"I've done my best, Hatherfield. There's simply nothing else to be done."

"There was," said Hatherfield, "but you refused to do it when you had the chance."

The carriage started forward again. The rattle of the wheels filled the air between them, the muted cacophony of horseshoes on pavement. A distant shout, a high peal of feminine laughter through the glass of the window. The familiar chorus of London, making the human silence bearable.

Southam said quietly, "I have in my pocket a note of hand

from Mr. Nathaniel Wright, requesting payment of a debt of honor incurred this past Friday, in the amount of forty-two thousand pounds, on or before the next quarter day."

"Forty-two thousand pounds?"

"Mr. Wright has kindly rounded off a hundred and sixty-eight pounds from the sum."

Hatherfield allowed himself a moment to catch his stunned breath. Forty-two thousand pounds. "Nathaniel Wright. That chap in the City, isn't it?"

"He is the owner of a considerable investment firm."

Hatherfield could almost hear the curl of his father's lip as he said the words *investment firm*. He stretched out his legs and examined the tips of his worn shoes. "*Your* debt of honor, sir? Or your wife's?"

"That, my boy, is none of your business. The point is that we shall be ruined by Christmas. Publicly disgraced, turned out of our house, and you will have only yourself to blame, Hatherfield."

"Me, sir?"

"When all of these problems, *all* of them, might be solved by a simple matter, a very straightforward alliance of the sort that built the very fortune on which your inheritance was founded. My God, Hatherfield! It's not as if I'm asking you to commit a crime! Marry a beautiful girl, get a child or two on her, and carry on as you like! Where is the hardship? You needn't even see her, except in bed and at dinner, from time to time."

"What an alluring picture you paint."

"Two hundred thousand pounds, Hatherfield!" The duke was breathless. He stamped his cane again, just as the carriage whirled around the corner of Sloane Square.

"Damn it, Father." Hatherfield put his hands to his temples. How did the man do it? Beat like this against his conscience, against his sense of honor: beat and beat, until Hatherfield could no longer tell what was right and what was wrong. His duty as a son; his duty as a human being. In the close air of the carriage, cold and dense with Southam's desperation, everything twisted and stuck together.

Marry Lady Charlotte. Could he do it, if he had to?

Marriage. A wife in his bed, Lady Charlotte between his clean white sheets, expecting his nightly arrival. Was the prospect really so dreadful?

For an instant, the image of young Thomas's sea blue eyes flashed in his head. Her face, hair loose, lines softened, lying against a pillow. His breath caught in his chest.

"Can you not put him off until the houses are finished, Father? You can have half the profit. All of it, if you need it." He'd have to start all over again, damn it all, but at least he wouldn't have this ball of guilt lodged in his stomach. This dangling prospect of Lady Charlotte.

The duke's cane struck the floor of the carriage. "Next summer, you mean! As if that would help!"

"It's all I have for you. Investments take time and effort, unlike gambling."

"At least say you'll think on it, Hatherfield." The duke's voice was unrecognizable: low and edgy, as if it might crack at any moment. "Think on it, my boy. My own son. For God's sake. You could save us all. Two unblemished centuries of dukes, the pillars of Great Britain, on whom thousands depend for their livelihoods. Do you really want to be the one who destroyed it all?"

Hatherfield didn't reply. The monumental white facades of Eaton Square passed by, behind their black iron fences and scanty November gardens. The carriage turned down Belgrave Place, and still he didn't speak, couldn't speak; he forced down the boiling rage with a heavy iron lid, until the carriage rolled to a stop before the magnificent double-fronted house of the Duke of Southam.

"Why do you put up with it?" he said quietly. "Why do you put up with her?"

The duke's voice snapped out as it always had, back to usual. "You will speak of Her Grace with respect, or not at all."

The carriage door swung open. Southam lifted himself from the seat. "You're not staying?"

"No. I'll take the carriage to my own lodging, if you don't mind."

"Your mother will not be pleased."

"Do present her with my compliments and deepest regrets."

The door slammed shut. The carriage moved off.

Hatherfield slumped back in his seat and watched London slide by. His dash of morning joy had proved short-lived, after all.

Stefanie drummed her fingernails along the edge of the leather briefcase on her lap. "You don't think there's anything the matter, do you?"

Sir John Worthington lifted his head from contemplation of a packet of densely written papers. A morning shadow slipped across his face from the carriage window. "I beg your pardon?"

"Lord Hatherfield. He wasn't at breakfast."

"Oh, one never knows when to expect him. He knows my door is open, whenever he should need it." Sir John's face turned back to his papers. How he could study them in this jouncing vehicle, lurching about the London traffic, wheeling heedlessly about the corners, Stefanie couldn't imagine.

Of course there was nothing to worry about. She'd just been expecting him, that was all. Had risen at half six, despite having gone to bed only five hours earlier. Had dressed herself and brushed her hair carefully with the help of a mirror. She had made sure her collar was clean and straight, she had pinched her cheeks for that irresistible rosy glow, she had rubbed her lips furiously together. For what earthly reason? Did she really want the Marquess of Hatherfield to admire the beauty of Mr. Stephen Thomas?

Well, yes. Yes, she did.

Illogical, wrongheaded, muddled, and dangerous in the extreme. But there it was.

And when she had bounded down the stairs and entered the breakfast room and seen only Sir John and a cross-faced Lady Charlotte, she had felt a huge tide of disappointment well up inside her. No smiling, broad-shouldered Hatherfield, the potent antidote to Lady Charlotte's venom. He had left her at Sir John's door last night with a *That's that, then, Thomas, pleasant dreams*, and an intimate smile that had hovered in her obediently pleasant dreams all night. Yes, all night. All night she'd kept company with the memory of Hatherfield's smile, all night she'd looked forward to seeing that smile again at the breakfast table. She'd simply assumed it would be there.

"I see," she said now, and Sir John made no sign that he'd heard her, no sign that she existed in this carriage with him. She fingered the fastening on her briefcase and looked out the window. They were jolting up the Strand, nearly there. Her paper lay on Sir John's desk. She couldn't even remember what it contained now; the last few pages had been composed in an exhausted blur.

Probably it was horrible. Probably he would read it in dismay. In horror. In—worst of all—amusement. She would be told to leave, to clear her desk, to clear her Spartan room on the third floor of the Worthington town house in Cadogan Square, and what would she do then? Make her way back to Olympia? Confess her failure? What then?

Oh, that Stefanie. Flighty, mischievous Stefanie, always getting herself in trouble, one scrape after another, and then charming her way out of it.

Only this time, there was no charming anyone. She wasn't a princess anymore, dispensing favors and charm, forgiven for all her faults. She was nobody. She was less than nobody, a fugitive, breaking the laws of Great Britain simply by wearing the clothes on her back. On Sir John's generosity, she was entirely dependent. And she had failed him.

The last of the morning's sweet exhilaration vanished into the London fog.

The carriage stopped. The door opened. Sir John climbed down without a glance at her and disappeared through the entrance of his chambers.

Stefanie dragged herself in his wake, carrying his heavy briefcase like the lowliest lackey, like the clerk she was. "I'll take that," said Mr. Turner, appearing out of nowhere with his threadbare black arms outstretched.

"And good morning to you, Mr. Turner."

"You may go to your desk, Mr. Thomas. There are a number of letters there awaiting transcription into clean copies." Mr. Turner gave her a triumphant look and headed off to Sir John's office, bearing the briefcase.

Stefanie turned to the desk in question and felt the room stir as four pairs of curious eyes dropped immediately away.

Her desk, which she'd left less than eight hours before. On this chair, she had sat and composed her case summary. On that chair, the Marquess of Hatherfield had sprawled his magnificent body and smiled at her. Had devoted an entire evening to ensuring she was fed and safe.

Well, that was something, wasn't it? She could take that memory with her.

Stefanie trudged down the aisle to her desk and squared the legs of the chair in an exact perpendicular relationship to the worn wooden surface. She inhaled the familiar smell of last night, that particular combination of leather and paper and wood, and her heart ached. A few forgotten bread crumbs lay in one corner. She lifted her hand to brush them to the floor and stopped herself. Hers or Hatherfield's?

She brushed them into her palm instead, and from her palm into her pocket.

In the center of the old blotter sat a stack of clean white paper and a few sheets of crisscrossed scribbles, topped with a plain black marble paperweight. Stefanie removed the fountain pen from the drawer, gave it a little shake, and set to work.

The pens of the other clerks scratched around her. Someone coughed, a strangled and desperate cough that its owner tried heroically to suppress. Stefanie concentrated on her handwriting, which had never been her strong suit, or even her middling suit, particularly when set next to her sister Emilie's perfect copperplate or Luisa's grand strokes. Stefanie was a scribbler, fond of dashes and exclamation points and sentences that had no point at all, just a *dotdotdot* at the end, an unfinished thought, a suggestion, a wink.

She frowned now at the phrase before her: *Therefore, it is my studied recommendation that the witnesses belong to one of two categories: Firstmost, those who will establish the character of the defendant as one who upholds the highest standards of moral and physical law; and, Secondmost, those who will establish the ability of the defendant to handle matters of bookkeeping and finance in a rigorous and arithmetically adept manner, without regard to his personal interest.* So dreadfully dry. How on earth did these legal chaps read all this without falling into a drooling catatonic stupor? Stefanie's pen hovered over the words *bookkeeping* and *finance*. She wondered whether anyone would notice if she changed them to *bookmaking* and *forgery.*

Clearly she wasn't cut out for this work. Clearly she should have been apprenticed to a newspaperman instead, or perhaps a theater owner, or even . . .

A shadow cast across the page.

Stefanie glanced up, expecting to find the beetle face of Mr. Turner sneering down at her, about to inform her that she might gather her hat and coat and find another set of chambers to darken with her slovenly habits and her intolerable cheek.

But the sight that greeted her was far worse than that.

Sir John Worthington. Stern, gray-faced, his impartial dark eyes burrowing through her forehead to root out the corruption within. Before Stefanie could so much as leap to her feet and perform a ritual genuflection, he barked out, "Mr. Thomas. In my office, if you please," and turned away in the obvious expectation of instant obedience.

Stefanie scrambled after him. On her back, she felt the weight of every clerkly eyeball, heavy with schadenfreude.

SIX

The telegram was waiting on Hatherfield's breakfast tray, after he had bathed and shaved in the private if rather sterile comfort of his bachelor flat in Knightsbridge.

"Nelson!" he called out. "When did this telegram arrive?"

His manservant appeared soundlessly and miraculously sober in the bedroom doorway. "While you were bathing, sir. I have taken the liberty of putting out the brown tweed suit, sir, and the blue necktie."

"Very good, Nelson." Hatherfield selected a daggerlike silver letter opener from the secretary in the corner and tore open the thin white envelope with a neat slash across one side.

PERCEPTIVE STOP EXPECTED NOTHING LESS STOP GUARD WITH ALL DUE VIGILANCE STOP RETURN LONDON LATE TONIGHT STOP EXPECT YOU AT NINE SHARP TOMORROW MORNING STOP YOURS OLYMPIA

Hatherfield tapped the edge of the telegram against the secretary and swore.

Guard with all due vigilance. What the devil did that

mean? Guard the secret of her disguise? Or guard young Thomas herself?

He pictured her again, her sleek auburn head bowed over her desk and then turning up to greet him in delighted amazement. The way his blood had jumped in his veins at the sight. And later, her face shadowed and exhausted in the anemic glow of the Cadogan Square gas lamps, as she disappeared up the steps of Sir John's town house. He thought of the clerks scratching away in those damned legal chambers, in full proximity to her dancing eyes and curving posterior, and the answer to his question rose up so violently in his throat, he could taste it.

Both.

As he had been doing, without instruction, already. Watching over her like a hen with a particularly adventurous chick, guarding her travels and providing her supper.

He looked down at the telegram once more. *Expected nothing less.*

Damn Olympia. He'd planned it all out, hadn't he? No accident at all, Hatherfield's being present in that godforsaken castle in Devon when Mr. Stephen Thomas made his introduction to his new household.

Which begged the question: Who the devil was she, really? And what the flying hell was Olympia up to?

"Nelson!" he called out. "Ring down for my hansom at once, please."

"Right away, sir."

Hatherfield gulped his coffee and reached for his shirt. His manservant, who knew better than to attend him while in the act of dressing, disappeared into the other room to ring the mews.

Half an hour later, Hatherfield's hansom was zigzagging nimbly through traffic on its way to the City. He had an errand to dispose of first, before he could attend to Miss Thomas.

Sir John Worthington had already positioned himself behind his desk, stiff-necked and imposing, by the time Stefanie stepped bravely after him into the office.

"Close the door, if you will, Mr. Thomas." Sir John lifted the ends of his jacket and lowered himself into his chair.

The door made an awful echoing thump as Stefanie closed it, as of a prison gate shutting tight. This was because the office itself was large and high ceilinged and remarkably free of the usual layers of bookshelf and wainscoting, a spacious box of a room, uncluttered and well lit, with Sir John's substantial desk positioned in the center and flanked by two chairs upholstered in leather. Also, the door was four inches thick of solid British heart of oak.

Sir John gestured to one of the leather chairs. "Sit, please."

As if she were a dog. Stefanie stalked up to the chair and crashed into the seat with equal parts vim and vigor. If one were about to be dismissed summarily, one should face one's fate with stubborn chin tilted.

"I have here before me your summary of the unfortunate case of Mr. Harding and the dustman," said Sir John.

"Mrs. Harding and the dustman, really," said Stefanie. "The husband seems to have played an ancillary role, at best."

"Ah. Yes." Sir John's eyes dropped to the papers before him, ran over a line or two, and then lifted back up to meet Stefanie's steady gaze. He stroked the tip of his beard. "I don't know quite how to begin."

"At the beginning, I should think."

"Yes. Quite. In the first place, this summary is an absolute mess, Mr. Thomas. In all my years of judicial practice, I have never encountered a paper less organized, less sensible, less"—he lifted up one corner and eyed it with distaste—"less *legible* than the one before me now."

"Handwriting was never my strong suit."

"Evidently not."

Stefanie rose to her feet. The chair legs scraped an excruciating track along the wooden floor. "Very good, then, sir. May I say that my time here in your chambers, while brief . . ."

"What the devil are you doing? Sit down."

"I see no reason to prolong this interview, Sir John. As you yourself have observed, I'm not cut out for the practice of law, which is exactly what I told His Grace, and might have saved us all a great deal of trouble if he'd . . ."

"For God's sake, Mr. Thomas. Sit. I wasn't going to sack you."

Stefanie halted her finger in mid-thrust. "No?"

"Sit down, please, and leave off this theatrical gesturing,

for God's sake. If there's one thing I can't abide, it's a theatrical gesture."

Stefanie flipped up the ends of her jacket and settled back in her chair. Her pulse was giving off odd nervous flecks in her throat, making her just a tiny bit light-headed.

Sir John steepled his fingers atop the illegible and poorly organized mess she had left on his desk last night. Stefanie fought the urge to rip it from beneath his hands, wad it into a ball, toss it into the wastebin, storm to the door, and say, fingers stabbing the air rudely: *How do you like this theatrical gesture, Sir John Worthington, Q.C.?*

"Now," said Sir John, in perfect composure, "aside from the obvious errors of composition, organization, presentation, orthography, and punctuation, this paper is a work of extraordinary legal genius."

"Well, sir, if you hadn't been such a dashed rigid-arsed martinet and had given me a sufficient time to prepare, instead of . . ." Stefanie blinked. "I beg your pardon?"

Sir John tapped his right forefinger against the paper. "Genius. Unschooled, obviously, and quite unaccustomed to the, er, to the rhetorical terms in which the law expresses itself . . ."

"Bloody boring, you mean."

"Yes, Mr. Thomas. Bloody, bloody boring. Dry, passive, riddled with clause. You've expressed yourself here in entirely too straightforward and dramatic a fashion, but the content itself—your lines of argument, your grasp of the subtleties of the legal principles involved, your ethical insight—it's all brilliant. It's—how do I describe it? A sort of cognitive leap, extraordinary in one with no previous exposure to the law."

Extraordinary. The word rang against the sides of Stefanie's skull.

Six months ago, Stefanie had been sitting in the Holstein Castle schoolroom, staring out the window as Miss Dingleby read over her latest composition. Stefanie couldn't now remember the subject, but she did remember counting the gardeners outside in the clean summer air, an extraordinary number, all of them harvesting immense quantities of roses and lilies from the royal gardens in preparation for her sister Luisa's nuptials the following Wednesday. She could hear their laughter as they worked, could smell the dense June-warm fragrance of the flowers drifting up from the soil below. Miss Dingleby's voice, when it finally carried across the stone room, had sounded distant: *Really, Your Highness, you must endeavor to put a little more effort into these essays, the way your sisters do. You must concentrate a little. You haven't the brains to keep up with Emilie; you have to focus your meager faculties, for God's sake, or you'll never be good for anything other than flirting with unsuitable men and getting yourself into scrapes.*

Now, in this chilly box of a November room, not a flower in sight, Sir John's voice sounded equally distant. Echoing. *Genius. Brilliant. A cognitive leap.*

Extraordinary.

"I'm sorry," she said softly. "I don't believe I quite understand you."

"It's masterful, Mr. Thomas. You've a talent, a natural talent for this kind of thing. The only thing wanting is a little discipline, of which any idiot is capable. Look at Mr. Turner, there." Sir John waved his hand to the door. "Thick as a plank, poor chap, but he keeps everything in order and that's what I need from him. You, on the other hand, Mr. Thomas, have a different sort of mind altogether, a very valuable mind, and with a certain amount of cultivation, I don't doubt you might eventually prove one of the most eminent men called to the bar this decade."

Stefanie's head felt as if it were floating. "Sir?"

Sir John rose to his feet. "I intend to take a close and personal role in your development, Thomas. I want you to brief yourself on all my current cases and accompany me to court. I shall be asking you to dine with me, inviting other members of the bar, because that is the proper way to learn, Thomas. Discourse."

Stefanie lurched upward. "Discourse. Yes, sir."

"For now, you will return to your desk and begin educating yourself. I shall want summaries of all my active cases, just like this one"—he held it up for a demonstrative jiggle—"except with perhaps a little more attention to organization and clarity, Thomas. Clarity."

"Clarity, sir. Of course. Organization and clarity. There is one difficulty, however, sir," Stefanie said, a little numbly, for she felt rather as if she were dreaming this episode instead of actively participating in it.

"Difficulty, Mr. Thomas?" Sir John's thicket of eyebrows hefted upward. "What possible difficulty could there be?"

"I have a few letters to copy, sir. On my desk this minute."

"Letters? Letters, you say?"

"Yes, sir. A dozen or so."

Sir John waved his hand and sat down. "Never mind the damned letters, Thomas. Do your duty, that's all. Now off you go."

Stefanie turned her body and walked slowly to the four-inch portal through which she'd passed a few minutes ago, in another lifetime, as another Stefanie. At the very last step, she turned.

"Sir."

He looked up, a little crossly. "What is it, Thomas?"

"Are you . . . are you quite sure, sir? One of the most eminent this *decade*, sir? That's . . . that's quite an assessment, based on a single poorly organized paper."

"Damn it all, Mr. Thomas. Are you suggesting I'm wrong? I am never wrong. Now off you go, and close the door behind you. I've the devil of an amount of work to get through before I attend sessions."

Stefanie floated through the door and shut it firmly behind her. She made her way back to the desk and sat down, staring blankly at the half-finished letter before her. She knew, somewhere at the back of her mind—her *valuable* mind, had he really said that?—that the other clerks were staring at her, that the incessant scratching of pens had unaccountably ceased, but she couldn't bring herself to care.

"Psst! Thomas!"

She turned her head to the side. Her neighbor clerk leaned toward her, shifting his eyes watchfully back and forth to Sir John's door, his brown whiskers bristling with mutton-chop curiosity on his jaw.

"Thomas!" he hissed again.

"Yes?" she heard herself whisper.

"The lads are I are headed to the pub this evening, after old Turner makes his disappearance. Care to join us in a bit of shenanigans?" His eyebrows gave off a waggle. He tapped his fountain pen against the side of his jaw.

And all at once, Stefanie was as light as air, as free and wind-drunk as a bird on the wing. She wanted to laugh out loud with the joy of it.

Instead, she smiled at the clerk in his identical black suit.

"No, thank you," she said. "I'm afraid I've a great deal of work to do."

By the time the Marquess of Hatherfield reached the offices of Wright Holdings, Ltd., on London Wall, it was nearly ten o'clock in the morning, the result of an overturned delivery wagon in Cheapside that had brought all wheel-bound traffic to an immediate and fatal halt. After ten minutes of fruitless waiting, he'd gotten out and walked, despite the clogging yellow fog and the stagnant water collected in the rutted pavement.

"Mr. Wright is attending a meeting at the moment, your lordship," said the secretary, concealing his surprise with impressive self-control at the sight of the plain ecru card Hatherfield had handed him. "Do you have an appointment?"

"I do not, as I'm sure you're well aware," said Hatherfield. "A certain matter has come up, an urgent matter. I should appreciate the opportunity to speak to Mr. Wright at the earliest possible instant."

"I see, sir." The secretary glanced at the clock. "If you'll do us the honor of taking a seat, Lord Hatherfield."

Hatherfield settled himself in a chair. The minutes ticked away in the silent interior of the reception room, an elegant space, furnished in serene colors with simple richness. Hatherfield had the impression of an immense amount of activity taking place behind the quiet door at the other side of the room, a beehive made of ticker tape with accountants buzzing about in green eyeshades. The door opened, and a man popped out, looking flustered, and strode without pause to the hat stand. The secretary jumped to his feet.

"If you'll excuse me, your lordship. I'll see if Mr. Wright is available."

A moment later, the secretary returned.

"Mr. Wright has ten minutes, your lordship."

If Hatherfield was expecting the notorious financier to own a grand office, stuffed with important furniture and lined with priceless Old Master paintings in gilt frames a yard thick, he was disappointed. The room was neat and small and businesslike, anchored by a quite ordinary desk, a few maps decorating the walls. Mr. Wright stood at Hatherfield's entrance.

"Your lordship," he said, in a voice no less powerful for its quiet volume.

Hatherfield shook his outstretched hand. "Mr. Wright."

"Please sit down. May I offer you refreshment?"

"No, thank you. I'll be brief. I understand you're a busy man."

Wright smiled and made a deprecating motion with his hand. Hatherfield had met him once or twice, at this or that party. A tall man, robust, blunt boned, and not unhandsome. His dark hair was brushed back from his forehead with a touch of pomade, and his mustache was clipped and modest. His eyes shone dark and keen from beneath his straight eyebrows. What had Hatherfield heard? That he was the bastard son of one aristocrat or another, brought up in genteel obscurity in some unfashionable quarter of London. He had that look, watchful and predatory and a little hungry. A touch ruthless, when he had to be. Or perhaps that was only his reputation. Reputations could be so often mistaken.

Hatherfield sat down. "I understand from my father, the Duke of Southam . . ."

"I know who your father is, Lord Hatherfield."

"Very good. Then perhaps you know why I've come. You hold my stepmother's marker for forty-three thousand pounds."

"Forty-two, I believe."

"I presume you know that my family has no possible means of paying it."

"There are always means, Hatherfield, if one's willing to find them."

Hatherfield leaned back and studied the man before him. "I suppose a man in your position knows everything that goes on in this little world of ours, don't you?"

A shrug. "I hear many things, of course."

"May I be so bold as to inquire why you drew a woman, a lady, deep into play, when you knew she had nothing at all to back up her markers?"

"On the contrary. Her Grace assured me that the family would soon be in possession of a handsome fortune, as a result of an advantageous alliance on the point of being announced."

"Her Grace was mistaken, as I'm sure you well knew."

Mr. Wright settled himself more deeply into his chair and rested his chin in one hand. *Tap tap tap* went his finger against the corner of his full mouth. His dark eyes studied Hatherfield, the brows above them slanted in thought.

A sensation passed through Hatherfield, a vague and fleeting sense of familiarity.

"I do have an investment of my own," said Hatherfield.

"Ah yes. Your houses in Hammersmith. Quality homes for the middle classes, instead of the usual job-work rubbish being raised all over the suburbs. A clever idea, and serves the purpose of keeping your own capital away from your father's grasping paws. I admire your thinking, your lordship." Mr. Wright smiled, not a particularly pleasant smile.

"If you can hold my stepmother's marker until summer, when the houses are finished and sold, I'll pay you myself."

Mr. Wright shook his head. "Too late, I'm afraid."

"Then I'll grant you a quarter-interest in the project now. This very instant."

Another shake. "Too risky. Estate prices are so variable."

"A half-interest. You might have twice your forty-two thousand quid by September."

"I have no need for another investment, Lord Hatherfield. With respect."

Hatherfield spread his hands. "I have nothing for you, then."

"What an unfortunate predicament for the duke and duchess," said Mr. Wright. "A knotty sort of conundrum."

"You could solve it in an instant, Mr. Wright."

"What, tear up the marker? A debt of honor? Come, Lord Hatherfield." Mr. Wright shook his head in sorrow. "We both know that's impossible. Perhaps a small matter, a trifling amount, between friends. But forty-two thousand pounds? A man's word is his word. It is the bedrock on which all else stands."

"The duchess is not a man."

"The principle remains."

What an implacable face the man had. Hatherfield, who had learned to detect every minute clue of expression, who could tell if a man was lying by the flicker of his eyelids and the movement of his pulse in his neck, found himself frustrated. Nathaniel Wright was as smooth as a mask.

But that in itself was a clue, wasn't it? Only a man with something to hide kept his face from revealing anything at all.

Hatherfield's nerves leapt to life. He leaned forward and rested his elbows on his knees. "Tell me, Mr. Wright. What is it you're really after, here? You've refused a perfectly good alternative to the debt in question. You're already as rich as Croesus." He gestured to the understated interior around him, the office of a man who owned so much wealth, he knew no urge to display it.

Wright spread his hands innocently. "I want my rightful forty-two thousand pounds, or at least some certain guarantee of it, by the next quarter day. That is all, Lord Hatherfield. Nothing could be easier, really." He smiled, a singularly wolfish smile, crammed with even white teeth.

"And if Her Grace proves unable to pay?"

"I am afraid I would, with the very greatest regret, be obliged to take measures." Wright's elbow was propped thoughtfully on the arm of his chair. He leaned his temple into his forefinger.

Measures. A man like Wright might have all sorts of measures at his thoughtful forefingertips, not all of them executed through official channels.

Hatherfield remained silent, a slight puzzled smile on his face, as if not fully understanding the weight of Wright's meaning.

"Of course," said Wright, "you could always marry the lady."

"That, my dear fellow, is none of your affair."

Wright shrugged. "No, it's not. Only a little friendly advice, man to man. An easy and straightforward remedy for the problem at hand. Eliminates the need for further trouble on all sides."

Hatherfield rose to his feet. "Man to man, eh? That's good of you, Wright, to assume such a tender interest in my personal affairs, but I've taken enough of your time this morning as it is.

Much obliged, your allowing me the interview and all that. I believe I understand your position with absolute clarity."

"Unless your affections are engaged elsewhere, Lord Hatherfield?"

Hatherfield went still. "I beg your pardon?"

"Your affections, Hatherfield. Are they engaged elsewhere? I ask as a businessman, of course, with an investment to protect."

Hatherfield pulled his watch from his pocket and consulted the face. "Affections? Gad, no. What a chap you are. Affections, indeed. Now if you'll excuse me, I must confess to a pressing appointment at the other end of town. Houses to inspect, you see, builders to consult. Can't waste another moment on this charming conversation. Good day, Mr. Wright."

Nathaniel Wright rose from his chair and extended his hand. "Your servant, Lord Hatherfield."

Hatherfield shook the offered hand and returned his smile, wolf to wolf. "Indeed, Mr. Wright."

Hatherfield returned to the reception room and found his coat and hat. Outside, in the street, his driver had finally made his way through the traffic and stood waiting next to the hansom.

"Hammersmith, if you will," said Hatherfield, and then he fell back against the seat and studied the small square window on the cab roof with grim eyes.

For he had, at the very end of the interview, at the words *You could always marry the lady*, suddenly placed where he'd seen that particular gesture before, that patient and rather predatory tapping of the corner of the old mouth.

Lady Charlotte Harlowe affected it, from time to time, when she was pondering a particularly complicated move at whist.

SEVEN

Old Bailey
July 1890

By the third day of the trial, the section of the courtroom closest to the dock was filled with young women—heaven only
knew from which shop room they had obtained leave—who
regularly swooned at the entrance of the Marquess of Hatherfield
into the courtroom and swooned again when he left it.

Such abuse of maidenly privilege did not improve Stefanie's mood.

Not that Hatherfield appeared to notice his bevy of dizzy
damsels. He appeared as he always did, negligent, a bit distracted,
exuding golden animal spirits like a lion left on display at the
London Zoo. Not even the entrance of Mr. Nathaniel Wright into
the witness box caused his radiance to dim an iota.

"Mr. Wright." The prosecutor drummed his fingers on the
table in a kind of anticipatory prelude. His eyebrows were
high, his lips pursed and smiling both at once, as if a bowl of
syllabub had just been placed before him.

"Mr. Duckworth," said Wright, in exactly the same tone, causing the entire courtroom to come down with a case of the titters.

The judge banged his gavel. "Order!"

Mr. Duckworth continued hastily. "Mr. Wright, I understand you have a sister."

Mr. Wright cast a lazy dark eye across the courtroom,

lingering with particular interest on the ladies assembled near the dock. "I understand I have several," he said, "though in the natural course of things, I am only acquainted with one." A telling emphasis on the word *natural*.

Mr. Duckworth's cheeks had the grace to turn pink. "And will you have the goodness to identify this sister, for the information of the court?"

"I would rather not."

Another bang of the gavel. "Answer the question, Mr. Wright."

Wright shrugged. "Her name is Lady Charlotte Harlowe."

A gasp swept across the courtroom.

"Your father, then, was the Earl of Montclair, God rest his soul?"

Mr. Wright brushed a speck of invisible dust from his cuff. He turned to raise a devilish black eyebrow at the damsels. "So I have reliably been informed."

This time, a mixture of gasps and titters. One of the damsels hesitated, and then swooned.

Mr. Duckworth crossed his hands behind his back and began a studious journey across the courtroom. A few hairs had escaped from the snug white curls on his wig and waved faintheartedly in the passing air. "You are close with Lady Charlotte Harlowe?"

"A rather vague word, that."

Mr. Duckworth stopped and turned. "Do you see each other often? Do you bear a fraternal affection for her?"

"I do." Wright's voice turned to steel.

Mr. Fairchurch leapt to his feet, causing the nearby papers to flutter in alarm. "Objection, my lord! I don't see how this line of questioning has anything to do with the case at hand."

The prosecutor raised his hand. "My line of questioning has everything to do with the case at hand, as I will shortly demonstrate."

The judge said, in a dry and fatigued voice, "Proceed, Mr. Duckworth, but bring us to the point."

"Oh, I shall, my lord. Mr. Wright, you are a wealthy man, is that true?"

"Another vague word, Mr. Duckworth. I'm disappointed. I understood lawyers to be precise and exacting. I pay my own solicitors a great deal of money for this precision, so my valuable time is not wasted."

The pinkness returned to Mr. Duckworth's cheeks. "Are you the owner of Wright Holdings, Limited?"

"I am."

"You are engaged in financial dealings?"

"I am."

"Do you have in your possession a promissory note in the amount of forty-two thousand pounds from the late Duchess of Southam, which she was, in fact, unable to pay?"

A veritable wave of gasps engulfed the courtroom.

"I do."

Another damsel swooned.

"And is it true, Mr. Wright"—Mr. Duckworth was on his toes now, building to a mighty crescendo—"that you and the Duchess of Southam agreed that the promissory note should be considered executed in full if her stepson, the Marquess of Hatherfield, agreed to marry your sister, Lady Charlotte Harlowe, who was in love with him at the time?"

A wail of agony rose up from among the damsels, nearly drowned by the expressions of shock and horror rattling among the benches behind.

Stefanie's heart had frozen in her chest. She looked in horror at Hatherfield, for some sign of surprise, but his expression remained in place. The mouth a little compressed, perhaps.

"I don't deny it," said Wright, looking a trifle smug.

"And did the accused, the Marquess of Hatherfield, agree to this plan?" demanded Mr. Duckworth.

Wright shrugged. "I can't say, can I?"

"Let me rephrase the question. Was it your impression that the Marquess of Hatherfield looked favorably on the hand of Lady Charlotte Harlowe? This—you'll pardon the expression—this bargain between you and the Duchess of Southam?"

A silence settled upon the courtroom, so thick and heavy it lay on them all like a blanket of hot midsummer air. Stefanie's mind floated above it all. She twirled her pen around her forefinger and stared at the square tip of Wright's clean-shaven chin. Someone coughed, and the noise echoed and echoed.

Without moving his head, Mr. Wright turned his gaze to Stefanie. His eyes, to her surprise, were soft with compassion.

"No," he said. "I believe he did not. Not at all."

EIGHT

November 1889

The brothel was not Stefanie's idea, not at all.

In fact, she hadn't quite realized they were going to a brothel at all. They'd been slugging back ale at the Slaughtered Lamb, and someone had slurred, *I've got it, let's head over to Cousin Hannah's, I hear they've got exceptionally fresh pickings at the moment*, and Stefanie, who was not precisely an innocent, still assumed he meant that this Cousin Hannah's establishment, wherever it was, had just received a brand-new shipment of ale. And anything was preferable to this swill she'd been pretending to drink at the Slaughtered Lamb.

"Oh, splendid thought," she exclaimed, hopping from the booth, because Stefanie had been born and raised in Holstein-Schweinwald-Huhnhof, had cut her teeth sneaking out of the castle for adventures in the village with the son of the Holstein mayor, and she knew her hefeweizen from her doppelbock. "The fresher the better!"

She did feel a twinge of guilt, as she made her way along the damp and darkened alleys of London with her fellow clerks. She'd always felt a twinge of guilt, even back home, when slipping out the kitchen door of Holstein Castle and into Gunther's jovial company (and, later, his waiting arms). There was work waiting for her back at the chambers, duties to be performed, and this time those duties actually interested her. There was her father's death to avenge, when she had a spare bloody moment.

But her spirits had stirred, her damned restless spirits, as the clerks rose up in five o'clock unison and made for their black coats on the coat stand, all jumpy and smiling with anticipation of the amusements to come. Before she could stop herself, she'd thrown down her pen and called out, "Wait! Perhaps I'll come along for a bit, after all."

And after all, it was important to win the trust and confidence of one's colleagues, wasn't it?

But. This business of skulking down the alleyways, this Cousin Hannah's establishment with its fresh shipment of ale. Stefanie should have felt the familiar rising tide of excitement, the anticipation of new mischief, but instead she felt rather . . . glum. As if she were going through the motions, not really interested. Her mind kept returning to the case she'd been summarizing a few hours ago. And, more deliciously still, to the Marquess of Hatherfield, who never quite disappeared from her mind, all vibrant in his mesmerizing figure and his rich laugh, his bright eyes and wit. With the tantalizing sense that she'd barely shaved the golden skin of him, that there was so much more inside waiting for discovery.

So infinitely more interesting than sitting around another battered wooden table for a few more tedious hours with this drunken lot.

She should really be getting back to Cadogan Square and a good night's sleep. This enterprise had been a stupid mistake, a leftover instinct from her old unsatisfied life. She imagined Hatherfield watching her now, understanding and a little sorrowful, giving his head a little shake. Disappointed in her choice of company. She should find a hansom and head back, she should . . .

"Here we are, then!" one of the clerks called out cheerfully, and bustled her inside an unexpected and nondescript doorway, halfway along the street.

"You know, I really . . ."

But her comrades were already filling the hall, already laughing and flinging off their coats, already moving as a group into a warm and well-cushioned parlor, in which an electric chandelier hung with decadent brilliance from the ceiling and the surrounding upholstery had evidently been acquired from a factory positioned directly atop the world's largest deposit of red ocher.

"Oh dear," said Stefanie.

Evidently this Hannah was a kissing cousin.

The clerk who sat next to her, Bumby was his name, delivered her back a hearty thwack. "Look there! Cousin Hannah herself!" he called out.

The mistress of the house appeared in the doorway, not at all the florid female butterball of bawdy house legend. Cousin Hannah was tall and willowy, except for a pair of unnecessarily plump breasts perched atop an unnecessarily snug corset, and at the sight of the company in her crimson parlor, her face of fragile if rather mature loveliness opened up in a welcoming smile. She held out her hands. "Why, Mr. Bumby! Do come and give me a kiss. It's been ages. A fortnight at least!"

Mr. Bumby obliged with enthusiasm, and then he turned to a pink-faced Stefanie. "This is my young friend Mr. Thomas, Hannah. He likes them fresh, he says. The fresher the better, isn't that right, Thomas?"

"In fact," said Stefanie, "I believe that last beer at the Slaughtered Lamb has rather done for me tonight . . ."

"Oh, rubbish, Thomas!" said one of the other clerks. "Why, Hannah's girls will have your prick standing in no time, never fear. Once I staggered in here at two in the morning, drunk as a dockhand, couldn't put two words together, couldn't bloody walk for England, and in two minutes little Camille had me so stiff I could have ground pepper with my . . ."

"Yes, yes, Mr. Humboldt." Cousin Hannah tilted her head and assessed Stefanie from under her thick black lashes. "But Camille is not for everyone, you know. Are you certain you want someone so young, Mr. Thomas? I think an older girl might suit you better. A girl of experience."

"Or no girl at all," said Stefanie, "for I'm really quite . . . shattered. Been an exhausting day, an exhausting few days really, and . . ."

"Oh, that's balls, Thomas," said Bumby. "Do go up for a quick one, at least. You can't just sit about the parlor waiting for us with your doodle hanging down mournfully around your ankles, can you?"

"That's . . . that's unlikely, really," said Stefanie. "In any case, I can find my own way home."

Cousin Hannah took a step closer. She laid her hand on Stefanie's arm, light as a silken feather, ladylike and lascivious all at once. "I think I understand your difficulty, Mr. Thomas."

"I really think you don't."

She bent her pretty head to Stefanie's ear and spoke so softly, Stefanie almost couldn't hear. "It is your first time, isn't it? A little nervous, perhaps?" Her breath smelled of chocolate.

"No! No. I mean yes. I mean . . ."

Her hand slipped down Stefanie's arm to grasp her fingers. "Come with me, Mr. Thomas. I have just the thing for you." She spoke more loudly now, and the other clerks whooped with gentlemanly approval.

"Go on, Thomas!"

"Up you go, old man!"

"Poke her a good one, Thomas!"

Cousin Hannah tugged her out of the room. Stefanie followed, thinking perhaps this was her chance, she could make a break for it, find a back entrance. But the stairs loomed up immediately, tall and steep and carpeted in plush crimson. Cousin Hannah gripped her wrist like a manacle and yanked her upward, in a gesture quite unlike her ladylike deportment in the parlor.

Stefanie took a few stumbling steps after her and cast a glance back down to the entrance hall, and an enormous beef-armed man glared back up at her, as if to say, *Don't even think about it, ye posh fragging twit.*

Stefanie gulped back a yelp of dismay and continued on in Hannah's determined wake. Her mind invented and discarded a dozen excuses, and finally settled on disease. Nothing a prostitute dreaded more than disease, wasn't it? Inconvenience, lost profit, disgruntled customers, that sort of thing. She would make her confession in the privacy of the room itself. Pay the woman a sovereign, or whatever the going rate was, and ask to be excused.

On the other hand, Stefanie found her natural curiosity

rather awakened as Cousin Hannah, those corseted hips swaying like lifeboats, dragged her down a hallway lined with doors, all of them shut tight. A bawdy house! A genuine, honest-to-goodness bawdy house! An establishment built for the sole purpose of fornication by the hour. What were the ladies like? What were the customers like? What were the rooms like? Did everybody get down to business straightaway, or was there any sort of farcical courtship first, a few words of affection or at least attraction, a human connection of some kind before the necessary parts made the necessary contact with the inevitable result?

Did they change the sheets between customers?

And what on earth was that oblong object on the hall table?

"Wait a moment," said Stefanie, rather breathlessly, but Hannah had already reached the room at the end of the hall and turned the knob.

"Here we are, sir. All private and lovely."

Stefanie stumbled across the threshold and caught herself on a lamp table. She gazed around her in astonishment. A torrent of faded crimson wallpaper coated the walls, peeling at the corners and at the chipped baseboards, which had once probably been painted in white, and which were now a sooty gray. Atop a stain on the thick red rug stood a tripod table, on which a half-empty bottle of sherry perched with two smudged glasses. There was a wardrobe in the corner, for what purpose Stefanie could not possibly imagine.

And the bed. Of course, the bed.

Sized for two, made up with gray white sheets and a few thin blankets, dominating the room and made double by a large oblong mirror attached to the wall beside it. The four wooden posts rose up like pillars, nearly touching the slanted ceiling.

"Look here . . ." Stefanie lunged for the doorknob, but Hannah shut it tight and turned the key.

"Now, then," she said. "There's nothing to be afraid of, my lad. It's the greatest pleasure in the world, isn't it? You've given yourself pleasure before, haven't you?"

"I . . . yes, well . . . you see, I . . ."

Hannah smiled beautifully. "Don't worry. No one will ever know, will they? And I'll take special care of you. You've come to the right place for it, Mr. Thomas. Nobody takes on a new boy like I do. But you knew that right enough, or you wouldn't have come, would you? Every young fellow knows to come to Cousin Hannah's for his first poke."

"But that's the thing! It's all a dreadful mistake!" Stefanie said, in desperation.

Hannah wandered to the table in the corner and poured the sherry into one of the glasses. The electric light tried and failed to catch the dirty facets. "Have a little sip, now, Mr. Thomas. It will relax you."

"I don't need to relax. I say, do you mean you make a specialty out of this? Deflowering boys?"

Hannah drifted back toward her. Her eyes gleamed the same color as the sherry. "Drink, Mr. Thomas."

"I can't possibly. I really must be getting home. I . . . Good God, madam!"

Hannah's hands, working deftly at her back, had just released the bodice of her dress. She cupped her breasts invitingly atop her corset, not that all that overflowing flesh required much additional upward momentum. "You see, Mr. Thomas? Lovely, aren't they?"

"I . . . yes, they are, quite lovely indeed, but I really . . ." Stefanie angled her foot toward the door.

Quick as a flash, Hannah interposed herself between Stefanie and the door. "Only a single sovereign, dear boy. One golden sovereign. Imagine sinking your head between these beauties." She gave her handsome pair another jiggle.

"Yes, quite," said Stefanie. "But . . ."

Hannah reached behind again, and an instant later the whole dress slid free in a whoosh of silk gown against satin petticoat.

"How the devil did you do that?" Stefanie asked, incredulous.

"I am very skilled at what I do, Mr. Thomas." The petticoats were dropping now, one by one, to be kicked aside in turn by Hannah's adroit satin-slippered feet.

"Yes, but the tapes! The fastenings! Surely there must be some sort of trick to it, because I've never . . . Let me examine that bodice . . ." Stefanie bent to retrieve the frock, and a petticoat landed frothily atop her head.

"Do you want me to take off my corset, dear boy?" purred Hannah, from somewhere above.

"Not really. I . . . Good Lord, where does it end?" Stefanie scrabbled at the lace obstructing her vision.

"Just imagine yourself lying atop them, sweetheart. Soft and lovely."

Stefanie drew away the petticoat at last and found Hannah's plump white thighs, covered only by stockings and a perilously thin chemise, nearly brushing her nose.

"I assure you, madam, I . . ."

Hannah took her by the shoulders and hoisted her upward. "Come along, now. Don't be shy."

"I'm not shy! I'm only . . ." Stefanie's mind raced. What was that excuse again?

"Right here, dear boy." Hannah's hands grasped the back of her head.

". . . ill!" Stefanie burst out, but the word was muffled by the endless pillow of Hannah's breasts, scented powerfully with rose.

"What was that?"

Stefanie jerked back her head and gasped for air. "Ill! I'm ill! I . . ."

"Of course you are! Ooh, that's it, isn't that lovely, Hannah will make it all better . . ."

". . . have a . . . disease of some kind . . ."

". . . ooh, I'll cure you straightaway, never fear . . ."

". . . an . . . an itchy sort of thing . . . itches like the devil . . ."

". . . ooh, scratch *me*, then . . . ooh, you're so strong, Mr. Thomas, such a fighter . . ."

". . . and . . . and pustules, I think . . . yes, great pustules of . . . of pus . . ."

". . . ooh, don't fight so, don't . . . *PUS!?*"

The door crashed open, just as Hannah thrust Stefanie away with such ferocious energy she tumbled on her back atop the thick red sour-smelling rug.

Stefanie stared at the ceiling, wheezing for breath. Every atom of air seemed saturated with rose water. Her head ached with it, or perhaps that was only the influence of the floorboards beneath.

Really, the evening could not possibly get any worse.

But no sooner had this thought crossed her aching brain, when the voice of the Marquess of Hatherfield broke above her, like an avenging archangel. "Mr. Thomas! What the devil do you think you're doing?"

She placed her palms against the rug and attempted to rise. "Isn't it obvious?"

Hatherfield fought to maintain a suitably avenging expression as he surveyed the scene before him. Poor young Thomas, lying on the floor, gasping for breath, his face as red as the rug beneath his head. The prostitute—the rather shapely and bountiful prostitute, it must be said—stuffing her bounty with some difficulty back into its rightful place in her corset, as a housemaid might stuff a few more feathers into a pillow already packed with down.

"Dear me," he said. "What a scene of corruption. Do sit up, Thomas, and attempt a little dignity."

"I want him out of my house!" screeched the prostitute. "Him and his diseased parts!"

Hatherfield lifted an eyebrow. "Diseased, Mr. Thomas?"

"Yes, sir." Thomas stood slowly, a little dazedly, and cast his shamed eyes down toward the rug. "Quite . . . quite dreadfully diseased, as I informed Mistress Hannah. Not wishing to . . . do her an injury."

"An injury! Very serious, Thomas. I own myself appalled. We shall have to get you to a doctor instantly and have this problem corrected. In the meantime, I think it best if . . ."

A series of shouts floated through the open door. A rattling crash. Another.

"What the devil?" said the prostitute. She gathered up her petticoats and dress and made for the door.

"May I . . . may I assist you, madam?" Hatherfield inquired, averting his eyes from her bosom.

"It's the police! Police, by God!" She thrust her legs through her petticoats.

"Police?" said Hatherfield.

"Police!" gasped Mr. Thomas.

"The dirty bastards! I paid them off, I did! The stinking

arseholes!" The room shook with the force of Cousin Hannah's indignation. No sign now of her ladylike air down below in the parlor. "Pigs. You can't trust nobody anymore!"

The dress was on, a few petticoats short. Hannah performed some feat of dexterity at her back and darted from the room.

Young Thomas stared after her. Her face was wide and still with shock. She pressed her mustache with her first two fingers. "Quickly, Hatherfield! We've got to run!"

"I'm quite certain . . ."

But Thomas had already grasped his hand and was tugging him out the door. "We'll find a back exit!"

The hall was already full of half-dressed women and men with gaping trousers, stuffing their shirts and swinging their jackets. "This way!" someone shouted, and a stampede ensued toward the back staircase.

"Come along!" Thomas pulled at his arm.

"No! The back exit will be guarded, you fool! That's how they take everyone!"

"How the devil do you know that?"

"This way. Back in the room." He turned around and pulled Thomas's spindly body behind him, back down the hallway.

Thomas yanked himself free. "We'll be sitting ducks in there! We've got to run!"

"Calm down, Mr. Thomas . . ." Hatherfield grasped her wrists.

"Let me go! You don't understand! They can't catch me, I can't be found out . . ."

There was no time to argue with her. Hatherfield bent and gripped Thomas behind the knees with one arm and across the back with the other. With a single giant heave he tossed her flailing body over his shoulder.

Her fists pounded his back. "Put me down at once!"

"Now, Mr. Thomas. Calm yourself. Just trust me."

"What the devil do you think you're doing? Back to that room? Are you mad?"

He didn't dare answer that question. He carried her back down the hall, against the tide of panicked sinners, ducking and staggering and apologizing. "Beg your pardon. Yes, back to the room, certainly not going to—excuse me, madam—dash out into that damned turkey shoot about to take place in the—watch the leg, there!—back courtyard."

The flailing limbs stilled around him. "Good Lord, Hatherfield. You're not thinking of shimming us out the window, are you?"

"Nothing to it, Thomas. It's only the first floor, after all." He ducked under the doorframe. "And in any case, we're not simply going to drop right down, into the turkey shoot. That would be foolish."

"We're not?"

Hatherfield slung her down in the center of the floor and closed the door behind them. "Of course not. We're going to lark across a few rooftops first."

"Across *what?*"

"The rooftops. Easy enough, really. We'll drop to earth somewhere around Frith Street, and then . . ." He unlocked the sash and pressed his fingers under the frame. ". . . And then get you . . . get you safely back . . . to the safe . . ."

"What's the matter?"

He stepped back with a frown. "The window. It's stuck."

"Oh, for God's sake. A big fellow like you." Thomas marched up next to him and positioned herself underneath the window. "Just put a little . . . a bit of . . . effort . . . like . . . like this . . ."

"Thomas . . ."

"It's . . . I felt it give a bit . . ."

"It's nailed shut, Thomas."

Thomas drew away and stared at the window. "Nailed shut? Why the devil would anyone nail a window shut?"

"To keep the customers inside, I presume." Hatherfield set his lips in a firm line and turned around. Ominous rattles vibrated the walls. The shouts were growing louder. "They're coming upstairs."

"You see! I told you we should head for the back exit! Now we're stuck here! Like . . . like rats in a trap!" Thomas's hands thrust into her hair.

"Rubbish." Hatherfield took her hand, went to the door, and opened it. A hail of shouts met his ears, the faint screeching of trapped humanity. No escape there.

"They're coming!" said Thomas, in a hiss. "Close the door!"

"No. No, leave it open. Come here."

"What the devil?"

Hatherfield dragged her to the wardrobe, opened the door, and bundled her inside. An outraged cry emerged, muffled by cloth.

Hatherfield stepped in after her and pulled the door shut.

"What do you think you're doing?" she whispered in his ear. Literally in his ear, for the wardrobe was tiny, stuffed to the gills with clothing, cheap silk from the feel of it, and Thomas's lips were so close he felt their warmth brushing his ear.

"Be still," he whispered back, and just to be sure of her obedience, and *only* to be sure, he wrapped his left arm around her and pulled her right up flush against his body.

She made a tiny yelp and went silent.

The wardrobe was narrow and deep. Hatherfield maneuvered her against the backboard and laid his own body protectively atop her, the blades of his shoulders brushing the door, his arms and shoulders surrounded by displaced silk. He ignored the feel of her limbs against his, her warm breath into his neck. He ignored the tantalizing swell at her chest, covered by wool and cotton and God knew what, but unmistakably softer than muscle. He ignored the scratch of her mustache at his collar, perversely and intensely arousing. He concentrated entirely on the sounds thudding through the wood and plaster, the pattern of footsteps on the stairs and the hall.

Oh, all right. He was doing his best, anyway.

His body had other notions. According to the mounting evidence.

Concentrate. The police were starting from the top of the house, no surprise, but there would certainly be guards posted at every stairway. No more screeching now. Had all the prostitutes and clients left in the first rush?

Bang, bang, bang. Doors opened and slammed shut above him. The police were searching the rooms, then, one by one. Bloody hell. A fitting end to a frustrating day.

And yet.

God, she felt good. She felt delicious. Her rigid muscles were softening now, taking his bones and sinews into the shelter of her, inviting exploration. Her skin smelled like honey. He imagined himself licking the hollow of her throat, tasting her pulse, and the seams of his trousers nearly split in response.

He tried to angle his hips away, but only managed an inch or so before his buttocks nudged the wardrobe door. Would she notice the thickening bulge? Damn it all, of course she would notice. The question was whether she would know what it meant, and he rather thought . . .

Concentrate. Spike the senses, coil the muscles. Ready to strike. He leaned his ear against the wood, the better to hear the progress upstairs, but now his mouth was full of her hair, loosened from its pomade grip, falling silky and scented about her face. A tiny noise escaped her. She moved her hips forward, just slightly, as if . . . God help him.

As if seeking the return of his own.

He flipped his other cheek to the wood, away from her tempting hair and head, trying to listen to the wood and not the beat of his own desperate pulse, but his traitorous hips could not resist the inviting shift of hers, like the rock of a cradle, and he fit himself against her, a perfect match, good God, brain spinning, thumbs brushing against her shirt, the distant pounding and slamming of impending disaster in his ears. Madness.

"Hatherfield," she whispered, right into his neck.

Do not kiss her.

A warmth touched his waist, beneath his coat. Her fingers, sliding along the seam where his waistcoat met his trousers.

You sweet thing. Did he say the words, or think them?

"Hatherfield," she whispered again. "Is it safe?"

"Not yet. Shh."

That was her heart, he realized, pumping through the layers between them. Thomas's heart. Her handprint turned hot at his waist, right there in the most sensitive spot. Her thumb nudged past the hem of his waistcoat to find his shirt. His skin, a few linen threads away.

Do not kiss her.

The alarm beat in his brain, danger clanging against the white light of sexual desire, the familiar scorching need that electrified every muscle. He was a satyr, a monster, just as his stepmother had always said. What kind of beast held a young lady's life in his hands, charged to protect her, and in that same moment pushed his shamefully erect cock into her innocent hips? He had probably maneuvered her into the wardrobe on purpose, if he were honest with himself. Tucked her in his arms and covered her with his body not to shield her, but because he'd been thinking of nothing else but bedding her since he'd met her. He had done this all for his own prurient sexual interest, hadn't he, when he might have bustled her safely outside with only a little more effort and ingenuity.

Hatherfield turned his head and let his lips hover at her temple. His eyes, adjusting to the darkness, began to pick up the faint shadow of her, not even vision really, more the sense of her, her outline against the black wood.

She tilted her head, ever so slightly, just enough that Hatherfield's lips met her temple.

Turn away.

But his lips, his guilty lips, stayed there on her skin, and she didn't move, either. Didn't jerk away, didn't gasp in shock.

He couldn't breathe, couldn't think. She must know, then. She must realize that he knew she was a woman, and if she did . . . well, then what?

Then he was in even more trouble than he'd imagined.

Thump, thump. Footsteps in the hall outside.

Hatherfield held his breath in his chest, held his lips against her temple, everything still and hot and waiting. A sense of crystalline expectation, the instant before the glass shattered.

The door banged open against the wall.

Hatherfield absorbed the flinch of Thomas's body. She pressed herself into him, her forehead tucked against his jaw, both hands around his waist. His aroused flesh nestled in the hollow between her hips.

He closed his eyes, the better to detect the movement of booted feet about the room. One man. Not urgent. He took a few deliberate steps and stopped. The floorboards creaked beneath the rug. A heavy shuffle, as he turned about. Perhaps picked up and examined Hannah's discarded petticoats.

After that first flinch, Thomas lay perfectly still. Not a whimper escaped her lips, not a ripple moved her muscles. Only her finger went on with its tiny up-and-down motions at his waist, as if to remind him that she was still alive, still there in his arms, making his skin mist and his heart pound. Her breath in his neck was steady and brave. Hatherfield might have thought she'd been hiding out from police in brothel wardrobes all her life.

Who knew? Maybe she had.

The floorboards creaked again. Slow, deliberate. Closer. Closer.

Thomas's finger stopped its caress and dug into his skin. Hatherfield thought he could hear the policeman breathing, heavy and rapid, through the clothes and the wood between them.

Another step. A long pause. Another step.

And then, in a rush, the boots thudded back across the floor and out the door.

NINE

Stefanie could not stop chattering as the Marquess of Hatherfield's private hansom rattled through the London streets toward Cadogan Square. "I really thought I should slip on that last rooftop, with all the shingles missing. Really, people ought to take better care of their houses, don't you think?"

"Indeed."

"How fortunate you were behind me, instead of in front. You quite saved me. Of course, I've no doubt the gutter would have stopped me eventually, but it would have been an exceptionally bumpy ride in the meantime."

"Indeed."

Hatherfield spoke in exactly the same tone he'd maintained since opening the wardrobe door some half an hour ago, after a minute or two of massive silence in which Stefanie had been expecting his kiss at any instant, had been deciding what to do when it arrived. (*Kiss him back*, was her brain's happy conclusion.) But the anticipated kiss had not, in fact, landed upon her lips. Only his body, heavy and hot, had lain against hers, with that steely bulge that made her want to crawl out of her own skin and into his, made her feverish and almost sick. Made her want to rub her hands and feet and body over every inch of his beautiful flesh, and especially those several thick inches pressed potently into her lower belly.

She had contented herself with a single finger at his waist.

Oh, all those feverish feelings, which had gotten her into such trouble before! They'd now returned at tenfold strength. Just sitting beside him now, she could hardly restrain herself from touching him. She should know better, she really should.

Especially since Hatherfield thought *she* was a *he*.

She went on speaking instead. "I hardly dare ask how you happened upon the establishment, and my room in particular, at exactly that moment. Followed closely by the police, I might add."

He roused himself a fraction. "The police were a surprise, in fact."

"And you?"

"I was looking out for you, young man. Isn't it obvious?"

Stefanie straightened her shoulders. "I'm not in need of a nursemaid, your lordship."

"Aren't you? You seem to have gotten yourself into a right mess on your own. What the devil were you doing in a brothel to begin with, for God's sake?" he demanded, with a little more vim, which was decidedly better than all those grim and ominous *Indeeds* he'd been sporting before.

Well, she wasn't about to admit the truth. "Oh, you know how it is. Out with the lads for a pint or two, looking for amusement. Isn't it obvious what I was doing?"

"You were on the floor when I arrived, Mr. Thomas. Looking considerably discomposed."

"The lady didn't suit me."

Hatherfield snorted. "I daresay not. That doesn't change the fact that you were there, in that bawdy house, an innocent . . . young person, when you should have been safe at home in your bed."

"Safe at home? You sound like a dowager."

"You need a dowager, Mr. Thomas."

The words burst out. "No, I don't! I'm not innocent. Not some damned lily-white virgin, after all."

The carriage slowed, making the turn around Hyde Park Corner. Hatherfield placed his large gloved hand on the edge of the door, as if to steady himself. When he spoke, his voice had returned to that grim tone of before. "I see."

Did he believe her, or not? She looked down at her hands, knotted together in her lap, atop the thick folds of her dreary black overcoat. Her breath exploded in a gust, and she realized she'd been holding it. She gathered herself and spoke defiantly. "Anyway, I don't see why I shouldn't have any amusement at all. I'm not the sort to lie quietly in my bed at night."

"No, I daresay you're not."

"But you are."

Hatherfield's hand hadn't left the hansom door. He rubbed his thumb slowly along the edge. "You make me sound rather dull," he said, a little amused.

"I daresay you could use a little adventure, now and then."

His laugh sent a cloud of fog into the London night. "You're adventure enough, believe me, Mr. Thomas. It will be hard going for me, tomorrow morning on the river."

"Well, it's not as if you have to do it, do you?" Stefanie said. "You could stay home and sleep another hour or two."

"No, I couldn't," he said softly.

"What, just for one morning?"

The hansom jounced over a rut and came to a sudden stop, where the traffic had thickened in its mysterious London night way. Hatherfield sighed. "Little one, you wouldn't understand. Sometimes there's just one thing holding you to your sanity. One true and honest thing in your life, and the rest is all pretense and ceremony and the face one wears in public. The face one's obliged to wear. So you have to escape somewhere, every day, or you'll go mad."

The vehicle started forward again. *Little one*. Somehow it hadn't sounded diminutive, in Hatherfield's voice. Stefanie closed her eyes. "You're wrong. I understand exactly what you mean."

A little pause, and then, "Well, maybe you do, at that."

"Anyway," Stefanie went on quickly, because every one of these little pauses seemed to carry the weight of what had happened between them in that wardrobe, "Sir John thought my summary showed a great deal of promise."

"I don't doubt it. You have an exceptional mind, Mr. Thomas."

"So I shall be working very hard indeed."

"I certainly hope so. Long hours, safe in those chambers of Sir John's. I can't think of anything better for you."

Stefanie frowned. "I don't know about that."

"I do. I'm quite certain of it. You shouldn't be let out at all."

"Not at *all*?"

"Not once." Hatherfield sounded positive. "You should devote yourself entirely to the practice of law, with occasional breaks at mealtimes, to be eaten at your desk or at Sir John's table in Cadogan Square. Or your room, more preferably. Yes, that's the ticket. With a double guard at every door."

Stefanie folded her arms. "I've changed my mind. You are dull. Worse than dull, in fact. I think you're in a rut. And do you know what else I think?"

"I can't imagine."

"I think you had fun tonight."

"Fun!" He laughed, a bit raspy this time, dark edged. "I suppose you could call it that. Fun." He finished in a mutter.

"So we'll do it again, won't we? Not a brothel, necessarily," Stefanie added hastily, while a part of her brain was screaming, *What are you doing, you idiot? He'll find you out in no time, the game will be up, he'll be furious, you'll put the whole scheme in jeopardy, you're mad!* and the other part was jumping up and down, screeching, *Yes! Yes! Delightful idea! More Hatherfield, please! More more more!* "But some other outing. Something exciting."

"I have quite enough excitement in my life already, thank you."

"No, you don't. In any case, if you don't go along, I'll simply have to go off on my own. And you know what scrapes I get into." She looked back modestly at her fingertips.

"You wouldn't."

"I might."

The hansom turned into Cadogan Square. A rumbling sound filled the space between them, and Stefanie realized that Hatherfield was laughing. Well, chuckling. But an expression of amusement, in any case.

The vehicle rolled to a stop. "Well?" said Stefanie.

"I want you to return home directly after your work is finished, every day," said Hatherfield.

"But . . ."

He held up his hand. "But. I shall invite myself to dinner, and then we'll see."

Stefanie's smile broke across her lips. She flung her arms around his shoulders. "Oh, you're marvelous, Hatherfield! We'll have such fun, I promise. You won't regret it."

"I am quite certain I will come to regret it acutely. However, that's of no consequence. Come along." He swung open the cab door. "I'll escort you inside."

"Escort me?"

But Hatherfield's hand was firm on her arm as she climbed out of the hansom. The touch reminded her again of that moment in the wardrobe, when his lips had pressed against the thin skin at her temple and hadn't let go, and she'd felt as if she were drowning.

The hand dropped away as they crossed the pavement to Sir John's front steps. Hatherfield jumped in front of her and let the knocker fall, and the door was opened an instant later by one of the footmen.

"Good evening, your lordship. Good evening, sir. Sir John is in the library."

"Thank you," said Hatherfield, "but I believe I'll be on my way."

The footman melted away. Hatherfield turned to face her. The light from the lamp cast a soft glow along one side of his grave and flawless face, and everything clogged in Stefanie's throat, every word she wanted to say.

"About the wardrobe," said Hatherfield.

"Yes! I . . ."

"It won't happen again, I promise. I am quite capable of controlling my baser instincts. You may rely on me, Thomas, to put your own interests foremost in the future."

Oh God, he was so beautiful, speaking to her in that grim voice, his blue eyes so terribly serious, his eyebrows set at a remorseful angle beneath the brim of his hat. Stefanie wanted to press her palms against those high cheekbones, to press her lips against that sensuous mouth.

"Yes, of course," she said. "Naturally, that would be best."

He reached forward and took off her hat. "I do want to apologize for . . ."

"Why, James!"

Stefanie and Hatherfield jumped like a pair of startled alley cats. Which, she reflected, as the wallpaper slid past her eyes, was not far from the truth.

Lady Charlotte stood in the hallway, tiny and exquisite and tremulous, her wide eyes bright from the lamp on the hall table just before her. One hand lay upon the newel post, the other fisted into her skirts. The flawless hourglass curve of her waist seemed impossibly minute against the busy flocks of the wallpaper behind her.

Hatherfield recovered first. He made a little bow of his head. "Lady Charlotte. Good evening."

She took a few steps forward. "We're in the library. Do come and join us." Her eyes were fixed on Hatherfield's face, as if Stefanie didn't exist.

"I'm afraid I can't. I'm up far too late as it is." Hatherfield's voice sent a distinct chill through the air.

"We missed you at breakfast this morning."

"Family duties, I'm afraid, Lady Charlotte."

Her gaze slid at last to Stefanie. "I see."

Hatherfield lifted his hat politely. "You'll forgive me, Lady Charlotte." He turned to Stefanie. "Mr. Thomas. I shall see you both in the morning."

Stefanie forced her lips to move. "Good evening, Lord Hatherfield."

"Good evening, James." Lady Charlotte's voice rang out with authority.

When the door had shut behind Hatherfield's swinging coat, Stefanie turned and braced herself for the expected swing from Lady Charlotte's elegant bat. "Your ladyship, I . . ."

"Mr. Thomas. My dear Mr. Thomas." Lady Charlotte's face transformed into softness. She stepped forward and linked her arm through his. "You must come and join us. It's the oddest thing. I feel as if you're part of the family. Not a servant at all."

At nine o'clock sharp the following morning, the Marquess of Hatherfield followed the immaculate ebony back of a footman into the Duke of Olympia's study on Park Lane.

The duke, looking up from his desk, threw down his pen

and rose with a broad smile. "Hatherfield! There you are. What a very great pleasure."

Hatherfield ignored his outstretched hand. "Olympia, you scoundrel. What the devil have you got brewing now?"

Olympia waved his hand. "Coffee? Or something stronger?"

"Coffee will do."

Olympia pressed his finger to a button on his desk. The footman reappeared. "Coffee for his lordship," said Olympia cheerfully.

Hatherfield stalked to the window.

"Come now," called the duke. "There's no need for sulking."

"I'm not sulking. I'm making bloody well certain I haven't been followed."

"You're perfectly safe here."

Hatherfield turned. "Am I? But that's not the question, at the moment. What I want to know is this: Who is this Stephen Thomas, and why in God's name have you dressed the poor lady up in men's clothing and set her to work for Sir John Worthington, of all people?"

"You find her position unsuitable?"

"I beg your pardon. Have you gone mad?"

"Not at all, not at all."

A knock sounded on the door.

"Come in, come in," said Olympia, and the footman swept through with a large silver tray, on which a large silver coffee service gleamed with the light of a thousand polishing cloths.

Hatherfield folded his arms and glowered as the footman set out cups and saucers and creamers, with all due ceremony appropriate to the private study of the Duke of Olympia. In exactly those same movements had a footman—possibly the same footman—set out the coffee on Hatherfield's first visit to this study, what was it? Four years ago, when he was just out of university. He'd received a note in his rooms, his brand-new rooms at the Albert Hall Mansions, a safe distance from Belgrave Square, and he'd looked at the thick paper blankly and thought, Penhallow's grandfather? What the devil would Penhallow's grandfather want with me? "My grandson Penhallow speaks highly of you," the duke had said, once the first greetings had been exchanged and the first sips had been taken.

"Your quick wits, your physical fitness, your sound moral character. I thought perhaps you might be willing to assist me with an important task. A discreet task, for which Her Majesty's government would be deeply grateful."

Hatherfield looked out the window again and tapped his finger against his upper arm. The weight of the passing seconds drummed against his brain.

The door closed at last.

"Come now," said Olympia. "Have your coffee, there's a good chap."

Hatherfield stalked back across the room and snatched a cup. "Well? Her name, at least."

Olympia's smile revealed a neat row of smug white teeth. "She is Her Royal Highness the Princess Stefanie, youngest daughter of the Prince of Holstein-Schweinwald-Huhnhof, who—as I'm sure you know—was murdered two months ago, along with the husband of his eldest daughter, the Crown Princess."

The cup froze in Hatherfield's hand, a hairsbreadth away from his waiting lips. He stared at Olympia's teeth, while the world swirled around him. "Princess?" he croaked at last.

"And my niece," said Olympia. "My sister Louisa was Prince Rudolf's first wife."

Hatherfield set his cup into his saucer and the saucer on the table. He selected a pastry from a flowered plate as fine as glass, popped it into his mouth, chewed, swallowed, reached for his coffee. He took a sip, replaced the cup, and said, "Where are Her Highness's sisters?"

A flutter of the ducal fingers. "Elsewhere."

"Are they in danger?"

"Obviously, or I should have left them in place in Germany."

Hatherfield drank his coffee. His brain was quite calm now, quite orderly. "And *this* is your plan? To keep the princesses safe by dressing them as young men and setting them loose, unattended, across England?"

"But they're not unattended, are they? You have been keeping my dear Stefanie in perfect safety." The duke sat back in his chair and beamed.

Hatherfield's cup crashed in its saucer. "My God! You *are* mad! What if I hadn't noticed Mr. Stephen Thomas was a girl, hmm? What if I hadn't known a few tricks of your trade? What if I hadn't bothered? The *risk* you were taking!"

"I believe I calculated the risks well enough." Again, the smile. "I trained you myself, didn't I? I've kept you honed with the odd assignment or two. I know exactly where your skills lie, Hatherfield, and I had every possible confidence that . . ."

Hatherfield stalked forward and crashed his fist on the desk, making the duke's pens rattle in their holders. He said, between clenched teeth, "You will tell me everything you know about the danger facing Her Highness. You will not leave out a single detail. And then *I*, Olympia, *I* will tell you how *I* wish to proceed with the matter, keeping the young lady's safety above all other considerations. *All* other considerations, do you hear me? You and your damned political intrigues."

The Duke of Olympia steepled his fingers together and leaned forward. His blue eyes met Hatherfield's with the intensity of a bolt of lightning. "I assure you, my dear fellow, nothing is more important to me than the happiness and well-being of my precious niece."

"Nothing, Your Grace?" Hatherfield said bitterly.

The duke spread his hands. "My dear, dear Hatherfield. Why else do you think I entrusted her to you?"

TEN

Hatherfield's barrister was not pleased, and he let his client know it.

"I am not pleased, Lord Hatherfield. You attend these proceedings as if they were a tennis match, and not a trial for murder in which your own life hangs in the balance." Mr. Fairchurch had a broad face full of luxurious brown whiskers, and he twitched them all with the force of his discontent.

Hatherfield leaned back in the chair and crossed his legs. "I assure you, Mr. Fairchurch, the weight of the matter lies heavy upon my shoulders. I haven't the slightest intention of seeming—oh, what's the word, Mr. Thomas?" He swiveled to Stefanie with a smile.

She did not return it. "Blithe. Insouciant. Unnaturally cheerful." She sat between two enormous piles of documents, and in the shadow of this crevasse the strong bones of her face looked almost gaunt. She leaned another inch toward him and said accusingly, "Lighthearted."

He snapped his fingers. "That's the word. But I see no reason to be downcast. Look at the pair of you, like moping owls. Have you no confidence in the British system of justice? The finest in the world."

"Only if the defendant takes a proper interest in his own case," said Mr. Fairchurch.

"I do. I listen to every word, I assure you. Even the Latin ones."

"To say nothing of this nasty surprise from Mr. Wright. Why the devil didn't you say anything of the business? Weren't you aware?"

Hatherfield looked at Stefanie. "I was well aware."

"Then . . ."

"Mr. Fairchurch," said Stefanie, without looking away from Hatherfield's face, "I believe your meeting with the judge and prosecution takes place in another two minutes?"

Mr. Fairchurch thrust his hand into his pocket and produced a watch. "Dash it all! I shall return shortly. Do try to talk some sense into the man, Mr. Thomas, and get to the bottom of this Harlowe business."

When the door clicked shut behind him, Hatherfield cast aside his careless air and reached across the table to take Stefanie's hands. "My dear . . ."

Her hands jerked away. "Stop that. If anyone were to see us . . ."

"He's just left."

"Don't be a fool." Her eyes were wet. "Don't you understand? You're on trial for your life, Hatherfield. Your life."

"There's no danger. I have every confidence in . . ."

Stefanie rose from her chair so quickly, she almost overturned it. "In the British justice system. I know. But we have nothing, Hatherfield. Nothing but your word. And why on earth did you never tell me that Mr. Wright was bribing your stepmother to arrange a marriage between you and Lady Charlotte?"

"He was bribing the both of them, as I understand it."

"But why didn't you say anything? All of a sudden, the prosecution has an actual motive!"

"Because I didn't think anyone else knew. It was a private matter."

She rose from her chair and went to the small window, overlooking an alleyway. "I wish Sir John himself were defending this case. Fairchurch is competent enough, but . . ."

"You know he couldn't. He was right there in Belgrave

Square, the night of the murder. We're fortunate that Fairchurch agreed to take you on as his clerk; at least this way Sir John can pass along his unofficial advice."

"I doubt he'll be pleased about today's developments. I wouldn't want to be in Lady Charlotte's shoes, if Sir John decides she knew about this arrangement of her brother's." She ran her finger along the dusty edge of the window sash. "Is there anything else you haven't told me?"

He said nothing. She turned, arms folded, and found that he was watching her intently. "How are you, Stefanie? How are you getting on? Nelson is looking after you, isn't he?"

Stefanie made a short laugh. "Nelson is a bulldog. He's waiting outside this very door, I daresay."

Hatherfield let out a long sigh, as if he'd been holding his breath for a week. For the first time, Stefanie noticed the lines about his blue eyes, the delicate trace of strain on his pale golden skin. "Good man."

She dropped back into her chair. Her eyes hurt with the effort of holding herself together. Not allowing the shameful tears to break free in the face of him. "Hatherfield, please. You have to do your best. You have to fight this. For my sake, if not for yours. My uncle has left town, I've no idea where to find my sisters. Even Miss Dingleby has cut off all communication. You cannot leave me alone, do you hear?"

"Sir John will take care of you."

She slammed her fist on the table. "I don't want Sir John. I want you!"

He rose to his feet slowly, as if keeping himself in check by the most herculean effort of self-control. He said softly, "A man with the stain of a murder accusation in his past? Even if I'm acquitted, Stefanie, I'm no longer suitable for you. If I ever was."

She leaned forward, across the narrow table, and grabbed his hands. "Don't say that again. Ever. I will fight for you with everything I have, Hatherfield, every ounce of brain and muscle I own, and I expect you to do the same for me. As you did, before all this. As you fought so hard for me when I needed *you*."

The light leapt into his eyes at last. In the flash of a leopard capturing his prey, he snatched her face between his broad hands and said, next to her mouth, "Stefanie, little one, you don't know what it costs me to . . ."

The doorknob turned.

Stefanie fell back in her chair, heart pounding, ears ringing.

"Well, gentlemen?" said Mr. Fairchurch. "Have we come to a satisfactory solution?"

"Yes, sir," Stefanie said stoutly, tunneling her gaze between Hatherfield's fierce eyes. "I believe I've put the matter to Lord Hatherfield in the clearest possible terms."

ELEVEN

Cadogan Square, London
November 1889

Every lamp and chandelier in the drawing room of Sir John Worthington's Cadogan Square mansion glittered brilliantly upon the company scattered across its cushions, but the Marquess of Hatherfield, pausing at the threshold, felt a cold shadow close over his chest.

"My dear boy," said his father, looking up from his glass. "There you are at last."

"Father. Good evening." He crossed to the woman occupying one side of the sofa, in intimate conspiracy with the dainty figure of Lady Charlotte Harlowe. "Your Grace." He took her outstretched hand and brought it near, but not quite touching, his lips.

"My dear Hatherfield," said his stepmother. She smiled beautifully. "You're late."

"I beg your pardon. I was escorting young Mr. Thomas home."

"How good of you to take such an interest in our protégé," said Lady Charlotte. "And where is the dear fellow now?"

Hatherfield turned to her. She held her hand out expectantly for another almost-kiss, another not-quite greeting. "Lady Charlotte. Mr. Thomas is upstairs, I believe, changing into a dinner jacket."

"A dinner jacket! Does he have one, indeed?"

"So I would imagine." Hatherfield pivoted back to where the two men stood, holding their drinks, shirtwaists stiff and necks stiffer. "What a tremendous surprise, Father. I had no idea you were dining with Sir John tonight."

"A pleasant surprise, I hope."

"Of course."

"We see you so rarely, Hatherfield, that we thought perhaps the mountain must come to Mohammed." The duchess's voice was as clear and cold as an Alpine lake.

As her heart, Hatherfield thought grimly.

He glanced at the doorway. Where the devil was Stefanie? He needed a friendly face, a single conspiratorial glance, a sense of some sort of kindred spirit. They'd hardly exchanged a word in the hansom, returning from Temple Bar. He had sat waiting for her on the street, counting the other clerks as they filed out, until at last her figure had emerged from under the soot-smeared lintel. Mr. Stephen Thomas. Her Royal Highness, Princess Stefanie, dressed in her plain black overcoat and bowler hat, her bristling little mustache and worn dark shoes. She'd glanced up and down the street, as if looking for him, and he'd stepped forward and blinked away the sheen that had somehow materialized in his eyes at the sight of her. Her brave jaw and slight shoulders, her sharp eyes and delicate note, her strength and her vulnerability. He wanted to press her safe into his heart, he wanted to press himself safe around her. "Good evening, Thomas," he'd said instead. "Let's get you home, shall we?"

And that was that.

Now, he'd have given his left arm for a glimpse of her.

"Working late again, was he?" said Sir John. "Good lad. Needs a bit of discipline, of course, but his mind is first-rate. Absolutely first-rate. Sherry?"

"Please."

Sir John addressed the liquor tray. "I do appreciate your taking an interest in the boy. Just what he needs, a bit of polish. A sterling example."

"I don't know about that." He took the glass from Sir John.

"Nonsense," said Lady Charlotte. "Mr. Thomas is immeasurably fortunate to have found such a well-placed sponsor. So fine and virtuous a gentleman as you, James."

He drank deep. "You flatter me."

"Naturally!" the Duke of Southam said jovially. "Naturally she does! The dear girl."

"Very dear." The duchess took Lady Charlotte's hand and squeezed it fondly.

Lady Charlotte cast her eyes downward and blushed. "You are all so terribly kind."

"Because we love you, my dear girl. So beautiful and charming and accomplished. The perfect young lady. Isn't she, Hatherfield?" The duchess smiled at him.

He polished off the sherry and glared at his father. "Indeed."

"Is everything quite all right, James?" asked Lady Charlotte. "You seem distracted this evening. Not your usual warm and engaging self."

"Aren't I? It must be the chill in the air." He went to the drinks tray and refilled his glass.

"The chill? I don't feel any chill. Do you feel a chill, Your Grace?"

"Not at all, my dear," said the Duchess of Southam. "Perhaps it's all this sherry Hatherfield is drinking."

"My dear stepmother. At the moment, I don't believe there's enough sherry in the world."

"Hatherfield! What the devil do you mean by that?" said the duke.

"He's not at all himself," said the duchess.

"Perhaps he's ill," said Lady Charlotte. She rose to her feet in a rustle of silk and hurried in his direction. "He did say he felt a chill. My poor James." She came up from behind and reached upward to lay a pair of cool fingertips upon his forehead.

He brushed them aside and stepped away. "I am not ill. For God's sake. All of you. I am simply . . ."

"Exhausted, isn't that right?"

The voice from the doorway floated out cheerfully, causing everyone to jump and the duke to spill his sherry with a vulgar oath that hung in the air in a most unseemly fashion.

Mr. Stephen Thomas—Stefanie—stepped forward with a brilliant smile. "My fault, I'm afraid. I kept him up far too late last night. I won't say what we were up to"—a devilish wink,

as she stepped past several pairs of astonished eyes on her way
to the drinks tray—"as the subject is not at all suitable for
ladies." She poured her sherry to the brim and clinked her
glass against Hatherfield's with a happy crystalline *chink*.
"Your health, sir."

"By God," said the Duke of Southam, stunned. "Who the
devil's that?"

"My new clerk," said Sir John.

Hatherfield gazed down at Stefanie's face, amused and a
little flushed, the slender mustache dark against her creamy
skin. Her black tailcoat squared neatly atop her shoulders;
her white shirtfront spread crisply across the smooth swell of her
chest. Her auburn hair shone dark with pomade, sleeked back
to expose her forehead and cheekbones, high and strong and
fearless. She looked back at him with those large, bright eyes
of hers, rimmed with extravagant black lashes, dancing with
shared secrets, and something whooshed in Hatherfield's ears,
as if a hurricane were galloping past, spinning and roaring and
tumbling him off his feet.

The sound of a man falling in love.

He smiled back at her and set down his glass.

"Your Graces," he said, "may I present Mr. Stephen Thomas,
kin and protégé of the Duke of Olympia himself. Mr. Thomas is
the cleverest chap in London and, so I've heard, the next great
colossus of the English bar."

Three sharp taps rang through the snug air of Stefanie's
third-floor bedroom, the instant she had struggled out of
her tailcoat.

She went still, both hands poised at her necktie, and looked
about the room.

Tap tap tap. A touch louder.

Stefanie frowned at the door. Who on earth would be wanting her company at this hour? Surely not Lady Charlotte, who
had been casting such murderous glances across the dinner
table whenever she thought Stefanie wasn't looking. In the
first place, an unchaperoned nocturnal visit would be highly
improper. In the second, her ladyship couldn't possibly think
she could get away with violent homicide in her uncle's own

house, what with modern techniques of criminal science and that chap with the deerstalker running amok across London, making his uncanny deductions.

Stefanie opened the door and peeked out.

Nobody there.

Tap tap tap.

Stefanie slammed the door shut and whipped about. Eight feet away, the face of the Marquess of Hatherfield pressed against her wet windowpane, his beauty rather smashed and distorted by the glass and the lurid shadows.

She let out her breath in a gust and crossed the room. "You might have said something," she said, thrusting open the sash. "You nearly killed me with fright."

"Nonsense. You're not susceptible to frights of that kind. Thank God." He crawled through with an expert twist of his sleek body and leapt nimbly to Stefanie's floor. A cascade of droplets shook forth from his golden hair.

Stefanie tossed him a hand towel from the basin. Her heart was thumping so quickly, she thought she might be dizzy. He seemed to take up all the space in the room, all the air, as if the sun itself had popped through her window to land, still burning, on her rug. "You know, there's this delightful invention called a staircase. Paired with a door, it's a really remarkable way of gaining entrance to someone's room. Or exit, for that matter."

"I'm trying to reform my dull ways, per your instruction." His face emerged from behind the towel, grinning widely, his damp hair tousled as if he'd just emerged from his bed. "Also, I didn't want to be seen."

Thump thump, went Stefanie's heart.

She snatched the towel and hung it back next to the washstand. "Why not?"

"Why not what?"

"Why didn't you want to be seen?"

"Oh, that." The window was still open. Hatherfield closed it with care and turned back to Stefanie. "Because if I'd been seen, I might have been followed. And if I'd been followed . . ."

He stood directly before her, all warm and glowing from having climbed up gutters and scuttled across rooftops in the dreary London drizzle. The line of his lips was softer now, more tender. "If you'd been followed?" she said breathlessly.

He took her hands and kissed each one. "If I'd been followed, someone might see me do this." He placed his warm palms along her cheeks. "And this."

He bent his face and kissed her lips.

Stefanie gasped into his mouth. He tasted of brandy and cigars, as she did, but on his breath the combination seemed a thousand times more potent, more masculine. She savored it for an instant, until he lifted his head.

"Oh," said Stefanie.

"Again?"

"Yes, please."

His lips were soft and gentle and deliciously damp. He reached a little deeper this time, slowly, a rich and wavelike movement that spread like flame through her head and chest and belly. The most sensuous kiss in the world. She slid her arms underneath his overcoat and upward along the back of his ribs, his hard and muscled shoulders, and his hands slid into her hair, his fingers caressed her scalp, and his mouth, *oh God*, his hot brandy mouth! Hatherfield's mouth. She ran the tip of her tongue along the tender inner skin of his upper lip, and he groaned from deep in his chest.

The sound of that groan stirred some alchemical reaction inside her, something dark and transformative. She raised her right knee and wrapped her calf along the back of his oaken thigh; her hands scrabbled along the edge of his jacket, seeking out his waistcoat and the shirt beneath, the warm skin she wanted ferociously to touch and kiss and devour.

He murmured something and drew back, just an inch or two. But it was enough.

Stefanie slid her leg back down to the floor. She was panting; so was he. His eyes were soft and serious as he searched her face. His lips parted slightly, as if he were about to tell her something, some declaration, and she realized in horror what she'd just done. The deception she had just willfully practiced on him; not like in the wardrobe, where she had no choice, but out here in the open, touching him with her tongue, wrapping her leg around him. Letting him believe she was something she was not. Letting him believe she was something he wanted.

He would hate her. He would thrust her away in disgust. But he had to know the truth.

The awful truth.

She reached up behind her neck and took his hands and held them next to her chest. She whispered, "Hatherfield, there's something I have to tell you."

"Little one, there's something I have to tell you."

". . . I shouldn't have kissed you like that . . ."

". . . I shouldn't have kissed you like that . . ."

". . . I shouldn't have let you kiss me . . ."

". . . shouldn't have let you return my kiss . . ."

". . . but I couldn't help myself, because it will never happen again . . ."

". . . but I had to do it, just once, because now that I know who you are, Stefanie, Your Highness, I can never hope . . ."

". . . once you know who I am. I'm . . . What did you say?"

He lifted his hand from hers and touched her cheek, her temple. "I can never hope to deserve you."

"Not that. I mean before. What did you call me?"

"Stefanie. Your real name, isn't it?"

She stumbled back. "You knew? All this time, you knew?"

"Well, I didn't know the details until this morning. Until Olympia told me. Obviously I knew something was up; a young lady doesn't masquerade as a law clerk without a damned good reason—I beg your pardon, a *jolly* good reason . . ."

"All this time, you knew I was a woman?"

His eyes widened into horrified blue moons, traveling across the sky of her, from the top of her head to the tips of her stocking feet. "You thought *I* thought you were a *man*? Just *now*?"

"Well, yes!"

"Yesterday? In the wardrobe?"

"I . . . Yes. Yes, I did. I felt dreadfully guilty to disappoint you . . ."

A chuckle escaped Hatherfield's lips. And another.

Stefanie crossed her arms. "Well, if you weren't so devastatingly handsome, you blasted Adonis."

Hatherfield threw back his head and roared.

"Be quiet. You'll wake the house." But her lips twitched.

Hatherfield's chest shook with the force of his laughter. He took a step back and collapsed on the bed, making the bedsprings creak in alarm.

"Look here. You're getting your damp overcoat all over my blankets."

"I . . . I can't decide whether to be offended or . . . or flattered!" he gasped, spearing his hands into his hair.

"I can't imagine why."

The quivers of chest began to slow. "Offended that you would think me such an imbecile as not to fathom your disguise in an instant."

"Look here, I believe I make a most convincing young man. My mustache is impeccable, and I managed that cigar tonight with aplomb, Hatherfield. Aplomb."

"You did indeed. That attempt at a smoke ring was most credible. But I happen to be trained in the examination of human details, princess. The telltale clues. Your hands, for example. Your very charming legs. Or perhaps it was something in the moon-eyed way you gazed at me." He stared up at the ceiling, still smiling.

Stefanie tossed her head. "Well, then. I see why you were offended. I hardly dare ask why you might have been flattered."

Hatherfield went up on his elbows and presented her with his most wolfish grin, a knee-weakening display of white teeth and gleaming eye. "That you wanted to kiss me so much, you went on regardless."

She made an outraged gasp and reached for the pillow.

Stefanie struck quickly, but Hatherfield was quicker. He rolled away and leapt to his feet, knees bent, eyes bright, hands at the ready.

"You are a beast." She swung the pillow into the empty space that, an instant earlier, had contained Hatherfield. "An insufferable"—another swing—"self-assured"—another swing—"delusional"—up against the wall now, nowhere to run—"beast!"

Hatherfield caught the final mighty swing of the pillow with one hand. He held it above his head and smiled at her.

"Give me that!"

"I think not. Spoils of war."

She tugged.

He tugged, and she crashed into his chest and forgot about the pillow. "Hatherfield, I . . ."

Knock knock. The door.

A high feminine voice floated through the wood. "Mr. Thomas, are you quite all right?"

Lady Charlotte.

Stefanie's eyed widened. Hatherfield shrugged.

"Quite all right," she called out.

"Because you're making the most dreadful thumping. Your room is directly above mine, Mr. Thomas, and I was beginning to grow alarmed." Her voice was peevish and curious, both at once.

"No cause for alarm, your ladyship," said Stefanie. "I was . . . I was only . . . There was a mouse. A very persistent and irritating mouse."

"To say nothing of delusional and self-important," whispered Hatherfield.

"What was that?" said Lady Charlotte. "Are you whispering?"

"No. No, that was . . . the wind. I left the window open. A little fresh night air."

"It's raining, Mr. Thomas. You'll catch a chill."

Hatherfield still hadn't let go of the pillow, and neither had Stefanie. She stood there against his chest, looking up at his amused face—the wretch—not daring to move. Not wanting to move. His body was so warm. Lovely and warm and firm.

Growing warmer and firmer by the second, if she wasn't mistaken.

Stefanie gasped out, "Yes. Quite. A chill. You're quite right. I'll shut it directly and go to bed."

Lady Charlotte made a little harrumphing noise, right up against the door. "Well, then. See that you do. No more thumping, Mr. Thomas. If you find another mouse, for heaven's sake call a servant instead."

"No more thumping," said Stefanie. "Call a servant. Right-ho."

"Good night, Mr. Thomas."

"Good night, your ladyship."

The soft tread of Lady Charlotte's footsteps retreated down the hall.

Stefanie released her breath. Hatherfield lowered the pillow and gave it back to her. "No more thumping," he said gravely.

Her arms closed around the pillow. It felt cool and shapeless, a poor replacement for the heat of Hatherfield's sturdy chest.

Stefanie frowned. "Trained."

"What's that?"

"You said before, you were trained in human details. What did you mean by that?"

Hatherfield walked across the room and retrieved his hat, which had fallen on the other side of Stefanie's narrow iron bedstead. "What I meant," he said, "or rather, what's relevant to Your Highness's own peculiar situation, is that you needn't concern yourself with threats to your person, whilst I am charged with your protection."

A rather formal speech. Her frown deepened. "I'm not that concerned, actually. I'm the youngest daughter. Not of much account. It's Luisa they're after, these anarchists."

He turned. "What do you know about it?"

"I'm not a fool, Hatherfield. I do listen in, from time to time. I expect it's this Revolutionary Brigade of the Free Blood, isn't it? They've been meddling in royal successions rather successfully this past decade. Promoting political instability—*executing the tyrants*, I believe they call it—so they can presumably step in and institute their own ideas, whatever those really are. They don't seem to agree with each other much over how governments *should* conduct themselves; they only agree on how bad the existing systems are. Not especially helpful, but there it is. Anyway, if you're one of his agents, I expect my uncle's told you all about it already. I expect he had it all planned out, throwing me in your way. Clever, clever uncle."

"Good God," said Hatherfield. He stared at her as if she were mad.

"Ha. You're just like the rest of them, aren't you? Oh, that Stefanie, she's nothing but an empty-headed mischief-maker, getting into scrapes. Well, I'm more perceptive than you think. And I daresay I know a great deal more about what the common man thinks than any of you do. What they say in the taverns and the squares."

"Do you, now."

"Yes. Anyway, it's Luisa they're really after. She's the heir, the Crown Princess. Father went and changed the succession laws so she could inherit, and naturally that upset all of that wretched Brigade's plans. They were counting on Father not having any sons, on the instability of an uncertain succession. So they murdered Father and Luisa's new husband, and they tried to kidnap Luisa, and they failed. All of which means I'm only in danger if both my older sisters are killed first, and if they are . . . Well, I don't suppose I'd care much about living anyway." She threw the pillow expertly into place at the head of the bed, whistling right past Hatherfield's rigid body. "You see? No danger at all. At ease, soldier. Go home and pour yourself another brandy."

She knew Hatherfield was looking at her, examining her for—what was it? Human details. The tone of her voice, the set of her jaw. Trying to determine if she was all bravado, or if she meant it. Trying to get to the bottom of her. Stefanie went on fixing her eyes at the pillow, which had landed a bit awkwardly, a trifle askew. Rather like herself.

Hatherfield spoke quietly. "They won't harm a hair on your head, Your Highness. I swear it."

"Don't call me that. Anything but that."

"Stefanie, then. But you can't deny who you are, you know. You can't pretend to be a clerk forever."

She looked at him sharply. "I'm not pretending."

Hatherfield let out a long sigh and shook his head.

"I mean it. I was angry at first. I wanted revenge. But now, I don't care. They can have my castle and my country, if they want it. I don't care. I've never wanted to be a princess. I hated it. This is who I am now, and the truth is, I'm happier. I happen to like the law. I happen to like you."

"Stefanie . . ."

She took a step toward him. Her body craved him, craved the return of his solid flesh against hers. His sensuous brandy mouth, kissing her deliciously. "And now that the air's clear, now that the secrets are out, I think we should pick up exactly where we left off."

"How, exactly? Sneaking about town, with you in your disguise, working all day in law chambers? For how long? To what end?"

"I suppose we'll find that out together."

He shook his head again. "Stefanie, no."

She took another step, and another, until she was right up bravely against his chest again, looking up at him. Trying to reclaim that look of his, that look of concentrated desire in his blue eyes. That look that made everything inside her heat and heat until it melted and reshaped itself into something altogether different.

But the expression on Hatherfield's face remained bleak and distant.

Undaunted, she placed her hands on the lapels of his overcoat and looked him squarely in the eye. "Are you worried about my honor? Because there's no need. I was telling the truth, back in your hansom. Last night. I'm no innocent."

He didn't blink. "Neither am I."

"You see? There's nothing in the way. No stupid old-fashioned notions. I'm not a princess any longer, I'm not a pristine marriageable young lady. That's all gone now. We're just two people, a man and woman, who . . . who find each other . . ." She lifted her face to kiss him. "Irresistible."

Hatherfield's large hands closed atop hers, and gently he set her away. "No, Stefanie. Not irresistible. I can resist you, and I will. Because you *are* a princess, you have a birthright. A birthright to which I intend to restore you, not to render you unfit."

She whispered fiercely, "I don't want it. I don't want my birthright. I've always wanted to be free, Hatherfield. Don't you understand? Don't you have any idea of what it's like? All my life I spent trying to escape from that damned castle, that bloody edifice, sneaking out night after night, and now I'm free, by God, and I intend to live my life the way I want to live it."

"What, by taking a lover?"

"Not any lover. You." She was hot and blushing, but she went on anyway. "Don't tell me you don't want it, too."

"Of course I do. My God. But it's not right, you know it's not. Not for either of us." He put his hat on his head, as if placing a barrier between them, and edged past her to the window.

She turned and stared at his back while he slid up the window sash. "I suppose you think I'm improper. This. All of this, the disguise and the clerking. My mustache. The bawdy house, the brandy and cigars. My . . . my unchaste state. Throwing myself at you, offering myself as a lover. You're disgusted. Any gentleman would be."

He whipped around. "Don't talk rot. When I'm barely holding myself together right now."

"You look composed enough."

"Because that's what I do, Stefanie. I look composed. Everybody's favorite chap, that Hatherfield, such a charming lighthearted fellow. Bloody hell. Disgusted by you? I want to strip you to your skin and take you to bed and make love to you until neither of us can stand. You incandescent woman. I'm blinded, I'm entranced, I'm . . . damn it all, I'm falling in love with you, the one thing I can't afford to do. For my sake, for your sake. Don't ask me again." He gripped the window frame behind him, with such force she could count the bones of his knuckles, if she could have torn her gaze away from his face.

"Then why did you kiss me like that?" she whispered.

"Because I'm only a man. Because I had to do it, just once. To kiss you once." He turned to duck through the window. "I'll see you at breakfast. Sleep well."

Stay. Please stay. I need you.

You need me.

But the old regal pride returned most inconveniently to stiffen her neck, and the words remained unsaid while Hatherfield slipped from her room to the roof, and she closed the sash behind him.

For the second night in a row, the Marquess of Hatherfield returned late and discomposed to his rooms at the Mansions. This wretched affair was going to be the death of him.

On this occasion, however, misery had company.

"Why, hello, Father." Hatherfield tossed his hat on the stand before Nelson could stagger across the room to perform the office. The overcoat, however, was forced to endure a proper divesting. "What an unexpected delight. Does Her Grace know you're here? I daresay she won't thank me for stealing you away at such an inconvenient hour, when every chap in his right mind should be home in bed with his wedded wife."

The duke remained in his chair, next to the fire. "Don't be impertinent."

Hatherfield shot a look to Nelson, which might best be interpreted as *Do yourself a favor, mate, and light on for the far side of the world.*

Nelson hurried away through the swinging door to the dining room.

"I daresay a fellow's got a right to be impertinent, at such an hour." He yawned extravagantly.

"I suppose you were in bed with your lover."

"My lover? I beg your pardon?"

"That boy. That . . . that clerk of Sir John's. I could see it, all through dinner, the way you were looking at him. The way he looked at you, damn it all."

The duke spoke in a fury of disgust. Hatherfield narrowed his eyes for a closer look. His father's face, ordinarily a flushed sort of object, now presented itself with something of the aspect of a freshly plucked tomato. His hands fidgeted in his lap, of which the legs were decidedly crossed. Even his hair had come unhinged from its pomade vise, swinging down in a metal gray sheet to meet his cheekbone.

"My lover," Hatherfield repeated slowly.

Southam jumped to his feet and rushed to the window. "I should have known. The signs were all there. Not a single whisker on your face. No desire for a wife. No mistress, not a hint of a doxy of any kind, high or low. This baffling obsession with physical exercise. Your bloody damned *beauty*." As he might say *your weeping abscess.* He whipped out a slim gold cigarette case from the inside pocket of his tailcoat.

"I didn't know you smoked."

"And I wondered why you wouldn't have her. Wouldn't even entertain the idea. Ha-ha." He lit a cigarette with shaking hands. "The prettiest girl in London, and two hundred thousand pounds to go with her, and you wouldn't hear of it. My God."

Hatherfield leaned against the wall, just beneath a framed engraving of the start of the 1876 University Boat Race—"*ARE YOU READY?*"—and crossed his arms.

"Of all the problems in the world. Of all the ways for

everything to come undone. This. Damn it all. I can't even look at you. Sodom and bloody Gomorrah. My own son." The duke sucked on his cigarette and stared out the window.

"Come, now," said Hatherfield. "There's no need for melo-drama." A feeling was beginning to invade his chest, a lighter-than-air feeling, and he hardly dared to say a word for fear of disturbing it. Or laughing aloud. Or doing anything that might hinder his enjoyment of this extraordinary moment.

"Every plan, every hope. Ruined. My God. A dynasty, the great dukedom of Southam, brought to its knees because you— *my* son, mine!—because *my own son* prefers pretty young men to a pair of proper English tits." His fist slammed against the window frame, making the panes rattle against the rain.

"The shame of it," Hatherfield drawled. "Whatever will you say to the chaps at the club?"

The drizzle rattled softly against the window. Southam went on smoking in jerky little movements. Hatherfield pulled his watch out of his pocket. Eleven o'bloody clock. In another minute, he would fall face-first into the carpet.

The duke said, in a low voice, "Just tell me this, Hatherfield. Do you not think you can marry her at all? Bed her at all? Not at all? Just once a month, for God's sake, a cock's a cock, it just needs . . . needs a . . ." Words failed him. He stubbed out his cigarette on the glass and buried his face in his hands.

Hatherfield plucked his father's coat and hat and cane from the stand, walked over to the bent figure at the window, and held them out.

"No, Father," he said. "I really don't think I can."

TWELVE

The prosecution had rested its case the day before, winding up with a bravura performance by an inspector from Scotland Yard, who had reenacted a veritable Shakespearean swordfight to demonstrate his contention that the killing had been an act of passion, committed by a man with great strength, so gruesome and extensive were the wounds upon the Duchess of Southam's deceased body when she was found by her maid at a quarter to eleven, draped across a chaise longue in her boudoir.

After that staggering drama, Stefanie was the one to suggest that the defense begin its case with a counterdemonstration of Hatherfield's gentler side, his capability for tenderness. Witnesses had been duly shuffled about. But now that Eleanor, Viscountess Chesterton, sat in the witness's box, her black mourning dress draped about her slender figure, her lace-edged handkerchief dabbing at her eyes, Stefanie wondered whether she should have left well enough alone.

"The dearest brother in the world," she was repeating to Mr. Duckworth, in cross-examination.

"Indeed, madam. As you described earlier, in full detail. Pony rides, picnics, et cetera. Presumably your mother shared in this . . . this shower of attention he bestowed on you and your sisters?"

"Well . . . that is . . ." Her hands played about with her handkerchief. "My mother wasn't the sort of mother who . . . What I mean to say is . . ."

"No, she didn't?"

Lady Eleanor looked down. "She did not."

"I see. Did she and Lord Hatherfield engage at all in an affectionate manner, common to happy families?"

"Not often." A whisper.

Mr. Duckworth nodded thoughtfully. "I see. Despite his affectionate behavior to you and your sisters. How curious. And did you notice anything unusual about his behavior, in the weeks leading up to your mother's murder?"

"Why . . ." She cast a quick glance at her brother, where he stood in the dock, watching her with a kind expression. "No more than . . ." She stopped.

"Yes, your ladyship? There was something?"

"Nothing of consequence."

"May I remind you, your ladyship, that you are under oath? That your own mother's murder demands justice?"

"But he didn't do it! He couldn't do it, not James!" She made a wretched sob against her handkerchief.

"Your loyalty to your brother does you credit, of course," Mr. Duckworth said greasily. "But he was acting a bit out of character, wasn't he?"

"A bit, but that was only because . . ."

Mr. Duckworth tilted his head and smiled. "Yes, your ladyship?"

She gathered herself. "He was a little less attentive to us, that's all. To his sisters. He was in the habit of seeing me often, after my marriage, and when my little daughter was born, why, he was the most devoted uncle. He would read her stories and let my dear, sweet baby fall asleep on his shoulder. He . . ."

"Yes, madam. But in the weeks before the murder?"

Lady Eleanor twisted her handkerchief and cast another nervous glance at Hatherfield. "He didn't visit as much."

"How often?"

"Not . . . Well, not at all. But he had many affairs to attend to. His houses, and . . ."

Mr. Duckworth cupped his ear. "Yes, my dear?"

"And I don't know." She said it emphatically.

Mr. Duckworth lowered his hand and captured it with the other, twiddling his thumbs together as he paced across the courtroom. "I see. Let us turn, if you will, to the events of the night of the murder. You were in attendance at the house of your parents, in Belgrave Square, were you not? At the ball?"

"I was."

"And how would you describe the behavior of Lord Hatherfield that evening?"

"He was . . . He was as he always is. Dear and charming. He danced with me."

"And then what did he do?"

She wet her lips. "He danced with another guest."

"And who was this other guest?"

"Why, I don't know. None of us knew her."

"Was she lovely, this mysterious lady of Lord Hatherfield's?"

Another glance at her brother. "She was wearing a mask, of course. But yes, I would say that she was very beautiful."

"Ah. Now then. Let me summarize all this, for the better understanding of the court. You say that Lord Hatherfield had appeared distracted, during the weeks previous to the night in question. In contrast to his earlier habits of frequent visitation, of attentiveness to you and your daughter, his infant niece, Lord Hatherfield did not visit you at all. And then, on the night in question, his lordship, the accused, spent much of his time dancing with a beautiful young lady, with whom you and your family were not acquainted."

Stefanie's cheeks burned. She didn't dare look at Hatherfield. She turned her face down to the paper before her and pretended to scribble earnestly at her notes.

"Not all his time. They disappeared . . ." Lady Eleanor stopped short, and a flush, not dissimilar to that on Stefanie's cheeks, spread across her face.

"Oh! They disappeared together. I see."

"But not . . . It was well before my mother retired . . ." She checked herself again, and her blush grew even rosier.

"There's no need to continue, your ladyship. I believe we have established the sequence of the night's events to the satisfaction of the court."

Lady Eleanor settled herself more comfortably into her seat. "Of course."

"Oh. One further question, your ladyship, if you don't mind."

"Yes, Mr. Duckworth?"

"The purpose of this ball."

"The purpose?" This time, Lady Eleanor stared directly at Mr. Duckworth, avoiding the sight of her brother with studied determination. "Why, to amuse ourselves, of course. That is what balls are for, Mr. Duckworth."

"Yes, yes. But balls are generally held in honor of some person, some event, are they not, your ladyship? A birthday, a young lady's coming of age." He smiled faintly. "An engagement."

"Yes, they often are."

"And this ball. Did your parents have some particular object in mind, to your knowledge?"

Lady Eleanor drew in a deep breath, and exhaled slowly.

"Yes, your ladyship? What was the object of this particular ball, on this particular night? Some surprise announcement, was it not?"

She looked down in her lap.

"Your oath, your ladyship," Mr. Duckworth said gently.

Lady Eleanor raised her head and looked helplessly at her brother. "They were going to announce his engagement. My brother's engagement to Lady Charlotte Harlowe. They said he had agreed to it at last."

THIRTEEN

Putney Bridge, London
Mid-February 1890

Stefanie arrived at Putney Bridge at a quarter past four, just to be safe. The sky was still ash dark and the cobblestones slick with fog, and she nearly fell on her arse twice as she made her way down the lane to the riverside.

Possibly she shouldn't have dismissed the hansom quite so soon.

Still, a sort of Gothic magic did lurk about the river at this hour. A quiet expectancy of heavy gray stone and yellow mist and lapping wavelets. Behind her, on the high street, a set of hooves and wheels clattered wearily along a delivery run. She pulled her hat low on her forehead and walked along the riverbank, until the steep edge gave way to a slope suitable for the launching of boats. A row of houses lined the other side of the lane, with large carriage doors facing the water, all closed tight. The boathouses.

Stefanie found a seat on an overturned barrel and crossed her arms against the February chill. Inside her jacket pocket, the sheet of folded newspaper from last night's evening edition lay crisply against her chest. She took out her watch: four twenty-eight. The ungodliness of it.

She leaned against the wall of the boathouse and let her eyelids sink downward, just for a second.

"Stefanie! What the devil are you doing here?"

Stefanie scrambled to her feet before the outraged face of the Marquess of Hatherfield.

"There you are!"

"Of course, here I am! You're supposed to be safe in Cadogan Square!" His hands were planted firmly on his hips, and his eyes, beneath the brim of his hat, flashed and snapped in the dim glow of the streetlamp. "Instead of asleep on a barrel next to the damned river at five o'clock in the morning!"

"I had to see you." She paused. "Was I really asleep?"

"Out like a light, you numbskull. Come on inside, before you catch a chill." He turned to the carriage door and fumbled with the lock.

She smiled at the sight of him, all tall and trustworthy in his thick black overcoat, heaving the massive door open. She couldn't help it. Even in his outrage, he was outrageously handsome, and he was *hers*. All hers, every golden hair and charming wink and taut sinew of him.

Oh, very well. True, he hadn't kissed her since that night in her room, three months ago. He avoided every possible point of physical contact with her entirely, to be perfectly honest. But he was there, every day, in the breakfast room in Cadogan Square. He waited outside Sir John's chambers as noon chimed the nearby tower of St. Martin-in-the-Fields, ate lunch with her at a tavern or tea shop—never the same establishment two days running—and returned her safely to her place of employment, except on the days she accompanied Sir John to court. Everywhere she went, he followed her like a faithful old hound, safeguarding her against every possible threat, casting a suspicious eye at every shadow in her path. At mealtimes they talked and talked, about the law and her work with Sir John, about European politics and palace intrigue, about Stefanie's childhood in Holstein Castle, about books and science and gossip. On weekends they rode in the park and went on outings to Hampton Court and Windsor and Hampstead Heath. He showed her Eton, where he went to school, and pointed out the playing field where he'd had a tooth knocked out playing rugby. He'd showed her the replacement and tapped it importantly. "Not a bad facsimile, is it?" he'd said, and when she said she might have to make a closer examination, he'd laughed and pulled away.

Laughed and pulled away, every time. But she knew what

it cost him. The more lighthearted and charming his manner, the more he wanted her; each laugh covered an inward groan of desire. And made her adore him even more, because how could you not love a man of that much strength? Of that much pure devotion?

Except at certain moments, when they were unexpectedly alone, and surrounded by darkness and privacy, and the intimate tension between them wound so tight it seemed the air itself might shatter into pieces.

Such as now. When he pulled her inside the boathouse and took her by the shoulders.

"What were you thinking? Coming here alone, falling asleep on the street like that!"

"I didn't mean to fall asleep." She smiled. How could she not smile at his passionate face, fraught with worry for her? "Anyway, I knew you'd be along any minute."

"And what if I hadn't?"

"Hatherfield, it's Putney. Nothing ever happens in Putney."

"You'd be surprised." He set her away grimly and turned to the boats, stacked up high along the walls. "So what brought you here, eh? Risking life and limb?"

"Yes. That." She reached inside her coat, brought out the newspaper clipping, and poked his arm. "Read this."

He unfolded the page. " 'LOST PRINCESS FOUND! GER-MAN ROYALTY LIVING IN LONDON WITH DUKE OF OLYMPIA; RUMORED ROMANCE WITH ENGLISH LORD; PRIME MINISTER ASSURES PARLIAMENT "WE HAVE NO INTEREST OR INFLUENCE" IN MATTER OF HOLSTEIN-SCHWEINWALD-HUHNHOF.' " He put down the paper. "I see."

She grabbed the clipping back and shook it at him. "But look! It's not me they're writing about. It's Emilie!"

"Your sister. Yes."

"My sister! Hatherfield, she's here in London! London! With my uncle!"

He took the paper back. "So it appears."

"She's living in Park Lane this very minute, she's out of her disguise. Something must have happened, Hatherfield, because I had a letter from her a fortnight ago, and she was still in Yorkshire somewhere, tutoring, and everything was fine." She strode to the door and looked out across the dark river to the anemic yellow glow of London. "Something's happened, Hatherfield, someone's discovered her, or she'd never have come back to our uncle's house."

"One of Olympia's plots, I expect."

She turned. He was frowning ferociously at the newspaper, as if to frighten the truth from its pages. Stern, fierce. But not surprised.

"You knew!"

"What's that?"

"You knew she was here! You knew about all of this! You and Olympia and . . . oh! And you didn't tell me!"

"There was no point. You can't see her. You can't have any sort of contact with her."

She strode up and took him by the lapels. "How long have you known? How long?"

"A week or two." He had the grace to look guilty. "We didn't want you to go off and do something harebrained . . ."

She gave him a good shake. "Harebrained! How dare you! You know I wouldn't have done anything without consulting you first."

He plucked her hands away, one by one. "But then you'd have gone off and done the harebrained thing anyway, regardless of my advice. My expert advice, I might add. I do know what I'm doing in these matters, Stefanie."

"Ooh." She turned away. She couldn't speak, she was so angry. All last week, all those breakfasts and dinners, those hansom journeys, those rides in the park. They'd gone to the theater on Saturday. *David Copperfield.* And all that time, he knew. He knew where her sister was, he knew she was—good God!—not even a mile away!

"Don't be cross, Stefanie. Olympia agreed with me, we both thought it best. The thing is . . ."

"Who is he?"

"I beg your pardon?"

"The man she's supposedly in love with. The English lord. I presume it's the man Olympia placed her with. He seems to have a knack for matchmaking of that sort, the old meddler. I suppose he thinks it will keep us distracted and out of trouble."

"Stefanie . . ."

"I know already that he's from somewhere in Yorkshire. Miss Dingleby told me, before we all left. A widower, obviously. He's got a son, about sixteen or so, the one she's tutoring. I could find out myself, so you might as well tell me."

Hatherfield made some restless movement behind her. "It's Ashland. The Duke of Ashland. I've only met him once or twice, but he was legendary in his time, absolutely untouchable, until he was injured in some godforsaken mountain pass in Afghanistan a dozen years ago. She's in good hands, I assure you."

"Oh, I have no doubt of that. Look at the magnificent specimen Olympia chose for me. You've done your job perfectly."

"Don't be unfair. You know my sole object is your safety."

She turned back to face him. "Well, obviously something's gone wrong, or my uncle would never have taken Emilie out of her disguise and gone public like this. Something's happened. What is it?"

He hesitated only slightly. "I don't know, actually. Olympia's asked me to stay away from it. He's got his own men on the case, and frankly, I want you well away from it."

"I'm not a fool, Hatherfield."

"It's the truth. I believe the duke found her out, that's all, and . . ."

"And brought her down to London, and put her in danger."

"I rather think it's the opposite. If I know Ashland, he wants to end things, once and for all."

Stefanie took him by the arms. "We've got to find out. You've got to help me, I've got to speak to her!"

"Now, wait a moment . . ."

"You don't understand. If she's in danger . . ." She let the sentence dangle. The possibility was too awful to contemplate.

Hatherfield folded the newspaper and handed it to her, forcing her to release his arms. "She's well protected. She's got Olympia and Ashland by her side, and I'd like to see the bloody fool anarchist who thinks he can get through the two of them combined. No, she's well enough as she is, for the time being." He picked up her fingers and held them lightly between his own, right next to his chest. "The question is you. Whether you're in danger. Because if this Revolutionary Brigade of yours has discovered your sister's disguise . . ."

"They might have discovered mine."

The faint clatter of hoofbeats invaded the heavy silence between them. Stefanie held Hatherfield's gaze as they listened together to the rhythm of iron on cobblestone, to the squeak of axles in need of oil, louder and louder and louder, the harness now jingling. Hatherfield's hands tightened around hers; his keen eyes grew keener, the eyebrows nearly meeting, as if he were trying to transmit some sort of message across the *cloppity-clop, jingle-jingle, rattly-rattly-rattle*, louder and louder.

And then, almost imperceptibly, softer. Softer and softer, and then it was gone, and only the waves slapped against the boat landing, and a dustman hallooed to another.

Stefanie let out her breath. Hatherfield bent his head and pressed his lips into her knuckles, and his breath spread warmth across her skin.

"Hatherfield," she whispered, because she couldn't speak.

He lifted his head and drew one hand away from hers to cup her cheek. "I will not let them harm a hair on your head, do you understand me? Not a hair. You have nothing at all to worry about."

"But my sister. I have to see her. You have to help me. If she's in trouble . . ."

"She's well taken care of, I assure you."

"Please." Tears leaked shamefully from the corners of her eyes, and she never cried! What was happening to her? As if some bandage had been ripped away from the surface of her heart, leaving it raw. She felt Hatherfield's thumb move on her face, brushing at a tear. "Please. She's my sister. Please help me see her. Just once, just to see she's all right."

He closed his eyes. "Christ, Stefanie. Don't ask this. The danger . . ."

"Please. You don't understand. She's my sister." *My Emilie, my sweet Emilie, my confessor and protector. Loyal Emilie.* Stefanie had been so busy these past months, so consumed with her new life and with Hatherfield, that the pain of missing her sisters had receded to the background. Now her arms ached with the need to hold Emilie again, to confess all her new secrets, to hear all of Emilie's secrets. Emilie in love! She wanted every detail, every look and kiss and word.

"I do understand," said Hatherfield. "I have four sisters of my own, God help me. I love them very much; I'd do anything for them, if they needed it."

"But it's more than that, with us." She choked on a sob. "Emilie and I, we shared a room. We slept in the same bed. It's not even love, Hatherfield, it's as if we're made of the same clay, just . . . just opposite somehow, and yet we understand each other, she understands me, she kept all my secrets, she . . ."

"Shh. Stefanie. Shh. It's all right."

Hatherfield drew her close, and then she was in his arms, against his chest, his solid ribs moving her as he breathed. She buried her nose in the scent of damp wool and Hatherfield, a bit of soap and London smoke, his warm human skin, and she was understood again, she was accepted, she didn't need to say a word. She was part of him.

"It's all right, Stefanie," he whispered in her hair. "I'll do it, I'll arrange something. I'll talk to Olympia . . ."

"No! He'll say no. He and Miss Dingleby. We'll have to find another way."

"Write a note to her. I'll get it to Ashland. He'll give it to her."

"Oh, thank God. Yes." She rubbed her cheek against his overcoat, trying to absorb more of him, before he drew away again. As he would.

"Give me a little time to work something out first."

"Yes. I'll write the note. We're in court this afternoon, but you'll be there afterward, won't you?"

His hands moved to her shoulders, and he set her gently apart. A fond smile lifted his mouth, and his head made a single shake. "In court this afternoon. Look at you."

"What's that?"

"You're extraordinary, that's all. I love watching you in the courtroom, with that serious expression on your face. The way you scribble notes back and forth with Sir John. If only they knew, those men in their wigs."

"Well, *you* know," she said tartly, "and it doesn't seem to affect you at all."

She knew she was fishing. She wanted him to say, *God yes, it affects me, I dream about you all night, I think of you constantly.* She needed to hear him say again, *I want to*—what was it?—*strip you to your skin and take you to bed and make love to you until neither of us can stand.* Those words he'd

said to her three months ago in her tiny bedroom on the third
floor of Sir John's Cadogan Square town house, words that had
revolved and magnified in her mind ever since, repeating endlessly as she lay in bed at night, flushed and aching, imagining
him there with her, naked and magnificent, on top of her,
below her, at her side, at her back.

But Hatherfield, as always, refused to rise to the bait. He
only smiled again, that patient smile, and looked at her wisely.
"Stefanie, you know better than that." He released her shoulders and turned to the wall of boats. "Now come along."

"Come along?"

"Help me pick out a boat and an extra pair of blades."

Stefanie's blood ran cold. "An extra pair of blades?"

"Oh yes. I can't leave you alone and unprotected in the
boathouse at this hour of the day, assassins on the loose and
all that. You, my dear, are about to learn how to stroke a pair."

She wasn't bad, not at all. A quick learner, Stefanie, but then
he'd known that already. Once he showed her the basic
motion, she dug right in and pulled her weight; a little awkward
and inefficient in her deployment of the oars, of course, but at
an innate and steady rhythm, matching his stroke for stroke.

He didn't take her out far—for one thing, they'd wasted
enough time in the boathouse, and for another, she wasn't
exactly in condition for it. At Hammersmith Bridge he turned
them around, laying his right blade in the water as the boat
swung a pitching arc in the frigid river.

"How are you doing?" he said, watching her back carefully.
He had bundled her up against the frozen February air in a
thick wool jumper and gloves, but he could still see the movement of her respiration, the faint white puffs as they left her
mouth.

"Quite well!" she gasped. She was breathing hard, but not
quite labored. Hanging in gamely.

"You're looking jolly tolerable. Are you certain you haven't
done this before?"

She shook her head. "Just rowing about in the Holsteinsee
with Emilie during the summer."

He steadied the boat in the water. "Look there. No, the

other bank. That row of buildings, to the left of the bridge. Do you see them?"

She peered into the shadows. "I think so. By the gas lamps?"

"That's the one."

"They look a bit skeletal, don't you think?"

"They're not finished yet." He wrapped his hand more snugly around the oars. "They're mine, in fact."

"Yours!"

"An investment project. My mother's money. It was part of her marriage settlement; it went into a trust for her children upon her death. There was only me, of course, so I came into it on my twenty-fifth birthday, and . . . well, there you have it." He watched her face anxiously.

"But that's marvelous! Look at them!"

"Yes, they're coming along nicely. We tore down a row of damned slap-up jobs, a slum really. There are plenty of luxury developments out there, and then cheap rubbish for everybody else, but I wanted something different. Something of genuine quality for the middle classes, in an area close to town, convenient and well situated and all that, but not what you'd call exactly fashionable." The boat was drifting upstream in the rush of tide; he made a few quick strokes. He added, almost under his breath, "Yet."

"But why? Why go to such trouble?"

He skimmed the water. "Because I had to, I suppose."

"Had to? But you're heir to a dukedom."

"That's exactly why I had to. Because the dukedom's a shambles. I don't suppose you know our history, but the Southam title, it was legendary once. And then my grandfather mismanaged things, and my father made it worse, and now it's all mortgages and falling rents and idiocy. I want . . ." He stared at the dim blur of the rooflines. "I want to save it. I know how to save it, I *will* save it. Build and sell these houses, and more like them, and I can reverse the tide. I can give our—I can give my children a name to be proud of. An inheritance worth inheriting."

The water slapped against the boat. A shrill whistle carried across the bank, a boatman preparing to cast off. London rising up and blinking into the February dawn.

"Why haven't you told me this before?" she asked.

"I don't know. Never got round to it, I suppose."

"Will you take me there on Sunday? Can I go inside one of them and have a look?" She turned around in her seat to look at him. Pleadingly, as if she really wanted to go.

He smiled. "Yes, if you like."

"I'd like it very much." She smiled back, and her teeth shone white in the darkness against her full lips.

"Anyway, we'd better head back," he said. He straightened out the boat to head back downstream. Stefanie turned and found her oars, and he dug into the water with both blades, relishing the resistance of the rising water as it fought back the natural river current. He said, "We're going against the tide, now. If you need a rest, just ship your oars for a bit and I'll carry on. You're doing marvelously."

Stefanie muttered something.

"What's that?"

She tilted her head over her shoulder. "I said, you'll pay for this, Hatherfield!"

He laughed aloud. "I expect nothing less!"

The landing was still deserted, a bit crispy with the beginnings of ice. Rowing in February was a dicey affair; Hatherfield was one of the few members who took a boat out at all, and if London experienced a particularly cold snap, with ice actually on the river, he had to content himself with the rowing apparatus indoors. But Hatherfield didn't mind. He liked the loneliness, the immense physical challenge, the way he departed the landing cold and stiff and returned warm and alive. He maneuvered the boat carefully to shore, keeping her narrow length as steady as he could in the swirling Thames eddies, guided in the blackness by the single gas lamp burning at the door of the boathouse.

"That's it. Keep your oars up and clear." He reached down and unlaced his feet from the stirrups. "Now steady on. I'll get out first and hold her for you."

From his right came the sound of a heavy steam engine, chugging some unknown ship along the fog-shrouded blackness. In a moment, the wake would hit them. He jumped out and shut his senses to the shock of the cold water. The boat rocked, and Stefanie made an outraged cry.

"Hurry, now! Unlace the stirrups!"

"I can't! They've got wet!"

"I'll help." He worked his hand down the wooden edge and plucked at Stefanie's laces. One foot came free, and the other. His own were turning numb. He found the pair of rubbers he'd stashed in the stern and held them out for her. "Put your feet in these as you come out of the boat," he said, but just as the words left his mouth, the steamship's wake hit the shell.

Stefanie, half rising and off balance already, pitched into the water.

"Oh!" she exclaimed wetly.

Hatherfield tossed the boots up the landing, let go of the boat, and grasped Stefanie beneath the shoulders. The water was only a foot or so deep, but she'd managed to fall backward in a thorough splash, smashing the tissue-thin crust of ice on the river's edge.

An instant later, as the coldness of the water penetrated her wool clothes, her howl of pain splintered the air.

At the sound of that cry, Hatherfield's body went electric with instinct. He hauled her into his arms and carried her up the landing. He'd left the boathouse key . . . where? In his pocket. He dug frantically into his trousers. She was already shivering violently. *Key!* He shoved it into the lock and threw open the door and bounded to the back of the boathouse and the stairs leading upward to the social rooms.

In the summer, the boathouse employed a full-time caretaker, and his room sat off to the side of the main commons. Hatherfield tried the door, and it slid open, thank God. He dumped Stefanie onto the cot and ripped off her soaking wool jumper, her trousers, her waistcoat.

"Oh my God!" Her lips were blue, her teeth rattling. She gazed up at him, eyes huge and dark and pleading, like an injured fawn. "F-fr-freezing!"

His chest went hollow.

"Here." The blankets were stacked on the bare mattress. He wrapped two of them around her shivering form. "I'll be back in a minute!"

"Wh-wh-where the d-devil are you going?"

"To get the bloody boat back!"

FOURTEEN

Hatherfield thundered back down the stairs to the sound of Stefanie's outraged howl. A loose boat on a dark and frigid river might mean death for some unsuspecting barge or fisherman. How long had he been gone? A minute? Two? Where the devil was the boat?

Upstream, in the rising tide.

He didn't see the rubber boots on the landing, God help him. He rolled up his trousers to the knee and plunged into the water. A hint of dawn rested on the horizon in a thin line, just gilding the tops of the houses across the river, but not enough to see by. He thrashed upstream through the water, blocking out the cold, his brain filled with the image of huge-eyed Stefanie shivering in her wool blankets.

She's fine, she's fine, he told himself, *just a little cold soaking*, but the fear in his veins knew no logic. The room was unheated. The water had been ice-cold. If he didn't find that bloody boat in thirty seconds, he would leave it in the water and let the river traffic keep its own damned watch, let the . . .

His knee bumped against something solid.

The boat.

Thank God.

He found the sides, readied his arms, and hauled it up and over his head.

In less than two minutes, he had the boat on its horse and the blades in their stack. The boots could go hang. He ran back upstairs and flung open the door to the caretaker's room.

"Stefanie!"

She sat huddled in her blankets on the floor before the tiny fireplace, stacking coals. She gazed up at him piteously. "T-tr-trying to s-st-start a fire," she whispered.

His legs were like icicles; he couldn't even feel them. He dropped to his knees next to her and took the coal basket. "I'll do that. Wrap yourself up."

He stacked the coals and the kindling and struck a match into the pile. A tiny flame leapt up.

"H . . . Hatherfield," whispered Stefanie. "I . . . I c-can't s-seem to get warm. Hold me."

He wrapped his arms around her. "My poor love. It's all right. Give yourself a moment."

"Hold me tighter. Tighter, Hatherfield!"

He did. As tightly as he could, willing his warmth into her frozen body. "I'm so sorry, Stefanie. My fault. I should have been more careful."

"You're all wet," she whispered.

"I'm sorry. I had to bring the boat in."

She snuggled even deeper. "Oh, G-God, I'm so cold! Why can't I get warm? Help me. *Help* me, Hatherfield."

"Shh. I'm so sorry." He rubbed her back, her arms beneath the blanket. She was nuzzling him now, making his head spin, and then the blankets slipped just a little and he became aware of a certain fact. An awful, unavoidable, and most inconvenient fact.

"You've taken your clothes off." A strangled whisper.

She tilted up her face, with that injured-fawn look in her eyes. "They were w-wet."

Oh, hell.

Do not look down.

She said softly, "Do you mind?"

Did. He. Mind. He could see them, just below his horizon of sight, in the gap between blanket and skin: two perfect breasts, curved exactly right to fit in a man's broad palm, the nipples just hidden into the wool.

His throat went paper dry. "You did that on purpose," he croaked.

She opened up the blanket. Her eyes, if possible, grew larger. "I'm so cold, Hatherfield. Just look at me."

Don't look.

He looked.

"Yes," he croaked again to her nipples, deeply pink and astonishingly erect and altogether too close to his woolen chest. "You are." And just like that, in the snap of the twig holding the whole structure in place, his self-control crashed and tumbled in a heap, somewhere on the floor between them.

He wanted to tear his eyes away. He really did. But his mind could not quite encompass the reality of Stefanie's breasts, the perfection even more splendid than his imagination had drawn them, so flushed and round and firm and . . . well, lonely. Needing a hand to hold them.

Without even thinking, Hatherfield lifted his palm and brushed his thumb against the very utmost tip of her rightmost nipple.

"Oh." She shivered. "I'm warmer already."

He brushed again. Small and hard as a tiny pebble, soft skinned as velvet.

He bent and licked it. Just the very tip-top, an infinitesimal speck of skin. Surely there was nothing wrong with that.

"Hatherfield."

He couldn't stop the thoughts in his brain now. Let the world damn him for them. Stefanie's white and pink body, soft in his arms, under his fingers, under his lips, touching her, kissing her, thrusting into her. His cock, already rigid, pushed fiercely against the placket of his trousers.

He licked the other nipple. Cool and hard and smooth under his tongue, tasting sweetly of Stefanie.

She made a little sound in her throat and wrapped her arms around the back of his head, cocooning them together in the blanket.

If he kept his clothes on. If only he kept his clothes on, it would be all right, he could stay in control of himself. He could touch her, kiss her, in perfect command. Discover the curves and scents and textures of her body. Warm her chilled body by the most efficient means he knew.

Surely there was nothing wrong with that.

She had asked for his help, after all. It was the gentlemanly thing to do.

Without her masculine clothes, her body seemed delicate by contrast, as fair and flawless and translucent as a curving Ming vase, almost too fragile to touch. And yet he knew she was sturdy. She had just rowed two miles up and down an unruly tidal river. He fitted his palms around her breasts and closed his eyes. She felt like heaven, heavy and just yielding to the gentle pressure of his hand, her skin damp and soft. "You are so beautiful," he whispered.

"I love your hands," she whispered back. "I love your lips."

He leaned forward and kissed her, as softly as he could, nudging her lips in a tender rhythm until she opened them for him, a fraction of an inch, a fraction more. He took her sweet breath deep into his lungs. More. He wanted more. He found the tip of her tongue and stroked it with his, as delicately as he might stroke the nose of a kitten, and the sound she made as he stroked her was very much of the kitten variety, a kind of eager mewl at the back of her throat.

A sound so tantalizing, he wanted to call it forth again.

So he stroked her tongue again, and again she mewled for him, and his hands at her breasts spread apart into individual fingers, each caressing her skin. He swirled his forefingers around each nipple. He sent each thumb to explore each thin-skinned underside, and Stefanie's hands pressed into his back, and her kitten sounds turned into growls of pleasure.

More. He wanted more.

He sent his tongue deeper into her slick mouth, tangling with her, and she tangled right back, and her fingers, still somehow clutching the blanket, speared into his hair and rubbed his scalp with eager knuckles. She arched her back, pressing her breasts into his hands. He should stop now, she was warm and flushed in the snug blanket-wrapped space between them, she had recovered perfectly.

More. He wanted more.

"Hatherfield." Her lips moved to his cheek, to his jaw. "Oh God, Hatherfield. Don't stop. I'm burning for you, I need you."

"I thought you were freezing." He couldn't resist.

She took him by the head and pulled him downward, until

they were sprawled on the floor inside her blanket, the air cold on his legs and hot everywhere else. He ran his hands up her chest to her long neck, into her short damp hair, around the pure curve of her ear. He was lying on top of her, holding himself up by the elbows. He pushed her hair back from her face. She was gazing at him, half lidded.

He could stop now. His layers of clothing lay thick between them; he could feel the tantalizing shapes of her body against his, but not the silk of her skin, the texture of her. He could feel her legs wrapping around him, but not the friction of her sliding flesh. He could feel the bursting strength of his erection inside his trousers, but it was all contained, all caged in by cloth and civilization. So far, he had done her no actual ill. He should stop now.

She was warm now. She was as hot as a coal under his fingers.

"Please, Hatherfield," she said, and let go of the edges of the blanket.

His breath stopped in his chest.

She was fair all over, a ginger's creamy pale skin, dotted here and there with delicate freckles. He wanted to kiss each one. Something beat in his head, something about stopping while he could, but he ignored that irritating voice and concentrated on her freckles, the ones on her shoulder, the ones just below the hollow of her throat, the sprinkling of them on her chest. Her fingers scrabbled at his back, pulling at his jumper, pulling at the cotton shirt beneath. He reached around and grabbed her hands and pinned them to the floorboards, above the edge of the blanket, and he kissed her deeply on the mouth.

"I stay dressed," he said. "Do you understand?"

She nodded.

He lifted his body and trailed his mouth down the line of her neck to her breasts, her beautiful siren's breasts, and he sucked one nipple into his mouth. She gasped hard and arched her back.

"More?" he said.

"More!"

He bent his head again and used his lips to suckle her, his tongue to rasp the sensitive rosy pink tip, until she was crying out and her hips bucked beneath him.

He moved to the other breast, while he caressed the first, mimicking with his fingers what he did with his mouth. Her cries rang like music in his ears; her fresh skin tasted of Stefanie, pure and undiluted, falling into no known category of saltiness or sweetness, floral or mint or spice: just her, just Stefanie, just life.

"Hatherfield, please," she said, almost sobbing.

"What is it, Stefanie? What do you want?" He wanted her to say it, he wanted the proof of her desire in his ears.

"You know. You know what I want." Her fingers, freed from his enclosing hands, flew down to the waistband of his trousers.

"No!" he snapped.

Her hands fell back. Her eyes flew open.

"No," he said, more softly. He kissed his way back up her neck to her ear. "Let me help you, Stefanie. I know what you need. I'll give you what you need. Just lie back and let me take care of you."

"I need you. I need you inside me."

I need you inside me. The words burned through his skin.

"I'll take care of you. Trust me." He swept his hand down her breast, across her belly, to rest on her hip. With his thumb he brushed the tiny curls.

She exhaled a long and heavy sigh.

He rolled to her side and allowed his gaze to follow his hand. The sight nearly did him in. Her pale hips made a graceful curve under his large hand; a neat auburn triangle pointed to the parting of her legs. He moved his hand and spread the fingers outward, until his thumb brushed one side of her hip bone and his pinkie just nudged the other, and the swell of her mons fit precisely into the hollow of his palm.

He turned his head and met her round eyes.

"You are the most beautiful sight," he said. "The most beautiful woman."

"Even when I'm wearing my trousers?"

"Even in your trousers, and most especially without them." He brushed her lips with a kiss.

She placed her hand atop his. "You've done this before, haven't you? You know what to do with me."

"I've done this before, but never with you." He kissed her again. "Tell me how."

"I . . . I don't know, exactly. Slowly?"

"Slowly, then." He moved his hand slowly through her curls, down her mound, until his forefinger found the soft flesh within. He touched her swollen clitoris with a hummingbird's lightness. "Like this?"

"Yes!"

"How many fingers?"

"One. Two. I don't care."

He slid one finger down the channel, already slick with arousal, and searched out the small fissure at her center. He circled around the rim and brought his finger up to his lips. The rich scent made his blood jump; he sucked it into his mouth and then found her again, that immaculate sweet flesh, and this time he pushed his finger inside her an eighth of an inch, just wetting the tip, until her hips moved restlessly and he pushed a little farther, a little farther, until his first finger joint was inside her and she made a carrying call, a wild sound, and her knees drew up and back down again, and her muscles closed hard around the fortunate first quarter of his finger.

"More?" he said.

"Yes, damn you! More!" she shouted.

Another quarter inch, and another, and another. Now his finger was halfway inside her, so that his thumb could easily rub against the nub above.

Her hand wrapped around his wrist. The nails dug into his skin.

"MORE! DAMN YOU!"

God, she was magnificent! He kissed her, he massaged her in lazy strokes, feeding his finger into her channel. "Do you know what amazes me?" he said. "How you can grip my single finger so tightly, and yet I could still fit my cock into you. My cock, Stefanie, which is about the size and strength of a brass cannon just now."

"Hatherfield!"

His finger was all the way inside her now, right up to the knuckle, buried in hot silk. He held it there, while his thumb went on with its rhythmic teasing, rubbing in light and tender circles, while her hips rose high.

"Open your eyes, Stefanie. I want you to look at me when you spend. I want to see what you're thinking."

She opened her eyes, looked at him, and climaxed hard and fast, her wet flesh clenching around his finger, her chest gasping for air. "Oh God, oh God! Oh *God*, it won't stop, it . . . *oh!*" Her head fell back on the blanket. The pulses died slowly away on his finger, until her release was only a distant flutter, a final half-remembered twitch.

He slid his finger out of her and drew up the side of the blanket to cover her from the cold air of the room. She turned her head into his shoulder.

She might have slept for a moment. He wasn't sure. Her breathing steadied against the wool of his jumper; her heartbeat took on a slow thud. The fire behind him seemed to have taken. He could feel its warmth at his back, could hear the familiar sizzle of burning coals.

"Did that help?" he asked at last, when she stirred.

"Yes," she said. "But what about you?"

"I'll manage." In fact, he was shortly going to die of spontaneous internal combustion.

She reached again for the waistband of his trousers, and he rolled away in a flash and jumped to his feet.

She struggled upward in a tangle of blankets and pale limbs. "What's wrong? What did I do?" Her short hair fell away from her face, exposing her pale face, her darkened large eyes. He turned away from the sight.

"Nothing. Just give me a moment." He went to the window and braced himself against the sill, staring at the cold back alley. The chill of the air penetrated his clothes. He thought of ice and snow, of cold river water, and when that didn't help, he thought of his stepmother's haughty face. Her triumphant eyes.

He turned. "Cover yourself. You'll catch a chill."

"Hatherfield?" She rose to her feet. "What's wrong?"

"I told you, nothing's wrong. We need to dry your clothes, get you dressed . . ."

"You're acting like an ass. Stop it now."

"I'm only being practical. You'll be late . . ."

"You're acting like an ass, Hatherfield! And I will just . . . I will just *slap* you in a moment, if you don't stop!" She was starkly and unashamedly naked. Her hands were fixed to her beautiful hips. Her eyes, good Lord, they shamed him.

"I'm sorry," he said softly. "Wrap yourself up. Please, Stefanie. There is absolutely nothing wrong. With you."

She looked at him a second or two longer, and then she picked up the blanket and wrapped it wantonly around her body, which was worse somehow, which made him imagine her wrapped in his own blankets in his own bed in his own damned bedroom. He bent and found her clothes and laid them out next to the fire. He was still erect as hell, but at least he could move.

"His name was Gunther," she said.

He turned. "What's that?"

"The man I was with before. Well, he was a boy, really. I was eighteen, he was about the same. I'd known him all my life. He was the mayor's son, a minor aristocrat I suppose, and we played together as children."

He ran his hand through his hair. "Why are you telling me this?"

"He understood me, in his way. The only one who did, apart from Emilie. He knew why I needed to get away, that the castle was like a prison to me. He helped me sneak out at night, and I was free then, I wasn't a princess, I didn't have duties and decorum and a life mapped out for me. I think we were about thirteen the first time we went larking. It was all innocent. And then that summer, the summer I turned eighteen, it all changed." She sank onto the cot and stared at the fire.

He studied her for a moment and sat down next to her, a foot or so away.

"I felt so restless. My latest stepmother had just died giving birth to another stillborn, and I really loved her, she was wonderful, almost a sister. Father was away at some spa or another, probably looking for another wife. I was going mad, I thought I would burst from my skin, and Gunther . . . I suppose he'd filled out a bit, he'd grown taller. His spots had sorted themselves out at last. And I convinced myself I was in love with him."

"Were you?"

"I suppose I was. Yes. The way one is at that age, all heedless and delirious. So one night I let him kiss me, and a few nights later I let him touch me, and then . . . I don't know. I suppose I'm just wicked inside, a wanton. I just wanted it so badly, like a burn below my skin. Like I did now, as if I would die if he didn't . . . if I didn't . . . well, I don't think I even knew what I wanted. He didn't really know what to do, either. It wasn't very successful at first, and then by the time we had finally learned how to get it right . . ." She shook her head.

He picked up her hand and held it between both of his.

She gathered her breath. "His father . . . I don't know if he realized what was going on or not. But he made Gunther marry another girl, a daughter of a factory owner, large dowry. Large breasts, too. I thought . . . I was stupid. I thought Gunther would say no, and we would run away together. I thought, maybe I'll be with child, and he'll have to marry me and take me away from all this. But I wasn't, and he did. Marry her, I mean. So that was that. A ruined woman. A useless princess, really, because if anyone knew, I could never be married off for the betterment of my country. No gentleman would want me."

"I want you."

"Not to marry."

He bit back his next words, because he couldn't say them. Had no right.

Instead, he said, "You're not ruined to me. It doesn't matter. I'm glad, at least, that . . ." He paused, because how did one phrase such things? He didn't want to offend her.

"Glad that what?"

"That you cared for him. That he cared for you." And especially glad that she—and he—would never see this wretched Gunther fellow, this infinitely lucky rascal, ever again.

"Yes. Well. Here's my point; I do have a point. My little affair with Gunther was very nice, the last time or two, when we had finally worked out how to do it all properly. But it wasn't like . . . like what happened just now. He wasn't like you at all. That was all very much *that*, and this is . . . *this*. And I want to tell you that whatever it is—or I suppose I mean *whoever* she was, the one who came before me, the one who makes you spring away like that afterward as if you loathed the very thought of what we've just done—well, that was that."

Hatherfield let out his breath, and it was as if his insides released themselves, too, leaving him hollow and shocked and raw. "And this is this."

"So the next time, you needn't jump up and tell me to get dressed, without my even seeing you, or touching you. Whatever you're hiding, whatever you don't want me to see, I don't care. I'm Stefanie, I'm not *her*, and I . . . I care for you, very much, far more than I ever cared for Gunther, and there is nothing, Hatherfield, nothing, nothing in this world and out of it, *nothing* that could make me think less of you. Do you understand?"

He lifted her hand and kissed it. "I understand you perfectly."

"Good, then." She jumped up from the cot. "And now, if we don't leave straightaway, I'm going to be late for work, and Sir John will probably beat me. These are still wet. Is there anything else I can wear?"

He cleared his throat. "There are rowing uniforms, of course. I'll find one to fit you. And Stefanie?"

"Yes?"

He wanted to reach out and fold her in his arms. He wanted to tell her she was the most extraordinary woman he'd ever known. That he was honored beyond words to have spent this past intimate half hour with her. That her kindness, just now, when she had every right to storm away, had meant everything to him.

He wanted to tell her that there *couldn't* ever be a next time. He wanted to tell her that there *must* be a next time, and another, and another, perhaps all in the same night, because once he unleashed himself he wouldn't be able to stop.

But for once, the charming Marquess of Hatherfield found no adroit phrase at the tip of his tongue. His shocked and hollow insides seemed to have swallowed them all up.

Instead, he said, "You seem to have forgotten your mustache."

FIFTEEN

As always, it took Sir John quite some time to work his way through the throng of colleagues in the overheated courtroom and the chilled corridor outside.

Stefanie bore her burden of books and papers and hung respectfully back, as every possible member of the English bar shook her employer's eminent hand and congratulated him with the same words: *Splendid show, Worthington. Had me riveted. By God, what an extraordinary case.*

She shifted the stack to one arm and lifted her hand to stifle a yawn.

"Quite a crowd here today, isn't there?"

"Hatherfield! Don't sneak up on me like that!" Stefanie juggled desperately, struggling to hold her precious legal resources while her skin flushed hot and her heart scrambled upward to attempt escape through her throat. She had parted from Hatherfield in perfect composure at the area entrance to Sir John's town house at seven thirty-five this morning; now, at four o'clock, all she could remember was the fervid beauty of the marquess's face when she had opened her eyes on the floor of the boathouse and climaxed around his thick finger.

His finger, which was now joined with its brothers to pry the books and papers from her hands. "I'll take those for you."

She pulled away. "You will not! What are you thinking?"

"I'm thinking you're about to drop those papers, and then where will your poor Mr. Northcote be? In the dock, a proven molester of hard-pressed wives, with God only knows how many years of prison to come."

There was an unmistakable irony in his voice.

She gathered her wobbling stack securely. "You witnessed the opening arguments, I presume."

"I had that honor. Though I must admit, I mostly witnessed you." He lifted his thumb and brushed the very end of her cheekbones.

"What the devil are you doing?" she hissed.

"Admiring you."

"You're not supposed to be doing that. At the moment, I mean."

"How can I help it? I . . . oh, I say. Mr. Wright. Can it really be you, out of the countinghouse in the middle of the day?"

Stefanie whipped around, setting the papers to wobbling again. A tall and saturnine man stood before them, dressed in charcoal gray, glowering keenly at Hatherfield.

"Hatherfield," he said. "What a charming waistcoat."

"Isn't it, though?" The marquess spread his arms. "I do love this particular shade of rose pink, don't you? I had my tailor search for weeks. Marvelous fellow, my tailor. Have you met my charming young companion, Mr. Thomas? Law clerk to none other than Sir John Worthington himself, and a more extravagant set of eyelashes you'll never encounter. Just look at the delightful curve of them."

The books and papers fell to the floor in a catastrophic cascade.

"Oh, my poor dear fellow!" Hatherfield dropped to his knees and began to gather them up. "Mr. Wright, do leave off that scowling. You're flustering Mr. Thomas's delicate nerves."

"My nerves are not delicate," said Stefanie. "I'll take those papers, if you don't mind."

"I beg your pardon," Mr. Wright drawled. "Is that a carnation in your buttonhole, your lordship? Wherever did you find it, at this time of year?"

Hatherfield straightened with his arms full of books, which he placed tenderly in Stefanie's arms. "I find, Mr. Wright, that if one wants something badly enough, deep down in the heart of one's soul, why, one must have it. Whatever the cost."

"I can't imagine what you mean," Stefanie said.

Hatherfield bestowed a fond glance on the top of her head. "My dear Stephen. Such ironic wit. Did you enjoy today's proceedings, Mr. Wright?"

"I found them rather distasteful, in fact. That Northcote fellow ought to be hanged."

Hatherfield smoothed his well-tailored sleeve. "Forbidden love is not to your taste, then? You've never felt the harsh shadow of society's disapproval on your choice of companion?"

"I disapprove of adultery, Lord Hatherfield, and whatever the actual facts of the case, adultery itself is not in dispute."

Hatherfield sighed and looked lyrically into Stefanie's eyes. "One cannot choose whom one loves."

"I beg to differ. One chooses what one bloody well decides to choose." Mr. Wright's voice matched his expression: as hard as marble.

"Ah, Mr. Wright. A man who can say that doesn't know what it means to love." He raised his chest for another sigh.

Stefanie cut it short. "What nonsense, Lord Hatherfield. I haven't the faintest idea what you mean. And I really believe I must be going; Sir John will shortly require my assistance." She peered through the crowd, as if expecting it to part and release her employer. Which, alas, it showed no signs of doing.

"Ah, work. What a ghastly word." Hatherfield shook his head. "I suppose you arrived here today for a respite yourself, Mr. Wright?"

"On the contrary. I had business here this afternoon."

"What sort of business?"

"I believe I'm conducting it right now, your lordship."

"Oh? I can't think what you mean. Are you speaking of the trial? Do you have a personal interest in our naughty dustman and his affairs? I urge you to discretion, as my dear Stephen is employed for the defense."

"My interest is not with the dustman. But I believe I have taken enough of your valuable time, Lord Hatherfield. My questions have been answered to my satisfaction, or rather to my dissatisfaction."

"Really?" Hatherfield spread his hands. "What question was that, Mr. Wright?"

"A certain rumor that had reached my ears. Of no consequence, really. I am not a man to be denied by mere trifles." He lifted his hat. "Good day, your lordship. Good day, Mr. Thomas."

He raked Stefanie over with his sharp black eyes, and melted into the crowd.

"What," said Stefanie, turning to Hatherfield, her face flushed hot enough to boil water, "the bloody hell was that?"

"Oh, Mr. Wright? An old friend."

"The way you were speaking to him. That tone of voice." She looked at the carnation in his buttonhole. She hadn't really noticed it before. How long had he been sporting such a thing? All winter? And his waistcoat. She thought it rather handsome, in fact, when she troubled herself to contemplate the clothes he was wearing, rather than the promising expanse of masculine bone and muscle that lay beneath.

But pink? With all those stripes?

Whatever did he mean by it?

"If you must know," said Hatherfield, "my father, or rather my stepmother, owes Mr. Wright a rather large sum of money. I believe they found the means to put him off for a few months, but he likes to turn up now and again, to make sure I haven't forgotten the obligation."

"But it's not your obligation, is it?"

"It will be, eventually, won't it?" Hatherfield was gazing thoughtfully at the spot where Mr. Wright had disappeared a moment earlier.

An awful suspicion took hold of Stefanie's heart. Hadn't she wondered all these weeks about his scruples, about his refusal to engage her affection, to even speak of an understanding between them, even this morning when he had indisputably demonstrated his attraction to her? And he was a son with a father still living, in expectation but without possession yet of his inheritance.

She leaned an inch or two closer. "Hatherfield, look at me. Are you in need of funds?"

He turned to her with an expression of mild horror. "Good heavens, Stephen. What a question. Of course not."

"Because . . . it doesn't matter." How could she phrase this, in a corridor full of people? She said, in a brusque voice, as if discussing the weather, "As it happens, I have a fortune."

"A fortune? How clever of you. Of no concern to me, however. Did you happen to regard the expression on your client's face, as the prosecution was listing his sins? They put the matter so tidily, I was tempted to string him up on the spot."

"Luckily, he has Sir John to defend him, or he would be at the mercy of the instant judgment of men like yourself," she said acidly.

Hatherfield looked away again, into the distance. "Yes. How good of him."

"Without a fair defense for all, our system of justice is nothing."

"Indeed. Do you have your note ready?"

Someone crashed into Stefanie's back, began to swear, and caught the expression on Hatherfield's face. "I beg your pardon, sirs!" he said, white-faced, and hurried away.

Stefanie tried to speak softly. "The note to my sister?"

"Yes. I shall endeavor to deliver it this week." He was still looking away. His eyes narrowed thoughtfully.

"This week? Why not tonight?"

"Because I have also received an interesting communication of my own on the matter. Something that rather changes the rules of the game entirely."

He said the words so calmly, it took Stefanie a second or two to understand his meaning. Her blood jumped in her veins. She had to restrain herself from dropping the papers again and grasping his arm. "A message! What sort of message? From my sister?"

He slid a square card from his pocket and handed it to her.

The Duke of Olympia
requests the honor of your attendance
Wednesday, the twenty-first of February
at eight o'clock in the evening

to celebrate the Engagement of his Niece
Her Royal Highness,
the Princess Emilie of Holstein-Schweinwald-Huhnhof
to His Grace, the Duke of Ashland

She looked up. "Oh, Hatherfield! Do you think . . ."

"You're not going."

"The devil I'm not!"

"We will discuss this elsewhere."

"But . . ."

"*Elsewhere*, Stephen." His voice went dark.

Sir John broke through the crowd at that instant. "Good Lord, what a crush. Like one of your stepmother's damned parties, Hatherfield. Is my carriage ready?"

"Yes, sir," said Stefanie.

"Excellent." He struck out in the direction of the doorway, without even bothering to ascertain whether the two of them were following him. He lifted his wig from his head and thrust it into his briefcase. An attendant swung open the door before him just in time to avoid being steamrolled. "You will join us for dinner in Cadogan Square, of course, won't you, Hatherfield?" he said, over his shoulder.

"Of course." He shook Sir John's hand. "Good afternoon, sir. Your usual fine performance in court today, defending the indefensible."

"Why, thank you, sir," said Sir John, with genuine pleasure. He paused, and Stefanie could have sworn that his jowls made a disapproving waggle. "Is that a pink carnation in your buttonhole, Lord Hatherfield? In February?"

The marquess looked down, smiled, and adjusted the flower. "Why, yes, Sir John. Yes, it is."

By the time Hatherfield arrived back at his rooms, Nelson had already laid out his soap and razor and dinner dress. He shaved and dressed and sleeked his hair neatly back. His scrubbed face gazed back at him from the mirror. How he had once hated that face. As a young man on the brink of adulthood, he had often longed to take that razor in his hand and slash away at all that perfection, all that symmetry and beauty. Surely a few good scars would do the trick.

He was glad, now, that he had not. He had this to give Stefanie, at least. Surely his beautiful face would compensate, in some small way, for the rot within.

Before leaving the room, he removed a set of papers from the false back of his shaving mirror and stared at them thoughtfully. There were fourteen in total. They had begun arriving at the end of November, written in an ornate and foreign hand, unsigned. The message was roughly the same, every time. The last one, delivered the previous Monday, read: *You and your pretty friend made a fine couple out ride in the park yesterday. The chestnut who bore your friend has being poison and is now dying. Good day.*

A knock on the door.

"Nelson, I am not to be disturbed. I shall call you when I require your assistance."

"Sir, it's your father."

Hatherfield sighed and shuffled the papers together. "Tell him I'm out."

The door swung open. "I heard that, you dog."

"Father." Hatherfield slipped the papers into his bureau drawer and turned wearily to the doorway, where his father stood in dinner dress, hair sleek and collar blinding. "I see you've returned to town. Have the charms of the country grown flat already?"

"I had business, and your mother wished to consult with her dressmaker."

Hatherfield nodded at the duke's tailcoat. "I'm afraid I'm already engaged."

"How delightful it is to return to town after a two months' absence, to be greeted by the usual excess of filial affection."

Hatherfield braced his arms against the bureau and leaned back. "I daresay you'd shrink away, these days, if I dared to approach you with my corrupt embrace."

"True." The duke folded his arms. "I only came to see for myself whether you've returned to your senses and your duty."

"I'm sorry to disappoint you, but I remain as I was in November."

"I understand from a mutual friend that you have been making a public spectacle of yourself with that boy of yours."

"I see." Hatherfield lifted his hand and tapped his chin. "Allow me to hazard a guess. Had this business of yours anything to do with Mr. Wright and Her Grace's gambling debt? Is your period of grace nearly at an end? I can only imagine how you contrived to fob him off in November."

"Mr. Wright was kind enough to allow us additional time."

"To convince me to marry his sister?"

"His sister!" The duke started.

Hatherfield turned to the shaving mirror and inspected the perfection of his white bow tie. "Didn't you realize? I spotted it at an instant. Mr. Wright is the natural son of Lady Charlotte's esteemed father. Which makes you and Her Grace . . . oh, what the devil is that word . . . something to do with chess . . . give me a moment, it's on the tip of my tongue . . . oh yes. That's it." He turned and fixed his father with a stony glare. "Pawns."

The Duke of Southam's face flushed an extraordinary shade of pink. "Nonsense."

"I will not be maneuvered into this marriage, Father. If you wish to dance at the end of Wright's puppet strings, I won't stop you. But I won't be dragged into the damned show myself. Now, if you'll excuse me, I have an engagement."

"With that boy," Southam spat.

"Yes. With that boy. How do I look, Father? As handsome as ever? Good. I should hate for my physical charms to fade, and leave me with nothing." He struck out past Southam without pausing.

"Wait, Hatherfield . . ."

"Can't, Father. I'm already late." Hatherfield found his overcoat on the hall stand.

The duke hurried behind him. "Your mother and I are holding a party next week. In Belgrave Square. The twenty-first."

"Isn't that the same evening as that royal affair at Olympia's?"

"Yes, it is. Your mother thinks . . ."

"Aha. Let me guess. Your Graces were not invited to the ball, were you?"

"Some damned mix-up, I'm sure. In any case, she wishes to hold a party of her own . . ."

Hatherfield threw back his head and laughed. "Oh God. I can picture it. Enraged, insulted, she decides she'll show them up, she'll call in every favor and ensure that Olympia's party is a complete failure."

"In any case, we—I—would very much like you to attend."

Hatherfield buttoned the last button and turned. "Why?"

"What the devil does that mean? Because you're my son. Our son."

"Oh, rubbish. You can't bear the sight of me." Hatherfield spun his cane elegantly. "I prefer the company of my own choosing, as it happens."

"Bring him, then! Bring your . . . your friend," Southam said breathlessly. As if he were pleading.

Hatherfield paused. He peered curiously into his father's eyes, which were wide and a bit too gleaming, a bit desperate. He said quietly, "What are you up to, Father?"

"Nothing. Nothing at all. A party, that's all, a masquerade, and I would like for my son to attend, for once. People are talking about our estrangement, and I want the world to know that . . . that . . ." His wobbly old throat swallowed. "That there is no estrangement. That we accept you and . . . and what you are. As I said, your friend is welcome."

"His name is Stephen. Stephen Thomas."

"Mr. Thomas is welcome to accompany you."

Hatherfield fingered his cane and regarded the duke's face, the angry flush now faded to an unwholesome winter pallor. In his mind, the picture of his father was frozen in time, a duke at the height of his power, strong shouldered and firm jawed, his hair dark and thick and his eyes glinting with confidence. Who was this old man, and when had he draped himself over the Duke of Southam's frame? The jowls swung low, the hair hung thin and white, the eyes crinkled with weary uncertainty. Even those doughty shoulders, which once seemed to brace the entirety of the British Empire, now sloped at a defeated angle.

Obviously something was up. The Duke of Southam did

not retreat from his entrenched positions; he did not forgive or forget; he did not welcome prodigal sons back to the Belgrave Square fold. Hatherfield knew this. He knew there was a noose there somewhere, into which he was placing his neck.

But he had never yet known the noose from which he could not escape.

And those defeated shoulders. That wobbly neck.

"A masquerade, eh?" he said.

"Yes. Everybody loves a masquerade, apparently."

Hatherfield fixed his hat more securely on his head. "Very well, Father. I'll put it in my diary. And now, I'm afraid you really must excuse me. My engagement is a pressing one."

He stood back, ushered his father through the door, and marched down the stairs to his hansom, which waited for him on the corner.

SIXTEEN

One week later

The westward traffic had already begun to thicken, and it was nearly five o'clock by the time the Marquess of Hatherfield's black hansom turned around the corner of Southam Terrace, Hammersmith, and came to a stop before the first house. "Wait here," he told the driver, and he leapt briskly to the beaten earth, where the pavement was marked out in stakes and long brown string. From within the buildings, in their various states of completion, came the echoing sound of hammers and shouts.

"Lord Hatherfield!" A rough-bearded man strode out the open door of the first house, tugging his cuffs down his frayed jacket sleeve. His gaze dropped for an instant to the carnation in Hatherfield's buttonhole. "There you are. Hoped my message would catch up with you before the evening."

"Mr. Brookside." He shook his manager's outstretched hand. "What seems to be the trouble? I left everything tight enough a few hours ago."

"Well, that's the thing, your lordship. Right and tight it was, until I came back after lunch when the new bricks was being delivered for the facing of numbers ten and twelve, sir." He nodded down the street, where the neat redbrick facades gave way to open timber framing. A pair of workers sat smoking on the stoop, staring at the stacks of bricks in the yard.

Hatherfield frowned. "There was trouble with the bricks?"

"Oh, the bricks was sound enough, sir. Best quality bricks, just as you directed. But there was only half of them. Half of what we ordered last week."

"Only half? Why? Some sort of shortage?"

Mr. Brookside's whiskers twitched voluminously. "Come along inside, sir."

Hatherfield followed the manager inside number two. The entrance hall was nearly finished, smelling of fresh paint and plaster; the electric chandelier sat in its wooden crate in the corner, waiting for hanging tomorrow. In a week or two, the house would be fully fitted up and furnished, pillows plumped and table laid, ready to serve as a model for prospective buyers. Just that morning, Hatherfield had inspected the plumbing in the bathroom and the W.C., had tested the hot and cold taps and the flush of the handsome wooden-seated commode, had gone into the boiler closet for a look at the newfangled beast squatting there with its dials and pipes. Central heating in every one of his houses, the most modern sanitary systems, electric wiring and refrigeration: He wanted his terrace to feature every possible convenience, every innovation for improved light and ventilation, for health and safety.

And, with luck, a flood of eager buyers on the half-finished doorsteps of Southam Terrace.

Mr. Brookside led the way into a small room off the kitchen, which was meant to serve as a pantry, and which currently did duty as a building office. "Your lordship," he said, fingering a stack of papers, "may I ask a private question?"

"You may, and I shall choose whether or not to answer it." Hatherfield crossed his arms and regarded Brookside's nervous movements with curiosity. His manager was not ordinarily a nervous man; Hatherfield had hired him firstly for his reputation for honesty and fair dealing, and secondly for his air of unshakable self-assurance.

"Are you having financial troubles of any kind, sir?" Brookside's gaze met his at last.

"None relevant to this project," said Hatherfield.

"Funding all in place, that is?"

"Yes. Ample funding, between my own capital and the loans I've secured on the property." Hatherfield removed his gloves. They'd turned on the central heating last week, and the contrast between the February chill outside and the warmth within caused his hands and arms and back to prickle with perspiration. "Why do you ask?"

"Because of them bricks, sir, I'm afraid. The bloke who delivered them, sir, he would only allow us half of what we ordered. I told him it was rubbish, that we was fully paid up, I would write him a draft that minute for the full amount. And the fellow, why, he scratched his head and said that there was a rumor about that we was in trouble here. That we hadn't the blunt to finish the building, that we was all on credit, house of cards, that sort of thing."

"Nonsense. Our financing is perfectly secure. I've funded fully half of the building with my own capital, and I sat down with the bank manager just last week, as the final loan tranche was deposited into the company accounts. You were right there during the inspection. They were delighted with our progress." Hatherfield spoke forcefully. In matters of finance, confidence was paramount.

"That's what I told him, more or less. And he agreed to deliver the rest of the bricks this week, once the draft's cleared the bank."

Hatherfield's blood rose high. "Once the draft's *cleared*! By God! The cheek!"

"What I thought, sir. But the point is, someone's spreading rumors about us, sir. Someone with enough mouth to make it stick, if you follow me. So I thought you should know about it." Brookside shrugged his shoulders and leaned against the bright white plaster, self-assured once more in the face of his employer's righteous anger.

Hatherfield's skin itched against his clothes in the warm room. Behind him lay the kitchen, bright and white, fitted with a handsome range and piped hot and cold water, well drained and ventilated. He'd overseen the design himself; he had put everything into this project, as if it held the key to his own salvation.

Someone with enough mouth to make it stick.

"You did well, Brookside. Thank you." Hatherfield replaced his gloves in short and angry tugs. "Obviously someone wishes to undermine our efforts. A competitor, no doubt. I assure you, I shall look into the matter with the utmost energy."

Like a ball of summer sunshine, the Marquess of Hatherfield burst through the doorway of the Worthington drawing room at three minutes to eight o'clock, just in time to save Lady Charlotte Harlowe from the receiving end of a faceful of Sir John's best sherry.

At the delivering end of the sherry, Stefanie's arm lowered. "Why, Lord Hatherfield. We were beginning to think you'd found a better offer."

Lady Charlotte turned to the door, and her peevish expression transformed into a flawless china-doll smile. "Nonsense. There is nowhere in England where his lordship is more welcome than in this house. Isn't that so, James?" She held out her hand.

Hatherfield's lips stopped just shy of the white Harlowe fingers. "Good evening, Lady Charlotte. Sir John." He turned to Stefanie, and the old smile broke across his face in a sparkle of mischievous white teeth. "My dear Stephen."

"Your lordship." Stefanie bowed stiffly.

"Have a glass of sherry," said Sir John. "You look as though you need it."

Hatherfield accepted the glass and tossed it down in an alarmingly thorough gulp. "I confess, it's been a rather complicated day."

"Complicated?" said Lady Charlotte. "What an odd word to describe one's time."

"No doubt it does sound odd, to a lady of complete and unremitting leisure, such as yourself, Lady Charlotte," said Stefanie. "But those of us engaged in gainful labor will understand exactly what his lordship means by the term *complicated*."

Lady Charlotte raised her eyebrows in alarm. "But James isn't engaged in gainful labor, are you, James?" As she might say *premeditated murder*.

"Heavens, no." Hatherfield shuddered. "Perish the thought.

Labor, indeed. How you joke, Stephen. No, fate merely tossed me an unconscionable number of rather tedious errands today. Nothing a well-bred lady of elegant habits would bother her dainty head about, I hope."

"How wretched for you. Couldn't you dispatch a servant instead?" inquired her ladyship. "I'm sure our Mr. Thomas would be happy to run messages about and that sort of thing, when he isn't copying out Uncle John's letters and dusting his desk."

Hatherfield sipped his sherry. "Alas, no. Much as I would have enjoyed Stephen's personal attention to my own affairs, he was employed in court today. I had only the glimpse of the back of his head, from several rows away. No, I suffered alone. Hammersmith, of all places." Another delicate shudder.

Lady Charlotte's scowl might have broken glass, had she hazarded a glance in the mirror. "I can't imagine why."

"Oh, I assure you, only the most urgent of matters could have torn me from the side of my very dear friend." Another smile at Stefanie, saturated with admiration. "But it seems some nefarious character has been spreading the most outrageous slurs on my character."

"Good God," said Sir John, properly shocked. "Was this your business today?"

Lady Charlotte clasped her hands. "Not a duel, I hope!"

"No, no." Hatherfield walked to the drinks tray and refilled his glass. The electric lamp winked provocatively on the facets. "Nothing so dramatic, I assure you. But these nasty sorts of attacks must be stopped in their tracks, don't you think?"

"Naturally," said Sir John. "If the law may be of any assistance in the matter of redress, I shall be happy to assist you."

Hatherfield turned and leaned against the cabinet, glass in hand, his body arranged in elegant long lines. "I thank you, Sir John, but in these sorts of affairs, a face-to-face interview tends to have the best effect. Don't you agree, Lady Charlotte?"

She adjusted a fold of her lemon yellow dress where it lay about her on the sofa. "I'm sure I wouldn't know."

"Quite sure?"

She looked up sharply. "Quite. That is, I haven't any experience in the spread of ugly gossip, but I daresay I should be ashamed to consult the law. Such needless public exposure to one's private affairs."

Stefanie had been watching the exchange keenly. "May I ask the nature of this slur, your lordship?"

His gaze continued to rest on Lady Charlotte: not at her face, but rather the top of her head, as if he were weighing whether to pop off the lid and examine the contents. He turned to Stefanie at the last instant before his reply. "A most outrageous attack upon my creditworthiness, dear Stephen. Of all things."

"But that's nonsense," said Lady Charlotte. "You're the heir to a dukedom. How could your credit possibly be in doubt?"

"How, indeed," murmured Hatherfield.

Dinner was called and eaten. Sir John, more than usually distracted with his current case, retired almost immediately after his first glass of brandy, leaving Stefanie alone in the dining room with Hatherfield. The instant the door closed, he moved his chair closer to her and slid her brandy out of her hand.

"Not tonight," he said. "You'll need your wits about you."

She looked up at his face in amazement. His eyes were glowing; his mouth wore a small smile at the corner. "My sister!" she whispered.

"Yes. Tonight. I'll be waiting in the hansom on the corner of Cadogan Gardens at half eleven." He took a long puff of his cigar. "Wear dark clothes. Well-worn and nondescript, if possible, so as not to attract attention."

"Oh, thank you. Thank you so much. You don't know what this means to me." She wanted to fling her arms around his neck; she contented herself with a small puff of her cigar and a gaze of unbridled adoration.

"You don't know what this *does* to *me*," he said. "It's against my better judgment entirely. I've done my damnedest to keep you clear of all this, to let Olympia do his bloody business without my interference, or yours. I nearly ripped up the note when it arrived at my flat, just before dinner. If it weren't Ashland, I wouldn't have considered it."

"But you did, and you'll help me, and you're . . . You're an absolute darling, Hatherfield. I don't know how I shall ever repay you." She glanced at the closed door and let her fingers rest on his knuckles, in a way that explained exactly how she wanted to repay him.

"Yes. Well." He brushed her forefinger with his thumb and turned his attention to his brandy. "Never mind all that. I shall focus solely on getting you out of this encounter unscathed this evening. Your sister's no longer in disguise; she may be followed. Do you perceive that? The danger of connecting yourself to her?"

"Yes. Yes, of course."

"You must do exactly as I say, Stefanie. Exactly and without hesitation. If I say run for the bridge, you run for the bridge. If I tell you to jump into the river, you don't pause to calculate the tidal pull. Do you understand me?"

"Perfectly." Her heart pounded happily in her chest. An adventure! Hatherfield was taking her on an adventure. At night. In dark clothes. In his hansom. To see her sister!

"Good. Because if anything happened to you . . ." He stared at his brandy and shook his head. "Damn it all. You have me at your mercy, don't you?"

"You have me at yours." She reached up and touched his cheekbone with her finger. "Thank you for this morning. I don't think I said that properly. It was beautiful, you were beautiful . . ."

He put his hand atop hers and held it there, against his warm cheek. His eyelids lowered. "No, I wasn't. I was an ass, and I won't . . ."

The door swung open.

Stefanie jumped back, nearly overturning her chair. Hatherfield stood slowly, lifted his cigar to his lips, puffed out an insouciant cloud of smoke, and said, "Why, Lady Charlotte. Aren't you supposed to be tucked up snug in your maidenly bed at this hour?"

Stefanie, remembering herself, stumbled to her feet. "Your ladyship."

"Why, hello, James. I thought you'd left." Lady Charlotte's voice rose a key or two higher than usual. Her face seemed a little pale, but then she was naturally pale, a true alabaster English beauty. "I wanted to have a word with our dear Mr. Thomas."

Hatherfield stubbed out his cigar in the ashtray and swallowed the last of his brandy. "Jolly luck. As it happens, I was just leaving. Most grateful thanks for a lovely dinner. Your cook has a delicate way with a bombe glacée."

"You are always welcome at our table, James."

He took her hand. "Good evening, your ladyship. I'll see myself out. Stephen, my dear. Au revoir. Don't forget my instructions." He waggled his fingers at Stefanie and prowled from the room.

Lady Charlotte watched him leave, until the last glint of his golden hair disappeared into the darkness of the hallway. She turned to Stefanie with a bright smile. "How droll he is! Did you ever in your life meet anyone so droll, Mr. Thomas?"

"Once or twice, perhaps."

"Instructions, indeed. Whatever sort of instructions could he have for you? Some sort of trifling errand, I suppose?" Her fingers curled around the back of a chair.

Stefanie shrugged her well-padded shoulders. "Nothing to concern you, your ladyship." How strange. She felt powerful suddenly, a drinker of brandy and puffer of cigars, a member of the rarefied masculine world, a speaking part on the great stage of life. What a lovely feeling. No wonder the men protected it so passionately.

"No, I suppose not," said Lady Charlotte. "Tedious things, errands. What trouble it must be for you, keeping yourself at the beck and call of others. I am so dreadfully sorry for you."

Stefanie spread her hands. "One must accept one's lot with good cheer."

"Indeed." She ran her fingertip along the edge of the dining table. "Do you know, Mr. Thomas, though we've lived under the same roof for months now, I often feel as if I hardly know you. Your history, your troubles. The misfortunes that have brought you to such a lowly position in life, so thoroughly dependent on the charity of others."

"I'm afraid it's a long and tangled tale, of very little interest to your ladyship, and certainly not suited to our present surroundings." Stefanie gestured with her cigar to the walls of the dining room, the empty chairs, the cloth already removed. The void of attendants, which in itself contained a titillating element of the forbidden. In all propriety, the two of them might only stay alone together in the room a few cordial minutes.

"How I feel for you, Mr. Thomas. I should very much like to help you, in whatever way I can. I have my own troubles, you know, and it gives me great sympathy for the trials of others." Lady Charlotte pressed one hand against her lacy heart.

"No doubt it does."

"Lord Hatherfield, bless his dear and affectionate heart, takes such a close and fraternal interest in you. It gladdens my heart, to see the two of you so close. Sharing each other's company in such an intimate fashion."

Stefanie bowed.

"I don't suppose . . . perhaps you might tell me . . . does he ever speak of me?" Lady Charlotte's smile was rigid on her face; her eyes fixed on Stefanie, bright and hard.

"Speak of you?" Stefanie said slowly.

"As his friend. Perhaps you have heard him mention my name, or perhaps . . . perhaps he has allowed you into his confidence." Her hand wound tight around the back of the dining chair.

"If he has, your ladyship, I certainly would not betray anything he might have said to me there." She saw, too late, that Lady Charlotte's eyes were a little too shiny, a little too bright.

"I see. You will not tell me. You don't trust me."

"Your ladyship . . ."

"Mr. Thomas." Lady Charlotte smiled. "You may address me more familiarly, if you like. We are living under the same roof, after all. We have the same interests at heart, don't we?"

Stefanie stubbed out her cigar in the tray, right next to Hatherfield's. "Perhaps your ladyship will be pleased to speak plainly. What is it you want of me?"

"Ah. Yes. I do admire directness, Mr. Thomas." She took a step closer, and another, until she was only a foot or two away from Stefanie's chest, and Stefanie could smell the scent of perfume in the soft dark hair near her nose. Lady Charlotte tilted her beautiful face upward, as if asking for a kiss, and spoke in a husky voice that was very close to a whisper. "I shall be frank. You will forgive me, I hope, because a woman in love must be forgiven anything, don't you think?"

"Almost anything."

"I *am* in love, Mr. Thomas. I know it's improper to say so, but I don't care. I will not be denied. I am in love with Lord Hatherfield—yes, I admit it—madly and faithfully in love with him, and I would do anything at all to secure his affection. Do you understand me? Anything at all. You cannot conceive the strength of love I bear for him. I love every bit of him, every dear atom of his generous mind and his active person. I would defend him with my every power. I would die for him, Mr. Thomas."

"Your ladyship speaks passionately."

"I do. I am passionate, Mr. Thomas. I am a tigress in defense of whom I love." She placed her little hand on Stefanie's arm, as gently as a bird might nestle on a branch. "What I hope is that I may count on your support, Mr. Thomas. Your goodwill."

"Why, my dear Lady Charlotte. My goodwill toward you is as strong as it has always been, I assure you."

She showed her teeth. "What a great relief, Mr. Thomas. I do dislike to be thwarted. I am as fervent in my friendships as in my enmities. Do you understand me? With all my heart, I hope I may count on you to help his lordship understand how happy he would find himself in my love. How rich in everything such a man requires. I can give him money, position, assistance, and advice in his ambitions. Children, to carry on his noble line." She cast a quick eye up and down Stefanie's body. Her soft breath caressed her chin.

"Do you really believe Hatherfield wants all this?"

Lady Charlotte laughed and stepped away. "Of course he does. We would make a perfect match, he and I, so beautifully suited in every way. Surely you agree? He must love me, eventually, when all the scales have fallen away from his eyes and he sees the truth of it. I would live to make him happy."

Stefanie felt a curious pain in her ribs, as if Lady Charlotte had placed her two hands inside and wrung her heart to dry. She groped for her snifter of brandy. A flush was rising in her cheeks; she felt its heat like the draft from a fire.

Lady Charlotte lifted her chin and placed her hand on the doorknob. "You're a fine fellow, Mr. Thomas. With many sterling qualities, I'm sure. But I beg you to remember who you are. You're nobody, you're the son of nobody, and I am the daughter of an earl."

Stefanie crashed the brandy glass to the table. The contents of the room spun about her. "Are you, then? Well, I myself . . ." She checked herself just in time.

"Yes, Mr. Thomas?"

Stefanie, the notoriously impulsive princess of Holstein-Schweinwald-Huhnhof, counted to ten in slow beats of her red-misted mind.

Remember who you are. Remember whom you are meeting tonight.

The blood receded, drop by drop, from her flushed cheeks. The spinning room ground to a careful halt.

She made a sweeping bow before Lady Charlotte's haughty nose. "I am at your service, your ladyship. As always."

Her ladyship smiled and opened the door. "Excellent, Mr. Thomas. I really feel as if we understand each other. Don't you?"

SEVENTEEN

Old Bailey, London
Early August 1890

Even in mourning, Lady Charlotte Harlowe maintained her impeccable sense of drama. She waited until she had settled herself in the witness box before lifting her elegant black veil, and her beauty—pale, fragile, almost skeletal—caused an audible gasp to suck the air from the courtroom, a whoosh of veneration that she acknowledged with the merest tilt of her pointed chin.

Stefanie had not been the one to suggest calling Lady Charlotte to the stand. If she had been in charge of the case, instead of merely acting as Mr. Fairchurch's clerk, she would have banished her ladyship from Old Bailey and its surrounding streets for a solid five-mile radius.

But Fairchurch had been charmed into abject worship during his interview with Lady Charlotte a few months previous—God save the world from the charms of women like her ladyship—and so there she sat in the witness box, awaiting her questioning with the alert elegance and secretive smug smile of a self-satisfied house cat.

"Lady Charlotte," said Mr. Fairchurch, as he might say *Your Majesty.* "This court is deeply honored by your presence here this morning. I hope we find you well."

"As well as can be expected, thank you. The Duchess of Southam was like a second mother to me."

"We share your grief, of course. How long had you been acquainted with the family?"

"I met them in the house of my uncle, Sir John Worthington, several years ago. A natural extension of his friendship with their son, the Marquess of Hatherfield."

"And would you say you knew Lord Hatherfield well?"

She cast a brief and meaningful look in Hatherfield's direction. The smug little smile returned at the corner of her mouth. "I knew him very well indeed."

Stefanie fisted her hand in her lap, fighting the urge to slap that smile off Lady Charlotte's face.

Mr. Duckworth smiled. All this had been discussed in her interview: the friendship between the families, her admiration for Hatherfield's character, her certainty that he could not possibly have murdered the Duchess of Southam. He went on, confident of her response. "I am loath to ask an indelicate question of a lady, but the circumstances of the prosecution's case against the accused require it. Would you say there was any particular sort of affection between you and Lord Hatherfield?"

Lady Charlotte's eyes remained tuned in the direction of Hatherfield's golden head. "Yes, I would."

"A fraternal sort of affection?"

She was supposed to reply, *Yes, exactly.* That was what she had told Mr. Fairchurch in the interview, after all: She looked upon Hatherfield as a brother. Stefanie, afterward, had warned Fairchurch that this was not the case, that she was certain—quite certain—that Lady Charlotte bore a passion for the Marquess of Hatherfield that had nothing at all to do with sisters or brothers. But Fairchurch had looked at her with an amazed disgust. "That dear and innocent girl? I wonder at you, Mr. Thomas."

But here, now, in the stifling summer courtroom in Old Bailey, she gazed rapturously at Hatherfield, blushed, looked at her hands, and said, "I can't say, Mr. Fairchurch."

The courtroom rustled with interest.

Mr. Fairchurch coughed. "Lady Charlotte. You were not certain of your feelings, then?"

She looked up with pleading eyes. "I had hopes . . . That is, before he began behaving so oddly, so unlike himself."

Mr. Fairchurch turned as pale as his wig. He glanced down at his notes, the neat line of questioning he had developed, against Stefanie's advice, that ended with a triumphant, *Your witness, Mr. Duckworth.* "Well, then. That is. I see. Let us turn to the evening in question, the twenty-first of February. Do you remember what time Lord Hatherfield arrived at the ball in Belgrave Square, in the home of his parents?"

"I don't remember exactly, but I believe it was about nine o'clock."

"You saw him enter?"

"I did."

"Can you account for his whereabouts at the time of the murder?"

She smiled. "I lost sight of him, of course, as one does at a ball. But I did encounter him again, upstairs in the library."

The ball of worry began to spin in Stefanie's belly.

"What was Lord Hatherfield doing in the library?"

She smoothed her dress. "I would rather not say."

Another wave of excitement rustled across the courtroom.

"But he was engaged, was he not?"

"He was engaged." She looked at Stefanie and smiled, a white, even-toothed smile. "I left immediately, of course, not wanting to disturb him and his companion."

"And this was at what time?"

"At about ten o'clock. Perhaps a little after."

Mr. Fairchurch turned to the jury with a relieved smile. "Thank you, Lady Charlotte. That will be . . ."

"Of course, I did see him once more, after that," she said composedly.

Stefanie's fingers froze around her pen. She looked at Lady Charlotte, at Hatherfield, whose face had taken on a bewildered frown.

"I saw him upstairs at half past ten. The duchess had just retired to her boudoir and asked me to send Lord Hatherfield to see her. I looked everywhere, and I was on my way upstairs to tell her I couldn't find him, when I saw him disappear around the corner of the hallway."

A murmur began, at the back of the courtroom.

Fairchurch knit his hands behind his back. "I see. Thank you, Lady Charlotte."

She shrugged. "He was coming from the direction of the family bedrooms, so I simply assumed he must have seen her already, and went about my business."

The murmur transformed into a rumble of eager whispering voices.

"I'm sorry," said Lady Charlotte. "I haven't said anything to hurt my dear Hatherfield's case, have I? Because I'm quite sure he had nothing to do with the murder."

The judge banged his gavel. "Silence in the courtroom. Mr. Fairchurch, have you any further questions for her ladyship?"

Mr. Fairchurch took a handkerchief from his pocket and patted his blanched temples, one by one, and the gleaming skin above his upper lip.

"Warm day, isn't it, Fairchurch?" said Mr. Duckworth sympathetically.

"No further questions, my lord," said Fairchurch.

EIGHTEEN

Cadogan Square, London
February 1890

Stefanie spotted the familiar lines of Lord Hatherfield's hansom the instant she turned the corner of Cadogan Gardens. A tall figure stood next to the curbside wheel, clothed in black. She broke into a run.

"In you go," he said, lifting his hand near her elbow, stopping just short of helping her inside. The driver stared straight ahead from his perch high above, seeing no evil.

When the doors sprang closed and the cab jumped ahead, Hatherfield released a great sigh and settled back against his seat. Stefanie laid her hand helpfully next to his, but he didn't take the bait. She contented herself with the warmth of his nearby body in the close confinement of the cab, the delicious proximity of his thigh beside hers.

"Are you nervous?" she asked.

"Nervous? I'm shaking in my boots. What a damned fool idea. I don't know how I let you talk me into it. I don't know why Ashland agreed."

"But nobody knows except us."

"Us, and any member of that damned Revolutionary Brigade of the Free Whatsit . . ."

"Blood. Free Blood."

"Free Blood. Brilliant. Yes. As I said, any member of this

sterling organization who happens to read the newspaper, who then knows that your sister is currently residing at the Park Lane town house of His Grace, the devious and all-damned Duke of Olympia, and who might perhaps be keeping a casual watch on said town house as a result." He folded his arms. "No danger there at all."

"Oh, I daresay you're more than a match for any of them. Or all of them."

"You seem to have picked up the alarming notion that I'm some sort of heroic figure. I'm hardly a professional at all this, you know, not like some of them. Never swashed a buckle in my life. Only picked up the odd job or two, as needed. A spot of adventure here and there, to chase away the ennui."

"Ha. You wouldn't admit it if you'd saved the British Empire single-handedly."

He lifted his fist and coughed delicately into his glove.

"Anyway, my uncle would never employ less than the very best. He has an eye for that sort of thing. Why, look at Dingleby. Doing her governess best to force-feed us daily Latin and grapefruit, when in fact she was protecting us all along."

He didn't reply. His disquiet radiated about them both, saturating the cold night air as it streamed along Stefanie's face. The mansions of Belgravia slid past, silent and monumental, brick and stone echoing back the brisk *clop-clop* of the horse's shoes against the pavement.

"I spoke with Lady Charlotte, after you left," she said.

"Oh? My sincere condolences. I hope she wasn't too difficult."

"She's very much in love with you, you know. *Madly, faithfully*, she said."

He shrugged. "There's no accounting for taste."

"It's true. She nearly stabbed me with her pitchfork. She would do anything for you, she said. That she would not be thwarted."

A heavy pause. "Did she, now. Did she say anything else?"

Stefanie drew her rightmost glove more snugly over her hand and held it out for a critical inspection, one eye closed. "And then she reminded me of all the myriad ways in which she would make you the perfect wife. Money, connections, children."

Hatherfield smacked his forehead. "My God! The dear angel! How could I have been so blind?"

"Well, it's true, isn't it? She's terribly suitable. Whereas I'm nothing but a mess, stripped of everything, my title and my name, even my virtue . . ."

"I happen to like you stripped of everything."

"Everything?"

"Everything. Your shirt in particular. You have the most perfect . . ." He paused.

Stefanie's breath caught in her chest. "Perfect what?"

"Perfect everything." A husky whisper.

Stefanie curled her hands around her legs to stop herself from touching him. Her breath came out in a long cloud of fog, yellow white in the light from a passing streetlamp. "She's terribly beautiful."

"Who?"

"Lady Charlotte."

"Yes, she is. Lots of women are beautiful, Stefanie. That doesn't mean one falls to one's knee and begs for the honor, et cetera." He grasped the edge of the door as the hansom swung around the corner of the King's Road.

"She's also clever and rich."

"Good Lord, Stefanie! Why are we even talking about her? When all I want to do is kiss you. Kiss the daylights out of you, and then . . ." He leaned his head against the window and stared at the fender. "The thing is, she's great friends with my stepmother."

"Isn't that a good thing?"

"No," he said. "It's not."

The hansom bounced over a rut, dislodging them both. Hatherfield put out his hand to steady her. Before he could pull it away again, she laid her hand atop his sleeve.

"I want to kiss the daylights out of you, too," she said. "And then."

They breathed together, sharing the damp air. Stefanie looked down at her gloved dark hand against his woolen dark arm, the layers that separated her skin from his. What would he look like, without those layers? Lean muscle and golden skin. Wide shoulders and narrow hips. Long legs bulging with driven power. His carved face, his blue eyes gazing down at her with that look of passion he'd worn that morning. He would touch her. He would kiss her, and lay her down in a bed of clean white sheets, and she would run her palms over every beautiful inch of him. She lowered her eyelids for an instant and imagined his hips closing against hers. His arms braced on either side of her. His hot breath against her forehead.

"You have to decide, Hatherfield," she whispered.

His other hand, like hers, was curled around his leg. Digging into his own flesh. "Decide what?"

"What comes next. What you're going to do with me."

He pulled his arm away in a swift jerk. "What comes next is this. I'm leaving the hansom on the corner of Cheyne Walk. We'll walk from there. I don't want the vehicle recognized. He'll proceed on to the Brompton Road, where we'll meet him afterward. Give us time to feint if we're followed."

Stefanie swallowed back the ache in her throat.

"That seems reasonable," she said clearly.

"It doesn't have to seem *reasonable*, Stefanie. I could tell you to walk to the moon, and I'd expect you to start climbing that instant. Am I clear?"

"Perfectly clear."

"You'll have fifteen minutes. That's all. When I say it's over, it's over."

She clutched her seat. "It's true, isn't it? I'm going to see Emilie."

His voice softened a single degree. "You're going to see Emilie."

The fog was already thickening, spreading like a miasma from the foul-smelling Thames. Stefanie huddled deep in her coat as she crossed the Chelsea Embankment at Hatherfield's side, into the tree-shadowed elbow of the approach to Albert Bridge. The area was deserted. Stefanie squinted her eyes to make out the shapes in the darkness. A pair of benches sat beside the footpath, flanked by bushes. Hatherfield reached inside his coat and pulled out something that glinted dully in the distant gaslight.

"Is that a pistol?" she whispered.

He didn't answer. With his other hand he pulled her along behind him, until they reached the bushes next to the first bench. He paused, as if scenting the air. "We'll wait here," he said, drawing her onto the bench next to him, as if they were two lovers enjoying a discreet midnight rendezvous.

The sound of carriage wheels rattled into her ears. Stefanie's body tensed. Hatherfield laid his hand over hers, a heavy and reassuring weight.

The carriage went past without a pause, receding into the night. Her shoulders slumped with disappointment, and Hatherfield curled his fingers more snugly around her hand. "Don't worry. We're early," he whispered.

She felt tender and exposed, here in the black night with Hatherfield, waiting for her sister. She turned her face to his. She could just make out his features in the dimness.

He lifted his other hand and took off her round bowler hat. "In case anyone's watching," he said, and he lowered his face to kiss her.

Stefanie made a shocked noise, low in her throat, and then understanding dawned and she opened her mouth and took his kiss deep, playing her part with enthusiasm. A pair of forbidden lovers on a dark Chelsea park bench: What could be more ordinary? Less deserving of anarchist suspicion? She raised her hand to caress the back of his neck, for good measure. One had to make things convincing, after all. Hatherfield's lips traveled over hers, warm and soft, tasting faintly and familiarly of brandy. His tongue brushed like quicksilver against hers, and she murmured a delighted *oh!* that didn't quite make it out of her throat at all, and she gripped his collar with both hands and yanked him against her chest.

This time, she didn't hear the carriage wheels rattle to a stop on the nearby pavement. She only dimly recognized the sound of footsteps on cobbles, and only then because Hatherfield had torn his delicious mouth away, the cad, and sprung with a leopard's grace to his booted feet.

"Holstein." The word carried low across the damp air, from the direction of the footsteps.

Hatherfield, in reply: "Huhnhof."

Stefanie stood and gripped the top of the bench with one hand. Hatherfield's agile body moved forward like a shadow. She craned her neck to see around him.

"Ashland, by God!" he said.

"Hatherfield?" A man's voice, deep and rich, coming from

an enormous human shape that blocked out all light behind it, except for a slight bobbing figure above one broad shoulder.

Emilie.

Hatherfield was speaking. "She's right in the bushes behind . . ."

But Stefanie was already flying past him, launching herself at the sister-shaped hole in the shadows.

Emilie let out a little cry as she took her in her arms. "Stefanie!" she gasped. Emilie wrapped her hands around Stefanie's shoulders and set her away. She put her cool gloved hands against Stefanie's face, and her round eyes gleamed in the distant gaslight, lurid and beautiful. "It's you!"

"It's me, it's me," Stefanie said, laughing and hugging her, taking her back and squeezing her to assure herself of the essential Emilie inside that thick wool coat, that round bowler hat identical to her own.

"Shh," said one of the men, rather harshly. Emilie's duke, no doubt, who radiated taciturn impatience and general ill humor. Even in the darkness, Stefanie could tell that his arms were crossed against his massive chest.

Stefanie took Emilie by the hand and dragged her to the bench.

"Fifteen minutes," Hatherfield called out.

"Yes, yes," Stefanie said, and she took Emilie's hands. "You have a quarter hour, my darling, so tell me all about him."

"About whom?" Emilie said innocently.

"This duke of yours. This Ashland. Hatherfield says he's legendary. Have you kissed him yet? Of course you have. You're engaged. What's he like?"

Emilie was laughing. "Oh, you're just the same, aren't you? He's wonderful, he's . . . well, he's rather taciturn at first . . ."

"I gathered that already."

"But inside he's loving and tender and . . . oh, Stefanie!"

Stefanie squealed. "You're in love, aren't you?"

Emilie squealed back and squeezed Stefanie's hands. "I am!"

"Oh, look at you!" Stefanie took off her sister's hat and fingered her golden hair. "Where are your spectacles?"

"I left them in the carriage. I was too excited."

"You look lovely. You're radiant. Are you really going to marry him?"

"I don't know. I don't know what's to be done. I suppose we'll have to marry." Emilie ducked her head.

Stefanie clapped her hand to her mouth and squealed again. "You're . . . you're *not*!"

Emilie whispered, "I am. I think I am. It's terrible of me, isn't it? But . . ."

"Oh! Oh! I don't know what to say. Are you happy? Oh, I don't believe it. You, of all people!"

"Shh! Stefanie, do be quiet. They'll hear you."

Stefanie leaned close. "What, doesn't he know?" she whispered fiercely.

"No! Not yet. I'm not even quite sure yet. That is, I am, but I'm not. Do you know what I mean?"

A queer pang struck Stefanie's ribs. "Well, no," she said.

"You must think I'm awful."

Stefanie gathered herself and held her sister's hands as tightly as she could. "You're dreadfully wicked, and I couldn't be happier. You beautiful thing. You broke free, you acted for yourself. Was it wonderful?"

Emilie leaned into her ear. "It was wonderful. He's wonderful. I never dreamed it would be like that. Oh, Stefanie. And we haven't . . . not since Yorkshire . . . and I miss it so. I miss him so. I want it all back. Isn't that strange? And we have our engagement ball tomorrow, and I should be thrilled, and all I want is to go back to Yorkshire and . . . and *sin* with him." She said the word *sin* with relish, in a way that made Stefanie's toes tingle with longing.

The duke's voice called out. "Five minutes."

They looked at each other and burst into a sisterly giggle.

"I'm glad, Emilie. I'm so glad. And I'll be an aunt!"

"Shh!" Emilie glanced at the men and back again. "Don't say that. You're scaring me to death. I can't even quite believe it myself yet, and everything's still so . . . oh God. I can't think about it. Tell me about this fellow with you. What's his name?"

"His name is James." The word sounded strange in Stefanie's ears. "The Marquess of Hatherfield."

"And . . . ?" Emilie's voice was rich with meaning.

"And what?"

Emilie nudged her. "And. Tell me about him. You can't hold back now; I've just bared my soul to you."

"Well, he's beautiful. That's what you notice first. Rather difficult to ignore."

"And?"

"And . . . well, he rows."

"Rows a boat?"

"Yes, a racing boat."

"Scull or sweep?"

"I haven't the faintest idea. He rows a boat. With oars. Very fast. A sort of champion. That's all I know."

Emilie sat back, mouth agape. "You're in love with him."

"Nonsense. He's beautiful, that's all. Well, quite extraordinarily beautiful. And I suppose his figure is admirable, if one happens to admire that sort of brutish abundance of muscles. A needlessly impeccable physique, when you come right down to it, though only to be expected with all that tiresome physical exercise, rowing and rowing, up and down, over and over." She paused. "Oh, and I suppose he's honorable and all that, I'll give him his noble character, a bit of the old-fashioned gentleman about him, really quite tedious to a modern thinker, as I am. And perhaps he drops the occasional witty line, when pressed, though he naturally expects a great deal of applause when he does. But no. I certainly haven't fallen in love with him."

Emilie burst into laughter.

"Two minutes!"

"Oh, Stefanie," said Emilie. "I miss this. I miss you."

"I wish I could be there tomorrow, to see you all dressed up and happy, on his arm."

"Well, it won't be like that, exactly. Olympia and Ashland planned the ball to . . ."

A shout rang out. "Hatherfield, secure the women!"

Stefanie half rose, just in time to see a blurred shadow race past the bench and into the bushes. In the next instant, a loud bang exploded the air nearby.

"Get down!" Hatherfield's hand connected firmly with her back, pushing her into the ground next to the bench. Emilie stumbled next to her.

"Where's Ashland? I've got to find him!" her sister screamed.

"Stay down!" shouted Hatherfield, planting his legs protectively before them, and even as he spoke the air filled with leaping shadows. He swung an expert punch into a jaw, whirled about, and delivered a fierce blow to another man's gut.

"There's too many!" Stefanie said. And too close—Hatherfield's pistol was useless.

Her blood fired. Anger filled her: fury at this group of men, linked undoubtedly with those who had killed her father, who now threatened Hatherfield. Threatened Emilie.

She was just beginning to rise when a hand grabbed the back of her collar and jerked her upward. She craned her neck and caught a glimpse of a hard face, a scar above a thick eyebrow, before the arm closed around her throat and drew her up against a stone wall of a chest and began to drag her toward the river.

Somewhere nearby, Hatherfield roared. A hard thump shuddered through her, and the hand loosened. She wrested herself free and spun about. Someone reached an arm about her neck, and she snapped her head to one side and bit the outstretched hand just in time. A howl of pain split her ears.

Emilie was shouting something in a strangled voice. Stefanie spun about, trying to find her sister in the shadow-crossed darkness, and for an instant that beloved white face floated into view between a pair of shoulders, braced at the jaw with a large wool-covered arm.

Ashland's massive body blurred past, swinging his fist in a fury. A loud grunt, and the man holding Emilie toppled backward. Ashland seized him with a knife to the throat—good God, how it glinted in the gaslight—and a hand closed around Stefanie's arm, spinning her around.

She raised her fist to strike, and saw it was Hatherfield. "You're all right?" he demanded.

"Yes."

Bang.

In a flash, Hatherfield gathered her under his own body and turned her away from the river.

"Damn it to hell!" Ashland shouted. "To the carriage!"

Emilie screamed her name.

"She's right here," said Hatherfield. His arms were still snug about her. "Shot came from the river."

Ashland drew out a pistol from his jacket. "Take the women to the carriage. I'll cover."

Hatherfield's arms fell away. "Right-ho. This way."

He urged her forward. She and Emilie ran hand in hand to the street, where a large four-wheeler stood waiting by the pavement. Another shot rang out. "Hatherfield!" she called, from her straining lungs.

"Right here," he said, behind her. "Keep going, damn it!"

She pounded on, legs stretched to their utmost, almost flinging Emilie along with her. The carriage loomed before her. Hatherfield's hand was at her back, his arm was reaching around her to spring open the carriage door.

"In you go," he said, and he threw the two of them inside and braced himself above them like a shield.

"Get in!" Stefanie screamed, tugging him away from the door.

Emilie squirmed out from under her. "Where's Ashland?"

"Here," said the duke, swinging himself inside, and the carriage lurched forward, and Ashland lifted Emilie into his lap, and Hatherfield's arms closed so tightly around Stefanie she could scarcely breathe.

A long and wordless moment passed, while the carriage jounced over the cobbles and the wet London houses flew past the windows. Stefanie breathed in the woolen scent of Hatherfield's jacket, clutched the material between her fingers. His shoulder lay under her cheek. His solid knee knocked against her leg at every bounce, but she didn't care. She hardly even noticed.

He was alive.

Emilie was alive.

"Where to?" asked Ashland quietly.

"The Brompton Road, if you don't mind." Hatherfield's voice rumbled against Stefanie's ear; she felt the words, rather than heard them. "I've got a hansom waiting there."

"Have you got somewhere secure to take her? Somewhere that won't give you away?"

What a voice the duke had, dark edged and baritone. Stefanie stole a glance at Emilie, who was curled up quietly against his chest, her hand on his lapel, as if she never meant to leave.

The carriage jolted around a corner. Hatherfield's arms loosened a fraction as he settled her more comfortably against his side.

"I believe I've got just the place," he said.

NINETEEN

The river fog had enclosed the row of boathouses so thoroughly, Hatherfield could only just make out the sallow glow of the lone gaslight outside his own club. He opened the window trap at the back. "This will do," he said brusquely, and the hansom stopped almost on the spot.

Stefanie leapt to the pavement the instant the doors had sprung. Hatherfield followed and turned to the driver. "The usual time tomorrow morning."

"Yes, sir."

"And Smith? Say nothing of tonight's doings."

"Of course not, sir. Good night, sir."

The cab clattered off. Hatherfield went to the door and pulled out his key. Behind him, the water lapped invisibly on the shore. Stefanie was shivering next to him, huddled inside her coat. She hadn't said a word, the entire journey. The lock released at last, and Hatherfield put his hand to her back and urged her inside. "We'll go upstairs," he said. "I'll start a fire."

The caretaker's room was exactly as they had left it a week ago, down to the slight wrinkle on the bed where they had sat, side by side. Hatherfield spared it a single glance and went to the grate. The small remains of the fire still sat there, a damp pile of ash and half-burned coal. He scraped it away and found new coal and kindling.

"Did you kill him?" Stefanie asked, in a clear and brave voice, not shaky at all.

He didn't look up. "No. I wish I had."

"I'm sorry. It was my fault."

The fire had caught. He rose and turned to her. She was sitting on the very edge of the bed, with a blanket wrapped around her shoulders. Her eyes were huge in her shadowed face, the blue faded to gray in the dim monochrome light. Her hat was gone, and her hair had come loose from its pomade, slipping around her face. She knit her hands tightly in her lap.

He went to her and knelt before her, taking her hands in his. "It was worth it. You saw your sister, you saw for yourself she's well."

Tears welled in her eyes. "I put you in danger. You might have been killed."

"It's not your fault that evil men want to hurt you, Stefanie. It's my fault. All these months, I could have been hunting them down, your father's murderers, and instead I did as Olympia told me and kept you to myself. I assure you, I won't make that mistake again. Tomorrow morning, Stefanie, I hunt them down. I'll meet with Ashland and together we'll . . ."

"No! No, Hatherfield." She slid down from the bed to kneel next to him, still holding his hands. She was so close, he felt her breath on his cheek. "You were nearly killed tonight, because of me. Killed. I won't let you do it. I won't let you put yourself in danger. If I'd known they wanted me, I never would have let you close. You've got to go away, Hatherfield, you've got to sever yourself from all this."

"I can't." He kissed her hands. "I won't."

"Then we'll both go away. We'll go together. We'll find a cottage somewhere, a dear little cottage, and we'll live there and . . . raise vegetables . . . and grow old . . ." She was sobbing now.

"Shh." He stroked her hair. "Shh. Don't be daft. You know that's not possible."

"Never mind the vegetables, then. I'm rubbish in the garden, to be perfectly honest."

"Christ. It's not the vegetables. You're a princess, Stefanie.

You have a duty to your country." He pressed her hands together within his. "As do I, one day."

She looked up. "Listen to me. I can bear the danger myself. It's what I was born to. But you, Hatherfield! I couldn't bear it if something happened to you. If you were hurt, or killed, because of who I am."

I couldn't bear it.

Her words burrowed through the wall of his chest to surround his leathered heart. She was so soft and willing in his arms, her skin like silk under his hands. His thoughts turned irretrievably to her warm female body beneath her clothes, her wet sheath pulsing around his finger a week ago. This ache of desire, this dull agony of longing, he felt it in every pore of his body.

Control yourself, his brain said sternly.

He put his hands to her cheeks and kissed her upturned mouth. Just once.

She moaned and burrowed her hands under the lapels of his overcoat.

Oh, very well. Twice.

She opened her mouth and caressed him with her tongue, while her hands attacked his buttons with nimble determination. The sensations came so fast and thick, he was helpless to do anything but kiss her in return, unbutton her coat, pull it from her shoulders, kiss her jaw and her neck, kiss the delicate hollow of her throat above her collar and her sweet-scented earlobe.

Somehow she had his jacket off, she was struggling with his waistcoat. At the touch of his tongue against her hammering pulse, she went still. Her hands fisted around his shirt, right against his skin, tightening and relaxing in a tantalizing rhythm.

He couldn't do this.

Oh, hell.

He was going to do this.

He unbuttoned her jacket, her waistcoat. The blood sang from his heart. She had left off the linen binding around her chest tonight, and her breasts rose beneath the thin white linen, unchecked, uncontrolled, young and firm, oh God! Her marvelous breasts, so ripe in his palms, making his blood sing and his ears roar and his prick thicken into steel. The tips turned into hard nubs beneath his searching thumbs, and she cried out and ran her hands upward to the back of his head.

Her gaze met his, soft with love. "Hatherfield, you're so beautiful," she whispered.

You're so beautiful, James. The old words echoed in his ears.

His limbs went stiff against her.

She kissed his lips, the corner of his frozen mouth. "Please, Hatherfield. Take me to bed. Now."

Now, James. Take me. Do it now.

He sprang to his feet.

She fell forward, catching herself with her hands just in time. "Hatherfield?"

The word tore another hole in the leather of his heart. His skin felt raw, as if he'd physically ripped himself apart from her. He stood and stared at her confused face, her short hair falling about, her open jacket and waistcoat and the tips of her breasts holding up her shirt.

By force, he turned himself away and fumbled for his buttons. His fingers would not obey him. He gave up and found the stack of blankets at the end of the bed and handed them to her. "Go to sleep, Stefanie. I'll keep watch downstairs."

She was on her feet, blazing. "You will not! What . . ."

"We will not do this, Stefanie. We can't."

"*I* can!"

He picked up his pistol from the table and slid it back into his jacket pocket. "And I can't. I'm here to protect you, Stefanie, not to ravish you. So go to sleep and let me do what I'm meant to do. Keep watch. Keep you safe."

He turned and strode to the door, and the sound of her whispered *Oh, Hatherfield!* echoed in his mind all the way downstairs, where he bent his forehead into a wooden hull and closed his eyes and wept.

For half an hour, Stefanie sat on the edge of the bed, staring at the red coals in the grate.

This pain she felt, the pain in her chest, squeezing her ribs. It wasn't the sting of his rejection. That had been sharp and brief, and it had ended when the expression on his face changed from disgust—horror, even—to . . . well, what was it? The hollow shape of his eyes, the clench of his mouth. It was torment.

Hatherfield was in pain.

She felt it herself. How strange, that you could feel another's pain as if it were inside your own body. If only she could relieve his suffering by taking it upon her soul, but suffering didn't work that way. Pain didn't exist in finite quantities that could be transferred to someone else. Pain was elastic, it stretched and grew. It found another host, another heart, and replicated itself there.

Like love.

Love, the opposite, the antidote.

The room was still chilly, still damp, but Stefanie felt a warmth stealing across her skin. The warmth of purpose. She slid off her jacket and her waistcoat, she pulled off her trousers and drawers, until she stood in her shirt and nothing else. She folded her clothes and set them on a chair, and she wrapped a blanket around her shoulders and left the room.

She found Hatherfield among the boats, leaning his sturdy shoulder against the wall, staring out the narrow window to the river. He said, without turning, "Go back to bed, Stefanie. There's nothing for you here."

She cleared her throat and tightened the blanket at her shoulders. "I only wanted to say something. Explain something. When I say you're beautiful, Hatherfield, I don't mean your face. You're a terribly handsome man, of course, but you know that. It's too obvious to be said, really. I expect you've heard it a thousand times, from a thousand women. What I mean is your soul. *You* are beautiful. When I kiss you, when you touch me, I feel your . . . your *radiance* down to my bones." She paused. There was no reaction on his face, no sign that he had heard a word. "I just wanted to make that clear."

Not a movement, not a single blink of his eye.

Stefanie stamped her foot. "And also. You broke your promise."

He came alive at that. "What?"

"You promised you wouldn't jump away next time. You promised to remember I wasn't her, whoever she was. You promised not to be an ass."

"I'd be an ass if I *did* take you to bed, Stefanie. Not by resisting my animal urges."

She stamped her foot again. "You can't do this. You can't flirt with me and make the entire world think we're lovers, and then when we're together, alone, you pull away. I realize I haven't come to you innocent, but I'm not defiled, for God's sake, I'm not some penny strumpet . . ."

"No! For God's sake, don't say that." He leapt away from the wall and paced down the cold length of the room. "It's not you. *I'm* defiled. I'm . . . God, if you knew."

"Tell me. Tell me. Do you think I won't understand? Haven't I told you there's nothing about you, nothing you could tell me that would make me think less of you?"

He stopped and spoke to the wall. "This would."

"Who was she, Hatherfield?" Stefanie spoke quietly, afraid to say the wrong word. "Who did this to you?"

He bent his head into the wood. "My stepmother."

Shock paralyzed Stefanie's throat. The room shifted about her, boats swimming past her eyes and ears, cold, damp air and her heartbeat like a distant crash in the center of it all.

"You see?" Hatherfield said. "I'm damned."

She forced herself to speak. "Tell me, Hatherfield. When did it happen?"

"It doesn't matter. It's done, it happened. There's no rewriting the page."

"It does matter. She hurt you. What did she do?"

He was silent.

"Tell me, Hatherfield."

"I've never told anyone."

"Then tell *me*. For God's sake. *Me*, Hatherfield. Stefanie, your Stefanie, standing next to you. I am not stainless. Please."

He braced both hands against the wall and spoke in a monotone, as if reading a page from a history book. "My mother died when I was five. Father married her a year or two later. I don't remember the early years very well. I was up in the nursery, the schoolroom, and she rarely came up. They had four little girls, my sisters, one after the other, and the last birth was difficult. I believe she nearly died; she was in bed for months. In any case, she couldn't have children after that. I was about twelve at that point, and when she recovered, when she was out and about again, she began . . . began to take notice of me."

Stefanie swallowed. "Noticed you?"

"She would tell me what a beautiful boy I was. My damned face. She would touch me, hug me, bring up sweets to the schoolroom. I had a tutor at that point. At first I didn't mind. I was so damned hungry, I hadn't had a mother in so long, my nanny was busy with the girls, and I . . . God, I just wanted a scrap, just a scrap of . . ."

"Of affection. Of love."

"Yes. Love." He soaked the word with irony. "So it was all very well, the hugs and sweets and affection, until she slipped into my room one night. To tuck me in, she said, as if one actually tucked thirteen-year-old boys into their beds at night. She said she wanted to look at me, to see how beautiful I was. I didn't know what to do. I hadn't had a mother since I was five, I didn't know what was normal."

"Oh, Hatherfield."

"It went on. She began touching me. Not every night, perhaps once a week she'd come in. And I hated it, and yet when she didn't come, I . . . I wondered why, wondered if she didn't care anymore. She played it all perfectly, I suppose. One night she took off her robe. I was fourteen, fifteen. By then I knew what she was getting at, and I was scared to death. Of her, of myself. I told her to go away. She said she would tell my father that I'd been making her do it, blackmailing her. She said she knew I wanted it. Then she put her hands on me and . . ." He shook his head. "My own stepmother, and I spent in her hand."

"You were a boy, Hatherfield."

"I was fifteen, Stefanie. Old enough and big enough to push her away, and I didn't. I couldn't. I was disgusted, and I couldn't stop, I couldn't, I let her do it. At that age, my God, a well-turned piano leg made me hard as stone. What was I supposed to do when a beautiful woman came to me at night and took off her clothes and . . ." His fist hit the wall. "I went off to Eton soon afterward, thank God. I couldn't even look at the other boys. I was dirty, I was different. *Oh, that beautiful Hatherfield, that golden creature, that angelic boy!* If only they knew."

"It wasn't you. It was her, she was the dirty one. You were a boy."

"Yes, but who would have believed my word against hers? Who would have believed I didn't want her there? I let her in. I let her in. I never said no." He shook his head. "I dreaded coming home during school holidays. I learned to make friends, so they would invite me to stay. I learned to put on a show, to play the proper role. Charming old Hatherfield. Just enough that everyone thought I was a regular chap, a good fellow to bring home to the old pile over Easter, or during the summer. When I did come to my own house, I prayed my father and the duchess wouldn't be there. That they'd be away in London and wouldn't send for me. Christmas was the worst. I couldn't avoid her at Christmas. I locked the door one year. She changed the lock, so it operated from the outside. She would come in and ask me if I'd met any girls, and what I had done with them."

"What did you tell her?"

"That I hadn't. Which was true, because I didn't dare, didn't trust myself even to look at a girl. I was seventeen when she got into bed with me. Boxing Day. I leapt out and ran for the door. She said she would scream for the servants, for my father. She actually started to scream."

The tears ran down Stefanie's cheeks. He hadn't moved from the wall. His hands still braced him up, as if his legs couldn't hold him. The sight of his bowed head pierced her with the purest agony. She walked toward him and stopped a few feet away, next to the wall. She knew better than to touch him.

"But I couldn't do it. I left. I ran out and went upstairs and hid in one of the old bedrooms in the servants' quarters. Nearly froze to death. In any case, I never spent another night under my father's roof. At some point I encountered Worthington, and he sheltered me from time to time, until I went to Oxford."

"And that's all. You were free."

He made a short bark of a laugh. "Free? Free of what? Free of sin, Stefanie? No, I was not. You see—and here's the irony—the very next time I went to stay with a friend, Easter it was, his mother seduced me in the conservatory Sunday afternoon, right after services, and that was that. Rather a relief, really. And it's a funny sort of pastime, because once begun, it carries on almost by itself, until you can't do without it. I'll spare you the details. Suffice to say, I made a career of it for a year or so, shagging restless matrons when they were available and visiting whores when they weren't. Not every night, I'd resist for weeks at a time, and then I'd go on a bender, two or three a night, one after another, sometimes all at once. I defiled myself in every possible way, I hated myself for it, but I couldn't stop. Eventually I got the clap, and *had* to stop for a bit, getting cured. That was about the time I met my friend Penhallow, Olympia's grandson . . ."

"My cousin Penhallow? Roland Penhallow?"

"Yes. Good fellow. He stroked for the Blues, and he told me I should try rowing, that I was built for it. So I did. I took it up with passion, and Penhallow took me in hand a bit. He was in his last year, frightfully clever, and he . . . well, he showed me it could be done. Being a decent fellow. Immersing myself in sport, in physical discipline. I stopped all the rest of it, I swear it. I never even . . ."

"Yes?" she said gently.

His arms relaxed at last. He laid his cheek against the wood, looking away from her. "Never even kissed a woman again, until you."

"Why not?"

"Because I couldn't. Couldn't trust myself not to . . . go back to what I was. And every time I got to flirting a bit, I would think, what if she knew? Knew what I'd done before. My own stepmother, my father's wife."

Stefanie shook her head. "It isn't what *you* did. It's what she did to you, when you were a lonely boy and she was a grown woman, someone with a sacred trust to protect you. You're not to blame."

"The fact is, it happened. I let it happen. And what I did after, all those women . . ."

Stefanie ventured a hand to his shoulder. "Listen to me. What you've told me, it's horrible. I want to put my hands around that woman's throat and strangle her. What she did to you, an innocent boy. How you've suffered, how you're suffering. But it doesn't change who you are, you radiant man, with your pure and magnificent soul, your immense and lonely heart. It was long ago, it's all past, and you have to grant yourself the forgiveness that God has long ago given you. Look at me, Hatherfield. Turn around and look at me."

He sighed and turned, and the misery stood there in his

exhausted face, so real and palpable that she moved forward without thinking and took him in her palms. The blanket slipped from her shoulders to the floor.

"Come to bed, Hatherfield."

He closed his eyes and shook his head, between her two hands.

"It will be different with us. You and I. What we do together, when we kiss, when we touch, it's right and good and beautiful. Because we are in love."

His eyes flashed open.

"Yes. It's true. And I need you, I need the comfort of your body, I need your strong arms and your passion. I suppose that's bold of me. I can't help it."

His mouth opened as if he wanted to say something, but not a word came out.

"I'm going upstairs now, Hatherfield. I won't seduce you, or beg you, or command you. I want you to decide for yourself. But I hope . . ." She swallowed back her fear and brushed his lips, very gently, with hers. "I hope with all my heart that you'll join me."

"Stefanie, wait . . ."

But she turned before he could speak, and made her way past all the silent boats to the stairway at the back of the room.

The Marquess of Hatherfield couldn't have said how long he stood there, in the midnight stillness, counting the boats on their horses, on their pegs along the walls. The air was still full of her, fragrant with the scent of Stefanie, echoing with her voice.

We are in love.

He spread his fingers out before him and stared at them. When he had first begun rowing, the pads of his hands were coated with ugly blisters, black and half healed, opened again the next morning. Eventually the calluses had formed, and they had never left. The only unsightly part of him. Whenever he thought about quitting the sport, or pausing for a few months over the winter, he remembered the agony of those first weeks on the water. How, if he relaxed his steely discipline even for a short while, the calluses would soften, his hands would grow tender once more, and he would have to relearn the pain all over again.

Above him, the wood creaked under the weight of Stefanie's footsteps. What was she doing? Readying herself for bed, perhaps. Making up the blankets and sheets, banking the fire. He closed his eyes and saw her before him again, naked except for her linen shirt, her breasts visible through the thin masculine material, unbearably erotic. He couldn't even look at her, while he had been reciting his sins. If she'd glanced down, she would have seen his arousal, his bone-rattling and barely contained desire for her.

What we do together, when we kiss, when we touch, it's right and good and beautiful.

To kiss her. To touch her. Hold her in his arms and make love to her. The heaven of it.

Because we are in love.

He opened his eyes and looked once more at his hands, his calloused and leathery hands, and without making a conscious decision, he walked to the stairs.

She was lying in the narrow bed. She sat up with a start when the door opened.

He opened his mouth to speak, and not a word came out. In lieu of speech, he removed his jacket and slung it over the chair. He unbuttoned his waistcoat, and laid that on top of the jacket. Piece by piece, layer by layer, he unclothed himself before her, studying her pale face against the dark wall, examining every telling movement of her body, waiting for the instant when the tide turned. When she found him unworthy.

But that instant didn't arrive. She gazed back with an expression of profound interest, one cat watching another, not moving a single muscle. The hushed glow from the fire illuminated her skin. He laid his stockings carefully over his folded trousers and reached for the end of his shirt, which tented over his raging erection with an abundance that might have provided shelter for a modest spring picnic.

He lifted the shirt over his head.

"Oh my God," whispered Stefanie. She rose to her knees and held out her arms.

He touched the very tips of his fingers to hers, pad to pad. "Tell me again. Say it again." His voice cracked alarmingly.

She pulled him in. "We are in love, Hatherfield. You and I, we're in love."

"Again."

"We are in love."

By some gargantuan effort of self-control, he kept the first kiss soft and featherlight, just tasting her generous lips, her sweet tongue. He drew his hands up her arms and tangled them in her hair. "Listen to me. I will try to be gentle . . ."

"It's all right. I'm sturdy."

"I know you are." He inhaled the scent of her hair, her skin, her warmth and delicate female roundness. "I don't think . . . once we start . . ."

Her hands caressed his back, his sides. "Once we start . . ." she whispered.

"I won't be able to stop."

"Then don't. Don't stop."

What he meant was that he would want her again, and again, and again; that his appetite was insatiable once he'd begun. But he pushed all that to the future and concentrated on the here and now of her, the present perfection beneath his hands and lips. He caressed her breasts through the fine linen of her shirt; he slid his thumbs across the velvet hardness of her nipples. He bent and covered one with his mouth, licking and then suckling it, while his cock pushed into her belly and her back arched toward him.

This woman. This Stefanie. He was going to have her at last. Take possession of that luscious body, and be taken in return.

The thought sent his blood shooting in his veins. He peeled back her shirt, up and over her head, and there she was, naked and blooming, her round breasts tilted toward him and her round hips cradling his stiffness.

He wasn't going to last. Already his stones were tingling, already the familiar flame was licking about the sensitive head of his cock. Stefanie's hands worked downward, reaching for him, and he grasped them just in time.

"You'll kill me," he said.

She looked up at his face, and whatever expression she saw there, Hatherfield feared to know: urgency, need, bestial desire. But she seemed to understand his predicament. She knit her fingers firmly with his and lowered herself back on the bed, drawing him with her, his heavy knees sinking between her legs, their hands linked together above her head. The sinful scent of her female arousal drifted up deliciously between them.

"Are you ready?" he managed.

God only knew what he would do if she said, *No, actually, not quite ready yet, kiss me a little longer.*

She lifted her knees and smiled. "Oh yes."

His prick was like solid iron, stiff and full. He was almost dizzy with the strength of his arousal. He brushed himself against her, and her readiness shocked him; she was slippery wet for him, her lips parted in an unerring channel that guided him home and clasped his tip. He braced himself above, poised, ready to strike.

"Oh God," she whispered. Her pleading eyes met his.

We are in love.

He slid inside her.

Ahhh, she groaned, long and luxurious, as he buried himself deep, a perfect fit, surrounding his cock from stem to stern with Stefanie. His mind went white with pleasure.

She was right. Of course she was right. How could he have doubted it? This was true and good and beautiful. This was Hatherfield joining himself to Stefanie, skin meeting skin, hand meeting hand, gaze meeting gaze, an act of loving union.

And at the same extraordinary instant, an act of pure carnal lust.

"Stefanie, I'm going to spend," he said.

She lifted her hips and dug her fingernails into the backs of his hands. The pain made an exquisite counterpoint to the ecstasy of penetration, holding his imminent climax just at bay. He pulled back and thrust again, and Stefanie cried out, and the sensation was so spectacularly good he did it again, and again, and again, until the pressure mounted so high he thought he would crack open. Stefanie's heels dug into the backs of his thighs, urging him faster, and this time there was no holding anything at bay, he was coming hard, he was coming *right now*, and he heard her call out his name, all drawn-out and singsong, *Haa-ther-field!*, and at that exact second, the climax rolled forth from his balls in long, reckless spurts.

TWENTY

Reason returned to Stefanie's brain in discrete little pings of awareness.

She smelled him first, warm and salty, his rapid breath tasting sweetly of kisses. She was surrounded with him, with the musky scent of sexual completion.

And then his hands. They were clasped in hers, high above her head, stretching her body to an exquisite sensitivity, a perfect vulnerability. Their fingers were twined together. Knotted in a vise.

And the rest of him, beautifully heavy, weighing her down into the mattress. He fit her just so, in the pocket of her torso, while her legs wrapped around his. His arms cradled her head; her ears fit neatly into the crooks of his elbows. His shoulders, tense with muscle, loomed like smooth-skinned hillsides near her lips. The warmth of his breath filled her hair.

She didn't move. She couldn't if she wanted to, and she didn't. She was pinned in bed by the Marquess of Hatherfield's magnificent body. Every sinew hummed, content with the echo of climax, like some sort of electromagnetic energy that kept on looping and looping about its circuit, held in place by the pressure of that rigid organ that still filled her below.

"Hatherfield," she whispered.

"Hmm."

"Are you awake?"

"Hmm. Of course I'm awake." Groggily.

"Your left hip bone . . . It's digging in just a bit . . ."

He shifted an inch. "Beg your pardon."

She waited for the flow of honeyed words, the praise and love, the vows of fidelity, the proposal of marriage, the honeymoon abroad, the hinted hope for children and grandchildren and pots of daffodils in the springtime.

Waited.

Waited.

Well, perhaps a small nudge was required.

"Hatherfield?"

"Mmm."

"That was lovely. That was . . ."—a word, a word, a word that would jolt him awake—"transcendent."

"Mmm."

"Magnificent. Divine. I would almost say sacred, if that isn't rather blasphemous, except that it *felt* like a sacrament to me, the two of us, consummating our passionate attachment with . . ."

An inaudible mumble.

"Yes, Hatherfield? You were going to say something?"

He lifted his head and kissed the tip of her nose. "I said, if you can come up with a word to describe all this, you're a better man than I am."

"Oh." She smiled. "Well done."

"Thank you." He pressed a lazy kiss to one corner of her mouth, and then the other.

An unfamiliar purring sound rose in her throat. She closed her eyes and absorbed him, his loving kisses, his warmth and weight and sensual beauty all draped atop her.

"You were right, however." he murmured, between kisses. "This was nothing like before. Different in every way."

"Stimulating?"

"Eternal." He kissed her ear.

"Earth-shattering."

"Life-giving." He was nibbling along the line of her jaw, kissing his way down her neck. His back arched effortlessly upward, the better to swirl his tongue in the hollow of her clavicle. "And completely insufficient for such a flesh-made sinner as myself. A man wholly and irrevocably in love with the most provocative woman in England."

"Hatherfield!"

"Mmm."

"You're still . . ."

"Ready and able. I'm well aware." He moved his hips and went on kissing her.

Her heartbeat rose to a flutter again. Her skin, already flushed, warmed anew. "You can't possibly mean to . . ."

"Yes."

"Without even . . ."

"Yes. Unless you have any objections." He released her hands and lifted himself away for an instant, just long enough to roll her over beneath him. He reached for the pillow, such as it was, and slipped it skillfully under her hips.

Her skin shivered, her limbs went heavy. Across the room, the molten glow of the fire roiled on the wall. "Well. If you must."

His hands closed around her hips and held her firmly in place. "I must, I'm afraid."

He parted her tender flesh and pushed deep, and the instant sensation of pleasure was so intense, so new and transformed from his penetration before, she cried out.

"All right?" he whispered in her ear.

"Yes!" She tilted up against him.

"I've dreamed of this. Every wretched night, since the day I met you, since the moment you tripped over that rug in Olympia's pile of ancient stone and landed at my feet." He began to move in a slow rhythm, holding her steady and helpless beneath him. Her hands clutched the end of the soft old mattress as her body accepted the thick invasion of his body. "Dreamed of you in my bed, beautiful as you are, your skin flushed and your throat making those lovely sounds as I drive my cock inside you." He spoke in a low voice, low and resonant and slow, in time with the thrusting of his body into hers, over and over, deeper and deeper, unbearably good.

Her hands curled into fists. "Faster, God, *please*, Hatherfield!"

"Oh no, my dear. Only just started."

She tried to push back, to hurry him along, but he wouldn't be tempted. He wouldn't stir from the controlled and massive beat of his lovemaking, as if he were stroking his boat in a marathon race and meant to finish every yard of it. She pictured his magnificent body upright behind her, his sinews flexing, his muscular hips thrusting against her bottom, and another howl escaped her.

"Don't fight it, Stefanie. Trust me. Just take me, take me all in. Let me show you what you can do." But his voice traveled on the edge of a razor. His hands gripped her hips as if to save his own life.

"I can't. I can't. Please."

"You can. Just take me in."

Oh God, it was good. It was so bloody, infinitely good. Each thrust struck her belly and radiated outward to her toes, to her fingertips. She couldn't move, she couldn't think. She could only open herself and receive him. Only accept the brute pleasure he delivered inside her.

She sobbed, "My God, I can't bear it, how can you bear this?"

He growled in her ear, "I warned you."

She squirmed her bottom into the cradle of his thrusting hips, begging for release, unable to endure the endlessly building ecstasy. She would die of it, she would shatter into a million pieces of exiled princess, each one pulsing with the relentless energy of Hatherfield's love.

He was right. He *had* warned her.

Once we start, I won't be able to stop.

What the devil had she gotten herself into?

An hour later, a lifetime later, she lay in a stupor in his arms, damp and hot and nearly senseless.

"You're insatiable." She tried to say it, but all she could manage was a humiliatingly raspy whisper.

"That's what I was trying to explain, before. You didn't seem to understand. I thought it best if I showed you instead."

"I hope you're not planning to do that again."

"Not for at least another twenty-four hours. You need your strength."

She turned her head into his shoulder. Her arm lay across his stomach. In the silence, she could hear his heartbeat, could actually feel it thud in a slow cadence against her eardrum. Hatherfield's heartbeat, his precious blood, his life flowing next to hers.

"In the meantime, I'll endeavor to go a bit easier on you," he went on. "Gentle as a lamb nibbling his favorite spring grass."

Stefanie swallowed.

"In the meantime?"

"Unless you'd rather waste your time sleeping."

"I would, rather," she murmured. "For just a few minutes. Please."

He laughed and stroked her hair. "You invited me, remember. I'm only indulging your wishes to the best of my humble ability."

She pinched his ribs. A slap would have been more effective, but it was all she could muster.

He laughed again and settled her even closer. If she closed her eyes, she could almost imagine slipping through his skin and merging herself with him, her luminous Hatherfield.

"I do mean it, you know," he said softly.

"Mean what?"

"I *am* insatiable. Base and carnal and rapacious. I want you again already. I can control myself—God knows I've had years of practice—but it's there. It's inside me, it's who I am. I want you so much, it strangles me. I want to take you day and night, in every possible way. I want to give you pleasure over and over. I want to have you again and again, until I'm stone dry."

Impossibly, something stirred inside her belly.

"Then have me."

"No." He kissed her hair. "You need rest. And we have a lifetime."

A coal popped in the fireplace. Stefanie's finger, which had been inscribing circles around the smooth skin of Hatherfield's gleaming left pectoral, dragged to a halt.

"A lifetime?" she whispered.

"My dear. I am insulted. Do you really think me so unscrupulous as to lie with you, to spend myself inside you, without offering my own hand in return?"

She summoned what little energy she owned and pushed

herself upward on his chest. "Hatherfield, I hope you don't feel obliged by all this. There are no chains attached to my bed, I assure you."

"Look. In the first place, this isn't your bed . . ."

"It is tonight," she said with dignity.

"And in the second place, I can't speak for your own intentions, my love, but as far as I'm concerned, this act of concourse in which we have now engaged twice . . ."

"Oh, is that how you describe it?"

"This—ahem—this transcendent act of ours, I happen to consider in the same nature as a sacred vow."

The word *vow* struck her dumb.

He tucked her hair over one ear. "A vow of loyalty, of fidelity. Of my constant devotion and protection, until death."

A stinging ache spread across the backs of her eyeballs. She tried to blink away the sensation, but it persisted stubbornly and spread to her throat.

"Oh," she whispered.

"As I said, I can't speak for your intentions. God knows you're the most unconventional woman I've ever met. But I want to be quite clear about *my* intentions."

His large and calloused hand spread gently across the small of her back. His eyes searched hers, unrelenting; she wanted to look away, but how could she break the spell of that fulminant blue gaze?

Hatherfield did it for her. He turned her head back into his shoulder and settled her in the shelter of his body. His voice was soft. "As I said, there's no hurry. Rest now."

Her body agreed. She knew that she was tired, she knew that she was sleepy. Hatherfield was so solid and delicious, and the bed so narrow, and the scratchy wool blankets made such a marvelous cocoon.

If only her mind would stop jumping about.

"Hatherfield."

His hand ran along her arm, delicate as a feather. "Yes, love?"

"How have you done it, all these years?"

"Done what?"

She laid her hand flat on his chest and stared at her fingers. "You're more cleverly disguised than I am, aren't you? No one knows. No one even suspects how passionate you are, how enormous your heart is. How much is packed inside that golden shell of yours. That angel's face."

He picked up her hand and kissed it. "Shh, now. Go to sleep. God knows you'll need it tomorrow."

Hatherfield woke before dawn, as always. But instead of startling awake in the grip of an unsettling dream, instead of lying there on his back while his heart pounded blackly in his throat, he simply . . . opened his eyes.

And saw her.

His princess. Tucked up against him, her back curving into his chest, her bottom snuggled into the hard cave of his lower belly. The fire was nearly out, and only a faint hint of ambient light drifted through the window glass, so he couldn't make out any details. Only his own arm draped possessively across her breasts, and the tip of her nose picking up a silvery gleam from some unknown source.

The familiar surge of desire enlarged his prick, but he ignored that. He breathed silently into her hair, not moving, not wanting to wake her. If she didn't wake, the day wouldn't begin. If the day didn't begin, their idyll would remain intact, and no unknown danger would lurk outside on the doorstep, no jumbled barricade of obstacles to their future together: her station, his family; her disguise, his past; Worthington and Olympia, Lady Charlotte and the Revolutionary Brigade of the Free Blood.

And just like that, the thought of those obstacles snapped his rosy contentment. His muscles flexed around her. The instinct to protect.

She was deeply asleep, her body utterly slack and trusting in the shelter of his own. His princess. His precious Stefanie, full of his love and his seed, who had given herself to him with such willing passion in the dark hours of the night, and taken everything he had in return.

He had made his choice. He had crossed the Rubicon. He had staked his all now, and there was no turning back.

In reluctant movements, he disengaged himself from her and slipped from the bed. He tucked the blanket around her and spread another one on top. He added a few coals to the fire and went downstairs for water.

When he returned to the room twenty minutes later, having coaxed the coal stove to its duty and heated two steaming pails, Stefanie was still asleep, clutching the pillow to her chest. He smiled at the sight. What if his future contained a thousand such moments, ten thousand mornings with a tousled Stefanie sleeping off a night's passion in his bed?

Was it possible? Could he be so fortunate?

"Wake up, sleepyhead," he called softly.

She mumbled a decidedly vulgar response.

"Ah. Not now, I'm afraid. Though the prospect is tempting, in an exotic sort of way." He brushed the hair from her face and kissed her lips. "I've brought your bath."

Her eyes blinked open. "Bath?"

"Well, not a proper bath. Strictly speaking, we have no tub, and the boiler for the showers takes ages to heat sufficiently after a long winter's nap. But I've hot water and a bit of soap and a towel." He gave her bottom a squeeze through the blankets. "Come along, now."

"You're sadistic."

"Only if you beg me."

She turned on her stomach and buried her face in the pillow. He laughed, tugged the blanket downward, and picked her up and over his shoulder in a single swing of creamy royal limbs.

She flailed. As well she might.

"You know, I'm beginning to suspect you're not an early riser by nature, my love."

"Not when I've been kept awake all bloody night, serving your endless beastly needs!" She wriggled her provocative bottom under his hand.

"I protest. Not all night, by any means. If I had, you wouldn't be able to stand." He set her down on the rug before the fire and ducked the soap into the first pail, working up a good lather.

"You're not going to *bathe* me!"

"With the most loving hands in the world." He lifted his soapy fingers to her breasts. "We can't have you waltzing into Worthington's worthy chambers at half eight in the morning, scented with musty blankets and carnal lust."

"Oh." She closed her eyes. "Well, perhaps not."

He washed her carefully, missing not a single curve or

crevice of her body, not a single tender inch, and then he stroked her clean with water from the second pail, until she was naked and rosy and shivering under his gentle hands, and the rug beneath them was thoroughly wet. For an instant, he imagined spreading her satiny new body out before the fire. He imagined stroking his tongue over the delicate anatomy between her legs, until she arched under his lips and sounded her barbaric cry of release, and then rising up to push his eager prick inside her and watch her face transform in the red gold glow from the coals.

He picked up the towel and wrapped her from chin to knee.

"Hatherfield." She was a little breathless. "Can't we . . . ?"

"Can't we what?"

"Please."

He kissed her forehead. "There's no time. The other chaps might start turning up any minute. It's nearly spring. The Boat Race is in a few weeks, and everybody's coming back to the fold."

She put her arms around his neck. "I'll be quick."

"Trust me, this pains me more than it pains you. As you can plainly see."

She breathed into the side of his throat. Her linen-draped breasts touched his naked chest. "Hatherfield. Then let me touch you."

He shut his eyes. His lips slipped against her silken hair. "We don't have time, my dear."

"All last night, we did the most intimate things together. We gave each other such joy. You've touched me everywhere, seen me everywhere, kissed me everywhere. I just want to *know* you, every inch of you."

His knees sank into the soaking rug. Stefanie's soft body fit into his arms, fresh and pure and smelling of soap. Her long-fingered hands rested against his chest. He was as hard as stone, as thick as a tree, as hot as a coal.

"Hatherfield, please. Let me worship you."

He rose to his feet. "Let's find your clothes."

H e managed to bring her back to Cadogan Square and through her third-floor window before the maid had come in to lay the fire.

"How am I supposed to sit next to you at breakfast, as if nothing's happened?" she said.

He produced a fresh shirt and collar from her drawer and unbuttoned her jacket. "That's easy enough. I won't be at breakfast this morning." He drew the crumpled old shirt up and over her head.

She snatched the long linen strip from her chest of drawers and wrapped it around her chest. "What? Why not?"

He was already popping the new shirt over her head, already stuffing the ends into her trousers. "I have a number of calls to pay this morning."

"What sort of calls? And I can dress myself, by the way."

"When I'm enjoying myself so thoroughly?" He pushed her hands away and attached her collar, and then he turned her around before the mirror and threaded her necktie underneath. "To answer your question, I shall first visit His Grace, the Duke of Ashland, and then His other Grace, the Duke of Olympia. And then I've got to bite the proverbial bullet and seek audience with His bloody damned Grace, my father, the Duke of Southam, during his party tonight."

"Why?" She was watching his expert hands in the mirror, as they folded her necktie. Her breath was becoming rather shallow.

"In the case of my father, because I have a certain matter to take up with him, related to my Hammersmith project. In the case of the other two, because I can no longer ignore the rather pressing need to track down this damned group of anarchists who attempted to kill you last night."

She spun in his arms. "You won't! You can't put yourself in danger like that. It's not your fight."

"If not mine, then whose?"

"My uncle and Miss Dingleby."

"Forgive me, but I believe they've had time enough to sort things out on their own. I want these men caught immediately and put somewhere—six feet underground, if possible—where they're no longer in a position to harm a single hair of your head."

"But I'm not in any danger. Not if I stay hidden."

He turned her around and wrapped his arms around her waist. Their tangled reflections gazed back at him, shirtsleeve against shirtsleeve, his broad forearms white against her dark waistcoat. "You can't stay hidden forever, you know."

"I know," she said quietly.

"Particularly if any consequences arise from our reckless night's work."

Her eyes in the mirror went wide and shocked.

"You hadn't considered that possibility?" he asked gently.

She whispered, "Yes, of course. But you needn't say it out loud."

He glanced at the clock. Five minutes to seven. He dropped a kiss on her temple and made for the open window. "I've got to leave, and you have breakfast down below, to say nothing of the conclusion of your case in court today. I've asked my driver to keep a close watch on you. He'll follow you and Sir John about in the hansom; discreetly, of course. He's well trained. You'll be in good hands. I'll return at nine o'clock to take you to the party. And for God's sake, keep your head down and your voice deep."

"But how are you to travel about town today?"

He angled himself through the window and turned to her with a last broad wink.

"Why, I'll take the Underground, of course. And Stefanie, my dearest?"

"Yes?"

"Don't forget your mustache."

TWENTY-ONE

His Grace, the Duke of Ashland, regarded the notes before him with a critical eye.

Eye, singular, for the duke possessed only one. The other had been blown from his face in the mountains of Afghanistan over a dozen years ago, and the empty socket sat beneath a black leather half-mask that lent his formerly handsome features a distinctly piratical flavor.

The remaining eye, however, was keen and blue and missed nothing. He raised his head and said, "The handwriting bears certain characteristics of the German Gothic script, don't you think?"

Hatherfield nodded. "My thought exactly. Do you recognize the hand?"

"No." The duke looked back down at the letters and adjusted one to a more perfect longitude against its fellows. Adjusted it with his left hand, for his right—like its corresponding eye—no longer existed, another casualty of clandestine warfare. "But I'm no expert in this damned organization. I do have my suspicions."

"Who?"

"There's a fellow who keeps watch over the house in Park

Lane. Hans, the old Prince's valet. Emilie swears to his fidelity—so does Dingleby—but I take nothing for granted."

"I'll investigate, then."

Ashland drummed his fingers on the edge of the desk. They were sitting in the study of his newly leased house in Eaton Square—the dukes of Ashland never had been much for town life—and the room lacked a certain air of lived-in comfort, to say nothing of furniture. Hatherfield perched on the edge of a rickety wooden chair that looked as if it had just been hauled hastily down from an attic for the occasion, while Ashland's desk gleamed with the sharp-edged newness of a shop room floor. The duke himself rested his massive six-and-a-half-foot frame on a leather-seated chair that might have looked substantial beneath any other man.

"There's no time for investigation," he said at last. A rare patch of late February sunshine rested on his close-cropped silvery hair, turning it brilliant. "Our engagement ball is tonight, lavish affair, Prince and Princess of Wales and all that. A tempting target, deliberately so, and we hope to catch the perpetrators in the act and end all this rubbish once and for all."

Hatherfield let out a long breath and turned his head to the window, overlooking the garden, where a groundskeeper was hard at work laying out fresh beds near the mews. Spring, just around the corner. "I suspected as much. Dashed risky, however."

"I shall be glad when it's over."

He turned back to Ashland. "What can I do, then?"

The duke's pale blue gaze locked with his. "Stay with the princess tonight. Do not, under any circumstances, let her out of your sight. I understand she has a reputation for impetuousness . . ."

"Perish the thought."

"See to it that she acquires no notions of presenting herself in Park Lane. Occupy her by whatever means you deem most effective." A certain emphasis on the word *occupy*.

Hatherfield coughed. "As it happens, my parents are holding a party of their own tonight, in protest at not having been invited."

"Good. Take her there and keep her busy."

"Exactly what I intended to do. But in the meantime . . ."

"It's too late to bring you into our plans, Hatherfield, or I would ask for your help. I've heard the most extraordinary praise of your abilities. But if things go awry, I hope I may count on your immediate aid." He rose and held out his left hand.

Hatherfield came to his feet and shook it. "We'll be in Belgrave Square, at the Duke of Southam's house. But are you certain?"

"Yes."

"Damn it all, I can't stand to sit around and wait . . ."

"Of course not. I daresay you're ready to punch the walls out. I don't blame you. But your task, your sole object, is to guard Stefanie. As mine is to guard Emilie, may God help us both."

"And the other sister?"

"Olympia won't say."

Hatherfield sighed. "I don't know whether to damn the old bastard or bless him."

Without warning, Ashland burst into laughter, a warm, rich laugh from the bottom of his chest. "Both, my friend. Both in the same breath."

Not guilty.

Stefanie accepted the celebratory glass of Madeira from Sir John's own hands; from what source he'd obtained it, she had no idea. They were sitting with the accused—the newly free accused—in a small anteroom at the Old Bailey, and Mr. Northcote grinned broadly as Sir John handed him a brimming glass of his own.

"Not guilty," repeated Sir John. "I congratulate you, sir."

"Ah, now, that's the stuff. Thank you kindly, Sir John." Northcote stopped smiling long enough to take a long draught of Madeira. "A relief, it is. Though I don't know what I'm to do next. Hardly seems fit to gather rubbish after all this."

"Any honest labor does merit to the man who performs it." Sir John finished off his own glass and gathered up his papers. "If you'll excuse me. I have a few matters to address with the court. The formalities of release and so on. You will wait here with Mr. Northcote, Mr. Thomas, until I return."

"Yes, sir." Stefanie set down her glass and looked across the wooden table at Mr. Northcote, who was polishing off his

Madeira with relish. She had never quite liked the man. It wasn't his lowly station—she had rubbed shoulders with all sorts in her madcap escapades back in Germany, and knew they were all made of the same clay flesh—but rather his manner. He hadn't yet thanked either her or Sir John for their efforts on his behalf, not once, though the Madeira had earned his appreciation. He had sat there throughout the proceedings with a slight smirk at the corner of his mouth, when he thought no one was watching.

Even now. Madeira finished, he stood from his chair and walked to the desk in the corner and picked up the bottle to refill his glass. "Good stuff, innit?" he said.

"Indeed." Stefanie took another small sip.

"Lord, I'm chuffed." He turned around and leaned against the table. He was wearing a brown suit, cheap but neat, and his shoes were polished. He pushed a greasy strand of hair from his forehead. "Did you see his face when they read the verdict? I looked over directly."

"Whose face?"

"Why, Hammond's, of course." Hammond was the wronged husband. "As black as sin, he was. I daresay she gets a good smacking tonight, when she's back home with him."

"I hope not. The matter has brought enough grief to all parties."

He threw back his head. "Oh, no doubt of that! No doubt at all. The way she carried on, when I first climbed in with her of a morning. Weeping fit to raise the dead."

Stefanie straightened in her chair. "What's that?"

"It took her a month at least to settle down proper and spread her legs nice and quiet-like." He shook his head. "And then when she was on the stand last week, wringing her hankie like it was the end of the blooming world. I thought we was done for. Good on you, Mr. Thomas. Good on the both of you for straightening out that jury afterward."

The edges of Stefanie's vision grew white and blurred.

Who would have believed my word against hers? Who would have believed I didn't want her there?

"Ha-ha," Northcote was saying. "Her face, when she heard them words. *Not guilty.* She knew what she were in for, that's . . ."

But he had no chance to finish his sentence. Stefanie had

marched across the room, grabbed the bottle of Madeira, and upended it over his greasy head.

"You, sir, are a disgrace," she said, and she left the room with a rattling bang of the door to await Sir John's arrival outside.

In the carriage afterward, they were both quiet. Sir John consulted his notes, and Stefanie stared out the window at the damp gray landscape, the gloomy passing London.

If only she'd paid closer attention. If only she'd given this case a fuller share of her attention, amid all the briefs and studying and escapades with Hatherfield. If only she'd been allowed to interview him herself.

In a few hours, she would be readying herself for a splendid ball, a marvelous party on the arm of the handsomest and most dashing man in the world. A mile or two away, her sister would be celebrating her engagement to an English duke, and the threat that loomed over them both, holding them prisoner, would—if all went well—be extinguished. She would be free to resume her old life, or something like it; free, perhaps, to begin a new life with Hatherfield. Heal his wounds and make him happy. The two of them, happy and rich and fruitful, while Mrs. Hammond endured the shame and disgrace and physical retribution of Northcote's *Not Guilty*.

"Did you know he was lying?"

Sir John looked up. His reading glasses perched precariously at the pink tip of his nose. "I beg your pardon?"

"Northcote. That he was guilty all along."

Sir John sighed and took off his glasses.

"I see," she said, and turned away.

"My dear Thomas," said Sir John, "our duty is to secure for the prisoner the very best legal representation."

"What about justice?"

"The British legal system is organized on the principle that justice is not perfect. That it's better to let a guilty man go unpunished than to let an innocent man be convicted for a crime he did not commit."

"I daresay Mrs. Hammond would beg to differ." Despite the dank air inside the carriage, Stefanie was growing warm beneath her clothes. *Stay calm*, she told herself. *Steady your feelings.*

"It's not our business whether Northcote is guilty or not, Mr. Thomas. In the absence of competent legal defense for all, the highest and the lowest, impartial and without regard for politics and station and wealth, we leave ourselves vulnerable to tyranny. Would you like to see an innocent man hanged because he could not stand against the might of his accusers?"

"I don't know how you can live with yourself," she said. "How can you look at Mrs. Hammond's face and live with yourself?"

With a desperate clatter of wheels against pavement, the carriage careered past a delivery van and around Hyde Park Corner. Sir John Worthington replaced his spectacles and turned back to his papers. "I begin to wonder, Mr. Thomas, if perhaps you might wish to reconsider your choice of profession."

The entry of Mr. Nathaniel Wright into the hallowed precincts of the Sportsmen's Club library on St. James, at a quarter past five in the afternoon, caused a ripple of shock to pass across the leather-scented membership.

I say, someone muttered indignantly.

Hatherfield rose from his armchair and held out his hand. "Ah! Mr. Wright. Jolly obliging of you to meet me here this afternoon. All sorts of affairs vying for your attention, I'm sure. I hope the Stock Exchange hasn't been set in a panic by your absence, or I should never forgive myself." He indicated the neighboring chair.

Mr. Wright shook his hand briefly and sat in the offered seat. "Trading is now concluded for the day, Lord Hatherfield. Pray relieve your mind of the burden." His eyes dropped to Hatherfield's waistcoat.

"Do you like it?" Hatherfield spread the ends of his jacket farther apart. "Purple's such a happy color, don't you think?"

"Indeed. The floral motif is abundantly pastoral. But I shall not delay you. I understand you have a ball this evening, for which to ready yourself."

"Why, yes! So I have. Clever chap. How did you know?"

"Because I shall be in attendance myself, of course."

"Ah! The Duchess of Southam's ball. What a delightful coincidence." Hatherfield spotted a waiter and signaled. "What color mask will you be wearing?"

"Mask, sir?"

"Mask. For the mas-quer-ade." Hatherfield said it slowly, for emphasis. "Traditional sort of nonsense, common among us vain aristocrats. Chases away the old ennui for a moment or two, I suppose. I'm thinking of wearing gold, myself. I do fancy a bit of sparkle."

"I see. Is it quite necessary?"

"They do come in handy, from time to time." Hatherfield winked.

"I suppose I'll find something, then." A waiter arrived, plunking two disdainful glasses of sherry between them. Wright picked up one of them and wet his lips with it. "Well, sir? I own myself curious. Why did the Marquess of Hatherfield invite me to his club this afternoon?"

"Oh yes. That. Had almost forgotten. This frivolous little noggin of mine. You see, Mr. Wright, the oddest thing happened to me yesterday"—good Lord, was it only yesterday?—"when I traveled to Hammersmith to inspect my little project."

"Your cottages, I believe?"

"My cottages. Houses, really. A terrace of them, snug and well built and coming along nicely, the entire endeavor perfectly planned with funds to spare. So imagine my dismay—horror, even—when my building manager informed me that my financial credit has been maligned from Richmond Bridge to the Solent."

"How unfortunate."

"Yes, isn't it? Credit is a delicate thing, as delicate as a lady's reputation. The slightest hint from the wrong quarter, and—poof." Hatherfield snapped his fingers.

"Poof, indeed." A trace of weight on the *poof.*

Hatherfield sat back in his seat and let his sherry glass dangle from his fingertips. He gazed at the famous carved Sportsmen's Club marble work, twenty feet above. "One feels so wronged, when such a false report circulates. One feels an almost unnatural rage. As if one might be capable of violence."

"I beg leave to point out that the Southam coffers are widely understood to be quite dry."

"But the Southam coffers have nothing to do with my project. Except to be filled by the proceeds, in due course."

Wright shrugged his shoulders. "As you said, credit is a delicate thing. Rumor runs rampant. Perhaps the report of an infusion of substantial funds might satisfy the nerves of your creditors."

"My dear Mr. Wright, I have no creditors. Every vendor has been paid in full."

"And the bank that holds the loan? You're confident it will not be persuaded to call in its capital?" Wright sat perfectly still, thick arms crossed, sherry sitting untouched before him since that first polite sip. His dark eyes looked as if they were made of granite.

Hatherfield lifted his hand and drained his sherry. He set the empty glass on the table between them, right next to Wright's full one, and rose to his feet. When he spoke, he pitched his voice low, without a trace of its customary negligent drawl.

"For a man who makes his living by judging the characters of others," he said, "you seem to have underestimated mine to a remarkable degree. Until tonight, Mr. Wright."

He turned and walked out the door, leaving Nathaniel Wright to face the curious hostility of the aristocratic Sportsmen's Club library alone.

Stefanie was standing next to the piano in the Cadogan Square music room, dressed in her formal starched black-and-white best, dragging her fingers over the sweep of ivory keys, when Lady Charlotte rushed through the doorway.

"There you are! Oh, Mr. Thomas! The most dreadful news!" Her eyes were wild and red rimmed. From one fist dangled a crumpled white paper.

Stefanie straightened. "Dear me. Has the ball been canceled?"

"Oh, don't joke! It's horrible!" She gazed up at the ceiling, her face wrenched in grief. She whispered, "It's Hatherfield. He's been killed."

"What?" Stefanie grabbed the edge of the piano to keep herself from falling. She was suddenly conscious of the smell of Lady Charlotte's hothouse flowers, sending off clouds of sickly sweetness from the crystal vase in the center of the gleaming black piano case. "No, it's not true. It's not."

Tears rolled down Lady Charlotte's pallid cheeks. She held up her hand, the hand with the paper. "It is! Would to God it weren't. A delivery van in Piccadilly. He stepped right in front of it. Oh God!"

The room swayed. Tiny black dots appeared in the center of Stefanie's vision. Impossible. She had just seen him. She had woken in his arms that morning; he had bathed her with his own hands. He had knotted her necktie and kissed her good-bye and ducked through her window.

"Dead!" moaned Lady Charlotte. She fell to her knees and put her face in her hands.

Stefanie's legs crumpled beneath her. She caught herself just in time. "It's not true," she said again.

"It's true, it's true."

Stefanie shut her eyes.

"You grieve?" whispered her ladyship.

Hatherfield dead. No. It couldn't be.

She moved her lips. "I will grieve forever."

She lowered herself onto the piano bench. She could not stop the whirling of blood in her ears, blocking her reason. She concentrated on her breathing, as Miss Dingleby had always instructed her to do in moments of shock: in, out.

In, out.

It couldn't be true. Hatherfield dead. It couldn't. Surely her own heart would have stopped beating, in the same instant.

Lady Charlotte whispered, "It's true. You love him. It's true."

Stefanie opened her eyes. Lady Charlotte was staring at her with a strange expression, an odd feral look, her eyes so wide the whites showed all around her dark irises. She was resplendent in her ball gown, a frothy pink so pale it was almost white, and a circle of pearls gleamed richly from the base of her pale throat.

"I? No, no . . ."

Lady Charlotte scrambled to her feet. "What if I tell you that it isn't true? That I made it all up?"

"What?"

"He lives. Hatherfield lives."

"He lives!"

Lady Charlotte gestured to the paper. "He's delayed, he's going to meet us there. There was no accident."

For a precarious second, her words dangled in the air.

There was no accident.

Hatherfield lives.

"Oh God! Oh, thank God!" The tears spilled without warning from Stefanie's eyes; she stabbed at them furiously with her shaking fingers, trying to stem the tide of hysterical relief. "Thank God! Thank God!"

"You do, then. You do love him."

Stefanie sprang to her feet. "How dare you! A trick, you tricked me, the basest trick . . ."

Lady Charlotte drew herself up. "*I* dare? You're the one who dares, you wicked thing, corrupting his pure heart with your disgusting lust. After all we've done for you! Wicked, wicked man!"

"Give me that paper."

Lady Charlotte pulled her arm away. "No!"

"Give me that paper!" Stefanie lunged forward and snatched it away from her.

"Wicked man. Don't you know who your rival is? You can't stand against me. You can't stand against what is right and good."

Stefanie turned her back and unfolded the crumpled paper. *Mr. Stephen Thomas*, it said, in Hatherfield's bold hand, and then a broken wax seal.

"It was addressed to me," Stefanie said. "You opened my note."

"Wicked man."

My dear, I've had a few unexpected matters encroach on my attention, and must beg you to travel to Belgrave Square with Sir J and Lady C instead. Will find you there and never leave your side. Last night was a miracle. Yours always, H.

"Yes, it's true. I love him," Stefanie whispered.

"You dare to admit it."

Stefanie turned. "I dare. I love him. I love him beyond reason."

"Oh, you wicked, wicked man," whispered Lady Charlotte. "I will destroy you, do you understand me? You cannot take this away from me."

Stefanie met her blazing eyes without flinching. "I don't understand. Why do this? You're happy, you're powerful. You're the child of good fortune, you have everything in this life."

Sir John's voice boomed through the doorway. "Charlotte, my dear! Mr. Thomas! The carriage is outside, for God's sake. We shall be *late*!"

As he might say, *We shall be showered in dung!*

Lady Charlotte's gaze remained locked on Stefanie. "Do you hear that? We're going to a duke's house, Thomas. My friends, the Duke and Duchess of Southam, Hatherfield's parents. They want me to marry him."

"Hatherfield is his own agent."

"There will be music and dancing. You will watch me dance with Hatherfield, you'll see how beautiful we look together. Everyone will be looking at me, Thomas. At *me*. Because I am the daughter of an earl, and you are nothing. You are a clerk. You are the dust under my slippers."

Stefanie took a single step closer. The faint smell of rose water caught the edge of her senses, drifting from Lady Charlotte's flawless skin. "Am I, your ladyship?" she whispered. "Are you quite sure of that?"

"I will be celebrated, and you will not. I'll be married to Hatherfield in a month's time, and you will have nothing. Nothing, do you hear me?"

"Charlotte! Mr. Thomas!" Sir John burst through the door. "What the dev—What in heaven's name is going on here?"

Charlotte turned. "Nothing, Sir John. Nothing at all. Mr. Thomas, are you quite ready?"

Stefanie returned to the piano. The air was a little cooler, so close to the window, and it soothed her burning cheeks. "Oh, the two of you go on without me. I find I have an unfinished task to perform, after all. Shall join you there shortly."

"A task? What sort of task?"

Stefanie sat on the bench and drew her hands over the keys. How long had it been since she had last played? Three months?

Four? She settled her fingers into the opening notes of the
Appassionata.

Lady Charlotte laughed. "I suppose Mr. Thomas has simply lost his nerve for the occasion. Isn't that right, Thomas?"

Sir John let out an exasperated sigh. "Regardless, we've got
to leave at once. You'll follow along later, Mr. Thomas?"

Stefanie went on playing.

"Rely upon it, Sir John."

When the front door closed with a bang, Stefanie rose from
the piano and lowered the cover over the keys. She put out the
lamp and climbed the stairs, two at a time, to her room on
the third floor.

A package sat unwrapped upon the bed, its brown paper
spreading out in stiff folds from the silvery contents. Stefanie
had discovered it upon her return home from court, right there
in the center of the woolen blanket, with a card slipped
beneath the string holding the parcel together.

Stefanie fingered the folded garments: chemise, corset, petticoats, stockings, a gown made of some silver gossamer that
shimmered in the lamplight. A pair of dainty silver shoes. A
spray of brilliants in a comb.

On top of it all, a silver mask.

She picked up the note and read it again.

*A princess should always appear to her best advantage
at a ball, even when hidden in disguise. Enjoy yourself
this evening. D.*

D. Miss Dingleby. God bless her from head to toe.

TWENTY-TWO

Old Bailey
August 1890

The cell occupied by the Marquess of Hatherfield in the historic depths of the Old Bailey Prison was, all things considered, not all that wretched an abode. He'd been allowed a few comforts of home: desk, chair, books in abundance. He'd made friends early on with the guards, and they left him to his business. When Stefanie came to visit, dressed soberly as the clerk to Mr. Benedict Fairchurch, Esquire, they allowed the two of them space and privacy and all the time in the world.

Which they spent going over the case, the progress of Southam Terrace, and sundry other business matters.

Still. She was there, she was within reach. He could drink in the comfort of her presence, could meet her eye from time to time. Could even, for a minute or two, hold her hand under the square table at which they worked, fingers tightly curled, so still and so close he could feel the tiny beat of her pulse through his fingertips. So perfectly united, it was almost worth the physical pain of separation when she stripped her hand away and rose from the table, eyes shining wet, and gathered her books and papers.

You shouldn't do this, he would whisper. *You should go back home.*

I have no home. You're all there is left.

After she left, he would pace the stone walls of his cell, from wall to wall. Where was Olympia? Where was this Dingleby of theirs? He'd written letters, he'd made every inquiry he could think of. Even bloody Lord Roland Penhallow was nowhere to be found. Ashland and Emilie were away on the far side of the world, enjoying a honeymoon in ignorant wedded bliss.

It was as if the entire universe had abandoned them.

He began to punch the wall in helpless fury. The pain of his bruised knuckles did nothing to ease his despair, but at least he was doing something. He was committing an act, instead of lying in his bed, staring at the ceiling, turning everything over in his mind. The soul-shredding worry for Stefanie, disguised as she was; the knowledge that any moment, some member of the Revolutionary Brigade of the Free Blood might discover her, harm her, and he could do nothing about it.

Tonight was the worst. He had fought with her, actually fought. "Don't you see? If you don't tell them everything, everything, you might be convicted," she said.

"By God, I won't say anything in that courtroom that will put you in danger! Your life's at stake!"

"Your life is at stake!" She said it in a low, intense voice, mindful of the nearby guards.

"I will not win my freedom at your expense. I gave your uncle my word . . ."

"Olympia's gone. Everyone's gone. Don't you see?" She laid her hand flat on the table, and her fingers were shaking. "I can't lose you. I'll go into that witness box myself, if you hold anything back that might save you."

He'd laid his hand on hers. "No, you won't. Just trust me, won't you? Trust that I can do this. I can give the jury what they need, without exposing you. I can do it, Stefanie. I can win them over."

She'd pulled her hand away and risen from the table. "Why the devil, Hatherfield, do you have to be so bloody noble? Do you know what it would do to me, if they hanged you?"

"They won't hang me."

She had gathered her things and left without another word. After the door closed behind her and her scent had dissolved, after throwing three good punches to three separate gray

white stones, Hatherfield braced himself against the abused
wall, head down, panting, and prayed.

Prayed that his testimony tomorrow would turn the tide.

Prayed that he could save himself without revealing Stefanie's secrets.

Hatherfield at his most charming. Hatherfield at his most
convincing. Nothing to see here but a careless garden-variety
aristocrat, a good-natured chap with nothing but sunshine
lighting his soul.

A peremptory knock rattled the door of his cell, and then
the jingle of keys in the lock.

"Visitor, yer lordship!" the guard said cheerfully.

Hatherfield lifted his head. His insides drowned in relief.
Thank God. She was back. He could see her again. Perhaps
touch her hand again—her single sweet hand, when he had
once held her entire body in his arms, had made love to her,
had fallen asleep to the rhythm of her breathing.

"Send him in," Hatherfield said.

The guard winked. "It's not a him, sir."

A small figure walked through the doorway, clothed and
veiled in deepest black.

Hatherfield took a step back. "Lady Charlotte! What in
God's name . . ."

The door fell shut behind her. She lifted her veil, and the
face beneath was extraordinarily pale, the skin almost translucent beneath the too-prominent bones of her face.

"Good evening, James," she said.

He crossed his arms. "You shouldn't be here. I don't know
how you managed to get through them all."

She made a bitter little laugh. "Don't you know, James,
there's nothing in this world one can't obtain with beauty, title,
and money? And I have all three."

"Almost nothing," he said.

"Have you nothing kind to say to me at all, James? Nothing? When I have suffered so."

He gazed at her in astonishment. "You've suffered? My
dear Lady Charlotte, I have been imprisoned and tried for a
crime I did not commit. I have been kept apart from the
woman I love . . ."

"Don't speak of her!"

"I will say her name with my dying breath."

"Then it *will* be your dying breath, by God," she said fiercely. Her veil trembled at the edge of her hat. Hatherfield looked at her sharp, frail bones, her bloodless lips. The way her rich black clothes hung from her body. No porcelain doll now, Lady Charlotte. She reminded him instead of a dangling ornament.

He said coldly, "Why are you here, madam?"

She held out her hands. "James, I know you're innocent. I know you didn't kill the duchess. I know what really happened, the night of the ball. I have . . . I have proof."

Proof.

The word rang in his ears, a siren's call, tempting and dangerous. *Proof.* What sort of proof could Lady Charlotte have?

And what price would she exact for it?

Hatherfield kept his voice even. "How unaccountable, then, that you failed to mention this heartfelt conviction in your testimony before the court. Instead, if memory serves, you did your level best to implicate me inextricably. *I saw him upstairs at half past ten*, you said, or words to that effect. *The duchess had just retired to her boudoir and asked me to send Lord Hatherfield to see her.* Convincing testimony, that. I shall have the devil of a time explaining myself tomorrow."

Tears welled at the corners of her eyes. "I was angry, I was hurt. I had seen you with her, embracing her, that woman . . ."

"You will not speak of her."

"I was consumed by jealousy. I admit it. But I can save you now. I can make up for my sins, if you'll let me." She reached for his hands.

Hatherfield stepped away. "You are perfectly welcome to inform the court that you have additional testimony. I only ask that you not reveal the single fact of Mr. Thomas's sex, which has nothing at all to do with the case."

"I will inform the court. I'll do it tomorrow. I'll tell them everything, and you'll be saved. I only ask, in return . . ." Her voice trailed off hopefully, making a slight echo on the stone walls.

And there it was. Hatherfield's chest went cold.

"Yes, Lady Charlotte?"

"Renounce her."

"Renounce her?"

"Renounce her, and I'll save you. You'll live, you'll be free."

"Never!" The word exploded from his throat.

She stamped her foot. "Don't be a fool! Do you want to die? You'll die, Hatherfield, they'll hang you. Either way, you'll never see her again. Why not save yourself? Are you mad?" She was trembling, despite the August warmth and her own black mourning clothes; the tears dashed from her eyes.

Hatherfield shook his head slowly. "You don't understand, do you? She has stood by my side, she's given me everything, she's fought for me with all her heart. She has loved me, she has put herself in the acutest danger for my sake. Renounce her? To save my own life?" He shook his head again. "I would slit my own throat first."

"Die, then!"

Her words revolved in the heavy prison air. *Die then die then die then.*

"What contrast," he said softly. "What contrast, between the two of you. Can you possibly wonder why I love her?"

She flinched, as if physically struck.

"Don't you see? I would lay down my life for her, if she let me. Because that's what love means, Lady Charlotte. What fidelity means. I am her servant before God."

She whispered, "You don't need to marry me. Only renounce her. Just tell me you won't see her again. That's all I ask."

"Why? Why not allow me happiness?"

She turned away to stare at the dull gray masonry, the encroaching walls of Hatherfield's cell. Her hands clenched and unclenched into the thick black folds of her dress. "Because I can't bear it. I can't bear her to have you instead. When I love you so."

The last faint flutter of hope died inside his heart.

"You must leave, Lady Charlotte. There's nothing for you here."

She spun about. "I'll tell them all. I'll tell them your pretty clerk is a woman, a cheeky little slut . . ."

In an instant, she was up against the wall with his fingers pressing the ends of her jawbone. "Do that," he said, in a tight whisper, "and you will not live to see another day. Not another hour."

Lady Charlotte's dark eyes blinked at him, wide and round. "You would strike me? A woman?"

"If you harm a hair on her head, you forfeit the privilege of your sex, Lady Charlotte. I will hunt you down like the vixen you are."

"You *are* mad."

He pulled his hand away. "Go."

She stumbled to the door and knocked. "Die, then. I could have saved you, I could have loved you."

"You must do as your conscience dictates, Lady Charlotte, and I shall do the same."

"I won't forgive you for this."

The door swung open. The guard filled the passageway, leering back and forth between the both of them. "Ready to go, madam?"

Lady Charlotte stood at the door, staring at him, her eyebrows raised proudly in her flawless forehead. "Well, Hatherfield?"

"She's ready," he told the guard.

She put down her veil. "Madman. And who will save your pretty face now?"

The door fell shut, and Hatherfield sank into the chair before his small wooden desk.

Who, indeed?

TWENTY-THREE

Belgrave Square
February 1890

At a quarter past nine, the Marquess of Hatherfield leapt up the front steps of his father's Belgrave Square mansion and tossed his hat and cape to the footman. "Has Sir John Worthington arrived yet?" he asked.

"Yes, your lordship. In the ballroom, I believe."

Hatherfield strode down the entrance hall to the ballroom, which stretched across the entire back half of the ground floor, its French doors open to the bare February garden. He had no trouble finding Sir John. There were perhaps thirty people assembled, including the musicians; in the center of the room, a few couples danced gamely to a waltz.

He started forward, and a hand appeared on his arm.

"Good evening, Hatherfield," said his father. "Arrived at last, I see."

Hatherfield turned. "Father. Good evening. A smashing success, isn't it? I can scarcely move for the crush."

"Don't be impertinent." The duke's face was flushed, as if he'd already had a few too many glasses of sherry.

"I heard the most thrilling rumor that Mr. Nathaniel Wright himself will be here tonight. What a magnificent coincidence. I hope you didn't go to such trouble for my sake."

"Needs must, I'm afraid."

Hatherfield flattened his eyebrows and looked keenly at his father. There was an odd note to his voice, or rather a missing note: that of belligerence. As if the grand old Duke of Southam had been defeated by some common foe at last. As if he had laid down his arms and now watched the conclusion of the battle in helpless woe.

"I don't suppose you happen to have seen Mr. Thomas lying about, have you?"

"Mr. Thomas?"

"My dear friend."

"Oh. Yes. Of course. I haven't, in fact."

"Didn't he come in with Sir John and Lady Charlotte?"

The duke's brow crinkled with effort. "No. No, I don't believe he did. Hatherfield, I . . ."

But Hatherfield was already striding off across the ballroom with a knot of worry tangling his gut. Sir John stood with Hatherfield's oldest sister, Eleanor, and his old granite face had rearranged itself into an expression of actual pleasure. The flirtatious sort of pleasure.

"I say, sir. I don't mean to interrupt," said Hatherfield, "but did you happen to bring Mr. Thomas with you this evening?"

"Well, hello, James." Eleanor lifted her cheek.

"I beg your pardon, my dear." He kissed her. "You're well."

"Quite. So is little Jane, if you're interested. You haven't been around in ages."

He arranged his face in contrite lines. "Terribly sorry. Things have been rather mad lately. Sir John, about Thomas."

"Thomas?"

"Your clerk, for God's sake. Did he arrive with you?"

"Thomas? Why, no." Sir John was still smiling. "Left him at home. Had an errand, he said, and would be along later. Hasn't he turned up?"

"No, he hasn't."

An errand. What did that mean? The obvious possibility burst at once into his brain. Stefanie had gone to Park Lane, to her sister's ball. Meddlesome, impetuous Stefanie. What was he thinking, leaving her to her own devices, even for an hour or two? A damned minute, for that matter. He should have set Nelson on her. His fist curled against his leg.

"Did he happen to reveal the nature of this errand?" Hatherfield said, with dry lips.

"Why, no. I expect he left something unfinished from today's case, or some damned thing. He and Charlotte were bickering in the music room, and . . ."

"Lady Charlotte!"

"Who's this Mr. Thomas?" asked Eleanor. "Do I know him?"

But Hatherfield was off again, this time at a run. Lady Charlotte was dancing in the formal clasp of a tall man with neatly clipped light brown whiskers—Eleanor's husband, he registered vaguely—and she did not look pleased.

"Cutting in, I'm afraid," he said, sweeping her away from her partner, and her face lit with instant delight.

"Hatherfield! I knew you'd arrive. How animated you look! I . . ."

"Where is he, Charlotte?"

"Who?"

"Thomas. What the devil have you done?" He executed a flawless turn.

She made a show of looking about the sparse ballroom. "Isn't he here?"

"You know very well he is not. Sir John tells me you were arguing with him, before you left tonight."

"Well, I certainly haven't seen him since." She tossed her head in a jingle of dark curls.

"What did you say to him?"

"Nothing of consequence. He was most insulting to me. Odious little wretch. I should have . . ."

"You left him at home, then? Did he say what he was doing? Where he was going?"

"Only that he would be along shortly. I don't know why you care so passionately. He has no manners, none at all, and as for his face, which some find so unaccountably handsome, I would never consider . . ."

Hatherfield flung her around another turn, this time landing her efficiently into the astonished arms of her previous partner.

She called after him. "Hatherfield! What on earth are you doing?"

"If anyone asks, I shall be in Park Lane."

He bounded across the acre or so of Italian marble and

through the columned passageway to the entrance hall. A cold draft of air flooded down the walls. His pulse was beating high, but his mind was clear and cold, mapping out the swiftest route to the Duke of Olympia's mansion on Park Lane at half past nine o'clock on a Wednesday evening, when the streets about the grandest ball in years would be piled deep with eager carriages, and then calculating what he should do when he arrived there. Sweep through the door and demand entrance, or else slip around to the back garden and seek her out from the discreet shadows.

The door was already flung open before him. He throttled down the hall almost at a run, past liveried footmen with trays of untouched champagne, past that damned suit of armor that Southam had insisted on bringing down from one of the more remote ducal outposts and installing there. His mind was buzzing so acutely he hardly noticed the pair of elegant silver slippers that appeared at the far end of his vision.

He heard a gasp behind him.

He looked forward and came to a dead stop.

In the more logical recesses of his mind, he knew this apparition was Stefanie. Above her silver mask, her pale forehead rose up in exactly that familiar way, high and smooth; her chin came to that perfect point he loved to kiss; her bare shoulders, her carriage, the glimpse of auburn hair that showed at the edge of her silver hood, crowned by a glittering spray of brilliants: They were all exquisitely Stefanie.

But this. This glorious gown, shot with moonlight, swirling about her curving figure. That long and slender cape, that filmy luminescent hood framing the angular bones of her face, her silver mask festooned with sleek white feathers. She was a spirit, a fairy, a darling sprite. She was magic itself, floating into his father's house in Belgrave Square as if to flood every cold and rotten corner with her light.

Including him.

Like Hatherfield, she had come to a stop. She stood about six or seven feet away, and her smile curved like a pink crescent moon below her mask.

Hatherfield was vaguely aware of the crowd gathering behind him. He didn't give a damn. His smile kept on growing and growing, until it threatened to split his face in two.

She smiled back.

He sank into a deep bow, straightened, and took two steps forward.

"Your Royal Highness," he said, under his breath.

"Your lordship." Her voice trembled with laughter.

He held out his hand. "I believe the first dance is mine."

Stefanie laid her white-gloved hand in his, and his fingers closed warmly around hers. How he loved her firm grasp, her unshakable optimism. Everything became possible when Stefanie's hand lay in his.

"If you must," she said.

The orchestra was just starting up another echoing waltz. Somewhere in the periphery of his sight, the other dancers were melting away in astonishment; somewhere at the far range of his hearing, the guests were whispering, and above them the querulous voice of the Duchess of Southam shrilled upward with the question: *Who the devil is she?*

But this all occurred at a great distance, in another universe from the one he occupied with Stefanie. He led her to the center of the floor and placed his hand at her waist, and without a word they spun into the first measures of the waltz. Her cape floated around them, a beat or two behind.

"You are the most beautiful woman in the world," he said, after a minute or two, when he could speak at last.

"Only with a mask on, apparently."

"You are beautiful any way and every way, but especially in that spectacular gown, with your eyes peeking through your mask, laughing at me."

"Shh. Everyone's staring."

"Let them stare." He twirled her again, almost giddy with the magic of her, the cheerful way she followed his movements, the exquisite knowledge of oneness with a well-matched partner. He gathered her a fraction closer and said, near her ear, "Marry me. Marry me tonight."

She laughed. "You're impossible. For one thing, we haven't a license."

"I'll find us one, if I have to break into the Bishop of London's bedroom and wake him myself. I don't want to sleep again until you're my wife."

"And you call me impetuous."

He loved the feel of her waist under his hand. "You haven't said no."

"I haven't said yes."

The waltz melted into another, and the two of them danced on without a pause. Hatherfield was vaguely aware that they had been joined by a few other couples, and then a few more, and when he could no longer swirl his princess about without knocking elbows with one or another of his sisters' husbands, he simply swirled her out of the room entirely and through the French doors into the garden.

"Oh no." Stefanie's words emerged in floating white clouds. "No, no. Far too cold."

He shrugged his black tailcoat down his arms and swung it over her shoulders. "Trust me. Now come along. Pay attention, there's a dodgy step in the middle."

The light from the ballroom lay across the terrace stones in golden rectangles. Beyond lay the murky garden and the shadows of the neighboring houses, the irregular pattern of illuminated windows. Hatherfield took Stefanie's hand and drew her along the width of the house until he reached the narrow wrought-iron staircase that spiraled upward to the library.

"Where are we going?" she whispered.

"Where we can be private."

She shimmered up the stairs before him. The rustle of her cape as it trailed along the metal made his blood hurtle in his veins. He caught a glimpse of the side of her throat, just above the collar of his tailcoat, and his heart hollowed into air.

She was his. Actually his. How was that possible?

When they reached the balcony, he slipped ahead of her and tried the door handle. It rattled without effect.

"I don't suppose you have a key?" Stefanie said hopefully.

He turned and reached around her hair, beneath the hood, fingers spearing gently through the silken strands.

"Oh! Mind the pins!" she exclaimed. "I had the most awful trouble securing that hood by myself . . . oh, I say!"

He drew out a pin and kissed it reverently.

"I hope you mean to return that," she said.

He inserted the pin into the lock, and an instant later the handle gave way. He opened the door and stood back to wave her inside, but instead she took him by the face and kissed him. He staggered backward into the darkened library, his arms full of Stefanie, laughing and kissing at the same time.

She lifted her lips away for a second. "That was marvelous." Another kiss. "Do it again."

"What, kiss you?"

"No. The lock. My entire life, I've longed to know how to pick a lock. Will you show me?"

"Absolutely not. I happen to have another lock in mind. Far more intricate. Mysterious. Devilishly clever."

She unbuttoned his waistcoat and ran her hands along his sides to his back. She looked up at him from beneath her decadent eyelashes and purred, "As bothersome as that? I can't imagine why you trouble yourself."

"Because of the treasure on the other side, of course." He slipped his fingers beneath her silvery bodice and closed his eyes in wonder at the plump welcome of her breast, the delicate hardness of her nipple. "A man might endure any hardship to taste such riches."

"He might fight off armed attackers in the middle of the night?"

"In an instant."

"He might fish a clumsy clerk out of an icy river at dawn?"

"With utmost dispatch."

"He might wash a woman with a bucket of soapy water and his own bare hands before the sun rises?"

"Every morning. Except on Sundays, perhaps, when a proper respect for the Almighty demands a genuine bathtub."

She laughed and put her arms around his neck. "I adore you. How do you manage it?"

"Manage what?"

"To be so full of life. To be you."

He reached inside her hood and untied her mask, placing it carefully on the round table next to the lamp, and then he eased the hood down to expose her short, newly freed auburn hair to the dim light. Such alluring shiny hair, curling just slightly around her ears. He lifted a strand or two and rubbed it between his fingers. "Because I have no choice, have I? One carries on regardless."

She turned her head and kissed his palm. The light caught a tiny glitter in her eyes. "Yes," she said.

"Yes, what?"

"Yes, I'll marry you. Whenever you like. However you like. I don't care, as long as I'm your wife."

"And the good people of Holstein-Schweinwald-Huhnhof? They won't mind?"

She smiled. "They'll love you."

He went on touching her silken hair, absorbing her ardent smile. As if the angels in heaven were bestowing this blessing on him, redeeming his tattered soul in an act of undeserved grace.

"My wife." Two small words, electric on his tongue. Warm around his heart.

Stefanie made a little tremor. Her blue eyes went round. "Did you feel that?"

"Yes."

"As if . . . as if it happened, right there. As if you bound us, just by saying it aloud."

Hatherfield kissed the hair in his fingers, and then he kissed her. "I believe, in certain cultures, that's all it takes."

His heart was pounding in a strong and confident rhythm. He placed a last kiss on her lips and walked to the magnificent paneled door, which stood just ajar. He looked out into the empty hallway. A lilting music drifted up from the staircase, a bustle of laughter and animated voices. He closed the door firmly and turned the lock.

Stefanie stood in the center of the room, resplendent and smiling, her hair glowing in a reddish halo from the lamp behind her. She held out her arms, and every bone in his body ached with desire.

In three long strides, he stood before her. He bent down and lifted her in his arms and carried her to the blue damask chaise longue that occupied the alcove overlooking the garden.

He placed her carefully on the cushions and settled himself above her.

"This is very naughty," she whispered.

"Singularly daring."

"And quite dangerous. Anyone might come in."

He was trailing kisses along the upper curve of her bosom. "Only the butler and my father have the key. And no one can see us from the door."

She craned her neck to verify this observation, and Hatherfield seized the opportunity to kiss the tender hollow beneath her ear. "There's something I want to do with you," he said softly.

She lay there with her head still turned, her neck still exposed. She closed her eyes, as if savoring his caress. "What's that?" she whispered.

"I want to taste you."

A throaty little laugh. "But you are tasting me. Am I delicious?"

His hands drifted downward and drew up her skirts, her petticoats. She wasn't wearing drawers. He ran his hand up her bare leg. "I want to taste you here."

She gasped. "Oh."

"Would you like that, Stefanie?" His forefinger eased inside her snug channel. She closed around him, wet and hot, and her hips moved restlessly beneath him. "May I kiss you here?"

"I can't imagine . . ."

"But I have. I've imagined it daily." He kissed her mouth, her chin, down her throat, down the silken crevasse between her breasts. He slid down between her legs and lifted her skirts high, parting her silvery gossamer skirt and her frothy petticoats and her transparent chemise.

She shivered as the cool air brushed her skin. Her hands found his hair. "Hatherfield," she whispered.

With his finger, he touched her auburn curls, the precious hood covering her hidden jewel, the delicate lips shining with arousal. Her warm feminine scent settled into his nose. "You're perfect," he said. He pressed his lips on her. He'd never done this to any woman. He wasn't quite sure where to start, where to begin sampling the riches before him. Stefanie lay quite still, her fingers latched in his hair, but he felt the rapid pulse of her breathing, nudging them both. Her legs rested uncertainly on either side of his shoulders.

He kissed her again and ran his tongue along her seam, from top to bottom.

Her hips jumped up from the cushion, her hands tightened in his hair. "Hatherfield!"

He swirled his tongue around her opening and darted inside, and out, and inside again.

"Hatherfield!" Breathless this time.

He lifted her legs and slipped them onto his shoulders, bringing her closer to his mouth, holding her secure so she couldn't thrash free. He ignored his own rock-hard arousal and explored her with a patient tongue. Each lick had its own effect, each stroke coaxed its own sound from her throat, and he wanted to know them all, he wanted to know exactly what she liked best, and how she liked it. A rhythm developed, back and forth between them, and her noises deepened into sobs, into half-coherent begging, while his tongue circled the bundle of sweet nerves at her center, lazy and then quick, and she was lifting her hips to meet him. She was going to spend, he could actually feel the trembling pressure beneath his tongue, and he brought his hand around her leg and inserted one finger into her wet slit while he sucked her softly above.

"Hatherfield!"

Her shout rattled the bookshelves as she came and came in rapid pulses around his finger, the sweetest climax, on and on. He was drowning in her, lapping her up, her salty tang of release, and all he could think was *beautiful, beautiful, beautiful.*

She sagged slowly downward. He followed her. The lace edges of her petticoats tickled his cheeks, and her hands released his hair at last.

He lifted his head and saw the tip of her chin pointing upward to the ceiling fresco, at the far end of her heaving silver chest. He prowled upward along her limp body. The lamplight glowed along the side of her face, casting her cheeks in shadow, but no shadow could hide the telltale pink glow on the skin of a well-loved woman.

God, he loved that flush.

"Well?" he asked.

"My . . . my goodness."

"Open your eyes."

She opened them.

"Stefanie. Little one. That was the single most exciting act of my life."

"I didn't—" Her flushed skin grew even more delightfully pink, but she didn't look away, not Stefanie. "I never even imagined."

He lowered his head and kissed her again, and then he pulled down the bodice of her dress and freed one perfect breast. "I want you to let your imagination run free, love. I want to make love to you in every way possible. I want to know what *you* want, to . . ."

A small noise jarred the still atmosphere of the library.

In a single smooth movement, Hatherfield pulled up Stefanie's bodice and leapt to his feet in front of the chaise.

Lady Charlotte Harlowe stood in the center of the room, her face white beneath her pale pink mask. A small key dangled from her right hand.

"Lady Charlotte. Good evening." Behind him, Stefanie was rustling quietly, arranging her clothes. He folded his arms and planted his massive legs like two protective trunks into the ancient Kilim rug before the chaise.

Lady Charlotte whispered, "I have been a fool."

He was silent. How could he speak into the waves of grief and shock that radiated from that small pale pink body, with its face of paper white?

"I'm sorry to have caused you any pain," he said at last.

"Very well," Lady Charlotte said. "I see where my duty lies."

She turned and walked to the door.

Hatherfield bolted after her. "You are not to say anything of what you've seen, is that clear?"

She shrugged off his hand. "You will not address me half dressed, Lord Hatherfield."

"She is my affianced wife. You will put her in gravest danger."

The door slammed shut.

He turned to Stefanie, who now stood tying her mask around her head with calm hands. He was already buttoning his waistcoat. She picked up his tailcoat from the floor and handed it to him.

"Go to her," she said. "Be kind. Forgive her. She loves you so."

He shrugged into his tailcoat and took her by the cheeks and kissed her hard. "My *wife*," he growled fiercely in her ear, as if saying the words really would make it so. "Stay here. Sit right on that chaise until I return. Do you understand me?"

She sank obediently on the chaise and lifted her hood over her hair. Her cheeks were still outrageously pink. "I understand you."

He dashed out of the room, straightening his tie as he went.

TWENTY-FOUR

Old Bailey
August 1890

By the time Mr. Fairchurch had finished his questioning, the afternoon was well advanced, and the audience in the packed courtroom—jury included—was beginning to doze off.

Hatherfield's outward face remained grave and guileless, but his interior walls smiled with satisfaction. Good. A complacent jury was a conservative jury, and a conservative jury might just be inclined to acquit him, in absence of any direct evidence linking the Marquess of Hatherfield to the crime itself.

Mr. Duckworth circled around his table, his hands tangled in a thoughtful knot behind his back. "Your lordship, your lordship," he said, as if puzzling to himself. "A very neat story. A neat story indeed, and delivered with convincing effort. I applaud you."

Hatherfield tilted his head expectantly.

"There is one . . . one small article of confusion. Or perhaps I've only muddled things in my head." He tapped the skull in question admonishingly. "Would you perhaps do me the honor, Lord Hatherfield, of repeating your account of your actions at your parents' house in Belgrave Square, on the night of February the—" he checked his notes "—the twenty-first of February?"

"I have already recounted them at length, Mr. Fairchurch. I should hate to weary the long-suffering gentlemen of the jury." Hatherfield turned his head to the nodding gentlemen in question, and nodded in sympathy.

"Nonetheless. A brief summary will do. Let me start you off. You arrived at the house in Belgrave Square at a quarter past nine and proceeded to speak with"—again, consulting the notes—"the Viscountess Chesterton, and then to dance with briefly Lady Charlotte Harlowe." He removed his spectacles. "And then our mysterious woman in silver arrived, and you danced with her until approximately ten o'clock, at which point you—well, it seems you disappeared from the witness account altogether. Do I have this correctly, Lord Hatherfield?"

Hatherfield smiled his best self-deprecating smile. "Not altogether. There was one witness."

"Oh?"

"The lady herself."

The gentlemen of the jury shifted about. The audience, under no obligation of dignity, tittered freely.

"Yes, of course. And this lady, where is she now?"

Hatherfield spread his hands. "I'm afraid she slipped away into the night, and I haven't seen her since." Which was true, in its way.

"Hmm. Slipped away." Mr. Duckworth's voice dripped with skepticism. "Let us suppose, then, merely for the sake of argument, that this lady of yours had been persuaded to stay within the circle of your charms, Lord Hatherfield"—cue the tittering—"instead of slipping away into the night." He made a skittering motion with his fingers. "Let us suppose that she has given us sworn testimony to the effect that she remained in your company for the rest of the evening. Why, then, does no one report seeing the Marquess of Hatherfield leaving the party that evening?"

Hatherfield shrugged. "It was a considerable crush, after all. Any number of guests milling about, most of whom I don't even know by sight. Come to think of it, any chap might have walked in off the streets that night, without being noticed by a soul." He delivered this point with particular emphasis in the jury's direction. "Besides, there was the lady's honor to consider."

"Oh, of course!" Mr. Duckworth snapped his fingers. "The lady's honor! You left discreetly, then. A rear exit, perhaps?"

Hatherfield paused. "Perhaps."

"You are under oath, your lordship."

"Yes. Yes, we departed from the mews."

"I see. Sneaking away, as it were." A glance at the jury.

Hatherfield willed himself not to look at Stefanie, but he could feel her energy, her scintillating need to spring to her feet and identify herself as the lady in question, to strip herself bare in an effort to save him from the snare Mr. Duckworth was evidently trying to lay. *Stay down.* He willed the word to her. *Stay low. Let me do this.*

He shrugged. "As I said, the lady's honor was at stake."

"Strange, that she never offered to return the favor. To save your honor, by testifying in your defense."

Stay down, Stefanie. Please.

Hatherfield brushed at his sleeve. "Perhaps she did make this offer, Mr. Duckworth. But a gentleman does not purchase his honor at the price of his lady's good name."

A sympathetic murmur traveled across the courtroom, concentrating with particular emotion among the damsels in the corner. Under the guise of acknowledging their support, Hatherfield gazed across the benches, and in the upper right quadrant of his vision he saw Stefanie's shoulders sink downward in relief.

Ah, little one. How could you doubt me?

Even Mr. Duckworth had the grace to look down and cough slightly into his closed fist. "Naturally. But the fact remains, your lordship, the court has no positive proof that you remained in the company of this lady throughout the course of the evening, and that you left the house in possession of her."

"Nor have you positive proof to the contrary."

The judge banged his gavel. "You are to answer the questions put to you by the prosecution, Lord Hatherfield, not to offer unsolicited statements of observation."

"I beg your pardon. Have you another question for me to answer, Mr. Duckworth?"

Another round of tittering.

Mr. Duckworth looked up. "Perhaps, your lordship, you can find it within the bounds of your honor to inform the court

which room you and the lady repaired to, when you first—
er—slipped away from the ballroom?"

Hatherfield hesitated. "To the library, I believe."

"You believe? You're not certain?"

"Yes, it was the library." Hatherfield smiled. "Quite certain."

Mr. Duckworth turned to the judge. "My lord, the prosecution wishes to recall an exhibit to the court's attention."

"For what reason, Mr. Duckworth?"

"For possible identification by the witness."

Hatherfield frowned. What the devil was this?

Mr. Duckworth was conferring with the officials in the
corner, bailiffs or whoever they were. Hatherfield drummed
his fingers against the rail and looked at Stefanie. She was
watching Mr. Duckworth, and her face had compressed into
grave lines. She leaned toward Mr. Fairchurch and whispered
something in his ear.

Like a premonition of evil, a vague sensation began to stir
at Hatherfield's gut. He studied Mr. Duckworth's lips, as if
he could somehow divine his words. Divine his purpose.

The courtroom stirred, too. Whispering, murmuring. The
gentlemen of the jury adjusted their collars in the hot afternoon air. Hatherfield remained quite still, his eyes fixed on
the activity among the prosecution, the gravitational shift of the
room from amused somnolence to anticipation.

An official emerged from the door at the side, carrying a
small silver object in his hand.

"The murder weapon," said Mr. Duckworth. "The object
used by the murderer to stab Her Grace, the Duchess of
Southam, several times, in a most brutal fashion."

The official held it aloft. A slender sword, a foot long, honed
to sharpness at one end. At the other end, a graceful handle,
engraved with the ducal crest.

"Can you identify this object, Lord Hatherfield?"

"I believe it's commonly used as a letter opener, Mr.
Duckworth."

"Ah. A letter opener." Mr. Duckworth smiled. "And where,
Lord Hatherfield, was your father the duke accustomed to
opening his letters?"

"Not having lived beneath his roof in many years, I don't
feel myself qualified to say."

"I will rephrase the question, then. Where, your lordship, do you last recall seeing this object, this letter opener, belonging to your father and with the crest of the Dukes of Southam plainly to be seen on its handle?"

Hatherfield set his lips.

"Your gentlemanly honor, no doubt, will compel you to answer me with the utmost honesty." Mr. Duckworth smiled again. "Your lordship."

The courtroom had gone silent. Astonishing, that so loud and so miserably restless a group of British subjects could hold themselves so entirely without sound. From the damsels, not even a sigh of trepidation.

Hatherfield sent a resigned glance to Stefanie.

"In my father's library. I believe I last saw it in the library."

TWENTY-FIVE

Belgrave Square, London
February 1890

Stefanie meant to sit quietly and wait for Hatherfield's return. After all, what else could she do, dressed as she was? Double disguised as she was?

But her nerves were jumping, her blood still rushing deliriously through her veins after Hatherfield's lovemaking. She couldn't sit still on the chaise, the sacred chaise they had occupied together mere minutes ago. *My wife.* The words still rang in her ears.

She jumped to her feet and walked along one wall, shelves over cabinets, stuffed with books that looked as though they hadn't been moved from their places in ages. Old leather bindings, long and obscure titles, mostly in Latin. A small collection of more modern novels. Stefanie concentrated fiercely on reading the titles. Occupying her mind, to keep her impetuous body from turning to the door and running outside and making matters worse.

It had been a mistake to come, of course. But how could she resist the urge to dress herself in her true colors? *You are nothing,* Lady Charlotte had sneered. *The dust under my slippers.*

Well, she'd shown Lady Charlotte, all right. Now the damage she'd done might be incalculable.

She wandered along the shelves and came upon the large

claw-footed desk at the end, heavy and substantial, like a great rectangular mahogany lion. Her fingers dragged along the gleaming surface, bare except for a lamp at one corner and a single framed photograph at the other.

Something about the photograph caught the corner of her eye. She reached out one hand and lifted it up.

Among the blurred sepia figures assembled on an unknown stone step, Hatherfield's face leapt out at her. His was the only smiling mouth, and she knew that smile, that automatic and charming social smile, familiar and yet different from the smile he gave her in private. He stood in the center, tall and muscular in his racing jersey, golden hair gleaming ivory in the sunshine, holding a silver cup in his broad hands. The caption, scratched in white on the photographic print, read: University Boat Race, 1883. Won by Oxford, J.M. Lambert, Captain.

Her eyes began to sting with tears. She'd put him in danger yet again, her gallant Hatherfield, and still he went running to chase down her enemies. To hunt and destroy every threat to her well-being. He would kill for her. He would die for her. If she spent her whole life pouring her love into him, if she gave up her crown and her birthright to live by his side, if she gave him children and laughter and the comfort of her body until the end of her days, it would not be enough.

Without warning, the door swung open, crashing into the wall with a fearsome thump.

Stefanie straightened and hid the photograph behind her back.

The Duke of Southam stood before her in an avenging thundercloud. His white hair sprang boldly from his head, and his fists clenched against the shining black wool of his tailcoat.

"Who are you, madam?" he demanded, in a booming ducal roar. "And what the devil are you doing in my private library?"

But Stefanie was a princess of Holstein-Schweinwald-Huhnhof, the daughter of Crown Prince Rudolf. She had danced with the Kaiser, she had faced down the Tsar at a state banquet and told him she didn't particularly care for Black Sea caviar. She outranked this puffy old English duke with one gloved hand tied behind her back.

On the other hand, he was practically her father-in-law.

She told him so.

"Tut-tut, sir," she said. "When I'm practically your daughter-in-law."

"What?"

"I'm afraid it's rather hush-hush at the moment. I suppose Hatherfield would rather tell you himself, in fact, but there it is."

He took two quick steps toward her and stopped. His face was deathly white. His blue eyes, paler than Hatherfield's, stared out from a pair of defeated red-rimmed sockets. "You have no right to spread such lies. My son is under a different engagement entirely, to Lady Charlotte Harlowe. We are about to announce the alliance, this minute."

She lifted her eyebrows in exactly the way Miss Dingleby used to do, when Stefanie presented her with a hastily scribbled essay and demanded to be allowed outside to play. "How extraordinary. Have you bothered to confide the fact of this imminent disclosure to Hatherfield himself? I'm sure he'll be delighted by the surprise."

The duke brought his fist down on the desk with a crash. "You have no right! No right to destroy this family. No right to destroy my son's happiness with your strumpet's costume and your loose ways . . ."

"Destroy his happiness? How dare you. How dare you, sir. It's you who have tried to destroy him, you and your evil wife. Do you have any idea what she's done to him? Or did you stuff your pillow over your head and pretend that her late-night expeditions were due to some digestive complaint, or some mysterious desire to repair to her boudoir and catch up on her correspondence?"

"What in God's name are you saying?" he whispered.

"*You* ruined him. She ruined him, and you let her. You failed in the single inescapable duty a father has to his son: to protect him. And he's suffered all his life for it, without ever saying a word, without once complaining. His noble soul, and she did her best to destroy it, except she couldn't. Because he's too strong for her, too good for her."

"It's not true."

"It is true. You know it's true, don't you? You've always

known, in your heart. Damn you to hell." She leaned forward.
"And if you harm him again, if that horrible woman even
speaks to him again, I will destroy you, do you hear me? You
don't even begin to know my power."

"Get out." But the note of command had vanished from his
voice. "You are not *welcome* here."

"Very well." Stefanie withdrew the photograph from
behind her back and placed it in his hands. "But look at him.
Just look at him, won't you? That smile of his. Just think what
it cost him, to smile like that. He's your son, Your Grace. He
needed you." She lowered her voice to a soft plea. "He still
needs you."

She left him there, standing by his own desk, with the
silver-framed photograph cradled in his hands and an expression of utter vanquish on his face.

Stefanie halted in shock on the curving marble stairs.
       The tepid party she'd left an hour ago had grown into a
crush of historic proportions. In the entrance hall below, a kalei-
doscope of silk dresses ebbed and flowed and shifted; a
thousand jewels glittered in the blazing light of the chandelier;
a frantic twitter of conversation threatened to raise the stained
glass dome at the very top of the staircase. The Duchess of
Southam's ball had turned into a success after all.

At least Stefanie wouldn't be conspicuous.

She skimmed down the remaining stairs and plunged into
the miasma of perfume and damp wool and perspiration.
Moving about was nearly impossible. She squeezed between
tailored black shoulders and bare powdered bosoms; she
smiled her best royal smile and pardoned herself for jostling a
dowager. The dowager appeared not to notice. She was discussing something in animated detail with her companion:
something about musicians and police. Stefanie didn't pause.
She soldiered on, searching out Hatherfield's golden head in
the crowd, or Lady Charlotte's spray of pale pink ostrich
feathers. Hardly anybody wore a mask. Perhaps they were all
too hot. Stefanie tried not to breathe the warm and stagnant
air. She had always hated these stifling long affairs, had
always escaped at the earliest opportunity to breathe the good

clean air of the palace garden. Emilie would come with her. They would bring cake and stolen champagne and set up a contraband picnic near the roses.

Emilie. Stefanie's heart squeezed painfully. If all went well tonight, this charade would be over at last. She could greet her sisters openly again. Everything would be as it was, only better, because now there was Hatherfield. Hatherfield and Ashland. What a lovely life they would have together, if only she could survive the night.

She spent nearly a quarter of an hour simply pushing her way to the ballroom, which proved little better. The musicians were still playing, sawing away at yet another waltz, but nobody seemed to be dancing. There wasn't room. She rose on her toes and scanned the room. No sign of Hatherfield's head, no glimpse of Lady Charlotte.

And where in all this chaos was the Duchess of Southam?

"Good evening," said a dark masculine voice, so close to Stefanie's ear she felt his breath on her jaw.

She pirouetted in shock. "Good heavens, sir! Who the devil are you?"

The man was tall and broad shouldered, as big as Hatherfield, with thick dark hair and a thin-lipped mouth. His eyebrows lifted high above his slender black silk mask. "What indelicate language. Are you a friend of the duke and duchess, or merely an acquaintance of their son?" He said the word *acquaintance* with a certain delicate emphasis that meant *whore*.

Stefanie straightened her shoulders and said, in her best state banquet voice, "I am the affianced wife of the Marquess of Hatherfield. You, sir, are not a gentleman."

He tilted his chin and laughed. Stefanie realized, on closer inspection, that the stranger's upper lip alone was thin. The bottom lip appeared rather decadently full. In fact, there was something decidedly familiar about him altogether, as if she had just seen him recently, somewhere in the City, that thin upper lip curled in disdain . . .

"Mr. Wright!" she gasped.

His smile disappeared. She couldn't see his expression properly beneath his mask, but she had the feeling his eyes had narrowed and were staring at her. Calculating her.

"I don't believe we've been introduced," he said. "My name is Nathaniel Wright, a friend of Lord Hatherfield's affianced wife."

"Really, sir? I don't recall counting you among my friends."

"I mean Lady Charlotte Harlowe."

"How very strange. Everybody here tonight seems to believe that Lord Hatherfield is on the point of announcing his engagement to dear little Lady Charlotte. Everyone, that is, except Hatherfield himself. Perhaps one of you might trouble to ask him about the matter yourselves. You might be taken rather aback at his answer."

Mr. Wright cast a slow gaze down her length, from the tip of her nose to the hollow between her breasts. "Are you quite certain of that, Miss—? Ah. I beg your pardon. I'm afraid I don't recall your name."

"Having accepted his heartfelt proposal scarcely half an hour ago, I have the utmost confidence in my engagement to Lord Hatherfield. Perhaps you have your ladies crossed, Mr. Wright. I've often observed that gentlemen who play with sums of money all day long become rather muddled about the relative qualities of the female sex."

For a moment, Mr. Wright stood absolutely still, regarding Stefanie with unblinking eyes while the crowd eddied about him. "By damn," he said at last, under his breath.

"If you'll forgive me, Mr. Wright." Stefanie turned to leave, but his hand closed around her arm.

"It's no use, you know," he said softly. "He's already gone upstairs with Her Grace to sort it out. The two of you, you're finished."

"I haven't the faintest idea what you mean. Kindly remove your hand."

"I mean we've got our man. The engagement will be announced any minute, you'll see."

"You're mad."

He shrugged his thick shoulders, as if the point were not worth arguing. He brought his masked face in close, until his lips nearly brushed her skin. She tried to yank her arm away, but he held firm. "You'll survive it. Look at you. You're too magnificent to let yourself be crushed down for long."

"You know nothing about me."

"Let me know when you're feeling yourself again, my dear. I'll give you whatever you want. You'll live like a princess."

She jerked her arm again. This time he released her, but before she could deliver his prominent cheekbone the stinging slap he deserved, he had melted away into the crowd with astonishing grace for a man so large.

We've got our man. What did that mean?

Stefanie struggled to look about her, to find a single familiar face, but there was none. A thread of cold fear wound its way through her ribs. Where was Hatherfield?

He's already gone upstairs with Her Grace.

What was going on? Surely the duke wasn't plotting against his own son.

Stefanie turned back toward the doorway to the entrance hall and pushed her way through with irresistible force. The guests fell away before her in their colorful dozens, tossing off expressions of mild contempt for her single-minded determination. She found the hall, the iron-railed staircase reaching upward in a noble curve. With an agile leap she laid her hands on the rail's base and levered herself around the throng of newly arrived guests pooling on the bottom steps.

. . .When the first shots rang out, someone was saying, but the words hardly registered in Stefanie's alarmed mind. She rushed up the stairs and found the landing. To the right was the library, where Hatherfield had told her to wait for him. But that was before the duchess took him upstairs, for whatever purpose she had in mind.

If Mr. Wright told the truth.

She hovered between right and left, and had just taken her first steps away from the library when an arm snaked around her waist and hauled her into an immense black-coated chest.

"Stefanie! Thank God!"

Hatherfield. Breathless, heated, his heart pounding against her ear. But here. Still hers.

"Oh, thank God, thank God." She wrapped her arms around his waist, her fists around his clothes. "I thought something had happened."

He grasped her by the arms and set her back against the wall. His eyes locked with hers, alert and full of purpose. "Something *has* happened. Listen to me. This crowd, Stefanie.

It's come from your uncle's house, from Park Lane. Something's gone wrong, the whole place erupted into fighting."

She gripped his lapels. "Emilie!"

"I don't know. I don't know anything. There were shots. The police arrived. Everybody was turned out in the streets, and naturally they came here, the only other party tonight." He ran a hand through his hair and took her hand. "Come along. I don't know what the devil's happened, but I do know I've got to get you away from here."

He tugged her down the hallway at a run. She followed him willingly, dizzy with anxiety. "She's not hurt, is she? Did anyone say anything about Emilie?"

"Nobody saw her."

"Is that good?"

"I hope so."

They had reached the back staircase. Hatherfield flew down the steps, drawing her with him, trusting her to move as swiftly as he did. His handsome face was fixed with grim determination. For a second or two, as they rounded the first landing, Stefanie thought about Mr. Wright's words, about Lady Charlotte and the duchess, but the question on her lips was instantly quashed by the image of Emilie—dear, gentle, scholarly Emilie—facing down bullets from an assassin's revolver.

They reached the bottom of the stairs, where a stream of harried servants was issuing from the kitchen with bottles and trays. "This way," Hatherfield said tersely, and he launched them down the passageway to the rear of the house. A blur of walls and doors went by. She stumbled up a set of steps and through a door, and they were in the garden, running down the pathway to the mews. Hatherfield stopped and let out a shrill three-note whistle.

Silence, backlit by a stream of merriment from the house behind them, by the sounds of the London street beyond.

Then a whistle, identical to the one Hatherfield had just made.

"Come along." He grasped her hand, led her through the gate and into the mews, and a moment later they were standing on the cobbles and Hatherfield's hansom cab was drawing up before them.

"To Park Lane," Stefanie said to the driver.

"To Park Lane," echoed Hatherfield, swinging in next to her, "but first we stop at Albert Hall Mansions."

The doors banged shut. "Your rooms?" said Stefanie. "Why on earth are we stopping there? To find a revolver for me? A change of clothes?"

The cab raced down the mews and around the corner to Belgrave Place. Hatherfield settled in beside her and placed his skin-warm tailcoat once more over her shoulders. "Perish the thought," he said.

"But then why . . ."

"*We* are not stopping at the Mansions. *You* are stopping at the Mansions whilst *I* proceed to Park Lane and find out what's happened."

Stefanie uttered an outraged gasp.

"Yes, quite. I thought you'd feel that way. That's why we're heading for the Kensington Road instead of Cadogan Square."

She tossed her head. "What difference does that make? You know I'll break away and follow you as soon as you've left."

"Because my home contains a generally drunken but nonetheless useful chap by the name of Nelson." He placed his arm over her shoulders and held her snug against him, as if concerned that she might make a flying bid to escape from his company altogether. "And not even you, my intrepid love, will be able to evade Nelson."

TWENTY-SIX

Stefanie woke up at a quarter past one o'clock in the morning, when some inner alarm warned her that someone had entered the flat.

She hadn't meant to fall asleep at all. She'd spent an hour pacing the five spare rooms of Hatherfield's home under the gimlet glare and crossed arms of Nelson, who proved as vigilant and barrel-chested as Hatherfield had advised her. Also, not terribly communicative. She had fired off a number of questions, until the last monosyllabic answer made her flounce into Hatherfield's bedroom and slam the door behind her.

She had gone to the pair of windows on one wall, but the sheer five-story drop offered no opportunity for escape. She'd folded her arms and looked about the room, Hatherfield's room, his large and neatly made bed and the chest of drawers on the opposite wall, topped by a simple mahogany shaving mirror. A desk and chair, a comfortable armchair upholstered in a rich blue that reminded her achingly of Hatherfield's eyes. A large wardrobe, its doors shut.

Well, he'd left her here, hadn't he? *Make yourself at home,* he'd said, dropping a kiss on her mutinous lips. *Run a bath, if you like.*

She wasn't going to run a bath, not with Emilie in imminent

danger, her whereabouts unknown, not with Hatherfield risking his life once more for her sake. But—she glanced down at her silvery ball gown, so lush and exquisite a few hours ago, now sadly out of place—she might just change her clothes.

She'd crossed to the wardrobe and opened the door. Several suits, expertly tailored and neatly brushed; a stack of hats on the shelf; shoes, polished to a liquid perfection. Behind the hats, a gleam caught her eye. She pushed aside the felt and straw and found a jumble of plates and cups, engraved with words like Queen's Prize, Henley 1886, and Winner's Cup, University Boat Race, J.M. Lambert. *James.* She'd never been tempted to call him by his given name. *James* belonged to the duchess, to Lady Charlotte, to the false intimacy of betrayal. What did the *M* stand for? Perhaps she could call him that, when they were married. When they were husband and wife and curled around each other in bed, and *Hatherfield* was too long and formal.

She ran her fingers down the shoulder of his brown tweed jacket, the one he'd been wearing last night, the one she'd slipped from his magnificent shoulders with her own two hands.

Hatherfield. The wave of longing struck her so hard and so sudden, she lost her breath. She pressed her hand against her chest and blinked back tears.

Let him be safe. Let them both be safe. Let Hatherfield return to her tonight, whole and brave, so she could take him in her arms and love him, love him.

And never let him go.

She had pulled a forest green dressing gown from a hook and struggled out of her layers of dress and petticoat and unaccustomed corset. She'd wrapped herself in Hatherfield's robe, and her heart had nearly stopped at the unexpected smell of his shaving soap, rising up from the endless folds of material. The silk lining slid like a caress against her skin, and she had sunk into the armchair in a totality of physical and emotional exhaustion.

Nelson had knocked on the door and pushed it open a watchful crack. "Everything all right, madam?" he said gruffly.

"Yes, quite all right, thank you."

And in the next instant, she was asleep.

When the sound of a shutting door awoke her a few hours later, she raised her head in confusion. The room was dark, and for an instant, she had no idea where she was.

And then the door opened, and Hatherfield stood before her, surrounded by light from the hallway, still dressed in his formal clothes from the ball.

He lifted one hand to loosen his tie and called over his shoulder, "Nelson, have some cocoa made up, there's a good fellow."

"Cocoa?" she whispered blearily.

Hatherfield dropped the tie on the floor, crossed the room, and knelt before her. "Look at you." He kissed her hands. "Don't you know what it does to a man, to walk into his home at the end of a shattering day, and find the woman he loves asleep in his chair, wearing his favorite dressing gown?"

"You're all right." She took his head in her hands and buried her mouth in his hair. "You're all right. Thank God."

"Everything's fine, love. Everything's fine."

"Emilie?"

He paused. "Your uncle will be around tomorrow to explain. It's all a bit complicated. But your sister is well, she's alive."

"Oh, Emilie! Oh, I'm so glad! Then everything's all right. We're free." She pressed kisses into his forehead and cheeks.

"Not quite, I'm afraid." He rose and lifted her effortlessly into his tired arms. "But Olympia will explain."

"What does that mean? These fiends, they're still out there?"

"Yes." He laid her carefully on his bed and shrugged his tailcoat from his shoulders. "But we'll find them, Stefanie. They're on the run, now. They can't hide from me."

She watched him toss his waistcoat on the floor and unbutton his trousers. She longed to do it for him, but she held back and observed his sinewy legs emerge from the sleek black wool, his broad hands roll down his stockings in impatient strokes. His flawless body, carved with impeccable lean muscle, honed by the river and his own iron discipline.

"What are you going to do?" she asked softly. "What are we going to do?"

"A very good question." He lifted the shirt over his head and sent it flying to join his waistcoat. "We'll discuss it tomorrow."

"Tomorrow?"

He knelt above her on the bed, naked and aroused and enormous, and pulled apart the lapels of the dressing gown. "Tonight we make love."

The cocoa had grown rather less than piping hot by the time Hatherfield rose from the bed to fetch it from the tray left discreetly outside the door by Nelson. He helped Stefanie rise to a sitting position against the pillows and handed her a mug, and then he dragged the armchair next to the bed and sank into it with a contented sigh.

She sipped her cocoa and studied him. When had it happened, that his physical beauty had somehow merged in her mind with the beauty inside him? She had almost forgotten how he actually looked, the objective symmetry of his features, the clean blades of his cheekbones and the angle of his eyebrows, the square line of his chin and jaw, the warm blue shape of his eyes. Now she looked at him, really looked at him, indolent as a lion after a day's hunting, stretched naked in the chair with his strong legs propped on the edge of the bed and the mug of cocoa resting at the seam of his sensuous lips, and the wonder of him filled her all over again.

He nudged her with his toe. "What is it?"

"You." The taste of chocolate warmed her mouth. Her body still strummed with release, with the echoing pleasure of his lovemaking.

He smiled and rose from the chair.

"Where are you going?"

He went to his chest of drawers and pulled out a piece of paper from somewhere inside the shaving mirror. He plopped it on her chest and returned to his former position in the armchair, smiling madly.

"What is it?"

"It's a special license. I've carried it about with me for weeks, just in case . . ."

She slanted him a look. "Just in case?"

"Just in case we needed it. To protect you. As my wife, you have the right to my name and my body to keep you safe." He drank his cocoa. "We can be officially married tomorrow, if you like. If you don't mind marrying the heir to a bankrupt estate, with only his ambition to recommend him."

She read the few lines on the paper and looked back up at Hatherfield. "*You.*"

"Me what?"

She folded the paper in precise lines, laid it on the bedside table, and rose to straddle him on the chair. His body was still hot to the touch, still radiant with carnal energy. She cradled the back of his head with her hands. "I love you. I will love you until I die. And then my spirit will rise up from the grave and *haunt* you with my love, until you give up and join me in the beyond and we will rattle heaven to pieces, you and I, because I love you so much . . ."

He chuckled. "And if I so happen to shuck off this mortal coil before you?"

"Don't you dare." She rubbed her cheek against Hatherfield's raspy golden skin, and closed her eyes. "I couldn't live without you. How can I live if my own heart stops beating?"

They sat there quietly for a moment, skin on skin, pressed together at every possible point. She breathed in deep and slow, taking giant lungfuls of Hatherfield into her body.

"What does the *M* stand for?" she said at last.

"What's that?"

"Your middle name."

"Oh. Mortimer."

"Mortimer?"

"My mother's maiden name."

"I see." She cleared her throat. "Er, do you perhaps have any other names? Names by which a wife might call you, in the intimacy of marriage?"

He stroked her back with gentle fingers, up and down, as he might soothe an infant. "My mother called me Jamie, before she died," he said.

"Jamie." She lifted her head and kissed him. "I like that."

He was growing hard again, thickening right there between her legs. She went on kissing him, running her hands over his shoulders. His fingers climbed around her ribs to caress her breasts. "Ride me," he whispered.

"Here?"

"Here."

"But how . . . ?"

"I'll show you." His hands closed around her hips, urging her upward.

She rose on her knees. He reached down and positioned himself beneath her, and she sank down with a slow moan of shock at the bone-deep penetration. "Oh God," she gasped. "It's . . . oh God . . . wait . . ."

"Shh. Just take me in."

She wriggled him inside another fraction of an inch. Her body softened and adjusted, accepting his massive invasion, stretching to accommodate him with an exquisite excess of bursting pleasure.

"Move with me, Stefanie." His voice was hoarse.

"I don't . . ."

"Just move. I'll show you." He nudged her with his hips, and she rose slowly upward, holding his fevered gaze as she went. "That's it," he said, "my own love, my beauty. And back down again."

Down she slid, along the hard column of his cock, slickened by her own body. Up again, and then down, and again, and again, until she found the rhythm and rode him with abandon, up *down* up *down*, the wet friction driving her wild, her head thrown back, her fingers digging into his shoulders, the tips of her breasts offered up for the thrilling rub of his thumbs and forefingers.

"Oh God, oh God, it's so much . . . I can't quite . . ."

He gripped her backside with his strong hands and lifted her with him, still joined, his hips locked against hers. He tumbled her back on the bed and stretched her long and tight. "Look at me, Stefanie," he rasped, and she forced her eyes to meet his. He hovered above her like a bowstring, drawn tight with anticipation, and kissed her lips. "Look at me loving you. As if . . ." His fingers curled around hers, high above her head.

"As if what?" she gasped out.

"As if I've loved you all my life." He thrust his hips into hers, and in a few heroic strokes he finished her off. She cried out, her back curved upward with the crashing force of her climax, and with a low roar he spent hard into her body, his buttocks clenching under her hands, his voice growling her name.

Afterward, drifting to sleep with his body still inside hers, his heavy shoulders draped protectively over hers, she thought how utterly they had united just now, how they were inseparable, bound and soldered together from tip to toe, and that nothing in the world could possibly come between them.

The pounding began shortly after dawn. Hatherfield's body tensed, and in the next instant he leapt to his feet and grabbed the dressing gown from the floor beside the bed.

Stefanie struggled upward. "What is it?"

"Stay here," he barked.

Well, she couldn't do otherwise, lying naked in Hatherfield's bed without a shred of clothing within reach. She sat up and clutched the blankets around her chest and stared at the closed door. Her pulse hammered hard. Was it the anarchists, her father's assassins, hunting her down at last?

She jumped from the bed and ran to the wardrobe. Oh God. Clothes, anything. Hatherfield's suits dwarfed her. She went to the chest of drawers and found a shirt, a pair of old breeches. She threw them on and wrapped a belt around her waist to hold it all together.

From beyond the closed door came the sound of brusque male voices, several of them, and heavy footsteps. The voices lifted almost to shouts, and then Hatherfield's stern tones cut through, low and implacable. What was he saying? Damn it all, what was going on? Were they fighting?

Stay here. But she couldn't just stay, when it was her fault. Her family's enemies.

Weapons. She needed a weapon, fast. Hatherfield must have revolvers about. But where? His drawers contained nothing but clothing and male haberdashery. The desk drawer? Locked. The wardrobe? She flung the door back open and searched the corners with frantic hands, while frantic ears craned to the sounds from the other room.

A firm weight came down on her shoulder.

She started and whipped around.

"Come with me," said Nelson.

"How did you—?"

"There's no time. Come." His hand grabbed hers and tugged her toward the door in the corner, Hatherfield's simple bathroom.

She resisted with fury. "I can't leave him! They'll kill him!"

"For God's sake! Now!" He bent down and flung her over his shoulder and ducked through the doorway into the bathroom. He opened the window and tossed her out.

Her scream was cut short when she thumped atop a wide ledge, a sort of balcony. Nelson's boots crashed into the stone next to her. "Down the stairs. Now."

"But—"

Nelson pulled out a revolver and looked over the ledge to scan the street below. "Go on, now! Master's orders."

A narrow metal staircase zigzagged downward to the alleyway below. Stefanie's feet flew along the steps. She could reach the bottom first and then run around to the entrance and come up, before the men discovered she was missing and hurt Hatherfield. Killed Hatherfield. Oh God! And he had sacrificed Nelson, his one ally, in order to make her safe.

The cold February air rushed across her cheeks and her shirtsleeves, but she hardly noticed the chill. She reached the bottom of the stairs and launched herself forward, but Nelson was ready. "Don't even think about it," he said, grabbing her hand. He dragged her down the alleyway, away from Hatherfield's building, until they came out to Prince Consort Road.

Stefanie looked up the pavement. A cluster of vehicles stood outside the entrance to the building. She strained against Nelson's iron grip.

"This way!" he said.

"Where are we going? I have to see him! I have to help!"

"You can't help." He was hurrying her down the street, without looking back, at a jogging pace just below a run.

"I can try!"

He stopped and spun her about. "You can't. It's the police, miss. We're taking you back to Cadogan Square before anyone knows you're gone. Before anyone connects you with the events of last night."

"But why? The police? What do they want with Hatherfield?"

They turned the corner into Exhibition Road. A hansom was clopping swiftly down the cobbles. Nelson raised his hand. "Because it seems a woman was murdered last night, at that ball."

"Murdered!"

The hansom clattered to a stop beside them. Stefanie looked up and saw with amazement that it was Hatherfield's hansom, Hatherfield's driver. His face was pale. "Get in, miss!"

"I can't!"

Nelson picked her up and hauled her into the seat. The doors banged shut.

"But were are you going?" she demanded.

"Back to the master."

"I don't understand! Will someone tell me what the devil's going on? Is Hatherfield in danger, or not?"

Nelson laid his hands on the metal doors and leaned forward. In the gaslight, the whites of his eyes glowed with sallow malaise, but the pupils were dark and tight and free of liquor. "Nothing he can't handle, I daresay, but there's trouble ahead, and it's best you're out of it."

"What sort of trouble? About the murder?"

Nelson's eyes locked with hers. "It's the Duchess of Southam, ma'am. Stabbed to death with a letter opener in her own boudoir."

The blood drained from Stefanie's head. She curled her fingers around the edge of the doors to steady herself. "Oh no! And do the police think Hatherfield has information about the murderer?"

Nelson's head made a single negatory shake.

"No, ma'am."

"Then why—?"

"They think he *is* the murderer, ma'am. They're taking him off to Scotland Yard this very minute, in a police van like a common criminal."

TWENTY-SEVEN

The gentlemen of the jury filed into their seats, one by one. By and large, their whiskers covered their expressions, though Stefanie strained hard to detect some clue among the springing hair of lip and jowl, some flicker of glance to reveal sympathy or sternness.

Hatherfield stood in the dock as he always did, hands braced lightly on the rail, on either side of his muscular body. She looked at him, and the shock of his blue-eyed gaze went straight to her chest, making her gasp for air.

"Have you reached a decision, gentlemen?" asked the judge.

The foreman stood. "We have, my lord."

The bailiff stepped forward and accepted the folded slip of paper from the foreman's hand. He bore it across the room to the judge's dais, high above the assembled crowd below, the orderly rows and squares of justice.

The judge took the paper, unfolded it, and studied it without expression.

He looked up. "Lord Hatherfield?"

"Yes, my lord."

"The gentlemen of the jury find you guilty of the crime of murder."

Guilty.

The blood left Stefanie's head in a sudden rush. She gripped the edges of the table to keep herself from falling. From the corner of the room came the sound of wailing.

Hatherfield's face, stark and shocked.

The wooden crack of the gavel.

The gray-haired voice of the judge: "Sentencing to take place tomorrow at noon in these chambers. Court is adjourned."

TWENTY-EIGHT

The guard's voice was respectful. "A visitor, your lordship."
Hatherfield went on staring at the stone ceiling above
him, the infinite pattern of round intersecting shapes. His
brain was still numb with shock, still unable to comprehend
this basic contradiction. That he was innocent, and yet he was
guilty.

Guilty, the judge had said. But he was innocent.

"Send him in," he said.

A creak of hinges, and then Stefanie's familiar footsteps on
the flagstones. The door closed with a gentle bang.

She hesitated near the threshold. He could feel the tender
weight of her indecision, a few yards away; the undulation of
her grief in the hot quietude of his prison cell. He held out his
hand.

"Oh, Hatherfield." She knelt beside the cot, holding his
hand to her cheek.

He sat up and bent over her head. The soft hair smelled of
soap and pomade and Stefanie, warm against his lips. "Shh.
Shh. It's all right, little one."

"It's not possible. Guilty. How could they think you
guilty? You?"

"Because a woman is dead, Stefanie. Murdered brutally in her own boudoir. Someone has to pay."

"It's not possible. Sir John . . ." Her back heaved. "Sir John said that was the point of the British system of justice. That sometimes the guilty go free, and that's the price we pay so that the innocent aren't convicted."

He closed his eyes and concentrated on every detail of her, every tremor of her body, every sob from her throat. "Listen to me, sweetheart. We haven't much time. I want to be sure you'll be taken care of, safe and sound. Nelson will look after you. I'm going to leave a letter for Sir John, explaining everything, and until your uncle turns up again . . ."

"Stop. Stop. Don't speak as if it's certain."

He stroked her hair. "The houses, everything I own, it's yours. I've already had documents made up . . ."

"Stop." She lifted her head and took him by the ears. "It's not possible. It's not possible. They can't do this."

He kissed her, because what else could he do? She was there, and time was short. He took her lips gently, stroked her cheeks gently. Her mustache tickled his lip. The softness of her skin was a miracle.

She pulled back an inch or two. Her eyes were wet. "I have something for you," she said.

"What is it?" He couldn't stop touching her face, her sweet skin.

She reached for the buttons of her jacket, her padded jacket that hid her feminine body from the watchful world. One by one she slipped the small brass knobs through their holes, while her wet eyes remained fixed on his, and the blood coursed like fire in his veins.

"Sweetheart, we can't . . ." The words struggled out, but there was something in the way she undid the last button, something in the way she parted the jacket, and in the instant before her swollen waistcoat appeared before him, he realized what she was trying to show him.

He whispered, "Oh God. Stefanie."

"I couldn't tell you." The tears were wandering down her face now. "I thought you might do something foolish, and by the time I knew for certain, we were already so busy, and I thought I'd tell you afterward, when you were free and we could . . ."

"Oh God. Oh God." He slipped off the cot, on his knees next to her on the hard stone floor. "Oh, my little one."

"I'm sorry."

"Don't be sorry. Oh God." He held her, rocking her against him, trying to encompass this new thought, this great and terrible miracle. Stefanie's belly nestled into his like a round little melon. His brain grasped at the sequence of months, trying to count them. Five? Six? "I am a selfish brute," he said.

"Don't say that." Her arms tightened around him. "I wouldn't change a moment. Not a single moment."

"How . . ." His throat was so tight, he could hardly speak. "When?"

"November."

There were things he should say, things he wanted to say. Joy and fear and pummeling grief. And gratitude to her, to Stefanie. And guilt, for what he had done to her.

He couldn't say any of them. The words had simply fled, leaving him hollow, leaving him crammed to bursting.

He thought, she shouldn't be on the hard stone floor like this.

He lifted her up and sat down on the bed and wept quietly into her hair.

He was used to the slow passage of time in prison, the eternal passage of seconds and minutes. You couldn't fight it. You simply accepted the hours as they were given; you anchored yourself in place and let the clock tick and tick around you. You paid attention to the warmth of the woman in your arms, the darling shape of her elbow, the shadow of her eyelashes on her cheek. You unbuttoned her waistcoat and loosened her shirt and laid your hand over the promising curve of her belly, and you thought to yourself, this is my child, my child who will be born and cry and love and live on after I am gone. This is the woman who will give him life, who carries my heart inside her body.

Stefanie lay quietly under his caressing hand, curled on his lap. Her hand wrapped around his knee. Every so often she let out a shuddering breath, and he stroked her hair with his other hand.

She turned in his lap to look up at him. "You have to live. We have to find a way to save you."

"They will hang me, Stefanie."

She sat up. "Let me save you. For God's sake. Let me tell them who I am, that I was the woman you were with."

"You can't."

"To save your life, Hatherfield!"

He hesitated, brushing her cheek with his finger. "It wouldn't change anything. Even if they believed you, it's not enough to call a new trial. And you weren't with me all the time. There was that gap, half an hour, right when the murder was supposed to happen. Right when the duchess went up to her boudoir. So it would all be for nothing. And you would expose yourself irrevocably, and I would still be here in this damned prison, unable to help you."

"There's been no attempt on me since the night of the ball. Nothing at all."

"Because they don't know who you are. Where you are."

"I don't care. I'll face that danger if it comes."

"You'll be put in jail yourself, then, for impersonation. For—I don't know, whatever the crime is, fraudulent representation to the court."

She took his lapels. "Better that, than your death!"

"I can't let you do it. I can't let you put yourself in danger . . ."

"You won't have a choice."

"Stefanie, no . . ."

She was running her hands over his chest, his shirtsleeves, back to his face. "Don't you understand? I need you. I'll do anything."

"Shh . . ."

"You are not allowed to sacrifice yourself for me. You are not allowed to do that to me, to make me live without you."

Her lips touched his. Her fingers found the waistband of his trousers, and he covered them with his hands.

"No," he said. "Not here, we can't . . ."

"Hatherfield. James. Jamie. My dear, dear love." She whispered the words into his mouth. "I need you so. Let me touch you, just once. Let me comfort you. Please."

"The guard." His resolve was disintegrating under the sensation of her touch, under the whispered word *Jamie*, under the pressure of desire that had settled into his loins for months now, unfilled and aching, a natural and necessary part of him.

"He's never interrupted us before, has he?" She undid the first button, and the next. His erection was already straining at the placket. Had been straining since she walked into his prison cell.

"Stefanie."

She looked up at him. Her eyes were large and round. "You'll let me, won't you? You'll trust me? You'll let me touch you?"

His hands went to her head. He ran his fingers along her short, silky hair, the delicate bumps of her ears, and said nothing. His breath had stopped in his chest, anticipation and fear and *need*, oh God, this craving for Stefanie, so acute and profound and lasting it was written on his bones.

She spread apart the placket of his trousers, and he sprang into her gentle hands.

A slow sigh rushed from his lungs, a gust of relief.

This was right and true and beautiful. This was Stefanie.

"You are so perfect," Stefanie whispered. She ran her fingers up and down his length, from base to tip, and then, without warning, she bent her head downward and took him into her mouth.

The wet heat of her lips and tongue surrounded him so unexpectedly, so intense and so pleasurable, he nearly came in that instant. His torso jerked, while his hands tightened around her head.

She didn't stop to ask if he was all right, if he liked it, if he wanted it, and he was grateful. How could he tell her how many times he had imagined this, aroused and shameful in his prison bed, when the lights were out and he had only the darkness for company? How could he say the base words? *God yes, suck my prick until I spend, work me with your tongue and your hot mouth and your sliding fingers until I lose myself in you.*

She had no rhythm, no skill at all. She had obviously never done this before. But this was Stefanie, this was her mouth on him, slick and firm and eager and loving, and in less than a minute his climax tingled in his stones and built and built, and he tried to pull away but she held on with the eager mewl of a kitten lapping a bowl of cream, and that single sound was his

undoing. He let himself go, he spent luxuriously in her mouth
as his hands cupped the curve of her head and his tears wet the
corners of his eyes.

When Stefanie arrived in Cadogan Square, dinner had
already been cleared and Sir John sat alone in the dining room, rolling the brandy about his snifter and staring into
the fire.

He looked up and saw her. "Come in, Mr. Thomas. I expect
you're just back from Old Bailey?"

"Yes, sir."

She stepped reluctantly into the room, which reeked of
smoke and melancholy. Sir John's face hung in folds of pasty
gray, and his eyes were rimmed in red. He sat with his shoulders slumped over the cloth. A cigar sat smoking in a tray near
his elbow.

"How is his lordship holding up? Were you able to buck his
spirits a bit?"

Stefanie raised her fist to her mouth and coughed. "A bit. I
had hoped to go out again, go over the evidence. Something
we missed, perhaps."

"I've gone over it a thousand times." He shook his head.
"The interviews with the witnesses, the physical evidence. If
only someone had seen something. And that's the devil of it.
There isn't any actual evidence, not a shred of it, that Hatherfield did the deed. The whole damned house was seething with
people. Fairchurch, I believe, did a decent job of establishing
that. And yet the jury convicted him. They wanted someone's
blood, I suppose. Wanted someone to pay. Or perhaps wanted
to believe that there wasn't some crazed murderer still on the
loose." He shook his head. "Poor fellow."

"I haven't given up hope. Somebody did this, somebody
murdered her. There's got to be some clue somewhere."

"After all these months? Something new?"

Stefanie shifted her feet. She was itching to be off, to go
upstairs with her papers and books, to find something, some
technical aspect of law, some overlooked statement that even
now might be presented before the court. She had to do something. Something to relieve this ache in her chest, something

to think about other than the feel of him on her lips, the knowledge that she might never feel him there again.

Because tomorrow at noon, if nothing else arose, she would have to play her last desperate card.

"Where is her ladyship?" Stefanie asked quietly.

"Out with her maid. I don't know where. I don't particularly give a damn." He picked up his cigar and drew in deep. "I'd wash my hands of her, if I could."

"She told the court what she knew."

"Spiteful bitch. That poor fellow. I sent off letters to the Queen today, to the Prime Minister, begging for some sort of clemency. I don't know if it shall have any effect." He went to stub out his cigar, and then thought better of it. His hand shook as he lifted the end to his lips. "Do you know something, Thomas? I don't believe I ever want to see the interior of a courtroom again."

Upstairs, she tore off her collar and her mustache and jacket. She undid the buttons on her waistcoat and drew a long sigh of relief. After months of blessed flatness, her belly had suddenly begun to swell a fortnight ago, increasing daily, fluttering and quickening with life. Soon she would be too big to hide, and what would she do?

She had to save him. She had to.

She turned to her wardrobe for a dressing gown, and in the corner of her eye she saw a small square envelope on her desk.

Mr. Stephen Thomas, Cadogan Square, London, read the address on the back, but it was not the words themselves that stopped her short.

It was the lettering.

The unmistakable copperplate of Miss Dingleby's cultured handwriting.

Stefanie had been gone half an hour when the guard announced another visitor.

Hatherfield rose to his feet and straightened his collar.

"Mr. Wright," he said. "Welcome. I'd offer you a glass of

sherry, but . . ." He made an apologetic gesture to the stone walls around them.

"Hardly necessary, under the circumstances." Nathaniel Wright removed his hat and set it on the table. "A rather decent system of civil bribery you've got in place here. I wasn't asked to grease a single palm."

Hatherfield shrugged. "They're good chaps, really. Expensive, but well worth the cost."

"I quite agree. What can I do for you, old man?" Wright's tone was that of one friend greeting another in the confines of a club library. Not a single note of awkward sympathy clouded his tone; not a single shade of softness obscured his dark gaze.

"You know the verdict that came down today."

"Yes, I heard. Hard luck. I'm sorry if my little testimony had anything to do with it. I wish I might have helped you."

"You did help me. You forbore to mention your encounter with . . . with the lady downstairs, and that has meant everything. Has quite possibly saved her life."

"While sacrificing yours." Wright's eyes were sharp as they regarded him.

Hatherfield motioned to the single chair. Wright settled into the hard wooden seat as if it were an armchair before the fire; Hatherfield lowered himself on the edge of his cot. "You haven't asked me who she is."

"It was not my affair."

"Would you mind particularly if I make it your affair?"

Wright picked up his hat from the table and fingered the edge. "In what way?"

How dim it was, in this cell. No matter how many oil lamps were brought in, it never seemed enough to chase away the dark summer, warm and oppressive. The skin of Wright's face was dusky, his eyes shadowed.

Say it, old boy. Go ahead. Your time's run out.

He began.

"I expect I shall be sentenced to hang tomorrow, and the execution will likely be carried out shortly thereafter. Stefanie . . ." He steadied himself. "She is five months gone with child, she is moreover in danger of her life, and I would go to my end with a far easier heart if I knew that someone capable—someone loyal, someone with the power and will to protect those under his care—were looking after her affairs."

The words, as he spoke them, caused a peculiar stabbing pain in the region of his heart. As if someone were slicing the organ from between his ribs.

"I see." Wright's fingers were long and brown as they circled about his hat. "Are you asking me to marry her?"

"That's not something I can ask of another man. In any case, the choice remains hers."

Wright spun his hat and watched him. "You love her," he said at last.

Hatherfield breathed quietly. When he could speak, he said, "More than my own life."

"So it seems." *Tap tap tap* went Wright's fingers on the smooth felt of his hat. "If I were to take this charge, I would need, as a practical matter, to know who she is. What danger threatens her."

"She is the youngest princess of Holstein-Schweinwald-Huhnhof."

Wright startled in his chair. "By God!"

"Yes. You perceive the peculiar nature of her case. Why I could not allow her to identify herself. At the moment, there is no one of her own family to protect her, no one to restore her to her birthright. The Duke of Olympia is her guardian, but he's left London entirely, and I haven't heard from him in months."

Wright rose from his chair and paced across the room. "By God."

"I have already endowed her with all I have. The houses, the rest of the money from my mother's side. The properties are nearly ready to sell, and I hope you'll assist her in obtaining the best possible price."

"I have a question," Wright said, facing the wall.

"What is it?"

"Why me? You will pardon my observing that we are hardly friends."

Hatherfield watched the back of Wright's dark head, his straight shoulders. "Because you're a man of your word. A loyal protector of a sister with no necessary charge on your duty or affection. The most trustworthy gentleman of my acquaintance."

Wright turned. His voice was low and respectful. "By God, Hatherfield. What a man you are."

Hatherfield rose to his feet. "Will you do it?"

Wright stood quite still, his large black body filling the space against the wall. He regarded Hatherfield with a peculiar expression. "I am honored beyond measure by your trust in me, Lord Hatherfield. I shall endeavor my utmost to carry out your wishes."

"And the child?" He could hardly say the words.

"Will be raised under my protection."

Hatherfield turned away. "Thank you," he whispered.

The wall stared back at him, gray and lifeless. How many days left? Hours of this life? How was it possible that you could count the minutes and seconds remaining to you in this world, with the woman you loved? How did you find the courage to leave, while your precious child grew inside her?

Behind him, Wright made not a sound.

"I have carried a special license in my pocket, in hope of a favorable verdict," Hatherfield said at last. "You may want to do the same."

"If she agrees."

"She will not, at first." Hatherfield held up his hands and stared at the palms, crisscrossed with old lines, thickened with callus. "She has a regal will. And the noblest heart in the world."

"I shall endeavor to be worthy of her."

Two knocks shook the door, closely spaced and urgent. The thick wood slid open.

"Sir." The guard's voice was laden with respect for the dead. "A message for you, express."

Hatherfield took the paper from his outstretched hand, and waited until the door closed again before opening it.

He read the few scrawled lines. For a moment, in the prison of his shock, their meaning was lost on him.

And then, as if charged by electricity, his brain burst back into life.

"Good news, I hope," said Wright.

Hatherfield looked up and turned. The blood was shooting in his veins, but it was a familiar sensation, the brilliant heightened awareness of purpose. The way he had once felt, in another lifetime, when steadying his boat at the start of a race. When a summons arrived in a plain envelope from the Duke of Olympia. "The opposite, I'm afraid."

"I am at your service."

Hatherfield refolded the paper while his thoughts assembled and resolved into clarity. He considered Wright's figure against the wall, his height and breadth and stance.

"My dear fellow," he said, "have you a taste for subterfuge?"

Wright crossed his arms and smiled, white toothed in the dimness. "Subterfuge? I am not opposed to it."

"In that case, I would be very much obliged if you would be so good as to lend me your hat."

TWENTY-NINE

The wide silver moon flashed on the cobbles ahead.
Stefanie gripped the frame of the hansom in anticipation of the curve around Trafalgar Square. The Nelson Column gleamed whitely above her for an instant, and then it
was gone.

Victoria Embankment, the note had said. Near the Temple
Underground station.

Miss Dingleby would help. Miss Dingleby would know
what to do. The wildest possibilities swung about her brain,
tantalizing her with hope. With Miss Dingleby's help, she could
perhaps spring Hatherfield from prison. Together they
could hide him, they could even spirit him back to Germany,
and bring her father's murderers to justice at last. He'd be safe
from prosecution behind the familiar old walls of Holstein
Castle. With Hatherfield by her side, she could face her old life
again. They could marry, they could heal the wounds brought
about by all the upheaval. A royal wedding, a new little prince
or princess. She put her hand protectively over the small swell
of her abdomen.

And perhaps, one day, they could clear Hatherfield's name.

The driver brought them expertly down the approach to the
Embankment. She hadn't had time to find Nelson and tell him

where she was going, but that didn't matter. Miss Dingleby could be trusted.

She peered ahead, between the horse's swiveling ears. In the distance, to the left, between the trees of the Embankment, she could make out the hulking box of the Tube station. She rapped on the roof. "Just there!" she said.

"I don't like it, sir," said the driver. "I don't think the master'd like it, neither."

"I'm meeting a friend, Smith," she said. "It's quite all right. And there's plenty of moon, at least." Thank God it was August; no cold miasma of fog and coal smoke. Only a clear night, a three-quarters moon, a few clouds drifting in a silver daze across the warm, dark sky.

"I don't like it." He slowed the horse to a walk.

Stefanie stood up on the floorboards and craned her neck. "Do you see anyone, Smith?"

"No one, sir."

"Keep going, then."

Her heart crashed in her ears. This couldn't be some sort of deception, could it? She knew Miss Dingleby's handwriting like she knew her own, and the passcode had been written at the top, exactly as they'd been instructed. No, it was Dingleby, all right.

It had to be.

Her palms were growing damp, making her hands slip against the black paint of the hansom doors. A movement caught her eye, a short figure in a bowler hat, weaving his way along the railing. He looked up as they passed him. "You're a fine lad!" he shouted. "Don't let them bugger you, them fine gentlemen what . . ." The rest was lost.

A cold shudder passed through her body, a vague presentiment. As if the bowler-hatted man had been a warning of some kind.

The horse walked briskly on. Another hansom passed them at a smart trot, and just as the driver's tall hat whisked out of sight, Stefanie spotted the familiar dark silhouette near the railing.

She thumped the roof. "Stop!"

Instantly, the horse wheeled to a halt.

"Let me out!" she said, and the doors sprang open.

"Wait, sir!" called the driver, but she was already jumping down to the pavement and running across the road to the railing, to the shape of Miss Dingleby against the rippling moonlit riverscape of the Thames.

The figure spread out its arms. "Stefanie, my dear!" called Miss Dingleby's well-remembered voice.

In the tumultuous course of Stefanie's adolescence, she and Miss Dingleby had not always been the best of friends. An incident rose to mind, even as she rushed to throw herself in those dark outstretched arms: Stefanie, forced on a dulcet summer's day to copy out all ninety-five of Martin Luther's theses, in the original Latin, while her sisters enjoyed a picnic expedition on the banks of the Holsteinsee, all because of some innocent prank involving a jar of paste, a pet ferret, and the visiting Prime Minister of Bohemia.

But all that was forgotten in the instant of Miss Dingleby's wiry arms closing about her back.

"You came back!" she said. "You came back."

"Of course I came back." Miss Dingleby put her hands to Stefanie's arms and set her away. "Of course I came back, my dear. How could you doubt me?"

"I didn't hear a word from you. Not a word."

"I was rather busy, investigating this matter of the anarchists."

Stefanie's eyes began to fill. "And all this time, the most terrible thing . . ."

"Yes, yes. This marquis of yours, getting himself in a dreadful pickle. I do hope it's all sorted out."

"It's not, I'm afraid. It's as bad as it could be. Today the court, the jury found him guilty of murdering his stepmother. Guilty! They'll hang him, and he's innocent, he's innocent, and we've got to save him . . ."

Miss Dingleby's hands gripped her arms with renewed strength. "What in heaven's name is all this? These tears, Stefanie! What's the matter with you?"

"They'll hang him, Miss Dingleby! You've got to save him!"

"By heaven, you're as flighty as a . . ." Miss Dingleby stopped. Her gaze moved downward. "Oh, by my old aunt Matilda. Not you, too."

"You have to help me, Dingleby," Stefanie whispered.

Dingleby rolled her eyes heavenward. "You, Stefanie? Even you? What the devil's in the English air? All of you, falling in love, getting yourselves with child at the first opportunity. I taught you better than this, by God!"

Stefanie straightened her back proudly. "You taught us to pursue our convictions with energy, and so I have. I have defended him in a court of law. You'd be proud of me, Dingleby. Every day, I've devoted myself to his case, I've studied and analyzed every aspect of the law as it relates to . . ."

"And for what? For love?" As she might say, *For raspberry trifle?*

"To save him. To save an innocent man from punishment, a good man, the best of men . . ."

Even in the haze of moonlight, Miss Dingleby's face of disapproval could melt iron. "This is not why I brought you to England, Stefanie. This is not what you were put on this earth to do."

For the first time, Stefanie heard the voices on the other side of the railing. The slap of water against surface.

"But you'll help me, won't you?" she asked.

Dingleby forced her face into sympathy. "My dear, of course I should very much like to help, but I'm afraid we haven't time."

"Haven't time? But what's going on?" Stefanie's gaze shifted to the railing, where a figure was drawing up from the riverside, a large male figure, placing his hands on adjoining cast-iron posts in preparation to vault himself over. "Look out!" She lurched forward and shoved Miss Dingleby out of the way.

A gasp of outrage. "Stefanie! What's the matter with you?"

"That man!" Stefanie pulled out the revolver from her jacket pocket, Hatherfield's revolver, the one he'd taught her to use himself.

"Put that away!" Miss Dingleby snatched the revolver. "He's ours, you fool. Always the impetuous one, Stefanie."

Stefanie fell back a single pace. "Ours?"

"Yes, ours." She motioned to the man, and he heaved himself over the railing and stepped toward Stefanie. His mouth, under the wide brim of his hat, was open in a large and familiar smile.

"Don't you recognize me, Stefanie?" he said in German, and he took off his hat.

Shock paralyzed the muscles of Stefanie's limbs. For an instant, she could only stare at him stupidly, not quite believing the evidence before her.

"Gunther?" she whispered.

In the early hours of the morning, before the verdict, when the Marquess of Hatherfield had risen and dressed, he had imagined walking out of the Old Bailey later that day, a free man, to join Stefanie in some private and predetermined location.

He had not, however, imagined doing so wearing the hat and jacket of Mr. Nathaniel Wright, natural half brother of Lady Charlotte Harlowe.

Astonishing how easy it had been. Men saw what they expected to see, he supposed, and as he and Wright were of roughly the same build, and wore the same hat, and flashed the same pass in the dim prison corridors to the dim prison guards, he found himself whisked through the front gates in surprisingly short order, a free man.

But not so free. He had to return before the guards discovered the deception. More imperatively, he had to find Stefanie on the Victoria Embankment before disaster struck.

And yet he couldn't deny the thrill of breathing in the warm night air. The loose and unfettered sensation of independence, no guard at his back, no company at all. A free man.

He struck off down the street, as hastily as he could without seeming suspicious. A hansom trotted by, passing like a ghost under the gaslight. "Need a taxi, mate?" asked the driver.

Hatherfield hesitated, and then remembered he hadn't any money. "Thanks, I'll walk," he said. It wasn't far, after all. Victoria Embankment, near Temple Tube station. Nelson would join him there. *Walking into a trap*, the note had said. How had Nelson discovered this? It didn't matter. All that mattered was reaching her in time.

He'd been given one last chance to secure her safety for good. He prayed he could succeed, for her sake. For their child's sake.

He turned the corner of Ludgate Hill and increased his pace, a man in a spot of hurry, nothing too remarkable. The Embankment wasn't too far away, a few hundred yards. He rounded down New Bridge Street and broke into a jog.

The moon came into view, a flattened orb, not quite full. His heart ached at the beauty of it. The buildings rose silent around him, commonplace London buildings, and while the front part of his mind was calculating the speed at which Nelson would have reached the Embankment, the relative distance there from Belgravia versus Old Bailey, the angles of vision and the height of the river tide and the degree of likely traffic, the rear portion of his brain followed each roofline, each column and grimy doorway with a loving eye.

How many times had he walked around London, never seeing its particular teeming beauty, never stopping to *treasure* that hour as he hurried to some appointment or another, some errand or task that had to be accomplished?

And now the hour had fled, his life had fled, and he had never loved London so much.

The Embankment trees lay ahead, silvered with moonlight. Hatherfield inhaled the brown brackish scent of the river, the pumping femoral artery of London.

He moved quietly in the lee of the buildings, down the approach, until the shadows of the Temple gardens massed to his right. He let out a low whistle.

A shape materialized out of the darkness. "Sir."

"Nelson."

A metal shape nudged at his hand. He accepted the revolver into his palm, a perfect fit, cold and familiar and reassuring.

"They're just ahead, sir. You can make them out by the railing."

Hatherfield narrowed his eyes. Two figures. No, three. Two men and a woman, except that one of the men was slighter than the other, carrying his head and shoulders in such a way that it could only be Stefanie.

Stefanie.

Hatherfield took an instinctive step forward.

Nelson held out his arm. "Wait, sir."

Hatherfield stilled himself by sheer force of will. The other man was opening his arms, and Stefanie—by God!—Stefanie was stepping forward, she was allowing herself into his embrace.

A wave of primal fury swept across his chest.

"What the devil?" he hissed.

"Sir! There they are, sir!"

A cluster of shadows emerged from the gloom of Temple Tube station.

Hatherfield broke into a run. Nelson panted at his heels, but Hatherfield was honed and fit from the rowing apparatus in his prison cell. His legs stretched out and flew, driven by fear and fury, as the shapes from the station resolved into men, and the men pounced on the three figures by the railing.

He cocked the gun as he went, as his legs pumped faster and faster and his lungs burned and flooded with oxygen. A man had grabbed Stefanie and yanked her arms behind her back. Fifty yards away, forty. Stefanie's scream carried through the air, and he roared from deep in his throat.

The men turned. "Drop them!" he yelled, and he fired at the man holding Stefanie.

A shout of pain, and the man fell to the ground.

But the others had sprung into action. "Get the princess!" someone yelled. "No, not her, the ginger, the one in the waistcoat!" Men were moving, they were vaulting the railing down to the piers and boat landings below.

In the blur of shifting bodies, he couldn't find Stefanie. He heard her scream again, and the sound shot through him like an arrow. He stuffed the revolver in his waistband and launched himself over the rail.

"Nelson!" he roared out.

"Hatherfield?" Stefanie's voice, amazed and frantic.

"At the railing!" he called.

To the boat! someone said, a woman. *Hurry!*

A mad stampede, a struggle. Stefanie flashed ahead of him, carried along down the stone steps to the landing below, struggling to fight the tide. Someone had her hand. A woman, a woman in dark clothes.

"Stefanie!" he called again, pushing aside the bodies, and then something hurtled into his back, knocking him flying.

"Hatherfield!" she screamed, the last sound he heard before he plunged headfirst into the oily River Thames.

Stefanie saw the water close over Hatherfield's shoes in a flash of reflected moonlight.

"No!" she screamed. She lunged forward to the edge of the pier, and a hand clapped over her mouth. She swung her limbs wildly, but it was no use. Arms clamped around her chest and heaved her over a heavy shoulder, and the world swirled around her in a chaos of men and shouts and water.

"Hatherfield!" she called out desperately.

Her abductor strode down the pier. The wooden edge of a boat swam past her bouncing vision, and down she swung to land on the smooth oak bottom with a gentle thump.

"Quickly!" said Miss Dingleby.

Stefanie struggled to her feet. "Hatherfield! He's fallen in the water! We've got to save him!"

"There's no time. I daresay he can swim." Miss Dingleby aimed her pistol at a man attempting to board. Around her, the crew of the boat were casting off rope, were picking up oars and shoving them into the chests and stomachs and hands of their attackers on the pier. Like corsairs, fending off a boarding party.

Stefanie ran to the stern of the boat and strained to see the shifting water. "We've got to go back! We can't just leave him to die!"

"We'll die ourselves in a minute! Did you bring your revolver?" Miss Dingleby's hand rooted in her pocket.

Stefanie cast off her jacket. "I'm going after him!"

"No!" A pair of thick hands jerked at her collar.

Stefanie spun around to find Gunther staring down at her with a ferocious expression. Gunther, fully a man now, large and meaty. "You don't understand! I love him! I can't just . . ."

Gunther picked her up and carried her to the wheelhouse. The boat had parted from the pier, the steam engine was rumbling them forward.

"Gunther Hassendorf! Put me down!" she screamed, and with all her might she kicked him directly in the stones.

Well, not directly. Her aim was off by an inch or two. But it was enough to make him howl with outraged masculinity, and in that instant of weakness she wriggled from his grasp and ran back to the stern of the boat, kicking off her shoes as she went.

But they were under way, and her path was blocked by a pair of dark-haired men. The one on the left lunged forward, and in the curiously elastic second before he grabbed her by the ribs and held a slim knife to her throat, she thought, *I know him.*

"Put your weapons away!" the man growled, in a thick German accent.

Miss Dingleby raised her pistol.

The other man kicked it out of her hand with the casual strike of a venomous reptile. He picked it up in the same arc of motion and aimed it at the advancing Gunther.

"Throttle back the engine!" said the man holding Stefanie. His voice vibrated her spine.

Miss Dingleby turned to the pilot in the wheelhouse. "Throttle back."

The pilot, white-faced, reached for the lever. The boat slowed to an idle.

The other intruder pointed his gun at Gunther. "You." Another man, another. "You. You. Into the water."

"I can't swim!" protested one of the chosen.

"I said, into the water, or the princess dies!"

Gunther folded his arms. "No."

The second man raised his revolver. Gunther flinched and fell back, but the deadly little barrel passed him right by, and came to rest in the direction of Miss Dingleby's bare head.

The man holding Stefanie said, "Order the men overboard, or your governess dies."

"Don't do it, Stefanie," said Dingleby. "I'm not afraid."

Stefanie tried to swallow, but the blade was sharp against her throat. "You're the men from last winter. The men who tried to kidnap me and Emilie."

"Don't talk," he said. He nudged the knife. "Tell them to go into the water."

"I won't!"

The other man fired the revolver. Miss Dingleby fell back, clutching her shoulder, and Stefanie tried to hurtle herself free. But the man only grasped her anew, crushing her against his chest. She grabbed at his arm, trying to free the knife.

And then a blur shot past her eyes and she was free.

She staggered forward and turned around.

"Hatherfield!"

There he stood, jacketless, shoeless, wet shirt plastered to his muscular chest. He punched her attacker with pistonlike shots to his jaw, driving him to the boat's edge, and with a last flying uppercut sent him flipping over the side and into the water.

Without a pause, Hatherfield spun about, and at that instant the other man launched himself at Hatherfield's back.

Stefanie's shocked muscles burst into action. At her feet, the knife gleamed silver in the moonlight. She picked it up and rushed forward.

"Stay back, Stefanie!" Hatherfield barked. He twisted his body and heaved upward, and the other man flew into the air to land with a groan on the bottom of the boat.

Hatherfield hauled him up by the collar and turned to where Miss Dingleby sat, white-faced, against the side of the boat, tended by Gunther.

"Do you need him?" Hatherfield asked coolly.

Miss Dingleby shook her head.

Without the slightest ceremony, Hatherfield lifted the man and tipped him over the side of the boat.

Hatherfield tied up the makeshift bandage with a neat knot and patted Miss Dingleby's other shoulder. "The ball passed straight through, thank God. The whiskey should help prevent suppuration, but you should see a doctor straightaway."

He straightened his aching frame and allowed himself at last to turn to Stefanie. She stood against the door of the wheelhouse, watching him with a peculiar expression, her eyes soft and her brow worried.

"How did you—" She shook her head and blinked.

Hatherfield's hands flexed with the need to touch her. He folded his arms instead. "I had a message from Nelson. Mr. Wright happened to be visiting me in my cell, and was happy to assist me with a little temporary deception."

She swallowed. "Temporary?"

"I have to go back, Stefanie. For one thing, I can't leave Wright there to be charged with aiding and abetting." He looked at Miss Dingleby, who was sipping her whiskey—a little internal application to complement the topical application—and watching them both with sharp eyes. "Can you tell me what's happened here tonight? Is she safe at last?"

"Yes, I believe so. Those men"—she nodded at the porthole—"were the ones sent from Germany to track the sisters down, the ones who escaped our net in February."

"And what were you doing here tonight, in this boat?"

She set down her empty whiskey glass and met his gaze. "I have a ship waiting in the Solent to take Stefanie back to Germany. Olympia and I have tracked down and eliminated the conspirators."

Stefanie gasped. "Just like that? We can go home to the old pile?"

"Yes. Your uncle awaits you at Holstein Castle. He's sent messages out to your sisters. You're all to return." She dropped her gaze to Stefanie's belly. "I suppose we'll sort out all the sordid details when we arrive."

From the shadowed corner of the wheelhouse, a broad-shouldered young man stepped forward. "I will take responsibility for Her Highness," he said, in pleasantly accented German.

Hatherfield turned to face him. The hair bristled at the back of his neck. "And who the devil are you?"

"My name is Gunther Hassendorf." He held out his hand. "A loyal friend of the Crown, and Her Highness's devoted servant."

Gunther. Stefanie's devoted servant.

Hatherfield held out his hand. "Hatherfield. A pleasure, Herr Hassendorf. I've heard a great deal about you from Stefanie. How is your wife?"

Gunther looked down. "My wife is dead."

"I see." He turned to Miss Dingleby and raised a questioning eyebrow. She shrugged her uninjured shoulder.

And then Stefanie strode boldly forward and linked her arm with his. "Gunther, my dear old fellow, wish me joy. Lord Hatherfield is my fiancé. A bit behindhand with rings and all that, but I believe I've trapped him rather expertly. We are expecting our first child in November."

Gunther's eyes widened. He looked at Stefanie's middle,

turned pale, looked up, and swiveled helplessly to Miss Dingleby. "But how are we to . . ."

Miss Dingleby rose, with only the tiniest wince of pain. "It seems there is a change of plan, Gunther. Lord Hatherfield, we welcome you to the family. No doubt His Grace will be eager to see you wed at the earliest opportunity." A slight emphasis on the word *earliest*. "Should your child prove a son, he will be the next Prince of Holstein-Schweinwald-Huhnhof. That is, unless one of my other appallingly fecund young ladies produces a boy, in which case he will merely be another useless prince, lowercase, clogging up the drawing rooms of Europe."

The words floated past his ears, dizzy with hope. Stefanie's hands grasped his, next to her chest. He looked down at her blankly.

"Yes! You see? The perfect solution. Come with us, leave England behind. You'll be safe, we'll be married, you'll have everything. Banquets, sycophants, perhaps even a small crown of some sort, if one can be dug up from the attics somewhere. Our people will adore you. Children and mastiffs will follow you about." She threw her arms around his neck and kissed him. "*I'll* follow you about, for that matter."

"Stefanie, it's impossible," he whispered. "I'm a convicted murderer."

She drew back. "But you're innocent!"

"You want me to flee like a criminal in the night? Turn my back on England? Renounce my own country?"

Stefanie gripped his shoulders. "I don't know if the fact's occurred to you yet—you're rather opaque about such things—but England betrayed *you*, Hatherfield. Don't be a fool. Come with me, live by my side. Our children will grow up away from all this democratic rubbish, in peace and security and lederhosen. And you'll finally have a decent mug of ale, which is no small consideration, in my judgment."

"And Wright? Simply leave him to rot in prison, for aiding my escape? He trusted me."

The soft hiss of steam covered his last words, as the pilot tended the engine.

Miss Dingleby spoke. "Gunther, my dear. I believe our guests need a moment or two of privacy."

"Stefanie," said Gunther softly.

She turned to the German. "Gunther, you silly ass. I love him."

Miss Dingleby took Gunther firmly by the arm and led him from the wheelhouse. When the door closed, Stefanie placed her palms on Hatherfield's chest and looked up at him with her blue eyes, her true eyes.

"Please. For the sake of what we've shared. For our child, Hatherfield."

He stared back at her, unable to speak. The temptation lay dangling before him, glowing with promise. A heaven that, by the very act of entering it, he could not deserve.

"I know how you feel. That honor of yours, that loyal and impractical British heart. But your time here is finished. We'll start fresh. My people will treat you as you deserve, Hatherfield. You'll be a prince, you'll be my love, my darling, my husband." There were tears, now, filling the corners of her eyes, hurting his heart. "Don't leave us alone. You can't even be thinking of it."

His throat strained. "You won't be alone."

"I am always alone, when you're not by my side."

He lifted his hand and caressed her cheek.

"You'll stay with me. You'll let me love you." She closed her eyes and leaned into his hand, and the immaculate curve of her cheek fitted his palm like the softest peach.

Hatherfield leaned down and kissed her.

"I will build you a throne next to the sun," he said.

He waited until she was falling asleep, curled up on the bench in the wheelhouse, while the pilot maneuvered the boat through the tidal eddies toward the Solent. "Just wait until you have your first sip of hefeweizen, Hatherfield," she murmured. "It will change your life."

"I know it will." He smoothed the hair from her forehead.

Her eyes drifted shut. "Oh. The baby's moving. Little chap seems to delight in fluttering about when I'm trying to . . . to rest . . ."

He laid his hand over her shirt, just above the waist of her trousers. The round bump was about the size of his spread fingers, firm and smooth.

A smile brushed across her lips. "You'll make a wonder-ful . . . father . . ."

Father.

He crouched there a minute or two, while her breathing stretched out to a steady rhythm. The baby seemed to have gone quiet, or perhaps it was still too small to be felt from the outside. His son. His daughter.

He leaned over to kiss the gentle salient of Stefanie's belly, and just as he lifted his hand away, he felt it: a flutter, a shift, like the beating of a butterfly's wings.

He placed his lips against the soft white linen.

"I'll keep watch," he whispered. "You'll never be alone."

Without another glance, he rose and slipped out of the wheelhouse.

He found Gunther and Miss Dingleby standing near the bow. Gunther's arms were crossed, and his face was earnest in the moonlight. As Hatherfield approached, he laid one powerful hand on the rail and flexed his fingers.

"Is there anything we can do to get rid of the murdering English bastard?" he said to Miss Dingleby, in German.

"You won't need to," said Hatherfield. He held out his hand. "Take good care of them both, Hassendorf, or I shall haunt you the rest of your miserable days."

Gunther had the grace to blush. He shook Hatherfield's hand once, and let it drop.

Hatherfield turned to Miss Dingleby. She was watching him closely, as if he were a previously undiscovered species of animal she could not quite place in order.

"Give Olympia my thanks," he said.

She tilted her head. "I will."

He turned, paused, and looked over his shoulder. "And best of luck with that shoulder."

"Lord Hatherfield . . ."

He dove cleanly into the water.

The guard's face turned white as Hatherfield approached his cell.

"You never saw a thing," said Hatherfield.

Inside, the prison chaplain was sitting in the chair by the table, next to a bottle of fine French brandy, and Wright was sliding about awkwardly on the rowing apparatus. He looked up at Hatherfield's entrance. "I can't make heads or tails of this machine," he said.

Hatherfield tossed the hat on the table. "It's all in the rhythm, old boy. Keep it, if you like. Reverend?"

Wright stood up. "I called him in. I thought perhaps you might want to make use of that special license, before tomorrow. Having had some experience myself with the life of an illegitimate child."

Hatherfield unbuttoned his jacket. This time, he accepted the anvil of grief as it pressed on his chest. "It won't be necessary. For either of us. She's gone back to Germany, in good hands. But perhaps . . ." He looked at the chaplain.

"Sir?"

"Perhaps if you've got one of those handy bits of verse lying about, the sort to buck up a chap's spirits, when he's a trifle low."

Wright handed him back his own jacket, and Hatherfield buttoned it slowly, concentrated on each shining weight beneath his fingers.

The chaplain cleared his throat. "Do you mean a psalm, sir?"

"A psalm. That's it exactly." He looked at Wright. "Any preference, Mr. Wright?"

Wright straightened his collar and shook out his cuffs. "Afraid you're asking the wrong man. The one with the shepherd and the valley of death and whatnot?"

"Oh yes. Rather. My own mother used to read me that one, in my impressionable childhood. There's comfort, for you."

The three men arranged themselves in the proper attitudes, the chaplain on the chair and Wright and Hatherfield on the cot, while the chaplain's low voice murmured the twenty-third psalm above their bowed heads, into the warm August darkness.

THIRTY

❦

In his first year at Eton, the Marquess of Hatherfield had been called into the headmaster's office for the unpardonable crime of having shaved a certain vulgar physical representation into the well-groomed coat of the headmaster's wife's French poodle.

Actually, he had not committed the crime in question—he harbored an affection for dogs, even ornamental ones—but the single unbreakable code of Eton was that you didn't snitch on another boy. So there he stood, one slender lad against a phalanx of outraged adults in grizzled gray whiskers, awaiting his sentence with his hands crossed contritely behind his back. He had never been more frightened in his life. And after the sentence had come down, and he had borne his twenty-five switches without a single sound, and his abused skin had finally healed, he knew that the worst part of all was the anticipation. The knowledge of impending harm.

The wanting it over with.

Funny, that he should think of that long-ago Eton day, as he stood in the sweltering midday courtroom, hands to rail, sweat percolating steadily down his spine, listening to the monotone recital of official procedure. He had been innocent on that occasion, too, and it hadn't mattered. Not even to him. A crime had been committed, and someone must pay. The pound of flesh must be exacted from humanity. And perhaps it was true, that in suffering for another's sake you achieved some sort of absolution for your own sins, uncounted and unpunished. You discovered some glimpse of your better nature, of the person you might have been, if this or that hadn't gone wrong, or you had taken another path at one of life's crossings.

Hatherfield watched the judge's lips move, watched the jowly folds swing back and forth, the grizzled gray whiskers shiver in the faintest of drafts, and he thought, *I love you, you scrap of humanity, you. You living relic of this world I am leaving. I love your whiskers and your jowly folds. I love each darkened grain of the wooden chair you sit on, and this unmistakably British courtroom with its columns and plasterwork and allegories. I love the sun that burns today like a white coal in the blue English sky, I love every cobble and drain in the London street outside. I love that hat one of the damsels is wearing, with its silly long ostrich feather quivering in fear.*

I love my princess.

I love my child.

His eyes stung at that, so he looked down at the defense table, where Mr. Fairchurch was scribbling frantically next to Stefanie's empty chair. *Where the devil is my clerk?* he'd asked that morning, during their conference, and Hatherfield had shrugged and said he hadn't the faintest idea.

Fairchurch had gone on about appeals and precedent, and Hatherfield hadn't paid much attention. What was the use? The outcome would be the same, he would be hanged.

Get it over with.

Mr. Duckworth was standing up and straightening his necktie, preparing to inform the court what a soulless scoundrel Hatherfield was, the depraved murderer of his own innocent stepmother, who only wanted the best for him, to marry him off to a lovely young lady with two hundred thousand useful British pounds sterling. And so on. Hatherfield assumed his most earnest expression, and allowed his eyes to travel among the spectators.

His father was absent, of course. The Duke of Southam, overcome by grief for his wife and disgust for his son, had only darkened the Old Bailey doorstep in order to testify against him. But there was Sir John, eyes still more red rimmed than the night before, and his clothing uncharacteristically rumpled

His sister Eleanor and her husband, Robert. Brilliant Robert, already a junior Cabinet minister. Great things were expected of young Lord Chesterton, and he looked it. Already his cheeks bristled with the beginnings of an ambitious set of whiskers; already his forehead had taken on a wise and serious pair of lines. *Well, best of luck to you, Robert. Knock them dead on the floor of the Lords. Keep Eleanor happy for me. That little spark of light that comes into her eyes when she sees you—don't let it fade.*

Next to Robert sat Mr. Nathaniel Wright, inscrutable as always, impeccably tailored. Wright, now. There was no telling where Wright might end up. Perhaps if . . .

A rustle was passing among the benches.

Mr. Duckworth shot an accusatory glance to the doorway, pushed up his spectacles, and continued. "The peculiarly savage nature of the attack, moreover . . ."

Hatherfield looked up at the soot-stained ceiling. The words droned in his ears. He wanted this over with. He wanted to go back to his cell to finish his letter to Stefanie. He wanted to do a bit of thinking, to sit and drink more of that excellent French brandy with the chaplain—a fine chap, that chaplain, it turned out—and make sure his affairs were in perfect order. He wanted to . . .

The judge banged his gavel. "I say, Mr. Fairchurch. Is that your missing clerk?"

Hatherfield's head snapped to the doorway, where the ripple of commotion had taken place, and as if by magic, the crowd parted to reveal an auburn-haired woman in a splendid silver ball gown and a bristling mustache.

With all eyes upon her, she lifted her hand and tore away the mustache in a single swift rip.

An instant's profound silence, and then the courtroom erupted into pandemonium.

Hatherfield couldn't hear the frantic banging of the judge's gavel; he could only feel it in his bones, a distant drumbeat, while Stefanie walked—no, strode—no, made her regal procession down the side of the courtroom, toward the defense table.

"No!" he shouted. "No, my lord! This is absolutely not Mr. Fairchurch's clerk! I have never seen this woman in my life!"

By God, she was smiling.

She turned, and her swollen silhouette made him dizzy.

This was not possible. This was *not possible*.

Bang bang bang went the gavel.

Stefanie approached the table. Mr. Fairchurch, stunned, rose and pulled out the chair for her. In times of crisis, the British male always reverted to habit.

Her lips moved. *Thank you.*

She sank into her seat and stared serenely forward.

The judge went on banging his gavel. "You are out of order, Mr. Thomas! I WILL HAVE ORDER!"

The noise began to simmer into a delighted expectancy. Hatherfield gripped the rails as if to split them with his bare hands.

"Mr. Thomas!" thundered the judge. "Rise and explain yourself, or I will hold you in contempt! If I don't already!" A few passionate droplets of spittle flew from his mouth.

Even blooming with pregnancy, Stefanie was still a princess, and Hatherfield was never more proud of her than when she rose to her feet before the judge in the most graceful movement he had ever witnessed. A smile hovered on her lips.

"My name is Stefanie Victoria Augusta, Princess of Holstein-Schweinwald-Huhnhof," she said, "and I am the lady who danced with Lord Hatherfield on the night of February the twenty-first of this year. I have worn the very same gown to this courtroom, to corroborate my testimony. And I can assure the court that while his lordship was indeed engaged most agreeably and single-mindedly in the library that evening, the silver letter opener remained on the desk when he left the room."

Mr. Fairchurch made a strangled noise and slithered to the floor.

"Good God!" said Sir John Worthington, who never spoke out of turn in a court of law.

A gasp came from the direction of the damsels, and another gasp, followed by a pair of swoons. Eleanor leapt to her feet. "It's true! That's the same dress. The same lady, I'll vow to it!"

Bang bang bang went the gavel. "Madam! Mr. Thomas!

This is most irregular. The trial has already finished. This court has neither the time nor the procedure to listen to additional testimony, from an evident lunatic . . ."

"I am not a lunatic. I am a princess. Hatherfield?"

All heads turned in his direction. Stefanie looked at him triumphantly, smiling with victory, her blue eyes bright in her beautiful face.

He cleared his throat. "The judge is correct. This lady is a lunatic."

An outraged gasp from Stefanie, drowned out immediately by the roar of the crowd and the *bang bang bang* of the gavel.

He held up his hand, and the courtroom went still.

He stared at Nathaniel Wright. "She is, however, the princess of Holstein-Schweinwald-Huhnhof, and I humbly suggest that Her Highness be removed from the courtroom immediately for her own protection, and with the respect and veneration that is her due."

Wright rose smoothly to his feet and walked toward the defense table.

Bang bang bang. "I am the one who gives orders in this courtroom," said the judge, purple-faced, clutching his wig with one hand and his gavel with the other. "This lady will be removed from the courtroom immediately for her own protection, and . . . I say, sir!"

Mr. Wright was reaching for Stefanie's arm.

"Look here, I will be heard!" Stefanie said.

"You are in contempt, madam!"

"I am a princess of Holstein-Schweinwald-Huhnhof, my lord, and I demand that that man be released . . ."

"You are a lunatic!"

Mr. Wright folded his arms.

Hatherfield sighed. "I say, can't a man simply be sentenced to death without bloody Bedlam breaking out?"

At which point, a voice screeched out above the pandemonium among the benches.

"Sir! My lord!"

Hatherfield threw up his hands.

The judge was on his feet, banging away. "Order! Order! What the devil is going on now? This is a British *court of law*! Remember yourselves!"

One by one, the spectators settled contritely into their seats.

"Now." The judge glared at Stefanie. "You, young lady. Young man. Whoever the devil you are."

"I am the princess of . . ."

"You are out of order. You will retire to . . ."

"My lord!" The voice broke out again, louder now and clearer.

The spectators turned to the aisle.

"And who the devil are you?" said the judge.

"Why, Mr. Turner!" exclaimed Stefanie.

Sir John, who had spent the last few minutes staring at Stefanie's head with an expression of appalled shock, swiveled his gray head to the center of the commotion. "What's this? *My* Mr. Turner? Interrupting the proceedings of a *court of law*?" His voice grew steadily more thunderous. "Explain yourself, Mr. Turner!"

The beetlelike Mr. Turner waved his exoskeletal arm. "News, sir! The gravest possible news!"

"Then it had better well have to do with the case before the court!"

Turner scuttled forward, his black jacket swinging with the force of his scuttle. "Oh, it does, sir! The message arrived express soon after you left, sir, and there were no hackneys to be had, so I took it upon myself to . . ."

Bang bang. "Silence! Bring your message to the bench, Mr. Turner." The judge held out his hand.

Mr. Turner walked forward and held out the paper to the judge, as if it were a live explosive.

The judge snatched it away and opened the folds.

A heavy silence descended over the assembly, as several hundred throats held back breath. Someone stifled a sneeze back into the recesses of his nose at the last instant, and the sound ricocheted off the walls like a gunshot.

The judge looked at Hatherfield from over the tops of his reading glasses. "Your lordship, I must ask you to brace yourself. I regret to inform you that your father, the Duke of Southam, passed away at ten o'clock this morning, the result of a self-inflicted wound."

The words struck Hatherfield such a sudden blow, he didn't realize at first what had hit him, and how hard. He felt it from a distance. Saw himself recoil. Thought, *By damn, that's a nasty blow, a real shock, I wonder how he takes it.*

"Jamie!" Stefanie cried, from an even farther distance, almost outside his hearing.

"I beg your pardon?" someone said. Himself, apparently.

The judge removed his glasses. "You are now the Duke of Southam. However . . ."

Mr. Fairchurch, who had since recovered his seat and his wits, rose instantly to his feet. "My lord, the defense moves that this case be thrown out entirely, as being beyond the jurisdiction of this court. The ninth Duke of Southam, as a peer of the realm, should and will be tried in the House of Lords."

Mr. Duckworth, not to be outdone, leapt from his chair as well. "My learned colleague is misguided in both principle and practice. The crime was committed while the accused merely held the courtesy title of Marquess of Hatherfield, and was therefore tried properly as a commoner. Furthermore . . ."

The judge stood up. "This has all gone on long enough. Princesses, suicides, pandemonium in my courtroom. This court is adjourned until tomorrow morning. Each side will prepare a brief, making its case and stating the applicable law, to be delivered to my chambers by six o'clock this evening. In the meantime, I will expect every member of this court and the public to behave itself with utmost decorum, and there will be absolutely no further interruptions to the proceedings. Is that quite clear?"

A meek silence greeted his words.

And then a firm female voice rose from the rear of the courtroom.

"Not quite."

A small black-veiled figure stepped into view.

Hatherfield—the brand-new ninth Duke of Southam—put his head in his hands and wished himself back at Eton.

S tefanie stared at the tiny figure of Lady Charlotte Harlowe as she made her way past the awestruck benches to the front of the courtroom. The rustle of her dress, the click of her heels on the marble floor expanded with unnatural strength to fill every nook and crevice of the electrified room.

She stopped just short of the counsel benches, her black sleeve mere feet away from Stefanie's own, and she raised her veil over the crown of her hat.

"My lord, may I address the court?" she asked.

The judge's whiskers made a resigned twitch above his jowls. "I don't suppose one more will kill us, at this point. Proceed, your ladyship. But for the love of heaven, make it brief."

"I understand the court has been informed of the tragic events of this morning in Belgrave Square, at the home of the Duke of Southam." She looked neither at Stefanie nor at Hatherfield, who stood pale and fixed in the dock, but straight ahead at the judge.

"Mere minutes ago," the judge said dryly. "Proceed."

She lifted her left hand from the folds of her dress and extended a small square of paper. "I have here the signed confession of the eighth Duke of Southam for the murder of his wife Maria, on the night of the twenty-first of February."

The courtroom, already numb from the tumult of the morning, looked at itself blankly.

Stefanie jumped to her feet. "A confession! But why . . ."

Lady Charlotte continued tonelessly. "If additional testimony is necessary to secure the release of the ninth duke, I offer myself as a witness, that on the night in question, after quitting the library in possession of the then Lord Hatherfield and his companion, I went to find the duchess and explain what I'd seen. She told me she would retire to her boudoir, and I should find Lord Hatherfield and bring him to her for a private audience. I followed her upstairs, but neither his lordship nor his companion was in the library. I went in search of him. By then, the ballroom was becoming crowded, and after looking for some time, I gave up and returned upstairs to tell the duchess, and that was where I saw Hatherfield in the hallway. He was looking for his companion and refused absolutely to attend me to the duchess's boudoir. So I proceeded to the duchess's rooms, and as I approached, I heard . . ." She paused, as if catching her breath. "I heard a series of strange sounds. I thought the duchess was choking. I went to knock on the door and the duke appeared. He was drying his hands on a linen towel. I saw a distinct splatter on his shirtfront, that I later realized was blood. He told me not to go in, that the duchess was indisposed. I left. And then, an hour later, the alarm was raised."

"By God!" said Hatherfield.

"Madam," said the judge, in a low and shocked voice, "do you know what you're saying? That you have committed perjury?"

She looked at him. "I have not. I answered each question truthfully."

"But not the whole truth," he said. "And there is the question of motive."

She bowed her head. "I have no idea why he might have killed her. I suppose he must have had some sort of mad spell. She was so dear and kind to me. I believe I refused to consider what I had seen for some time, to accept the truth—that a man I so admired could have committed such a deed—and by then, his lordship was already incarcerated, and . . ." She looked back up. "I was wrong. I hope my presence here will atone for the mischief my omission has caused. And I extend my deepest . . . my most heartfelt wish . . ." She turned to Hatherfield. Stefanie couldn't see Lady Charlotte's expression, but her hands pressed into her sides, buried in her dress. Hatherfield's face, watching her, was lined with pity. "For your happiness," she finished in a whisper.

"And I for yours," said Hatherfield quietly.

The courtroom waited for more. Even the damsels forbore to swoon, fearful of missing a single instant. Stefanie gazed in astonishment at the corner of Lady Charlotte's jaw, which was clenched tight beneath her pale skin. Her hand moved restlessly at her side.

Without warning, Hatherfield sprang into motion. He vaulted over the railing and launched himself at Lady Charlotte with a furious roar.

"No, don't hurt her!" screamed Stefanie.

They crashed to the floor together, struggling in a mass of black-clothed limbs, and it was not until the shot fired harmlessly into the ceiling, raining a cloud of plaster on the horrified spectators, that Stefanie noticed what Hatherfield had detected from the vantage of the dock.

A small silver pistol, hidden in her ladyship's tiny right hand, buried in the folds of her black mourning dress.

EPILOGUE

Paris
August 1890

The staff of the Crillon Hotel were having a hard time of it. "Every day, it is the same!" exclaimed the maid Hortense. "They do not leave the room until it is nearly noon."

"And the breakfast tray! To be left next to the door, not to disturb them!" Pierre, the room service waiter, shook his scandalized head. "The brioche, the chocolate, it will be as cold as ice!"

The maid propped her polished black shoes on a chair and sipped her coffee. "So at noon, Monsieur Henri tells me they have left. I rush in, I begin to clean, and then boom! The door crashes open, they are hand in hand, the duke begs my pardon and I am to come back later. Later! When is later, I ask? When they are left for dinner?"

Marie-Rose, the senior housemaid, settled down at the table with coffee and a wise smile. "They are on the honeymoon, the duke and duchess. Did you see them come in, four days ago? He carried her through the door like a prince from the fairy tale. And they are so much in love. It is natural they are insatiable for each other."

Little Marguerite, fresh from the provinces, broke in eagerly. "And doesn't the so-handsome duke give you ten francs when he asks you to leave? Soon you will be able to buy your own hotel, Hortense."

"It's scandalous," sniffed Hortense. "The duchess is already great with child. He should control his base desire. Her belly is so fat, I don't know what he sees in her."

"Ah, you don't know what it does to a man, to see the woman he loves grow round with his child," said René, the dining room waiter, with his long black mustache and his twinkling eyes. He made a gesture with his hand to illustrate his point, and kissed the fingers. "And the duchess, she is not so great yet, her belly is like the sweet melon in the garden. How she blooms, like the rose."

The room service bell rang. Pierre lifted himself up with a resigned sigh and left the room.

"Oh, Hortense only wishes the so-handsome duke would look at her, instead of his bride," said Marie-Rose.

Marguerite sighed. "Ooh, what I wouldn't give for a kiss from the duke."

"Hortense wants more than a kiss from him, believe me." Marie-Rose laughed.

Hortense tossed her head. "Well, and why not? He should know what it is to have a fine, fit Frenchwoman in his bed, instead of his fat English broodmare."

Marie-Rose leaned forward. "She's nothing like that. I hear she's a princess. A real German princess! And so beautiful, with her red hair and her blue eyes that sparkle . . ."

Hortense stood up and snapped her towel. "Princess or not, she's lucky to have a man like that, an English-German cow like her. Why, her hair's so short, she can hardly pin it back! And if I catch him by himself . . ."

Marie-Rose laughed again. "Well, you won't, Hortense, not if you stayed by the door like a shadow. And do you know why?"

Hortense tossed her head.

"Ooh! Why?" Marguerite bounced in her chair.

Pierre poked his head through the doorway and brandished a little square of paper. "For the honeymoon suite, a bottle of champagne and a bowl of raspberries. Raspberries! *Sacré bleu!*"

Marie-Rose turned her wise eyes on little Marguerite and chucked her gently by the chin.

"Because, my dear. They are in love."

* * *

The ninth Duke of Southam, after much consideration, placed the final raspberry in the hollow between the ninth Duchess of Southam's breasts and set the bowl aside.

"Don't move," he said.

His wife giggled, and the raspberries on her nipples rolled away.

"See what you've done!" He shook his head and replaced the raspberries with exquisite care. "There. Perfect. Ah, look at you. You are the most delectable dessert I've ever seen."

"But we haven't even had dinner."

"Hold still!"

Her laughing face assembled into a suppressed seriousness, and her limbs went still. But her eyes were wide and soft, and they gazed upon him as if he himself were her dinner, her feast, and she'd been fasting for weeks.

Which she hadn't. Not even for hours.

He flexed his arms happily and bent over the first raspberry, in the hollow of her throat.

"Ooh! That tickles!"

"Hold still, my love. This is delicate work." He lapped the raspberry into his mouth and tasted it, sweet berry and salty Stefanie. Exactly what he was hungry for.

He kissed his way downward to the next three raspberries, lined up in a flawless horizontal line: breast, cleavage, breast. He started from the left and nibbled his way right, gorging himself on the newly ripe fullness of her, the smooth slope of her blue-veined skin beneath his mouth.

His wife made a low sound in her throat and worked her hands into his hair. "I shouldn't want this again," she said. "We've hardly stopped all day. I believe the maid was scandalized when we came back in this afternoon."

"What's a man supposed to do when his wife gives him a look in the middle of the Tuileries?"

"Did I give you a look?"

"You most certainly did. And that dress you were wearing, with the lace about your breasts, reminding me how you looked while I made love to you this morning in your rakish new Parisian negligee. Anyway, I told you long ago that I was . . ."

"Insatiable."

"Mmm. So you can't say you weren't warned." He licked about her nipple, making sure every last trace of raspberry was gone, and then he suckled her in long pulses, until her back arched and a raspberry rolled away from the topmost point of her belly. "Haven't I told you to lie still?" he said. "The night is short, and I have so many raspberries left to pluck."

Stefanie took him by the shoulders and rolled him over, sending berries flying across the bed.

"Bother the bloody raspberries," she said, and she lowered herself downward on her husband's magnificent body.

Later, as they lounged on the bed, feeding each other a picnic supper delivered by a rather put-upon waiter, Stefanie set aside a torn-off piece of baguette and draped herself over her husband's chest.

He picked up the bread and gave it back to her. "You must keep up your strength," he said, waggling his eyebrows.

"Be serious a moment." She touched his chin. "I know we agreed not to discuss anything until after our little holiday . . ."

"Quite right. Far too serious for such a lighthearted occasion."

"But since we seem to have such trouble even leaving this bed . . ."

"Nonsense. Quite untrue. I walked off to retrieve the room service tray not half an hour ago."

She picked up a pillow and hit him with it, and then she nestled herself against him.

"But we should speak of it, you know. There's something I should tell you."

"What's that?"

"The night of the murder. The duke came in and spoke to me, and I told him . . . I don't remember exactly what I said, I was so angry. But I told him something of what your stepmother had done. And I think . . . I know that's why he did it. To avenge you."

"Or to punish her, for her infidelity."

She raised herself up. "You don't sound surprised."

He was staring at the ceiling. "I suppose I put two and two together. Perhaps I knew the truth all along, like Charlotte, and I refused to accept it. That my father would murder her, that he would very nearly allow me to hang for the crime. I don't know. I don't think I'll ever understand my father. He was always a selfish brute. A coward, who never had the courage to face his own shortcomings. I don't think I had a single loving word from him, and yet I suppose he loved me, in his way. He just loved himself more." He paused. "But in the end, you know, he couldn't do it. He couldn't let me hang for it. I suppose that's something."

"You'll be a much better father."

"God, I hope so. With you by my side, showing me the way."

She smiled and caressed his cheek. "We'll have to decide where we're going to live. Whether you can bear to keep the house in Belgrave Square, after all that's happened there . . ."

"We can live wherever you want, my love." He reached up and took her hair between his fingers. "You're like the sun, eclipsing all the old memories."

She might have had to blink, once or twice, before she could answer him. When she did, her voice might have held a touch of rasp. "I just want you to know that I don't mind. I don't need the splendor, if you don't want it. Belgrave Square or a flat above the boathouse, I don't care. I'll be happy wherever we are."

His thumb reached out to caress her cheek. "I know you will, sprite. One of countless reasons why I love you. But you read Mr. Wright's telegram of this morning. The splendid success of the sale of Southam Terrace houses. We shall soon have quite enough capital for a new start entirely. Just in time, for a chap with a growing family to care for."

"Mmm." She slid to his side and laid her arm across his muscular chest. "Which brings me to another thing."

"Oh? What's that?"

"I've been meaning to ask . . ." She swallowed. "Jamie, I know you have an important position, you're one of the foremost men in England now, and our child . . . our children . . ."

He was caressing her bare arm, up and down. "Go on, love. Tell me what you want."

"I know our children will be English, that their inheritance and destiny lie there, but I want . . . I would like . . . for this child at least, our first . . ."

He waited patiently.

"Would you mind terribly if I wanted to have the baby in Germany? With my sisters near? I know the future duke should rightfully come into this world in the state ducal bed and all that, but . . ."

He laughed out loud. "Is that all? For God's sake, Stefanie. We can have the baby wherever you like, so long as there are at least a dozen doctors available at a moment's notice. All I want, all I care about, pray for . . ." His voice grew soft. He moved on his side and took her in his arms. "Stefanie, when a man comes within a whisker of losing everything, when he's prepared himself to die, he learns what's vital. And all I want is a safe delivery, a healthy wife and baby. You, our child. You're everything in this world. You're all that matters. If you want to climb to the top of Mount Kilimanjaro and deliver the infant there, I'll carry the palanquin myself."

"Ooh, that sounds lovely! What a splendid idea! Think of the view!"

"Except that there are no doctors on Mount Kilimanjaro, so I expect we shall have to stay rather unimaginatively at sea level." He shrugged regretfully and lowered his mouth to hers.

A knock rattled the door.

The Duke of Southam, who was already engaged in kissing his wife senseless, lifted his head and called out, "Another time!"

Stefanie looped her hands around his head and dragged him back.

Knock knock knock. More insistent this time.

"I said, another time!" he called.

Knock knock knock. "A telegram, Your Grace! It is marked urgent!"

"Not nearly as urgent as making love to my wife," he muttered, nibbling his way to her ear.

KNOCK. KNOCK. KNOCK. "Your Grace!"

He lifted his head and sighed. "I suppose I'd better get that."

Stefanie sat up and watched him while he stalked across the room at his lion's pace, muscles flexing in the blue twilight that crept through the curtains. His beauty washed over her again, the powerful curve of his shoulder, the clean line of his jaw, the golden glint of his hair.

He was hers.

She placed her hands on her round middle and caressed her own skin in dreamy circles. "Well?" she said. "What is it?"

He looked up from the telegram. "It seems, my dear, you're about to get your wish."

"What wish?"

He returned to the bed and sat on the edge. "We've been summoned to Holstein Castle by the end of the week, by no less an authority than your own uncle, the Duke of Olympia."

Stefanie snatched the telegram from his fingers and scanned it. "He doesn't say why."

"Of course not." Her husband slid his arms around her, lifted her effortlessly from the bed, and carried her to the chaise longue by the window.

He opened the curtains and allowed the Parisian dusk to spill across her skin.

"But just in case," he said, lowering himself between her legs, "I'm going to bring my revolver, a bottle of brandy, and a pair of very fast horses."

NOTE

As a child, I was dragged—sometimes willingly, sometimes not—to evenings at the Seattle Opera, so inevitably
operatic shenanigans make their way into my books. I'm
afraid the entire Princesses in Disguise trilogy may have
originated in the plight of the captured princess Aida. The love
triangle connecting her, the warrior Radames, and the fiercely
jealous Amneris in an imaginary long-ago Egypt inspired the
dynamics between Stefanie, the Marquess of Hatherfield, and
Lady Charlotte in Victorian London . . . in this case, thank
goodness, with a much happier ending.

As I discovered, words sung beautifully in Italian often
wind up translating poorly on a written English page. Still, I
couldn't resist throwing in Radames's expressive declaration
of love: *Ergerti un trono vicino al sol* ("Build you a throne
next to the sun"). I think Hatherfield says it well, don't you?

Turn the page for a preview of
Juliana Gray's next book

HOW TO SCHOOL
YOUR SCOUNDREL

Coming in June 2014
from Berkley Sensation

ONE

❧

London
November 1889

The Earl of Somerton leaned back in his chair, steepled his fingers into an imaginary cathedral before his nose, and considered the white-faced man standing at the extreme edge of the antique Kilim rug before the desk.

Standing, of course. One never made one's underlings too comfortable.

He allowed the silence to take on a life of its own, a third presence in the room, a roiling thundercloud of anticipation.

The man shifted his weight from one large, booted foot to the other. A droplet of sweat trickled its lazy way along the thick vertical scar at the side of his face.

"Are you warm, Mr. Norton? I confess, I find the room a trifle chilly, but you're welcome to open a window if you like."

"No, thank you, sir." Norton's voice tilted queasily.

"A glass of sherry, perhaps? To calm the nerves?"

"The nerves, sir?"

"Yes, Mr. Norton. The nerves." Somerton smiled. *"Your* nerves, to be precise, for I can't imagine that any man could walk into this study to report a failure so colossal as yours, without feeling just the slightest bit" —he sharpened his voice to a dagger point— "nervous."

The Adam's apple jumped and fell in Mr. Norton's throat. "Sir."

"Sir . . . *yes*? As in: *Sir, you are correct, I am shaking in my incompetent boots*? Or perhaps you mean: *Sir, no, I am quite improbably ignorant of the fatal consequences of failure in this particular matter.*" Another smile. "Enlighten me, if you will, Mr. Norton."

"Sir. Yes. I am . . . I am most abjectly sorry that I . . . that in the course of . . ."

"That you allowed my wife—a woman, unschooled in the technical aspects of subterfuge—my *wife*, Mr. Norton, the Countess of Somerton—to somehow elude your diligent surveillance last night?" He leaned forward and placed his steepled fingers on the desk before him. "To escape you, Mr. Norton?"

Norton snatched his handkerchief from his pocket and dabbed at his temples. His narrow and unremarkable face—so useful in his choice of profession—shone along every surface, like a plank of wood left out in the rain. "Sir, I . . . I . . . I most humbly suggest that Lady Somerton is . . . she has more wits in her possession than . . ."

Somerton's fist crashed into the blotter. "She is my *wife*, Mr. Norton. And she slipped through your grasp."

"Sir, in all the weeks I've kept watch on Lady Somerton, she's traveled nowhere more suspicious than the home of her cousin, Lady Morley . . ."

"Who is undoubtedly complicit in her affairs."

"Oh, but sir . . ."

"And she has followed *me,* on occasion, has she not?"

"Yes, but . . ."

"Which means she has neither the good sense nor the propriety of a common shopwife."

Norton's massive jaw worked and worked. His gaze fell to the rug. "Sir, I feel . . ."

"You *feel?*" Somerton barked. "You *feel,* Mr. Norton? Allow me to observe that your *feelings* have nothing to do with the matter at hand. My wife, the Countess of Somerton, is engaged in an adulterous liaison with another man. It is my belief that she has carried on this sordid correspondence throughout the entire duration of our marriage. Your object—the task, the sole task for which I hired you, Mr. Norton, as the best man in London for clandestine work—your task was to obtain proof of this affair and bring it to me. You are not paid to have *feelings* on the matter."

"Sir, I . . ."

"Look at me, Mr. Norton."

Erasmus Norton, the most stealthy and deadly assassin inside these British Isles, known to have killed at least one mark with a single silent tap to the skull, lifted his dark eyes carefully upward until he met Somerton's gaze. For an instant, a flutter of pity brushed the inside wall of the earl's thick chest.

And then, like the butterfly snatched by the net, it was gone.

"Believe me, Mr. Norton," said Somerton, in his silkiest voice. "I understand your little predicament. She is a beautiful woman, isn't she? Beautiful and full of grace. You wouldn't think, as you watched her smile in that gentle little way of hers, as you watched her float about her daily business, that she would be capable of dishonoring a pet mouse, let alone her husband. I can see how you've fallen under her spell. I can hardly blame you. I fell myself, didn't I, in the most catastrophic manner possible. I married her." The word *married* came out in a growl.

"If I may say, sir . . ."

Somerton rose to his feet. "But you are paid to set aside these tender notions, Mr. Norton, these misguided ideas of yours, and see to your business. Otherwise, I shall be forced to consider, one by one, the various means by which your *feelings* may be forcibly exhumed from your incompetent breast." He leaned forward and spoke in a low voice, just above a whisper. "Do you understand me, Mr. Norton?"

Norton hopped backward from his perch like a startled brown-haired parakeet. "Oh, but sir! She's innocent, I'll stake my life on it . . ."

"Innocent?" The low simmer of fury in Somerton's brain, the fury he had battled all his life to control, flared upward in a roar of heat. "Innocent? By God, Norton. Do I hear you correctly? Are you actually saying I'm mistaken about my own wife?"

Norton's white mouth opened and closed. "Not mistaken exactly, sir, that's the wrong word, I . . ."

Somerton walked around the side of his desk. Norton's

eyes followed his progress, while his words drifted into a wary silence.

Somerton came to a stop next to the edge of the rug, mere inches away from Norton's blunt and unlovely figure. They were of about the same height, he and Norton. In fact, taken both together, they made a pair of brothers: tall, dark-haired, brute-boned, thick with muscle, crowned by faces only a particularly adoring mother could admire.

Not that the woman who had given birth to Somerton had been that sort of mother.

"Mr. Norton," he said, "I find this conversation has dragged on long enough. Either do your duty, or I shall exact the usual forfeit. There are no other choices. We've done business together before, and you know this fact as well as any man on earth."

Norton's dark eyes blinked twice. "Yes, sir."

"You may go."

Norton turned and dashed for the door. Somerton waited, without moving, until his black-coated figure had stepped off the rug and reached gratefully for the door.

"Oh! There is one more thing, Mr. Norton."

The man froze with his hand on the knob.

"As I observed, you have allowed Lady Somerton to follow me about my business in the evening, from time to time. A dangerous occupation, that."

"I have kept the closest watch on her, sir. As close as possible without revealing myself," Norton said to the door.

"Let me be clear. If a single hair on Lady Somerton's head, a single *eyelash* belonging to her ladyship's face is harmed, you will die, Mr. Norton. I shall perform the deed myself. Do you understand me?"

Norton's hand clutched around the knob, as if struck by the actual cold-blooded wind of Somerton's voice.

"I understand, sir," he whispered.

"Very good."

Lord Somerton returned to his seat without another look. The door creaked slightly as it opened and closed, and then there was silence, profound and merciful silence, except for the rhythmic scratch of Somerton's pen as he finished the letter in which Norton's entrance had interrupted him.

A double knock struck the study door.

He signed his name, considered it carefully, and blotted the ink on the page before he answered.

"Come in," he said.

The footman stepped cautiously through the doorway. "Mr. Markham is here to see you, sir."

"Mr. Markham?"

"For the position of secretary, sir." The footman's voice lifted just a single nervous trifle at the word *sir,* turning the statement into a question. Servants and peers alike performed a similar vocal trick when engaging Lord Somerton in conversation. He couldn't imagine why.

"Send him in."

Somerton folded the letter, slipped it inside an envelope, and addressed it himself in bold strokes of black ink. A wretched and time-consuming chore, that. He did hope this current secretarial prospect would prove capable of the position, but the hope was a faint one. For some reason, he had the most appalling luck with secretaries.

The footman dissolved into the darkness of the hallway. Somerton consulted the list he had prepared an hour ago—another damned chore he was eager to relinquish—and made a small check next to the word *Ireland*. Two more words remained: *Secretary* and *Wife*.

He was about to take care of the first, anyway. He preferred not to think about the second.

A coal popped in the fireplace nearby. The London air had taken a turn for the chillier this week, and the usual miasma of yellow fog had thickened like an evil enchantment about the streets and buildings of the capital, as millions of chimneys put out millions of columns of coal smoke into the damp English atmosphere. In another week, the household would retire to Somerton Park for the Christmas season. Hunting every day, drinking every night. His wife's uncomplaining mask at dinnertime; his son's brave *Yes, sir* and *No, sir* to the few questions Somerton could stretch his adult imagination to ask. The querulous voice of his mother, inquiring after his dead father.

In short, the usual jolly old Yule.

The door opened. Somerton flexed his fingers.

"Your lordship, Mr. Markham," said the footman.

A young man stepped through the doorway.

"Good morning, Mr. Markham." Somerton glanced at the clock on the mantel. "I hope the hour is not too early for you."

"Not at all, your lordship. I thank you for taking the trouble to see me." Mr. Markham moved into the lamplight, and something stirred in the pit of Somerton's belly.

Indigestion, no doubt.

They were all young men who came to interview for the position of personal secretary to the Earl of Somerton, but this young man seemed younger than all of them. He could not have been more than eighteen. A suit of plain black wool covered his coltish limbs a little too loosely. His face was smooth and unlined, without a single whisker; his dark auburn hair was slicked back from his head with a stiff layer of pomade. In the symmetrical architecture of his face, there was a trace of almost delicate beauty, a lingering evidence of boyhood.

But there was nothing childlike about the way he moved. He squared his thin shoulders, propelled his lanky figure to the center of the rug, and went on, in a firm, rich alto. "I have come to interview for the position of secretary."

Somerton set aside his pen in an exact perpendicular relationship to the edge of the desk. "So I am informed, Mr. Markham. I read over your references last night. Astonishingly fulsome, for a man so young."

"I hope I have given satisfaction, sir." In a voice that knew full well he had.

Cocky little bastard.

Not that cockiness was necessarily a fault. A secretary should approach his work with confidence. That cockiness could shove open more than a few doors in his employer's service; it could accomplish what timid self-effacement could not.

Just so long as the two of them were quite clear: That cockiness should never, ever direct itself toward the Earl of Somerton himself.

Somerton raised his most devastating eyebrow. "No doubt, Mr. Markham, you gave the,–er–, the attaché of this beleaguered ambassador of Holstein-Schweinwald-Huhnhof the very utmost satisfaction. I presume you left his employ because of the political revolution there?"

A slight hesitation. "Yes."

Somerton shook his head. "A shocking state of affairs. The ruler murdered, the heir snatched away from the funeral itself. Is there any news of the missing princesses?"

"None, I'm afraid," said Mr. Markham. "One hears they escaped to relatives in England with their governess, but it's only a rumor. Likely a false hope."

"My sympathies. Regardless, I should warn you that my standards are perhaps a trifle more exacting than those of a backward, corrupt, and regicidal Germanic principality."

Was that a flare of indignation in Mr. Markham's warm brown eyes? But the lad smothered it instantly, returning his face to the same pale symmetry as before. Another point in his favor: the ability to control emotion.

"That unfortunate state," he said icily, "is nonetheless most exact in its notions of ceremony and diplomatic procedure. I assure you, I am well versed in every aspect of a secretary's duties."

"And I assure you, Mr. Markham, that the duties required of *my* secretary will soon prove unlike any you have encountered before."

Markham's eyelids made a startled blink.

"We will, however, begin at the beginning, so as not to shock your tender sensibilities. I begin work directly after breakfast, which you will enjoy on a tray in your bedroom. I dislike company in the morning, and my personal secretary does not take meals with the household staff."

"I see."

"You will report to this room at half eight. We will work through until ten o'clock, when coffee is brought in and I receive visitors. Your desk is there"—he waved to the small mahogany escritoire set at a right angle to the desk, a few feet away—"and you will remain in the room, taking notes of the meeting, unless I direct otherwise. You can write quickly, can you not, Mr. Markham?"

"I have recently learned the essentials of shorthand notation," Mr. Markham said, without the slightest hesitation.

"We will take lunch here in the study, after which your time is your own, provided you complete your assignments by the time I return at six o'clock. We will work for another two hours, after which I dress for dinner. I invariably dine out. You may take your meal in the dining room, though you will likely find yourself alone. Her ladyship dines in the nursery with my son." Somerton congratulated himself on the absence of expression in his voice.

"Very good, sir. Do I understand you to mean that I have met with your approval?" Mr. Markham said. His face tilted slightly against the lamplight, exposing the curve of his cheekbone, prominent and graceful, in perfect balance with the rest of his face. His arms remained crossed behind his back, his posture straight. Almost . . . regal.

What an extraordinary chap. The thought slipped without warning between the steel columns of Somerton's mind.

He rose to his feet. "Approval, Mr. Markham? Nothing of the kind. I am in want of a secretary. You, it seems, are the only man daring enough to apply for the position."

"Rather a tight spot for you, then, sir."

The words were said so effortlessly, so expressionlessly, that it took a moment for Somerton to process their meaning.

What the *devil?* Had the fellow *actually* just said that?

Rather a tight position for you. The cheek!

Somerton's shoulders flexed in an arc of counterattack. "You have one week, Mr. Markham, to prove yourself capable of the position. A position, I hardly need add, that no man has held for longer than two months together. If you succeed in winning my—what was your word, Mr. Markham?"

The young man smiled. "Approval, Lord Somerton."

"Approval." He sneered. "You will be compensated with the handsome sum of two hundred pounds per annum, paid monthly in arrears."

Two hundred solid English pounds sterling. A fortune for an impecunious young man just starting out in his profession, clinging by his claws to the first rung of the professional ladder; twice as much as his wildest hopes might aspire to achieve. Somerton waited for the look of startled gratification to break out across Mr. Markham's exquisite young features.

Waited.

A small curl appeared in the left corner of Mr. Markham's round pink upper lip.

"Two hundred pounds?" he said, as he might say *two hundred disemboweled lizards*? "I no longer wonder that you have difficulty retaining secretaries for any length of time, your lordship. I only wonder that you have tempted any to attempt the position at all."

Somerton shot to his feet.

"I beg your pardon! Two hundred pounds is impossibly generous."

"You will forgive me, Lord Somerton, but the facts speak for themselves. I am the only applicant for the position. Evidently two hundred pounds represents not nearly enough compensation for an ambitious and talented young fellow to take on such an overbearing, demanding, bleak-faced despot as yourself." He uncrossed his arms, walked to the desk, and spread his long young fingers along the edge. "Allow me, if you will, to make you a counter-proposition. I shall take on the position of your personal secretary for a week's trial, beginning tomorrow morning. If the conditions of employment meet with my approval, why, I'll agree to continue on for a salary of three hundred pounds a year, paid weekly in advance. My room and board included, of course."

Mr. Markham's eyes fixed, without blinking, on Somerton's face. That unlined young face, innocently smooth in the yellow glow of the electric lamp, did not twitch so much as a single nerve.

"By God," Somerton said slowly. The blood pulsed hard at the base of his neck. He sat back in his chair, took up his pen, and balanced it idly along the line of his knuckles. His hand, thank God, did not shake.

"Well, sir? My time this morning is limited."

"You may go, Mr. Markham." He waved to the door.

Markham straightened. "Very well. Good luck to you, sir." He turned and walked to the door, at that same regal pace, as if leading the procession to a state dinner.

Somerton waited until his hand had reached the knob. "And Mr. Markham? Kindly tell my butler to arrange for your belongings to be brought over from your lodgings and unpacked in the suite next to mine."

"Sir?" At last, a note of astonishment in that imperturbable young voice.

Somerton took out a sheet of blank paper, laid it on the blotter, and smiled. "I suspect you shall suit this overbearing, demanding, bleak-faced despot very well, Mr. Markham."

L uisa closed the door to the study and leaned back against the heavy carved wood.

Her heart still thudded inside her ribs at an alarming speed, as if she'd just finished a footrace around the shore of the sparkling clear Holsteinsee. Thank God for starched white collars and snug black neckties, or else that man—that Somerton, that predatory prizefighter of an aristocrat with his keen black eyes and his impossibly thick shoulders—would have detected the rapid thrust of her pulse against her skin.

Her tender female skin.

He would have seen right through her mask of male bravado. He would have annihilated her.

How her chest had collapsed at the words *You may go*, as if the world had vaporized around her.

And then *Unpacked in the suite next to mine*, the point at which her heart had resumed beating, with this alarming and reckless patter of . . . what? Fear? Relief? Anticipation?

When Luisa was younger, before her skirts were lengthened and her hair arranged in elaborate knots and loops under a jeweled tiara, her father used to take her out in the Schweinwald to stalk deer. They would set out at dawn, while the grass still breathed out rings of silver mist, and the thud of the horses' hooves rattled the autumn silence. In those quiet mornings, Luisa learned how to hold herself still, how to be patient, how to listen and watch. She would study her father's movements and replicate them. She was Diana, she was the virgin huntress, wise and ruthless.

Until that October day when her horse had gone lame and she had fallen behind, unnoticed, and the familiar trees and vines of the Schweinwald had become suddenly and terrifyingly unfamiliar. She had hallooed softly. She had whistled. She had called out in mounting alarm, panic mottling her brain, and as she stood there with her hands gripped around the loops of her horses's reins, a black bear had wandered into view among the trees and came to a stop about twelve feet away.

They had stared at one another, she and that bear. She knew, of course, that you weren't supposed to stare. You were supposed to look away and back off slowly. But she couldn't remember all those rules of engagement. She couldn't leave her lame horse. She had nothing to fall back on, no rear position in which to shelter. So she stared back, for what seemed like an hour and was probably less than a minute.

She still remembered the absolute blackness of the bear's fur, except for a small patch of rufous brown where a miraculous ray of sunlight penetrated the forest canopy. She remembered the dark watchfulness of its eyes, the fingerprint texture of its round nose. She remembered the syrupy scent of the rotting leaves, the chilling handprint of the air on her cheek.

She remembered thinking, *I am going to die, or I am going to live. Which is it?*

"Sir? Are you going to see my father?"

Luisa opened her eyes and straightened away from the door.

A young dark-haired boy stood before her, examining her with curious black eyes so exactly like those of the Earl of Somerton, her heart jumped an extra beat for good measure.

"I beg your pardon?" she said.

"My father." The boy nodded at the door. "Are you going in to see him? Or has he tossed you out?"

"I . . . I have just finished my interview with his lordship." Luisa heard herself stammering. Children made her nervous, with their all-seeing eyes and their mysterious minds, occupied with infant imaginings Luisa could no longer even attempt to guess. And this one was worse than most, his pale face poised upward with unsmiling curiosity, his eyes far too reminiscent of that pair she'd just escaped. She scrambled for something to say. "You are Lord Somerton's son?"

The boy nodded. "Philip. Lord Kildrake," he added importantly.

"I see."

"I guess he's tossed you out, then. Well, buck up. That's what Mama says. Buck up and try again later, when he's in a good mood."

"I see."

Young Lord Kildrake sighed and stuck his finger in his

hair, twirling it into a thoughtful knot. His gaze shifted to the door behind her. "The trouble is, he never is. In a good mood."

From the entrance hall came the sound of feet on marble, of the butler issuing quiet orders. A woman's voice called out. The boy's mother, probably. Lady Somerton, summoning her son.

He never is. In a good mood.

In the end, that long-ago day, Luisa had lived, but not because she had stared the bear down. The thunder of avenging hoofbeats had filled the forest, and Prince Rudolf had appeared on his white charger. He had risen in his stirrups, dropped his reins, lifted his rifle, and shot the bear dead without a break in the horse's stride.

Luisa looked down at the little boy. He had lost interest in her now. He let out another long sigh, turned, and ambled back down the hallway, still twirling his hair.

Her father was dead. Her husband was dead. Her sisters, her governess, all scattered to the winds of England.

She was alone.

Luisa straightened away from the door and shook out her shirt cuffs. She had better get on with it, then, hadn't she?

*Three intrepid princesses find themselves targets
in a deadly plot against the crown.*

FROM
JULIANA GRAY

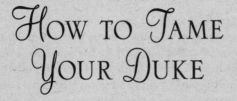

England, 1888. Quiet and scholarly Princess Emilie has
always avoided adventure, until she's forced to disguise
herself as a tutor for the imposing Duke of Ashland, a
former soldier disfigured in battle. When chance draws
them into a secret liaison, Emilie can't resist the opportunity to learn what lies behind his forbidding mask.

The duke never imagines that his son's tutor and his
mysterious golden-haired beauty are one and the same.
But when her true identity is laid bare, Ashland must
face the demons in his past to safeguard both his lady—
and his heart.

"Juliana Gray has a stupendously lyrical voice."
—Meredith Duran, *New York Times* bestselling author

julianagray.com
facebook.com/JulianaGray
facebook.com/LoveAlwaysBooks
penguin.com

M1348T0813

FROM
JULIANA GRAY

A Gentleman Never Tells

Six years ago, Elizabeth Harewood and Lord Roland Pen-hallow were London's golden couple, young and beautiful and wildly in love. Forced apart by her scheming relatives and his clandestine career, Lilibet and Roland buried their passion beneath years of duty and self-denial, until a chance holiday encounter changes everything they ever knew about themselves . . . and each other.

But Miss Elizabeth Harewood is now the Countess of Somerton, estranged wife of one of England's most brutal and depraved aristocrats, and she can't afford the slightest hint of scandal attached to her name. When Roland turns up mysteriously at the castle where she's hidden herself away, she struggles to act as a lady should, but the gallant lover of her youth has grown into an irresistibly dashing and dangerous man, and temptation is only a single kiss away . . .

PRAISE FOR JULIANA GRAY

"Juliana Gray has a stupendously lyrical voice
unlike anybody else."
—Meredith Duran, *New York Times* bestselling author

"Juliana Gray is on my auto-buy list."
—Elizabeth Hoyt, *New York Times* bestselling author

julianagray.com
facebook.com/JulianaGray
facebook.com/LoveAlwaysBooks
penguin.com

M1169T0912